www.wadsworth.com

wadsworth.com is the World Wide Web site for Wadsworth and is your direct source to dozens of online resources.

At *wadsworth.com* you can find out about supplements, demonstration software, and student resources. You can also send email to many of our authors and preview new publications and exciting new technologies.

wadsworth.com
Changing the way the world learns®

THE WADSWORTH COLLEGE SUCCESS SERIES

Clason and Beck, *On the Edge of Success* (2003). ISBN: 0-534-56973-0

Gordon and Minnick, *Foundations: A Reader for New College Students,* 2nd Ed. (2002). ISBN: 0-534-52431-1

Hallberg, Hallberg, and Rochieris, *Making the Dean's List: A Workbook to Accompany the College Success Factors Index* (2004). ISBN: 0-534-24862-4

Holkeboer and Walker, *Right from the Start: Taking Charge of Your College Success,* 4th Ed. (2004). ISBN: 0-534-59967-2

Petrie and Denson, *A Student Athlete's Guide to College Success: Peak Performance in Class and in Life,* 2nd Ed. (2003). ISBN: 0-534-57000-3

Santrock and Halonen, *Your Guide to College Success: Strategies for Achieving Your Goals,* Media Edition, 3rd Ed. (2004). ISBN: 0-534-60804-3

Steltenpohl, Shipton, and Villines, *Orientation to College: A Reader on Becoming an Educated Person,* 2nd Ed. (2004). ISBN: 0-534-59958-3

Van Blerkom, *Orientation to College Learning,* 4th Ed. (2004). ISBN: 0-534-60813-2

Wahlstrom and Williams, *Learning Success: Being Your Best at College and Life,* Media Edition, 3rd Ed. (2002). ISBN: 0-534-57314-2

THE FIRST-YEAR EXPERIENCE™ SERIES

Gardner and Jewler, *Your College Experience: Strategies for Success,* Media Edition, 5th Ed. (2003). ISBN: 0-534-59382-8

Gardner and Jewler, *Your College Experience: Strategies for Success,* Concise Media Edition, 5th Ed. (2004). ISBN: 0-534-60759-4

Gardner and Jewler, *Your College Experience: Strategies for Success,* Expanded Reader, 5th Ed. (2003). ISBN: 0-534-59985-0

STUDY SKILLS/CRITICAL THINKING

Longman and Atkinson, *CLASS: College Learning and Study Skills,* 6th Ed. (2002). ISBN: 0-534-56962-5

Longman and Atkinson, *SMART: Study Methods and Reading Techniques,* 2nd Ed. (1999). ISBN: 0-534-54981-0

Smith, Knudsvig, and Walter, *Critical Thinking: Building the Basics,* 2nd Ed. (2003). ISBN: 0-534-59976-1

Sotiriou, *Integrating College Study Skills: Reasoning in Reading, Listening, and Writing,* 6th Ed. (2002). ISBN: 0-534-57297-9

Van Blerkom, *College Study Skills: Becoming a Strategic Learner,* 4th Ed. (2003). ISBN: 0-534-57467-X

Watson, *Learning Skills for College and Life* (2001). ISBN: 0-534-56161-6

STUDENT ASSESSMENT TOOL

Hallberg, *College Success Factors Index,* http://success.wadsworth.com

Fourth Edition

ORIENTATION TO COLLEGE LEARNING

Dianna L. Van Blerkom
University of Pittsburgh at Johnstown

Australia • Canada • Mexico • Singapore • Spain • United Kingdom • United States

THOMSON

™

WADSWORTH

Publisher/Executive Editor: Marcus Boggs
Manager, College Success: Annie Mitchell
Assistant Editor: Kirsten Markson
Technology Project Manager: Barry Connolly
Advertising Project Manager: Linda Yip
Project Manager, Editorial Production: Emily Smith
Print/Media Buyer: Rebecca Cross

Permissions Editor: Sarah Harkrader
Production Service: Graphic World Publishing Services
Text Designer: Adriene Bosworth
Cover Designer: Bill Stanton
Cover Image: Jose Luis Pelaez Inc./Corbis
Compositor: Graphic World, Inc.
Text and Cover Printer: Phoenix Color Corp

Printed in the United States of America
1   2   3   4   5   6   7   07   06   05   04   03

For more information about our products, contact us at:
Thomson Learning Academic Resource Center
1-800-423-0563
For permission to use material from this text, contact us by:
Phone: 1-800-730-2214
Fax: 1-800-730-2215
Web: http://www.thomsonrights.com

Library of Congress Control Number: 2003100992

Student Edition with InfoTrac College Edition: ISBN 0-534-60813-2
Student Edition without InfoTrac College Edition: ISBN 0-534-60816-7

Wadsworth/Thomson Learning
10 Davis Drive
Belmont, CA 94002-3098
USA

Asia
Thomson Learning
5 Shenton Way #01-01
UIC Building
Singapore 068808

Australia/New Zealand
Thomson Learning
102 Dodds Street
Southbank, Victoria 3006
Australia

Canada
Nelson
1120 Birchmount Road
Toronto, Ontario M1K 5G4
Canada

Europe/Middle East/Africa
Thomson Learning
High Holborn House
50/51 Bedford Row
London WC1R 4LR
United Kingdom

Latin America
Thomson Learning
Seneca, 53
Colonia Polanco
11560 Mexico D.F.
Mexico

Spain/Portugal
Paraninfo
Calle/Magallanes, 25
28015 Madrid, Spain

To Sharon and Robbie.
You bring love,
laughter, and learning
to my life.

BRIEF CONTENTS

DETAILED CONTENTS

TO THE INSTRUCTOR

One of the challenges faced by instructors in orientation, college success, and study skills courses is that of helping students succeed in college. This task includes such things as helping students develop independence, improve relationships, manage stress, and learn their way around campus, just to name a few. Although all of these are important first steps to success, once students learn to balance their time among home, school, and work responsibilities, they must begin to focus their attention on their course work. Many orientation texts do a good job of preparing students to meet the social challenges ahead of them; however, few of them prepare students to meet the academic challenges they must face to succeed in college. I wrote this text to fill that gap—to provide students with a solid foundation of learning skills and strategies that will help them succeed in college.

During the past nineteen years, I've had the opportunity to work with freshmen and sophomores at several colleges. I found that they were often as unaware of the level of work that would be expected of them in college as they were lacking in the skills and strategies that would help them succeed. By focusing on learning skills and strategies and incorporating some of the traditional orientation topics, I found a formula that led to success for many of them. The emphasis on learning skills and strategies helped them make a good transition to college. I have tried to share this formula with others in the field through writing *Orientation to College Learning*.

Why is it important to focus on learning skills and strategies? Many college students say that no one ever really taught them how to study. Although they probably did learn some study skills during their twelve years of schooling, they may not have learned the study and learning strategies that are necessary for college success. College courses are typically more difficult, more intensive, cover more material at a faster pace, and focus on topics that are completely unfamiliar to new college students. Some or all of these differences may contribute to the difficulties that some students have during their first year in college. As a result, some students are dissatisfied with their grades or their performance in their courses, but they don't know what to do to correct this problem. Often they experience anxiety and frustration and may even begin to doubt whether they have the ability to succeed in college. For many of these students, simply learning how to study and how to learn strategically in college makes the difference between failure and success. Other students benefit by increasing their motivation, boosting their self-esteem, or learning better ways to study so that they can enjoy their college experience more. Becoming a strategic learner can help them achieve both their academic and their personal goals in college. If students apply what they are learning, they should see an improvement in their grades, have more time for other responsibilities or for leisure activities, feel less stressed about their academic work, feel better about themselves, and perhaps even begin to enjoy learning.

In order to succeed in college, students must learn to apply the strategies they are learning to real course material. Practicing these strategies on material in psychology, history, biology, and sociology, for example, will help students learn to modify and adapt the strategies to the lectures, texts, exams, and assignments for their other courses. This transfer experience will help motivate students to use these new strategies in their other courses, one of the goals of college success courses.

The activities at the end of each chapter can help your students facilitate this transfer. In addition, there are a number of text excerpts and practice activities available in the Activities Packet, available in the Instructor's Manual and on-line at the *Orientation to College Learning* Web site (http://info.wadsworth.com/vborientation).

UNIQUE FEATURES OF THE TEXT

You might expect to find many of the important aspects of this book in any college success, orientation, or learning skills text. However, I feel that there are many features unique to this text:

- Emphasis on strategic learning throughout.

- Excellent student examples help students using the text to connect to effective study strategies illustrated by their peers.

- Clear, in-depth explanations for each of the strategies presented.

- A step-by-step approach to success in college.

- Excerpts from college textbooks in many disciplines help students practice new skills immediately (available in the Instructor's Manual and on the *Orientation to College Learning* Web site).

- Exercises and activities for immediate practice of the concepts being taught.

- "Hands-on and experiential" approach, which supports best theories about how students really learn.

- Four full textbook chapters for additional practice activities (available on the *Orientation to College Learning* Web site).

- Longer selections for practice, which simulate the real college experience better than short excerpts found in competing texts (available in the Instructor's Manual and online).

- InfoTrac College Edition© available, bundled with this text.

- Internet and InfoTrac College Edition activities in each chapter.

- Boxed feature, "Tip Blocks," in each chapter for traditional and nontraditional students.

- Flexible, straightforward format and organization that appeals to a variety of instructors—full-time or part-time faculty, counselors, residence life personnel, or anyone in academic assistance.

IMPORTANT ASPECTS OF THE BOOK

This text provides a step-by-step approach to college learning skills. By breaking each of the topics down into smaller units, students will be able to master each of the steps before moving on to the next. Each chapter includes instruction in the skill, student examples, exercises for practice, and activities for self-evaluation.

INSTRUCTION

This text provides clear, easy-to-read explanations of how to study. Strategies for getting motivated, setting goals, managing time, improving concentration, taking notes, reading and understanding textbooks, and preparing for and taking tests. Because every student learns differently, a number of different strategies for taking text notes, preparing "To Do" lists, and preparing study sheets (just to name a few) are described in the text. Students are encouraged to try all of the strategies and then permitted to select the ones that work best for them. But learning to study effectively and efficiently requires more than just knowing a new skill; it also requires using that skill. In many cases, understanding why particular strategies work helps motivate students to use them in their other courses. Explanations and rationales for using these strategies are also presented so that students understand why one strategy may work in particular situations while others may not.

EXAMPLES

A large number of examples have been included in the text to show students how to use the strategies that are presented. For many students, seeing an example of what they have to do makes it much easier to do it right the first time. Since there are many ways to develop a study sheet, take notes, or even keep track of assignments, a number of different examples are shown for each of the different strategies discussed in the text. These models help students understand how to use the strategies and may also motivate them to complete their assignments.

PRACTICE

One of the most important goals of any successful college success, orientation, or learning skills course is getting students to transfer what they learn to other course work. In order to help students achieve this goal, more than 150 activities have been designed to let students practice what they have learned. In addition to the activities at the end of every chapter, the Activities Packet, available in the Instructor's Manual and online, contains additional activities and excerpts from other college textbooks. In this way, students are afforded practice with material that is similar to the course material they are currently using. Finally, many of the activities require students to practice the strategies using their own course materials. In this way, students transfer the skills they have learned to their other courses while at the same time increasing their understanding of the material for their other courses. In many cases, this leads to overall higher success, something that helps students see the real value of learning skills instruction.

SELF-EVALUATION

Many of the activities are designed to help students monitor their own learning. The "Where Are You Now?" activities provide a quick check of the number of effective strategies students have prior to beginning each unit and the number they have made a part of their repertoire at the end of the unit. The

"Where Are You Now?" activities are available online for "post testing." Some instructors choose to have students complete the end-of-chapter activity at a later date to allow more time for the students to incorporate the strategies. In addition, activities throughout the book ask students to evaluate many of the strategies that are presented in the text. It is only through self-evaluation that students can actually prove to themselves that one method of study is working for them. Once students know that a strategy is effective, they are more likely to continue to use it.

CHANGES IN THE FOURTH EDITION

The fourth edition of *Orientation to College Learning* contains new review questions, activities, and student examples in every chapter. Although additional changes were made in all chapters in this fourth edition, only the most significant changes are listed below.

CHANGED ORDER IN CHAPTERS

Former Chapter 10 (Improving Memory) has been moved to Chapter 5. Understanding how we learn and remember helps students better realize that they need to take good lecture notes (Chapter 6); read, highlight, and take notes on their text material (Chapters 7, 8, and 9); and use the Five-Day Study Plan and the active learning strategies that are described in the new Chapter 10 to succeed on exams. Many instructors have indicated that they have been introducing this chapter on memory and learning earlier in the course.

NEW ON-LINE APPENDICES

Four new appendices have been added to the Instructor's Manual and are available online for this fourth edition. Appendices A, B, and D originally appeared as sections of the former Chapter 15 (Communicating on Paper, Orally, and On the Internet) which appeared in the third edition of the text. Redesigning this chapter as individual appendices will better aid students in building skills at any point during the semester. The addition of Appendix C on studying math will be very useful for any student taking a math or science course, which includes math-based problem solving. All of these topics present valuable information that is best presented early in the semester rather than at the end of the course. Hopefully, this new format will make this material available to students as they need it.

NEW TOPICS

- Plagiarism (Chapter 1)
- Increasing level of interaction (Chapter 1)
- Study logs (Chapter 3)
- Components of concentration (Chapter 4)
- Taking notes on PowerPoint presentations (Chapter 6)
- Predicting quiz questions (Chapter 8)
- Organizing text information (Chapter 9)
- Using pacing strategies (Chapter 11)
- Studying math (Appendix C)

EXPANDED COVERAGE ON

- Evaluating time use (Chapter 3)
- Coping with procrastination (Chapter 3)
- Strategies for improving concentration (Chapter 4)
- Rehearsal strategies (Chapter 5)
- Affective and motivational strategies (Chapter 5)
- Writing recall questions (Chapter 6)
- Benefits of taking lecture notes (Chapter 6)
- Benefits of editing lecture notes (Chapter 6)
- Reviewing lecture notes (Chapter 6)
- Reading/study systems (Chapter 7)
- Reasons to mark your text (Chapter 8)
- Mapping (Chapter 9)
- Evaluating text notes (Chapter 9)
- The Five-Day Study Plan (Chapter 10)
- Study sheets (Chapter 10)

- Budgeting time (Chapter 11)
- Organizing information for essay tests (Chapter 12)
- Preparing for comprehensive finals (Chapter 14)

DESIGN FEATURES

- Updated review questions at the end of every chapter
- New updated *Orientation to College Learning* Web site
- More group activities in every chapter
- New self-monitoring activities in every chapter
- More journal activities in every chapter
- New Web site activities in every chapter
- New and updated text excerpts for practice
- New text chapters available on the Web site
- New wider margins
- New brighter blue for accents
- New online appendices

SUPPLEMENTARY MATERIALS

Instructor's Manual

The Instructor's Manual includes an overview of each chapter, teaching suggestions, course materials and handouts, journal and portfolio activities, quiz questions, and multiple-choice, essay, and discussion questions. Also included are excerpts from other college textbooks, additional student examples (including the activities packet), the four appendixes, and transparency masters.

InfoTrac College Edition

InfoTrac College Edition, an online database with current full-text articles from hundreds of scholarly and popular publications, is available bundled with this text. Both you and your students can receive unlimited online use for one academic term. Activities that help students use InfoTrac College Edition are now included in each chapter of the text.

Orientation to College Learning Web Site

Students using this text will have access to the *Orientation to College Learning* book-specific Web site. In addition to the activities and end-of-chapter review questions, students will have access to four full text chapters and a number of additional text excerpts from college textbooks for transfer practice activities, the entire activities packet of exercises, handouts on additional topics related to college success such as calculating your GPA, goal setting and action planning forms, time management calendars, a self-scoring version of the learning style inventory, sample lectures for note-taking practice, practice tests for multiple-choice, matching, and true-false tests, final exam planning calendars, updated Web sites for research, college success links, and many other special features.

College Success Web Site

Students using this text will have access to Wadsworth's College Success Web site. In addition to a wealth of online links and resources, students can access InfoTrac College Edition, a virtual library of hundreds of articles and links to many other useful sites.

ACKNOWLEDGMENTS FOR THE FOURTH EDITION

Many people have been instrumental in making the fourth edition of *Orientation to College Learning* possible. I am especially appreciative of the innovative ideas, concrete suggestions, and continued support of my editor Annie Mitchell. I am also appreciative of the support of the Wadsworth team: Emily Smith, Kirsten Markson, and Carol O'Connell have been invaluable in getting this book into print. Thank you all. As always, my husband, Mal, has been my greatest support. In addition to writing the first half of Chapter 5, he is always willing to help out at home, provide objective feedback, and remind me that I should be working. As a public speaking instructor herself, my daughter, Sharon, was able to provide concrete suggestions on the preparation and delivery of oral presentations for Appendix B. I am so proud to have her as a colleague. I am grateful to my students who have been eager to share their own strategies for success. Their enthusiasm, encouragement, and personal success have been very important to me. After teaching for more than twenty years, I am still learning from them. Many of the new topics and expanded coverage are a direct result of their requests, insight, and suggestions.

I have been very fortunate to have had a group of reviewers who shared their time, expertise, and wonderful suggestions for shaping this fourth edition. Thank you for your feedback on the strengths and weaknesses of the text and your excellent suggestions. Your insight and experience in teaching college study skills and college success courses have been invaluable in creating this fourth edition: Ralph Anttonen, Millersville University; Laura Bauer, National-Louis University; Mary Lynn Dille, Miami University; Mike Elias, Texas Woman's University; Zola Gordy, Maplewoods Community College; Margaret Hébert, Eastern Connecticut State University; Faith Heinrichs, Central Missouri State University; Barbara McLay, University of South Florida; Nancy Mills, University of South Florida; Cassandra Patillo, Santa Monica College; Curtis Ricker, Georgia Southern University; Barbara N. Sherman, Liberty University; Jaqueline Simon, Rider University; Will Williams III, College of Charleston.

TO THE STUDENT

As you are reading this preface, you are probably feeling excited about beginning your college career. You should be—being in college is an exciting opportunity. A few years ago, I heard someone talking about how foolish some people are to put so much emphasis on their college years. After all, the person said, it's only a few years out of an entire lifetime. But many students remember their college years as being very important and very special times of their lives. Perhaps it's because they are extremely important years. They open many new doors—both socially and professionally—and, in many ways, shape your entire future. Because your college years are such important ones, you may be feeling a little unsure of how successful you'll be as a new college student.

Many students begin college unsure of themselves. Some feel unsure about living away from home and being on their own for the first time. Others are uncertain about whether they can attend college while still working full time or caring for their families. Many students worry about how well they'll do academically. As you'll learn in Chapter 1, college is very different from high school. Many of the study strategies that worked for you in high school may not be as useful in college. In order to make the transition from high school to college as smooth as possible, you may need to learn more about how to study. This text introduces and explains many learning strategies that will help you achieve your academic goals. If you're using this text before or during your first semester in college, you should be well prepared for the challenges ahead of you. By learning and applying new strategies for dealing with college courses, you can achieve your academic goals.

Did you take driver's education in high school? When I ask my students that question, most indicate that they have and that, for the most part, it's still taught in much the same way as it was when I took it. You do the "book part"—learning how to operate the car and the "rules" for safe driving. You then do the "car part"—you actually practice driving in the driver's education car. To be a good driver, you need to do both well. Becoming a successful student isn't that different. You need to do the "book part" (learning new skills and strategies) and the "car part" (applying those strategies to your own college assignments). If you use the new strategies to complete your reading assignments, take your lecture notes, and prepare for and take exams, you'll be successful in college. By trying out each of the new strategies for managing your time, setting goals, taking text notes, and preparing essay answers, for example, you can evaluate the effectiveness of each method and choose the one that works best for you—you can become a strategic learner.

Once you put your newly learned strategies into practice, you should begin to see your grades improve in each of your courses. This kind of improvement does not result from just being told what to do differently but rather from hard work and persistence in applying effective learning strategies to your own course material. Becoming a successful student takes time and effort—there are no miracles involved. If you're willing to learn new skills and strategies and are also motivated to use them when doing your own course assignments, you, too, can achieve your goals.

Speaking of goals, I have four goals for you in your use of this text. First, I want you to learn new strategies that will make learning and studying much more effective. Second, I want you to use those strategies in your own course work, so that you can achieve your academic goals. Third, I want you to feel better about yourself both as a student and as a person—I want you to have self-confidence. Fourth, I want you to actually learn to enjoy school. Instead of dreading a class, an assignment, or even an exam, I'd like you to look forward to them because you'll know how to be successful in taking notes, writing that report, and preparing for and taking that exam. If you apply what you are learning, you should see an improvement in your grades, have more time for leisure activities, feel less stressed about your academic work, feel better about yourself, and, perhaps, even begin to enjoy learning.

HOW TO USE THIS BOOK

There are many resources available in this text to help you make a successful transition to college learning. Each of the following text resources will provide you with additional information to help you achieve your goals.

CONCEPT MAPS

The concept maps on the first page of the chapter are designed to give you a brief introduction to the main topics in the chapter. Think about what you already know about each of the topics before you begin reading the text. You may also find that they can serve as a template for your own map of the chapter. See Chapter 9 for more information on how to map the information in your textbook.

WHERE ARE YOU NOW? ACTIVITIES

By completing the "Where Are You Now?" activities before reading the chapter, you can evaluate your current strategy use related to the topics in each chapter. Once you identify your strengths and weaknesses, you can focus on those areas where you need the most assistance. You may notice after completing one of these activities that they provide you with an overview of some of the strategies that will be discussed in the chapter. After you complete the chapter or even 2 or 3 weeks later, complete the activity again in the text (using a different color) or do it online at the *Orientation to College Learning* Web site (http://info.wadsworth.com/vborientation).

TIP BLOCKS

The Tip Blocks found in each chapter include additional strategies for both traditional and nontraditional students. You'll find practical suggestions in each chapter that will save you time, help you apply your strategies to your other course work, or give you tips for making studying more interesting and challenging.

STUDENT EXAMPLES

The student examples shown in the text serve as models for many of the strategies that are described in each chapter. Although it has become almost a cliché, a picture is worth a thousand words to students who aren't sure how to take lecture notes, create recall questions, and set up study sheets, just to name a few of the applications you may find useful in this text. Occasionally, poor examples are included that contain common errors students make. These examples are designed to keep you from making those same mistakes.

TRANSFER ACTIVITIES

Each chapter contains two or three transfer activities. To complete these activities, you need to apply one or more of the new strategies described in the chapter to your other college course work. By using the strategies in your own work, you'll be able to determine which are the most effective for you, while at the same time improving your performance in your other courses.

SELF-MONITORING ACTIVITIES

Each chapter contains self-monitoring activities. By completing these activities you can learn how to monitor your learning. These activities help you monitor your performance in your other course work and the strategies that you're using. Knowing whether or not you're using effective strategies can help you make changes, if they are necessary, in order to be more successful in college.

GROUP ACTIVITIES

The group activities in each chapter are designed to encourage collaborative work. Many students enjoy working with others and find that they learn much more when working in a group. Sharing ideas, resources, and strategies all help you succeed in college. If you haven't already discovered the advantages of collaborative work, you may find that these activities will demonstrate how effective it can be.

JOURNAL ACTIVITIES

The journal activities in each chapter are designed to help you reflect on your learning experiences as you move through the text and your course work. By writing about how you applied each of the strategies to your own work, you can evaluate how effective they were in helping you achieve your goals. You may also find that noting any changes that you would make the next time you used the strategy can help you monitor your own learning and your progress toward success. Many students find that writing about their progress is very motivating and provides them with feelings of accomplishment as well.

INFOTRAC COLLEGE EDITION ACTIVITIES

The InfoTrac College Edition activities are designed to help you develop research skills so that you can make use of this powerful full-text database. Beginning with the activity in Chapter 1, each activity is designed to help you search the database in progressively more sophisticated ways. You will learn how to search using both keywords and by using the subject index. This will help you locate articles on any topic related to your own course work for papers, projects, and presentations.

INTERNET ACTIVITIES

The Internet activities in each chapter are designed to help you become familiar with using the World Wide Web to access information and do research. In each chapter, you will learn to use the Internet in progressively more sophisticated ways to locate the information that you need. If you aren't already familiar or comfortable with using the Internet, go first to Appendix D (available on the Web site). You'll find an easy-to-follow introduction to communicating on the Internet.

ORIENTATION TO COLLEGE LEARNING BOOK-SPECIFIC WEB SITE

The *Orientation to College Learning* book-specific Web site is a new feature to this text. It contains a wealth of information to help you succeed in college. You'll find answers to the multiple-choice and completion items from the end of chapter reviews. There are handouts on topics such as calculating your GPA, forms for setting goals and action planning, and calendars for time-management activities. You'll also find a self-scoring form of the Learning Style Inventory described in Chapter 1. There are sample lectures and text excerpts for note-taking practice and practice tests for objective and essay exams. You'll also have access to four entire text chapters from a variety of academic disciplines. Updated Web sites for research, college success links, and many other activities, in the Activities Packet, can be found on this new Web site. Check it out at http://info.wadsworth.com/vborientation.

REVIEW QUESTIONS

The review questions at the end of each chapter are designed to help you monitor your learning. You'll find a list of key terms you should know, and both completion and multiple-choice questions. You'll be able to check the answers to both the completion and multiple-choice items on the Web site listed above. Please keep in mind, though, that these questions do not cover all of the important information in the chapter. They are designed to provide you with some feedback on your reading comprehension and learning, but you need to predict additional questions to prepare for quizzes and exams. I recommend predicting about 25 to 30 additional questions for each chapter. By using the review questions as models, you should be able to generate these additional questions on your own or within a study group.

A FINAL NOTE

It's always exciting and rewarding when students tell me that the strategies in this book helped them. I'm especially delighted to hear about their success in their freshman year. I'm often as happy, I think, as they are when they make the Dean's List. If you were successful during your first semester, first year, or even during your college career because of your use of this text, I'd love to hear from you, too. Drop me a note and let me know how *Orientation to College Learning* helped you. Also, if you have any suggestions for how this book can be improved in order to help other students succeed in college, please let me know. You can contact me by writing to:

Dianna Van Blerkom
Thomson/Wadsworth
10 Davis Drive
Belmont, California 94002

Chapter 1

GETTING READY TO LEARN

"In the beginning of the semester, I was dead set against changing my ways. I thought my study methods were tried and true and would work in college the same as they did in high school. I was wrong. With the increased workload of college, I needed to change practically everything that I did academically. I was studying, taking notes, and writing papers the wrong way. Now that I've learned new study methods, I've changed my habits, and I am getting higher grades in college than I ever did in high school."

Carlos Becerra
Student

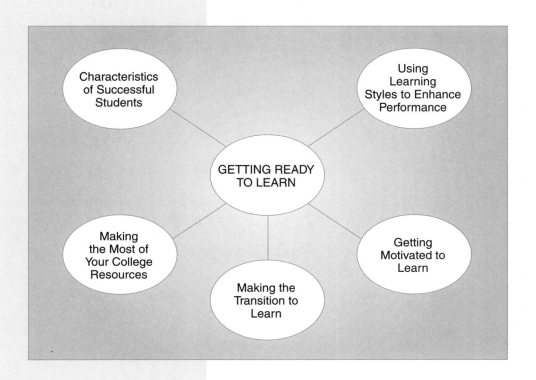

Where Are You Now?

Take a few minutes to answer *yes* or *no* to the following questions.

	YES	NO
1. Do you know how to increase your motivation?	_____	_____
2. Do you know where to go on your campus to get financial aid, a tutor, and information on clubs and organizations?	_____	_____
3. If you miss class, do you expect your professor to go over the material with you at a later date?	_____	_____
4. Do you know your preferred learning style?	_____	_____
5. Do you plan to take a lighter course load during your first semester in college?	_____	_____
6. Do you attend class regularly and stay up-to-date with your assignments?	_____	_____
7. Do you experience stress about getting your assignments done on time?	_____	_____
8. Do you make decisions without thinking about the outcome?	_____	_____
9. Have you really thought about why you are in college?	_____	_____
10. Do you expect college to be the same as high school?	_____	_____

TOTAL POINTS _____

Give yourself 1 point for each *yes* answer to all questions except 3, 7, 8, and 10 and 1 point for each *no* answer to questions 3, 7, 8, and 10. Now total up your points. A low score indicates that you need some help adjusting to college. A high score indicates that you already have realistic expectations.

CHARACTERISTICS OF SUCCESSFUL STUDENTS

What makes some students succeed in college and others fail? Faculty, administrators, and students have discussed that question for years. Although there is no exact formula for success, research indicates that there are some factors that do lead to success. Successful students are actively involved in their learning. In addition, successful students are more likely to plan, monitor, and evaluate their learning—they are strategic learners. Finally, successful students take responsibility for their own learning—they are independent learners.

BECOMING AN ACTIVE LEARNER

How do you typically prepare for a quiz or an exam? When I ask my students that question at the beginning of the semester, most say they read over the material. Is that what you said? You may be thinking that reading over the material worked well for your high-school exams. Many college exams cover two to three hundred pages of text and four weeks of lecture material. You can't learn all of that information just by reading over it a few times. Instead, you need to identify, organize, and condense the information. Next, you need to use active study strategies such as taking notes, predicting questions, making word and question cards, developing study sheets, participating in study groups, and self-testing to learn the material.

Active learners talk and listen, write, read, and reflect on (think about) what they are learning.[1] Talking about the information and listening to others discuss the information in a study group, for example, gets you actively involved in the learning process. In addition to reviewing the information, you are elaborating on it by putting it in your own words. You can also learn by reading actively. Active reading involves previewing, highlighting, predicting questions, and thinking critically about the material, all of which force you to interact with the printed word. These strategies help you activate your prior knowledge, identify the key information, check your understanding of it, and form connections within the material. Writing summaries, taking notes, developing concept maps and study sheets, and writing out answers to predicted essay questions help you organize and synthesize the information as you learn it. Reflecting on the information helps you gain a deeper understanding of the material and form con-

---

[1]Chet Meyers and Thomas B. Jones, *Promoting Active Learning: Strategies for the College Classroom* (San Francisco: Jossey-Bass, 1993).

nections between the new information and your prior knowledge. Getting actively involved in your learning is the first step toward succeeding in college. You'll learn many active learning strategies in the remainder of this text.

BECOMING A STRATEGIC LEARNER

Another way to be more successful in college is to become a strategic learner. According to Weinstein and Hume, "*Strategic learners* are students who view studying and learning as a systematic process that is, to a good degree, under their control."[2] Weinstein's model of strategic learning involves three main components: skill, will, and self-regulation.

Skill

Strategic learners possess a wide variety of skills to aid their learning. These *skills* include knowledge about yourself as a learner, knowledge about different types of academic tasks, knowledge about strategies for learning, prior content knowledge, and knowledge about the contexts in which that knowledge could be useful.[3] Let's look at the first three of these components briefly.

You already know many things about yourself as a learner. You know which subjects you excel in, which types of classes you like, and which types of assignments you do best. You know something about your ability as a student from your grades in high school or scores on standardized tests. However, you may not know much about your learning style—about how you learn best—and you probably aren't aware of many of the study and learning strategies that you'll need to use to be successful in college.

After completing twelve years of formal schooling, you have a great deal of knowledge about completing academic tasks. You know how to do math problems, write a paper, and read a chapter in a textbook, just to name a few. However, some of the tasks that you will be asked to complete in college are different from anything you've done before; they will require you to complete new tasks, complete some tasks differently, and apply new strategies for learning.

Although you've learned some study strategies in the past, you'll need to develop many new ones to succeed in college. In addition to the increased amount of information you'll have to learn, you also will be expected to understand the material rather than just memorize it. To achieve these goals, you must learn new strategies and learn how to match them appropriately to the task.

---

[2]Claire E. Weinstein and Laura M. Hume, *Study Strategies for Lifelong Learning* (Washington, DC: American Psychological Association, 1998).
[3]Claire E. Weinstein, Strategic Learning/Strategic Teaching: Flip Sides of a Coin, in Pintrich, Brown, and Weinstein, Eds., *Student Motivation, Cognition, and Learning: Essays in Honor of Wilbert J. McKeachie* (Hillsdale, NJ: Lawrence Erlbaum, 1994).

Will

Just knowing how to prepare for an exam or take lecture notes, though, is not enough. A strategic learner must have the will to put that knowledge into practice. *Will* involves setting goals, selecting appropriate study strategies, and believing in your own ability and in the study strategies that you have chosen. In addition, strategic learners are motivated—they are willing to work hard to achieve their goals.

Have you ever met a student who didn't do well in college? Most people assume that the students who fail or quit are those who can't do the work or don't have enough ability to succeed. However, most studies indicate that it's just as often the brightest students (as defined by test scores or academic histories) who do not succeed. Why does this happen? Look around your own classroom. You probably will notice that some students are absent. Not attending class, not doing reading assignments, not preparing for exams and many other similar factors contribute to college failure. These activities depend on your willingness to do what is necessary to be successful in college. Will is an equally important factor in college success.

Self-Regulation

Finally, strategic learners are *self-regulated learners*. They manage their time well, monitor their learning, evaluate the results of their effort, and approach learning in a systematic way.[4] Self-regulated learners are self-directed, not other-directed. They are what we often call *independent learners*—they take the initiative for their own learning. In high school, your parents and teachers often took the responsibility for your learning; they made sure that you completed your assignments, remembered to study for exams, and often felt responsible if you were not successful. You have to learn to do that on your own—you have to become an independent learner.

Self-regulated learners plan before starting a task, select strategies that they know are appropriate for the task, and monitor their own learning as they are completing the task and after the task is completed. Self-regulated learners know what they have to do to be successful. They set goals and design plans that help them complete their work on time. They also know a wide variety of study skills and strategies and choose the appropriate strategies for each task and testing situation. For example, self-regulated learners prepare differently for multiple-choice and essay exams. They use different strategies for completing a reading assignment that will be followed by a quiz and one for which they must only take lecture notes.

Finally, self-regulated learners monitor their learning. They pause to check their understanding when reading, ask questions in class when they don't

---

[4]Claire E. Weinstein and Laura M. Hume, *Study Strategies for Lifelong Learning* (Washington, DC: American Psychological Association, 1998).

understand something, compare lecture notes with friends, and self-test before exams. Self-regulated learners also make adjustments when they find their strategies are not working.

You'll have the opportunity to use many new learning strategies in many of the text activities, and, I hope, you'll use them in your other course work. By using the strategies in your own work, monitoring their effectiveness, and making changes when necessary, you can become a strategic learner.

USING LEARNING STYLES TO ENHANCE PERFORMANCE

Your learning style also affects your ability to succeed in college. Researchers in education and psychology have been investigating the issue of learning styles since the 1950s. In this section, you'll discover more about how you learn best, how to match learning strategies to specific tasks and subject areas, and how using your preferred and non-preferred learning style will affect your performance in college.

WHAT ARE LEARNING STYLES?

The term *learning style* refers to the preferred way that you acquire, process, and retain information—the way you learn best. We learn new tasks in different ways; we each have our own style or preference for learning. The time of day you study, the kinds of strategies you use, whether you work alone or with a group, and even the place you study are all aspects of your learning style.

However, your learning style involves more than these factors. Researchers have explored the nature of learning styles in many different ways. Some relate learning style to cultural factors that affect the expectations that teachers, parents, and students have about learning in the classroom and at home. Others have investigated the relationship of learning styles to whether we are left-brained or right-brained learners (whether we tend to process information in a linear, analytical manner like a computer or in a more holistic, visual manner like a kaleidoscope).[5] Many learning styles are based on Kolb's theory that some people approach new situations through "feeling" and others through "thinking."

---

[5]Sharon L. Silverman and Martha E. Casazza, *Learning & Development: Making Connections to Enhance Teaching* (San Francisco: Jossey-Bass, 2000).

Take the Learning Style Inventory in Figure 1.1 or the self-scoring version on the *Orientation to College Learning* book-specific Web site at *http://info.wadsworth.com/vanblerkom04.*

CHARACTERISTICS OF LEARNING MODALITIES

The Learning Style Inventory in Figure 1.1 is an informal inventory that can provide you with information about your preferred learning modality (learning through the senses). Are you a visual learner, an auditory learner, a kinesthetic learner, or do you have preferences in two areas. Before reading any further, turn the page and complete the Learning Style Inventory, or take the self-scoring version on the *Orientation to College Learning* Web site. As you read through the following descriptions, you may find that you have some of the characteristics of each style. You probably do. We all have some strengths in each of the three learning modes. As you discovered by completing the inventory, however, one of the styles is your preferred style for learning new information.

Visual Learners

If you found that you're a *visual learner,* you learn best by seeing things. Reading; looking at pictures, diagrams, and charts; and watching films, videos, and demonstrations are all ways that you can learn new information. You probably have found that you understand your professor's lecture better if you read the text chapter ahead of time. Think about how you study for exams. You probably reread your text and lecture notes, rewrite your notes, take notes, and fill in study guides or make study sheets. During an exam, you may be able to "see" the correct answer in your mind's eye.

Auditory Learners

If you're an *auditory learner,* you learn best by hearing information. Unlike the visual learner, you probably prefer to go to your class and listen to the lecture before you read the text chapter. Have you found that you can understand the text much more easily after you hear the professor's lecture? Reading difficult text passages out loud is also a good idea for the auditory learner. Discussing the course material, mumbling information as you read and study, asking and answering questions out loud, and listening to study notes on tape are some strategies that you may already use if your preferred learning style is auditory. You may find that you can actually "hear" the professor's lecture when you try to recall the specific point you need to answer a particular test question.

Kinesthetic Learners

If you're a *kinesthetic learner,* you learn best by doing things. You prefer hands-on tasks that allow you to touch and feel. Many of the strategies used by visual

FIGURE 1.1A

• • • • • • • • • • • • • • •

Learning Style Inventory

As you read each of the following statements, put a check mark for *yes* or *no* to indicate the response that describes you best.

	YES	NO
1. I remember things better if someone tells me about them than if I read about them.	_____	_____
2. I'd rather read about "tapping" (extracting the sap from) trees than take a field trip and actually tap a tree.	_____	_____
3. I enjoy watching the news on television more than reading the newspaper.	_____	_____
4. I'd rather build a model of a volcano than read an article about famous volcanoes.	_____	_____
5. When I'm having trouble understanding my text chapter, I find that reading it out loud helps improve my comprehension.	_____	_____
6. If I had to identify specific locations on a map for an exam, I would rather practice by drawing and labeling a map than reciting the locations out loud.	_____	_____
7. I tend to better understand my professor's lecture when I read the text material ahead of time.	_____	_____
8. I would rather take part in a demonstration of how to use a new computer program than read a set of directions on its use.	_____	_____
9. If someone asked me to make a model for a class project, I would rather have someone explain how to make it than rely on written directions.	_____	_____
10. If I were preparing for an exam, I'd rather listen to a summary of the chapter than write my own summary.	_____	_____
11. I would prefer my professor to give me written directions rather than oral directions when I have to do a writing assignment.	_____	_____
12. I'd rather listen to the professor's lecture before I read the chapter.	_____	_____
13. If I had to learn to use a new software program, I'd prefer to read the written directions rather than have a friend describe how to use it.	_____	_____
14. If I have trouble understanding how to complete a writing assignment, I prefer to have written directions than have someone explain how to do it.	_____	_____
15. I like to listen to books on tape more than I like to read books.	_____	_____
16. When I have to learn spelling or vocabulary lists, I prefer to practice by reciting out loud rather than writing the words over and over again.	_____	_____
17. If I had a choice, I would prefer to watch a video of someone else doing chemistry experiments than actually perform them myself.	_____	_____
18. When I have trouble with a math problem, I prefer to work through the sample problems rather than have someone tell me how to do them.	_____	_____

FIGURE 1.1B

· · · · · · · · · ·

Scoring Instructions

Your responses in both the *yes* and *no* columns are important in determining your preferred learning style. Tally your responses using the following scoring key and then use the chart to total your responses.

1. A (Auditory) style. Look back at your responses and count the numbers of the *yes* responses for items 1, 3, 5, 9, 10, 12, 15, 16 and the *no* responses for items 6, 7, 11, 13, 14, 18. Write the totals in the appropriate blocks in the A column on the chart.

2. V (Visual) style. Look back at your responses and count the numbers of the *yes* responses for items 2, 7, 11, 13, 14, 17 and the *no* responses for items 1, 3, 4, 5, 8, 9, 12, 15. Write the totals in the appropriate blocks in the V column on the chart.

3. K (Kinesthetic) style. Look back at your responses and count the numbers of the *yes* responses for items 4, 6, 8, 18 and the *no* responses for items 2, 10, 16, 17. Write the totals in the appropriate blocks in the K column on the chart.

	A (Auditory)	V (Visual)	K (Kinesthetic)
Number of *yes* responses			
Number of *no* responses			
Total points			
Cutoff score	8	8	5

Add up your score for each column. To determine your preferred learning style, compare your total score for each column to the *cutoff score* for that column. If your score is equal to or higher than the cutoff score, then you tend to show a preference for that learning style. The higher your score is, the stronger your preference for that style of learning. You may find that you have high scores in two areas; that's okay. You may learn well using more than one learning style. Note: Your total points for the A, V, and K columns should add up to 18.

Note: You may also take this learning style inventory online in a self-scoring format.

and auditory learners also appeal to kinesthetic learners. For example, in Chapter 9 you'll learn a strategy called *mapping*—creating visual diagrams or representations of written and oral information. Whereas the visual learner can recall the information from a concept map by seeing it, the kinesthetic learner will be able to remember it by the feel of how he or she created it. Kinesthetic learners also learn well from doing experiments, taking self-tests, or replicating the tasks they will later have to perform in the testing situation. Kinesthetic learners like to get actively involved in what they are learning.

Integrated Learning Styles

Although each of us has a preferred learning style, most of us learn information by using a combination of learning styles. In fact, some courses, assignments, or exams may require you to use one or more of your less preferred learning styles in order to complete the task. When you're forced to complete a hands-on activity, for example, you may find that using a kinesthetic approach is more successful. Even though it's not your best way to learn *most* material, it may be the best way to learn *that* material. Although my preferred learning style is visual, I always call the computer help desk when I run into a problem with a computer program. The advantage for me is that the technical support personnel tell me how to fix my problem, and they stay on the line and assist me as I complete each of the steps on the computer. By using my two less preferred learning styles together, I learn better than by using my preferred style.

Using a combination of auditory, visual, and kinesthetic strategies will help you benefit from all the ways that you can learn information. As you learn about note-taking, text-reading, and test-preparation strategies in later chapters, keep your preferred learning style in mind. However, the most successful students are often the ones who can use strategies that take advantage of all of the ways they learn or those who can switch styles depending on the demands of the course or the assignment.

Other Characteristics of Learning Styles

The inventory in Figure 1.2 should help you find out more about how you learn best. One of the interesting outcomes of completing this activity is that many students find that they aren't always aware of some of the characteristics of their own learning style. For example, you may have indicated that you learn best when you study in the morning, but in fact you actually do most of your work in the late evening. This may be a habit you established in high school or for some other reason. However, now that you know that you learn best in the morning, you should change your time schedule to work earlier in the day. When and where you work are often dependent on each other, so look at your rankings to items 1 and 2. If you find that you often do your assignments late at night, it may be because that's the only time you can find a quiet place to study.

Your response to question 3 may explain why you work best when you're asked to do group projects, or why, for you, they're often something you dread. Many students study best when they work by themselves, whereas others find that everything falls into place when they work in groups. Although question 4 appears to focus on how you should take a test, it really assesses how impulsive (acting without thinking) or reflective (thinking before acting) you are in learning situations. If you tend to be impulsive, you may have more difficulty completing certain types of academic tasks—especially problem-solving tasks. Students who are more reflective tend to think through things more slowly and carefully. Reflective learning styles are generally more suited to academic learning and success. If you tend to be an impulsive learner, you can learn to be more reflective by using many of the learning strategies that will be presented in the remainder of the text.

FIGURE 1.2

• • • • • • • • • •

Find Out More
About How You
Learn Best

> Rank the four responses to each item according to the following scale in order to determine more about how you learn best: 4 = best, 3 = good, 2 = fair, 1 = poor.
>
> 1. I learn best when I study
>
>   _____ in the morning.
>   _____ in the afternoon.
>   _____ in the evening.
>   _____ late at night.
>
> 2. I learn best when I study
>
>   _____ in complete quiet.
>   _____ with soft background noise.
>   _____ with moderate levels of noise.
>   _____ in a noisy environment.
>
> 3. I learn best when I study
>
>   _____ by myself.
>   _____ with my regular study partner.
>   _____ with a small group.
>   _____ in a large-group review session or recitation class.
>
> 4. When I take exams, I generally
>
>   _____ just guess to get done.
>   _____ pick the first answer that looks right.
>   _____ read all the possible answers before I choose one.
>   _____ eliminate incorrect responses before I select the correct answer.

A Word of Caution

The results of the learning style inventories that you completed in Figures 1.1 and 1.2 may not be accurate. These are informal surveys that have not been scientifically tested. In addition, these (and all) learning-style inventories are self-report questionnaires. That means that you determine your own score. Your mood, the way you interpret the statements, and how you feel at the time you do the activity all affect your score. You may want to do the inventories again, perhaps later in the semester or even next semester, to verify your results.

If you are intrigued by some of the ways of looking at learning styles that were discussed earlier, go to your college learning center, counseling center, or testing center and ask to take a formal learning style inventory. Some of the more common ones (which are much too long and complex to include here) are the LSI (Kolb's Learning Style Inventory); the 4MAT System developed by Bernice McCarthy; the Learning Style Inventory by Dunn, Dunn, and Price; and the MBTI (the Myers-Briggs Type Indicator).

WHY YOUR LEARNING STYLE IS IMPORTANT

Knowing more about how you learn best will help you improve your chances of succeeding in college. Do you tend to do well in some classes but have difficulty in others? For instance, let's say you're taking History and Biology this semester. Given the same level of effort and time spent in preparation, you may think that you should do equally well in both courses. However, if you earned an A in History but got only a C in Biology, you probably would feel frustrated and confused. You may have more difficulty in college biology because the instructor's teaching style doesn't match your learning style or because you didn't use your preferred learning style when preparing the biology assignments.

Many professors teach the way that they learn best; they use their preferred learning style. If you learn best through the method that your professor uses, you probably feel very comfortable, in control, or "in your element" in that particular course. If, on the other hand, your learning style doesn't match your professor's teaching style, you may feel uncomfortable in class, have difficulty completing assignments, and perform poorly on exams. This mismatch can lead to frustration and even failure.

Understanding how you learn best can also improve your concentration. When you're working in your preferred learning mode, you probably find that you're better able to concentrate on your study tasks. Approaching a task from your preferred style results in a better fit or match—studying feels right. When things are "going well" during a study session, you'll probably complete your work efficiently and effectively. Working outside of your preferred style or using a learning style that doesn't fit the task may be the reason you put in a lot of time on your studies but don't get the results you expect.

GETTING MOTIVATED TO LEARN

Psychologists have been trying to explain why some people work hard at a task while others choose not to do so. Think of a task that you recently completed. Did you put all your energy into completing it? Did you understand what you were trying to accomplish? Did you continue working on the task even though it was difficult? How you answered each of these questions may give you a better understanding of how motivation affects college success. Motivation affects whether or not you do your work, which study strategies you decide to use, when you do your work, how long you work on a task, how well you concentrate on it, how much effort you expend doing it, and what you learn from completing the task. *Motivation* can be described as something that energizes, directs, and sustains behavior toward a particular goal. Understanding more about the factors that influence motivation and the strategies that can be used to increase it can help you be more successful in college.

FACTORS THAT INFLUENCE MOTIVATION

Although many factors influence motivation, your goals, your self-efficacy, and your level of effort are perhaps the most important ones for college success.

Goals

Your goals influence your motivation to complete a task. Without challenging, realistic goals, you may not know where to direct your efforts. You may have noticed that your motivation (or lack of motivation) varies depending on the tasks that you need to complete. Many students find that they are more motivated to work on a task when they have a personal interest in completing it or find it challenging to do so. If you're personally interested in learning how to use a computer program, for example, you may be highly motivated to achieve your goal. Working on a task because you want to learn or do something (even when you don't have to) can be described as *intrinsic motivation.*

On the other hand, you may also be motivated by the promise or expectation of earning rewards, grades, or other types of external gain. Being motivated by external factors can be described as *extrinsic motivation.* If you were told to learn to use a computer program as part of a course assignment but have little personal interest in using it, you may find that you're less motivated. Many times, our efforts are motivated by a combination of intrinsic and extrinsic motivation. You may begin to read a textbook chapter, for example, because you're concerned about your grade in the course (extrinsic motivation). However, as you're reading, you may find that you become interested in the material itself and want to learn more about the topic (intrinsic motivation). Your increased interest in the material may actually increase your motivation to complete the task, perhaps with even more effort.

Self-Efficacy

Your belief in your own ability to successfully complete a task can also affect your level of motivation. If you believe that you can successfully complete a task, you're more likely to be motivated to work on it. This belief in your ability to successfully complete a task is often described as *self-efficacy.* Each time that you're successful in accomplishing one of your goals (completing a task), it increases your self-efficacy (self-confidence) so that you can complete a similar or even more difficult task in the future. Students who have high self-efficacy are also more likely to persist on a task when it's difficult. For these reasons, many psychologists believe that past successes lead to future successes.

Effort

Your motivation is also affected by the strength of your belief that the amount of effort you put forth on a task can affect your performance. If you attribute your successes and your failures to your level of effort, you're more likely to be motivated to work hard to complete a task. The amount of effort that you exert when working on a task is something that you can control. Unlike luck, which is out of our control, we can exert a lot of effort, very little effort, or no effort in completing a task. Many study skills experts believe that students need to work hard at the beginning of the semester so that they can see that the amount of effort they put toward their academic tasks does have a positive effect on their performance. Early success (knowing you can learn the material and achieve your grade goals) is very motivating for new college students. This early success can therefore lead to even more success. You may find the following formula will help you put all of this together: $M \rightarrow \uparrow E \rightarrow S$ (Motivation leads to increased effort, which leads to success).

STRATEGIES TO INCREASE MOTIVATION

There are hundreds of strategies that you can use to increase motivation. Just go to a bookstore and check out the reference or self-help shelf. Books on how to get motivated or increase your motivation at home, at school, and at work are plentiful. Many of the chapters in this text in fact contain strategies that will help you increase your motivation. A number of basic strategies can help you get more motivated now (see Figure 1.3).

GETTING YOUR MONEY'S WORTH

A college education is your key to the future, but it's also one of the most expensive investments you or your parents will ever make. A college education can cost anywhere from $20,000 to $100,000. If you break down your tuition costs, you may find that you're paying several hundred to several thousand dollars for each course you take. Divide that number by the number of class sessions that you have in each course. You may be astounded by the actual cost of each of your classes. What's the point of all of this math? Well, it's to help you realize that every time you miss a class, you're wasting money. Some students are excited when a professor cancels a class or doesn't show up. But students who are paying the bill or attending college on loans—which they'll have to repay—often feel angry because they believe that they're not getting their money's worth. In the same way, each time you skip a class, sleep through one, or show up unpre-

FIGURE 1.3

• • • • • • • • • •

Strategies to In-
crease Motivation

- **Set challenging but realistic goals.** We are more motivated to complete tasks when we feel that they are challenging and yet attainable, within our reach.

- **Set learning goals.** Decide what facts, concepts, or ideas you want to learn before you begin working on a task.

- **See the value in the task.** Understanding why you are doing the task—seeing the importance of the task—can help motivate you to complete it.

- **Have a positive attitude.** As you begin a task, think about similar tasks that you completed in the past. Knowing that you've done it before can increase your motivation.

- **Use positive self-talk.** You may find that telling yourself that you can do it, why it's important, or that you're almost done with the task can keep you going.

- **Work hard.** One of the most important steps in getting motivated is to work hard, exert effort, on a task. Not working on a task or exerting very little effort often results in reduced motivation the next time you need to complete a similar task.

- **Use active-study strategies.** Knowing which strategy to use for a specific task and that it will work can help you be more motivated to work hard.

- **Break down tasks.** Some students have trouble getting motivated to start a task that appears to be long and difficult. Breaking down the task into smaller parts can increase your motivation.

- **Monitor your learning.** When you know your time, effort, and study strategies are working to help you learn, you'll be more motivated.

- **Learn from your mistakes.** Find out what you did wrong when you don't achieve your goals. Knowing what you need to do differently can help you be more motivated after a "failure."

pared, you aren't getting your money's worth, either. You can get your money's worth and maximize your success by going to class, working hard, and staying up-to-date with your assignments.

Work Hard to Get Your Money's Worth

Working hard will also help you get your money's worth. In high school, many students did just enough to get by. Did you "cruise" through high school? Did you spend only one hour a day doing homework assignments or studying for tests? If you answered yes to either of these questions, you'll have to change your study patterns in college. To get your money's worth, you need to put school first; you need to spend twenty to thirty-five hours or more each week (if you're attending college as a full-time student) reading, doing assignments, and preparing for exams.

INCREASE YOUR LEVEL OF INTERACTION

You're probably wondering how you could possibly spend that much time studying. Think about how you completed your last reading assignment. Did you just skim it? If so, you probably exerted very little effort and put very little time into the task. Unfortunately, you probably didn't get much out of the chapter, either. During the first week of the semester, I try to get my students to increase their level of interaction with their reading assignments. I developed a hierarchy of tasks that shows increasing levels of involvement with the material. Take a look at my list (see Figure 1.4) and put a check mark at your level of involvement.

Some of you may find that your check mark is near the top of the list, and I'm sure that some of you are working somewhere in the middle. I hope one or two of you are working very hard and your checkmark is near the bottom of the list. You probably can't jump from the top of the list to the bottom overnight—you may not have a good knowledge of all the skills involved. However, as you move through the text and acquire many of the skills that were listed, I hope you'll increase your level of involvement as you complete your assignments. You'll also learn how to get more actively involved in taking lecture notes, doing math assignments, writing papers, and preparing for exams in later chapters. Re-

FIGURE 1.4

• • • • • • • • •

Levels of Interaction

When you read this chapter or another assignment did you:

• Just skim it?

• Just read it?

• Read it and highlight the important information?

• Read it, highlight, and take notes?

• Read it, highlight, take notes and predict questions in the margin?

• Read it, highlight, take notes, predict questions, and do some of the activities?

• Read it, highlight, take notes, predict questions, do some of the activities, and think about how you would use some of the strategies?

• Read it, highlight, take notes, predict questions, do some of the activities, think about how you would use some of the strategies and apply one or two of them to your own work?

• Read it, highlight, take notes, predict questions, do some of the activities, think about how you would use some of the strategies, apply one or two of them to your own work, and quiz yourself on the material to test your understanding?

member, the more actively involved you are with the task, the more you'll learn. If you work hard, you'll get your money's worth and a good education, too.

WHY ARE YOU IN COLLEGE?

As you're getting ready to learn, maintain a positive attitude toward your progress. Think about why you're in college and what you plan to accomplish during your college career. Take some time to visit the career services office on your campus and explore the job opportunities available in your major field of study. Talk to other students and to your professors about the options available to you. Having a clear set of goals can be very motivating and can help you over some of the hurdles that you'll have to face. If you haven't chosen a major yet, that's okay, too. Use your first year or two of college to explore various courses and majors. Make an appointment to discuss your interests with your advisor, the department chairperson, or with someone in the counseling or career services office. Colleges offer courses of study that you never even heard of in high school—one of them may be the right one for you. You may even think about changing your major. Most college students do change their major at least once; many change their major several times. The important thing to remember is that career goals help motivate you to set and achieve your academic goals, which help motivate you to set and achieve your study goals. Why are you in college? Think about it.

MAKING THE TRANSITION TO LEARN

Attending college requires a certain amount of adjustment for most students. If you started college immediately after high school graduation, you'll experience many changes in your life. You may be on your own for the first time—you may have to take on many of the responsibilities that your parents or teachers previously handled. If you're a commuter or a returning adult learner, you'll have to make adjustments, too. Although juggling work, school, and home responsibilities is a challenging task, many students do it every day.

PEANUTS is reprinted by permission of Newspaper Enterprise Association, Inc.

BALANCING SCHOOL, HOME, AND WORK RESPONSIBILITIES

The U.S. Department of Education has predicted that by 2011, 38 percent of all students enrolled in institutions of higher education will be twenty-five years of age or older.[6] If you work and have home responsibilities, you may need to attend college on a part-time basis.

Returning adult learners are often described as more motivated, more committed, more organized, more independent, and more self-directed than recent high school graduates. Many of these qualities come from their greater maturity, wealth of life experiences, and strong motivation to succeed in college.

If you're a returning adult learner, these characteristics will help you do very well in college. You're probably highly motivated to succeed, because you have clear career goals and are paying for your own education. You want to get your money's worth, so you take class attendance and your assignments seriously. Your high motivation, positive attitude, and willingness to work hard are all important factors that contribute to college success.

ACCEPTING NEW RESPONSIBILITIES

If you just graduated from high school, you may have spent the summer before college learning how to sort, wash, and iron your clothing. Did you practice scheduling your time, budgeting your money, or setting priorities? These new responsibilities are also critical to college success. Keeping track of your expenses can help you stay financially solvent throughout the year. Take some time to work out a realistic budget for each semester, and then stick to it.

Learning to set priorities is one of the most difficult tasks you will face. Everything seems so interesting, exciting, and new when you begin college. College life offers many opportunities to get involved in social, organizational, and sporting events. All these activities are appealing and interesting to new college students, and all of them take time—some a great deal of time. Although you should get involved in campus life, you need to start out slowly. Join one or two clubs instead of every club that your roommate or next-door neighbor joins. If you become too involved in campus activities, you won't have enough time to complete your academic tasks.

---

[6]National Center for Education Statistics, "Projections of Education Statistics to 2011" (2001 report).

AVOIDING PLAGIARISM

Many students unintentionally are guilty of plagiarism when they write reports and research papers. *Plagiarism* is a difficult concept but can described as taking someone else's ideas or words and using them as if they were your own. The easiest way to avoid plagiarizing is to carefully document all of the information that you take from reference sources. One method of documenting information involves putting quotation marks around any information that you copy directly from a book, periodical, or other source. Another method involves paraphrasing information from source materials. Many students think that as long as they put the information into their own words, they don't have to cite (indicate the source) the information. In most cases, even paraphrased information must be documented. The only time you really don't have to document reference material is in the case of common knowledge. Information that is included in every source or many sources that you referenced may be considered to be common knowledge. On the other hand, information that is contained in only one of your sources is considered to be the unique idea(s) of the author of that book or article. This information must be documented in order to give credit to the person who developed it.

You can cite a source by including the publication information of the article or book or other work in a footnote, endnote, or reference list. Since many different citation styles are used in college, you should check with your professor to find out which format he or she expects you to use and then use your style manual or handbook to verify the proper form for each reference work you're citing.

MANAGING STRESS

Attending college can be stressful for many students because they are forced to deal with so many new responsibilities, opportunities, challenges, and decisions. *Stress* can be described as feeling tense, overwhelmed, or under pressure. Identifying the causes of stress and learning some strategies for coping with it can help you manage the stress in your life.

Sources of Stress

Many college students experience stress because they are concerned about their academic performance. Most new college students experience stress when they realize that their courses are much more demanding and fast paced than were their high school classes. Some students experience a great deal of stress about achieving the grade goals that they have set for themselves or that their families may expect them to achieve.

TIPS FOR MAKING THE TRANSITION TO COLLEGE

BELIEVE THAT COLLEGE IS THE RIGHT DECISION FOR YOU. Many students come to college feeling uncertain of their ability to succeed. Give yourself at least one or two semesters to make the transition; don't give up too soon.

MAKE ACADEMICS YOUR TOP PRIORITY. Some college students get so caught up in social activities that their grades suffer. If you aren't working full time, you should have enough time to get your course work done and still have time for leisure activities. Set a goal to get your course work done before you participate in social activities.

TAKE A LIGHT COURSE LOAD YOUR FIRST SEMESTER. Many college freshmen think that taking five or six classes will be as easy as it was in high school. However, they don't realize how much time they will be expected to spend on each course outside of class. Taking the lightest full-time course load available will help you do well during this transitional semester.

MAKE USE OF THE RESOURCES AT YOUR COLLEGE LEARNING CENTER. If you find that you aren't getting the grades that you expected on papers, quizzes, or exams, go to your college tutoring or learning center immediately. If you wait until after you've gotten two or three low test grades, it may be too late to change your course grade.

TAKE A REFRESHER COURSE TO BUILD YOUR SKILLS. If you haven't used your math, writing, or study skills for 5 to 10 years or more, you probably have become a bit rusty. Taking a refresher course or two will help you upgrade your skills.

GET TO KNOW YOUR COURSE INSTRUCTORS. Stop by your TA's or professor's office to introduce yourself or chat about the course. Making this initial contact will help you feel more comfortable about asking for help when you have a question or problem.

DEVELOP A SUPPORT NET AT HOME. Talk to your family and friends about why you are in school. By sharing what you're doing, what you're learning, and how you're feeling, you can get their support, too. Plan activities with your family and friends at least one or two hours each week and during semester breaks.

TAKE CARE OF YOURSELF. It's important to eat well-balanced meals, get enough sleep, and get some exercise. If you don't take care of yourself physically, you won't be able to work hard.

LEARN TO USE COMPUTERS. You don't have to be a computer expert, but you do need some basic computer skills to make it in college today. Take an introductory computer course during your first semester or check into tutorials offered through your college learning center, adult reentry center, or the computer labs.

Lifestyle changes are another common source of stress for college students. Balancing work, home, and school responsibilities puts additional stress on students. Some students find that after they complete all of their class assignments, there is little time left for their families or themselves. At times, this leads to conflicts and may result in even more stress. Other students experience stress from living on their own. Besides being responsible for managing their time and setting priorities (perhaps for the first time), they are trying to form new relationships while maintaining connections with their families and friends at home.

Many college students also experience stress due to personal problems. Many students spend a lot of time worrying about money. They may be concerned about the sacrifices that they or their families are making to pay for their education. Along with these concerns, students may face problems with social relationships, family crises, or health problems, just to name a few. All these personal problems add to the stress of academic and lifestyle changes that most students experience.

Methods of Coping with Stress

Although there are many positive ways to deal with stress, some college students use negative, nonproductive methods of dealing with it. Some students attempt to ignore the problem or pretend that it doesn't even exist. Others try to avoid thinking about a problem by using escapist techniques like watching television, playing video games, or even using drugs or alcohol. Although these strategies appear to eliminate the feelings of stress for the moment, they don't bring about any productive resolution of the problem. There are, however, more positive and productive ways to cope with stress.

Take Action

One of the best ways to deal with stress is to take action to eliminate or reduce the stress itself. This may involve taking control of how you use your time. Making up a daily "To Do" list can reduce stress if you're worried about getting all of your work done on time. You may also find that making out a list of important due dates will help you organize your time and relieve anxiety. Chapter 3 contains many other effective strategies for better time management. If you're stressed out about money problems, go to your campus financial aid office. Getting more information about how you can apply for scholarships, grants, and loans can help you reduce your stress. When students experience conflicts about family, work, and school responsibilities, it may be time to make a few changes. Delegating some of your responsibilities (at home or at work) to others may reduce your stress dramatically.

Seek Social Support

Another method of dealing with stress is to seek social support. Just talking about your problem with someone else is often a good way to relieve some of the stress you're feeling. We often discover that when we share our concerns with someone else, we're also getting a better understanding of them ourselves. A friend or family member also may be able to provide some much needed emotional support or suggest a way of dealing with the problem that you hadn't considered.

If you aren't sure why you're feeling stressed, you may need to seek help from someone who has special expertise in dealing with your problem. Your professor, advisor, or someone in your college learning center may be able to help you deal with your academic concerns. The school counselor is trained to help students with personal problems. Although some students believe that they should solve all of their own problems, sometimes the most effective method of reducing stress is to seek help.

Balance Work and Relaxation

Developing a good balance between work and relaxation can also reduce or eliminate stress. Taking a break from a stressful situation can at times give you a chance to look at the problem more realistically or from a different perspective. When we're refreshed and free from pressure for short periods of time, it may help us cope more effectively with stressful situations as they occur.

DECISION MAKING AND PROBLEM SOLVING

During your first year of college, you'll be making many decisions. Each time you choose to read a textbook chapter or study for an exam, you've made a decision to complete an academic task instead of socializing, sleeping, or cleaning. However, even that decision involves making more decisions. You also need to decide what to study, what strategies to use, where to study, and how long to work on the task. Although most of these decisions can be made without a lot of reflection, other decisions may require more thought and planning. Deciding whether or not to change your major, what to do if you're failing a class, or which courses to schedule for the next semester require more consideration.

Making a decision when the choices are quite obvious, like choosing between chocolate or vanilla ice cream, is fairly easy. However, when some or all choices are unknown, you may need to use a problem-solving process. The five-step approach to problem solving shown in Figure 1.5 will help you make a more informed decision or find the correct (or best) solution to your problem.

FIGURE 1.5

• • • • • • • • •

Problem Solving
Process

1. **Define the problem.** Identify the problem or the choice that you have to make. If possible, break down the problem into parts. Think about how you would like to change things. Write down what you want to do.

2. **Consider the alternatives.** Think about all the possible choices that you could make or all the possible solutions to the problem. Gather all relevant information on each alternative and consider any obstacles that could prevent you from reaching your goal (the solution). Finally, consider all the possible outcomes that could occur for each alternative.

3. **Make a plan.** List each alternative that appears to be a reasonable solution to the problem. Decide which alternative you want to try first, second, third, or fourth. Be careful not to choose the most familiar or the easiest alternative on your list because these often don't lead to the best solutions to the problem. You may need to try several alternatives before you find the best solution to the problem.

4. **Take action.** Choose the best option from your plan and put it into action. Taking action itself requires that you make a decision. After developing a plan, some students choose not to act on it. They may be concerned about the outcome or afraid that the plan won't work. Deciding not to act is an alternative that must also be carefully thought out.

5. **Evaluate the results.** If you aren't satisfied with the outcome, try another option on your list. Think about what went wrong. Did you consider all the possible alternatives? Did you gather all the relevant information? Did you just use the easiest or most obvious solution to the problem? Did you take the time to implement your plan in a step-by-step manner? Finally, did you have a positive attitude—did you believe you could solve the problem?

MAKING THE MOST OF YOUR COLLEGE RESOURCES

Many resources are available on your college campus to help you succeed. By familiarizing yourself with the various student support services, the library, and computer labs early in the semester, you can improve your chances for college success. Your professors and your advisor are the first people you should contact if you have a question or a problem. If they can't help you personally, they'll know who can.

GETTING TO KNOW THE TURF

One of the most important steps in adjusting to college is feeling comfortable in your new environment. One way that you can speed this process is by getting to know your campus and the resources that are available to you. You may have already taken a tour of the campus during a college visit or during an orientation program, but that tour was probably one of many that you took. During the first week of school, take your own tour. The more that you know about your campus, the more comfortable you'll feel and the more easily you'll become a part of the college landscape.

STUDENT SUPPORT SERVICES

Some students are reluctant to ask for help; they think that they should be able to solve all their problems on their own. If you have a personal or an academic problem, a number of resources on your college campus are available to you. In most cases, you should probably begin to deal with your problem by talking about it with someone you trust—a family member, a roommate, or a friend. If you need to take some type of action to resolve the difficulty, you may need to talk to someone who has some authority on campus. Most colleges have professionally trained counselors who can help you with personal problems.

If you're having a problem in one of your classes, make an appointment to discuss it with your teaching assistant or professor. If you feel uncomfortable going to your professor, talk to your advisor or someone in your college learning center. Get a tutor if you're having difficulty understanding the course material or doing the homework assignments. Most colleges provide some type of tutoring services—find out where tutoring in your subject area is available and go sign up. Go to your college learning center if you're having difficulty with test preparation, note taking, reading your text, and so on.

YOUR COLLEGE LIBRARY

Learning to use your college library or library system is another important step in achieving college success. After you take the library tour, go back several times to get acquainted with the resources that you may need to use. Most college libraries have shifted from traditional card catalogs to computerized listings of their holdings. If you've never used a computer or a computerized card catalog before, you may find your first experience challenging or even frustrating. Some libraries provide instruction sheets next to each computer terminal, whereas others "walk you through" the instructions right on the computer screen. Of course, you may save yourself a lot of time and effort by asking one of the librarians to show you how to use the computerized catalog or database.

On your next trip to the library, you may want to focus on using some of the reference materials. Set up an appointment with one of the reference librarians to learn more about using the various online indexes, abstracts, and databases that you may be required to use when completing assignments for your courses. Knowing how to use these resources will save you a great deal of time when you're ready to do research for a paper or project.

YOUR PROFESSORS

College professors are different from your high school teachers, but they are not inhuman or superhuman. Although some college professors appear to be unapproachable in the classroom, they are often very different in less formal settings. At many colleges, graduate students may teach or may assist the professor in teaching the course. Even though they may not be much older than their students, they should be approached in the same way as other professors. If you have questions about the course content or any of the assignments, schedule an appointment during your professor's office hours.

Many students are afraid to talk in class because some professors appear to be annoyed by interruptions during class. However, most professors tend to invite questions at the end of the lecture or at the end of a particular topic. If you have a question, ask it. If you feel uncomfortable, ask the question after class or during office hours. Professors like students who are interested in the class and well prepared. They generally are willing to answer reasonable or thoughtful questions. They don't, however, respond well to questions that clearly show that you, the student, didn't read the assignment or missed the previous lecture.

If you miss class, *you* are responsible for the material and the assignment. Don't expect your professor to repeat the lecture for you privately at your convenience. Instead, you should ask another student for the notes. If you fail a quiz or exam, you need to see your professor to talk about your performance. Don't expect your professor to call you in for a conference. Instead, you need to take the initiative and schedule the appointment. Your professors expect you to take responsibility for your education.

YOUR COLLEGE ADVISOR

Most college students are assigned an advisor during their first year. Your advisor, generally a professor in your major field of study, is the person who will help you monitor your progress toward your degree. You're still the one responsible, however, for completing all the degree requirements. When you plan your schedule, your advisor will either approve your selections or make suggestions about alternative courses.

Although you probably have already completed your schedule for this semester, you may want to consider some of the following suggestions as you plan your schedule for next semester. First, it's important to remember that you can't always take every course offered in your major or every course that looks interesting during any one semester. You'll benefit in the long run if you balance your schedule between courses in your major and courses that fulfill your general education requirements. By taking one or two of your required general education courses each semester, you'll gradually fulfill your requirements while getting to sample a number of subject areas that you may find interesting. Balance these courses with one or two of the courses in your major or related to your major each semester.

You also should try to balance your classes by mixing heavy-reading courses with courses that emphasize more writing, problem solving, or lab work. Scheduling an English course or a math course along with several reading courses can provide you with a welcome change of pace when you're completing your assignments and preparing for exams.

SUMMARY

Many factors contribute to your college success. One of the most important, though, is your commitment to the academic demands of your course work. Becoming an active, strategic, and independent learner will help you achieve that success. Determining your learning style, how you learn best, will help you learn to select the appropriate study strategies to use for each of the study tasks you'll need to complete. Getting motivated to work hard and learn is critical to your college success. Choosing to use some of the strategies to increase your motivation can make a difference. Attending college involves making many transitions and taking on new responsibilities. If you're a nontraditional student, balancing your commitments at work, home, and school may be your most challenging task during your first year in college. If you're a traditional student, you'll have to learn to set priorities, balance a budget, and accept responsibility for your own learning. Many new college students experience stress during this transitional period; that's normal. However, too much stress can be harmful. Using effective coping strategies can help you reduce your stress so you can focus on your education. Learning to make good decisions using a problem-solving process may help you reduce some of the stress in your life. During your first week in college, get reacquainted with your campus; locate the various offices and services that are available to help you succeed. Don't forget to stop in the library and sign up for a tour. Get to know your professors, your advisor, and other support people personally—they are all there to help you succeed in college.

Activities

1. Make a list of at least ten strategies that college students need to use to be successful. Then share your ideas with a group of your classmates. As a group, select the ten strategies or activities that are most representative of successful students. Think about how many of the strategies you currently use and select three that you plan to use this semester to increase your success.

2. Complete the Learning Style Inventory in Figure 1.1A or use the self-scoring inventory on the *Orientation to College Learning* Web site (http://info.wadsworth.com/vanblerkom04). As you read each of the statements, check *yes* or *no* to indicate the response that describes you best. Then use the information in Figure 1.1B to determine your preferred learning style.

3. Find out more about what kind of learner you are by taking the quiz at the Personality Type Web site (www.personalitytype.com/quiz.html). This interactive quiz, based on the MBTI, is short, easy, and self-scoring. After identifying your type, be sure to take some time to explore the information available on the Web site.

4. List three academic tasks that you worked on recently. On a scale of 1 to 10 (with 1 being the least effort you ever put into a task and 10 being the most effort you ever put into a task) how would you rate the amount of effort you put into each task?

   Write a paragraph or two describing each of the tasks you rated and why you had trouble getting motivated or staying motivated when completing one or two of your academic tasks earlier this week. What strategies did you use to try to complete your work? Which strategies presented in this chapter may have been even more effective? Why?

5. Using your own paper, write an essay describing the reasons you chose to attend college. Did anyone or anything influence your decision?

6. Use the five steps in the problem-solving process to make a decision about a personal or academic problem that you encounter this week. Describe each step of the process that you used. How effective was this process in helping you reach a good decision? What changes would you make the next time you have to make a decision?

 7. Access your campus home page on the Internet and locate campus resources that you can use that will help you make a better transition in college. Create a chart (or use the chart in Activity 1-3 from the Activities Packet on the *Orientation to College Learning* Web site) and post it in a convenient place. Include office locations, phone numbers, and the names of contact people for each office. Are your campus calendar, student handbook, and faculty rosters available online?

 8. If you're using InfoTrac College Edition, access it using the Internet address: http://infotrac.thompsonlearning.com and type in your password (located on your access card available with this text). Click on the EasySearch Help button and click on the *link* (the underlined phrase) introduction. Use the BACK button on the top left-hand corner of the tool bar to return to the EasyTrac main screen to learn how to use it to do simple searches. Use the *subject* guide to locate information on the topic: college. Type the word *college* into the search entry box and click the SEARCH button. You'll find a long list of related topics. You'll need to view several pages. Scan the subject headings for one related to freshmen or college survival. View the list of articles and then click on the *link* to read one or two that look interesting. List three topics that most closely match the information you want to find. After reading several articles, list three practical strategies that you plan to incorporate in your survival plan this semester.

 9. Think of three examples of how you've applied what you learned in this chapter. Choose one strategy and describe how you applied it to your other course work using the Journal Entry Form that is located on the *Orientation to College Learning* Web site. Consider the following questions as you complete your entry. Why did you use this strategy? What did you do? How did it work? How did it affect your performance on the task? How did this approach compare to your previous approach? What changes would you make the next time you use this strategy?

 10. Now that you've completed Chapter 1, take a few minutes to repeat the "Where Are You Now?" activity, located on the *Orientation to College Learning* Web site. What changes did you make as a result of reading this chapter? How are you planning to apply what you've learned in this chapter?

Review Questions

Terms You Should Know:

Active learners	Learning style	Skills
Auditory learners	Mapping	Strategic learners
Extrinsic motivation	Motivation	Stress
Independent learners	Plagiarism	Visual learners
Intrinsic motivation	Self-efficacy	Will
Kinesthetic learners	Self-regulated learners	

Completion: Fill in the blank to complete each of the following statements.

1. Reading over your notes is an example of _____ learning.

2. The most common learning style for college professors is _____.

3. Strategic learners are students who view studying and learning as a _____ process that is, to a good degree, under their control.

4. You can get your money's worth in college by _____ all classes.

5. Taking a _____ course load during your first semester or first year can help make the transition to college easier.

Multiple Choice: Circle the letter of the best answer for each of the following questions. Be sure to underline key words and eliminate wrong answers.

6. Learning to set _____ is one of the most difficult tasks you will face.
   A. study goals
   B. time plans
   C. priorities
   D. a budget

7. A kinesthetic learner learns best by:
   A. reading.
   B. listening.
   C. doing.
   D. integrating all three learning modalities.

Short Answer–Essay: On a separate sheet, answer each of the following questions.

8. What are the three factors that influence motivation? Describe each briefly.

9. What is a self-regulated learner?

10. What are three ways to deal with stress?

Chapter 2

GOAL SETTING

"Goal setting has helped me in a number of ways. I have found that setting goals for myself creates a sense of excitement. I know that if I set my mind to accomplish something, I can. This has been especially helpful in planning long-term goals. I have a sense of knowing that I will accomplish those goals no matter what obstacles may come into view."

Maria Mardis
Student

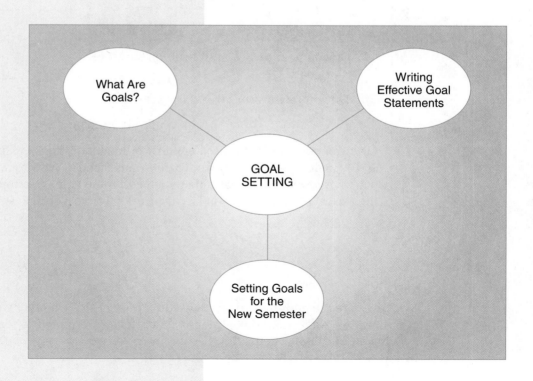

Where Are You Now?

Take a few minutes to answer *yes* or *no* to the following questions.

	YES	NO
1. Have you decided what grade point average (GPA) you want to achieve this semester?	_____	_____
2. Have you decided what grade you want to get in each of your courses this semester?	_____	_____
3. Have you written down the grade that you want to get in each of your courses this semester?	_____	_____
4. Are the goals that you set for your courses attainable?	_____	_____
5. Do you use words like *try* and *hope* when you describe your goals?	_____	_____
6. Do you set goals for yourself each week?	_____	_____
7. Do you set daily study goals?	_____	_____
8. Do you tend to achieve the goals that you set?	_____	_____
9. Do you tend to give up if you don't achieve your goals?	_____	_____
10. Do you revise your goals during the semester?	_____	_____
TOTAL POINTS	_____	

Give yourself 1 point for each *yes* answer to all questions except 5 and 9 and 1 point for each *no* answer to questions 5 and 9. Now total up your points. A low score indicates that you need some help in setting goals. A high score indicates that you are using effective goal-setting strategies.

WHAT ARE GOALS?

Goals are the ends toward which we direct our efforts. In other words, goals are things we want to achieve, things we aim for as we pursue a certain course of action. You have been setting goals since you were very young, although you probably weren't aware of it. Did you ever climb up on the kitchen counter to get a cookie out of the cupboard? Your goal was to get that cookie, and you worked out a plan to get it even though it was out of reach. You need to take the same approach in college. You must decide what you want and then figure out how to get it.

Goals are important in college because they help motivate you to do your work, attend classes, and study for exams. Even though you already may have set some goals for the semester, chances are you thought little about whether those goals were realistic. You can improve your academic performance in college by learning to set goals that motivate you to do well and that increase your chance for success.

CHARACTERISTICS OF GOALS

To be both useful and motivating, the goals you set must have some important characteristics. Your goals should be self-chosen, moderately challenging, realistic, measurable, specific, and positive.

1. **Goals should be self-chosen.** Goals that are set by your parents, teachers, or friends may not always work for you. You need to determine or choose your own goals; *you* need to decide what you want to accomplish. If you set your own goals, you'll be more motivated to achieve them.

2. **Goals should be moderately challenging.** You probably were told to set high or even exceptionally high goals for yourself in college; you may have been told to "shoot for the stars" or "go for straight As." In fact, this may not be the best advice. If your goal is to achieve all As during your first semester in college, you may be disappointed. As soon as you "lose your A" in one class, you may feel that you failed to achieve your goal, and you may be tempted to give up.

    One way to set moderately challenging goals is to consider what you have done in the past. Of course, everyone is different, but high school grades are fairly good predictors of college success. Why were you successful in some classes yet unsuccessful in others? You may have been more motivated, so you may have worked harder. Of course, if you didn't work very hard in high school, you can do better in college if you choose to apply yourself; increased effort can make a difference. Even so, you should set goals that are moderately challenging—goals that will require you to achieve more than you did before but will not place undue pressure on you. Goals can always be revised if you discover you can achieve more than you originally set out to accomplish.

3. **Goals should be realistic.** Think about whether your goals are attainable. It would be unrealistic to expect to get a B or better in Calculus if your math background is very weak and your high school grades in math were never higher than a C. To set realistic goals, you must carefully evaluate your chances of achieving each goal. Using the Five-Step Approach to setting goals (discussed later in this chapter) can help you make this decision.

4. **Goals should be measurable.** A goal is measurable if you can determine whether you reached it. It would be difficult to determine whether you achieved your goal if you just wanted to "do well in a course." How can you measure that? What does "well" really mean? It undoubtedly means different things to different people. It would be much easier to measure your success if you had aimed for an A or a B. At the end of the semester, you should be able to look at your final grade in a course and at the grade you set as your goal and compare them to evaluate your efforts.

   Goals for specific study sessions need to be measurable, too. Studying chemistry is not a measurable goal. "I will read pages 12 to 22 in my chemistry text and work all the sample problems" is a good example of a measurable goal statement. At the end of your study session, you will be able to determine whether you did what you planned to do.

5. **Goals should be specific.** The more specific your goals are, the more motivated you will be to achieve them. If you formulate vague or unclear goals, you will be less likely to accomplish them. Getting a B+ in College Algebra is a specific goal; getting a "good grade" in College Algebra is not. Study goals should be specific, too. The goal "I'll do my homework at 7:00" is rather vague. It is important to think of your homework as a series of individual assignments. You need to write separate goals for each of these assignments. A more specific goal statement is, "I'll do problems 1 to 20 in my chemistry text (page 54) at 7:00 on Tuesday."

6. **Goals should be positive.** Negative goal statements tend to make you feel that you can't really be successful; they aren't motivating. "I don't want to get any lower than a C in any of my classes," "I won't go to dinner until I get this calculus work done," and "I'm not going to fail this test" are all examples of negative goal statements. You will always do better if you are working *toward something*—when you have a positive attitude.

   Also avoid using words like *try, think, hope,* and *should* when you describe your goals. What's wrong with including those kinds of words? You're right if you said that they offer "a way out." If you state your goal this way: "I'm going to *try* to write my sociology essay tonight," and later push your paper away unfinished, you may say to yourself, "Well, I did *try*." Positive goals that emphasize success help motivate you to get your work done.

LONG- AND SHORT-TERM GOALS

Most students have long-term goals in mind when they enter college. Even if you don't know exactly what major you want to pursue, you have probably thought about getting a degree and getting a job. You may even know what field interests you most, whether it be education, engineering, nursing, or politics. Long-term goals are helpful to your success in college because they give you direction. However, there are times when long-term goals can seem awfully far in the future. That's where short-term goals can help. *Long-term goals* are the objectives you set for yourself for the end of the year, for 4 or 5 years from now, or even for a lifetime. *Short-term goals,* on the other hand, can be set for an hour from now, for the end of the day, the week, the month, or the semester. Short-term goals include things like completing a reading assignment, writing an essay, getting a B in a course, or making the Dean's List for the semester. Think of your short-term goals as steps toward achieving the long-term goals you've set for yourself. By accomplishing daily, weekly, and semester goals, you move closer to your long-range academic, career, and personal goals.

ACADEMIC AND PERSONAL GOALS

In college it's important to balance your academic and personal goals. *Academic goals* relate to your course work. They include things like going to class, completing assignments, and preparing for exams. To achieve your academic goals, you need to learn to set study goals, too. *Study goals* can be defined as the objectives you want to achieve during a particular study session. They may include reading your sociology assignment, reviewing your class notes, conducting research for a term paper, or preparing for an exam. When you write study goals, be specific about exactly what you want to accomplish. Your academic goals should be your highest priority in college. *Personal goals,* like making new friends, participating in clubs or sporting events, exercising, or even doing your laundry, are important, too. Although many students believe their personal goals cannot be changed, they can. Some household tasks can be postponed, eliminated, or delegated to other family members. If each member of your family accepts just one task, you'll be amazed at the time you'll gain. Although it takes

FIGURE 2.1

• • • • • • • • •

Goal Setting Improves Performance

1. **Goals direct our attention to the task at hand.** Goals keep you working on an assignment and direct you back to it if you begin to think about something else or are distracted.

2. **Goals mobilize effort.** Goals motivate you to work hard (to increase your effort) in order to complete the task.

3. **Goals increase persistence.** Goals help you continue to work on the task (persevere) even when the task becomes difficult.

4. **Goals promote the de   of new strategies when old strategies fall short.** Goals help you monitor (keep track of and evaluate) the effectiveness of the strategy or strategies that you are using to complete the task. Goals can help you determine whether the strategy is working, and, if it isn't, goals can motivate you to select another strategy to use.

some planning and flexibility, balancing academic and personal goals may be necessary. However, if you allow yourself to focus on your personal goals, you may find that you have little time left for study. By learning how to balance your goals, you can have time for both your academic work and your personal life.

GOAL SETTING IMPROVES PERFORMANCE

You learned in Chapter 1 that setting goals increases your motivation and that being motivated improves your performance. How does that actually happen, you may be asking? According to Locke and Latham, who do research on goal setting, there are four main reasons to explain the process (Figure 2.1.).[1]

WRITING EFFECTIVE GOAL STATEMENTS

By putting your goals in writing, you increase the chances that you will actually accomplish them. However, another factor that affects your success is how you formulate your goal statements. You can write down the first thing that comes to mind, or you can spend some time and explore each of your goals by using the Five-Step Approach to goal setting. Developing and implementing an action plan for each of your goals can also help you achieve them.

---

[1]E. A. Locke and G. P. Latham, *A Theory of Goal Setting and Task Performance* (Englewood Cliffs, NJ: Prentice Hall, 1990).

USE THE FIVE-STEP APPROACH

Writing effective goal statements isn't as easy as it sounds. You need to consider what you want to accomplish, any obstacles that could prevent you from achieving your goal, and the resources available to you. You then need to formulate your goal statement and polish it. Because each of your courses has different requirements, you must consider each course separately. If you are taking five courses, you must go through this process five times. See Figure 2.2 for an example of the Five-Step Approach to setting goals.

FIGURE 2.2

Tomi's Five-Step Approach to Setting Goals

COURSE: _____ Biology _____

STEP 1: Tentative Goal Statement
I want at least a B in Biology

STEP 2: List of Obstacles
1. There is a ton of reading, and I usually put it off.
2. I have trouble following the lecture, and I struggle to take notes.
3. Class would be easy to skip because it's in the auditorium and attendance isn't taken.
4. The book is very hard to read and understand.
5. The class is so big that I am easily distracted.
6. The subject matter is very difficult for me.

STEP 3: List of Resources
1. I will set up a schedule to read 15 pages each night.
2. I'll read the chapter before the lecture. I'll rewrite my notes afterward.
3. I can't afford to miss class. I'll go from my 8:00 class directly to Biology at 9:00.
4. I'll highlight and take notes as I read.
5. I'll read Chapter 4 on Concentration early and sit up front.
6. I'll get a tutor in the learning assistance center.

STEP 4: Revised Goal Statement
I'll try to earn a B in Biology.

STEP 5: Polished Goal Statement
I will achieve a B in Biology this semester.

Note: A full-size blank form is available on the *Orientation to College Learning* book-specific Web site.

STEP 1: Write Down What You Want to Accomplish

This initial description can be thought of as a *tentative* goal statement. The easiest way to begin your tentative goal statement is with the words "I want to." Think about what you want to accomplish.

STEP 2: Write Down Any Obstacles

Think about whether there are any course requirements, assignments, tests, or other factors that could jeopardize your success. Make a list of the difficulties you may encounter. Some students, for example, panic when they find out that their exams are going to be essay tests. You might consider this an obstacle if you know that you ordinarily don't do well on essay tests. Others may be concerned about attendance policies or oral presentations.

STEP 3: Write Down Any Resources Available to You

First, consider your *general* resources. You have successfully completed 12 years of school, so you have acquired some of the skills that can help you become a successful student. You have also acquired a background in quite a few subject areas. In addition, you probably earned some As and Bs, so you know that you can be successful in your academic pursuits. If you're a returning adult student, you also have developed skills in meeting deadlines, setting priorities, and managing multiple tasks—all necessary skills for college success. All these things are general resources that will help you achieve your goals. Next, consider each of the obstacles you listed individually. Think about how you might use your resources to overcome each obstacle. Write down *specific* resources you could use to achieve each goal. Specific resources include your friends and family, the faculty and staff members at your college, and you yourself. For instance, if you have difficulty with essay tests, you could go to your professor or to your college learning center to get some help before the exam.

STEP 4: Review and Revise Your Tentative Goal Statement

Now that you've thought about any possible difficulties and have figured out whether they can be resolved, you're ready to write your final goal statement. In some cases you may find that you don't change your tentative goal statement at all; in other cases you may do a lot of revising.

STEP 5: Polish Your Goal Statement

Check to be sure that your final statement is well written and takes into consideration the six characteristics of effective goals.[2]

---

[2]Based on some ideas from Walter Pauk, *How to Study in College*, 4th ed. (Boston: Houghton Mifflin, 1989).

DEVELOP AN ACTION PLAN

To achieve your long- and short-term goals, you need to develop an action plan. An *action plan* is a carefully thought-out method of implementing a strategy to achieve your goal—one that will help you get from where you are to where you want to be. Writing an action plan for a long-term assignment (such as a term paper, semester project, or portfolio) can help motivate you to work on the task throughout the semester because you have to identify each step of the process in advance. You can develop an action plan on notebook paper, on an index card, or by using the form shown in Figure 2.3, which can be found on the *Orientation to College Learning* Web site. By breaking down your goal into a series of smaller, more specific goals, you can develop a set of action tasks for your plan. *Action tasks* are the specific tasks that you need to complete to achieve your

FIGURE 2.3
. . . .
An Action Plan Sheet

Goal:				
Target Date	Action Tasks	Materials Needed	To Do Date	Evaluation
Outcome:				

Adapted from *Motivation and Goal-Setting*, 2d ed. (Hawthorne, NJ: Career Press, 1993), p. 38.
Note: A full-size version of this form is available on the *Orientation to College Learning* book-specific Web site.

original goal. To write a term paper, you might include action tasks such as choosing a topic, writing a tentative thesis statement, using a database to identify three to six good sources of information, taking notes on the source materials, developing an outline, and so on. Next, think about any materials you may need to complete your action tasks. For example, to take notes on your sources, you would need to have your laptop or index cards, copies of your articles or books (or if you can't check them out, a list of where each is located in the reference area of the library), and a pen or pencil. Next, set a target date for the completion of each of your action tasks.

Giving yourself one week to complete each step in the plan is a good guide for completing a term paper, for example. You may find that you can complete some of your action tasks in one day while others (such as taking notes for your paper and writing your rough draft) may take 2 or 3 weeks. You should also include a To Do date for each step in the plan. Once you establish your target date, it may be useful to set up a specific date and time to work on each of the tasks. Checking off each task as it's completed can help you see the progress you're making in completing your goal. Finally, include an outcome statement at the end of your action plan. After completing your plan (and your goal), you should describe how well your action plan helped you achieve your goal. You could list, for example, the date that you actually finished your term paper, any problems that you encountered using the plan, and the grade that you received.

SETTING GOALS FOR THE NEW SEMESTER

The most important time to set your goals and start using specific strategies for achieving them is during the first 3 weeks of the semester. If you make academics your first priority and get off to a good start in each of your classes, you will find you'll continue to do well throughout the semester. Setting priorities, planning for early success, planning rewards, and revising your goals periodically can all help you achieve the academic goals you set for yourself. It's important to start using these strategies right from the start of the semester.

SET PRIORITIES FOR THE FIRST THREE WEEKS

If you make academic goals your priority for the first 3 weeks, you will practically ensure your success for the semester. Many students think that the first few weeks of a new semester are a breeze; typically, there are no exams, and often there are few papers, projects, or presentations. What you do during those first few weeks, though, often affects your performance during the rest of the semester. If you start doing your reading and other assignments right from the beginning, getting your work done will become a habit. In the same way, attending classes and meeting with study groups and tutors will also become part of your daily routine. By working especially hard at the beginning of the semester, you'll learn to make your academic goals your top priority.

PLAN FOR EARLY SUCCESS

Another way to get off to the right start is to plan for early success. Getting an A or a B on the first quiz or first homework assignment should be one of your short-term goals for the semester. Once you get an A on one of your quizzes or assignments, you won't want to lose it. That first A lets you know you can do the work—increasing your self-efficacy. You know that by attending all your classes and by doing your assignments you can be successful. This also motivates you to keep working hard in all your classes.

If you try to breeze through the first few weeks of the semester, you may end up with a D or F on your first assignment or quiz, and that low grade can have a negative effect on your future performance. Some students begin to doubt their ability to succeed in a particular course or in college in general. Even though they really may not have applied themselves, the doubts still are there. Some students respond well to a low grade early in the semester; it shakes them up and they "start to hit the books." Others, though, just get depressed about their performance and eventually give up. It's much better to avoid those early low grades by striving hard for early success. The Tip Block on page 42 lists ten tips that should help you get off to the right start this semester.

PLAN REWARDS

When you think about achieving your goals, a 15-week semester can seem like a long time to wait. Unfortunately, there aren't a lot of "warm fuzzies" or immediate rewards in college. You may not get a grade on an assignment until the fourth or even the seventh week of the semester. You also may find that you miss that pat on the back or verbal recognition that you got in high school. It can be hard to stay motivated when no one is "telling you" that all your hard work is paying off, so you need to begin to reward yourself. Establish a method for rewarding yourself for knowing the answers to the questions that the professor asks in class, for being able to explain the solution to a problem, or even for being up to date on your reading assignments. If no one else is there to give you that pat on the back, you may need to give it to yourself.

TEN TIPS TO GET OFF TO THE RIGHT START THIS SEMESTER

BE SELECTIVE IN CHOOSING CLASSES. Choose courses your first semester that will help you build the skills you need to succeed in college or entry-level courses in your major. Taking a class you find interesting is another good way to start out. Your advisor will help you select courses that are appropriate for you.

GO TO ALL CLASSES AND TAKE NOTES. Your goal is to write down as much information as you can. Four weeks from now, you won't remember much of what you heard today. Edit your notes within 24 hours to organize and expand the information.

KEEP UP WITH YOUR READING ASSIGNMENTS. Break down long reading assignments into more manageable units of about 7 to 10 pages. Read the 10 pages and then switch to another subject. Take a short break; then go back and read 10 more pages. Remember to carefully highlight your text or take notes as you read.

LEARN TO SAY NO. While you're attending college, you don't have time for many outside activities. You may find that working, taking care of yourself and your family, and going to school is all you can handle. When you do say no, explain that when you complete your education, you'll be happy to help out.

CREATE A GOOD STUDY ENVIRONMENT. Find a quiet place to study. If studying in your dorm room or at the kitchen table is too distracting, find another place to do your work.

SET REALISTIC GRADE GOALS. Although students are very successful in college, they don't all get As their first semester in college. Earning a B or a C your first semester (or any semester) is fine. Consider what *you* can accomplish in each of your courses.

STUDY FOR EXAMS BY WRITING AND RECITING OUT LOUD. You won't learn the information by just reading it over and over. Writing and reciting are active strategies that help you learn the information.

LEARN TO PREDICT EXAM QUESTIONS. This is important for all exams, but it is critical for essay exams. After you predict 5 to 10 possible questions, plan the answers before the exam and then learn the main points.

WHEN TAKING EXAMS, RELAX AND BE SURE TO READ THE DIRECTIONS. Answer the easiest questions first, skipping the ones that you don't know immediately. Then go back and complete the ones that you skipped.

GO TO YOUR COLLEGE LEARNING CENTER WHEN YOU NEED HELP. Don't wait until it's too late. Stop in to talk about any classes in which you're having difficulty. Gathering suggestions on how to study or signing up for tutoring can improve your grades dramatically.

CONSIDER CONSEQUENCES

If you're having difficulty achieving your short-term goals, try using rewards as motivation. If this doesn't work, though, you may need to consider seriously the consequences of your actions. Think about how not achieving one or two of your short-term goals might affect the successful completion of your long-term goals. You learned earlier in the chapter that each of your goals is really made up of a series of steps or smaller short-term goals. If you leave out one or two of those steps, you may not be able to complete the larger task. Consider the steps to achieving your goal as rungs of a ladder. If you eliminate too many or even one at a critical location, you may never get to the top. Each step is crucial for achieving success.

REVISE YOUR GOALS PERIODICALLY

It's important to rethink your goals at some point during the semester. Some students tend to "play it safe" and set unrealistically low goals for themselves at the beginning of the semester. It may seem like a good idea to set safe goals; that way you always are successful at what you set out to do. However, "safe" goals can also hold you back because they don't challenge you to achieve all that you might be able to achieve. Some students have the opposite tendency; they set goals that may be completely unattainable. By doing this, they are setting themselves up for failure and disappointment.

Remember, goals should be moderately challenging; they should be just a little out of reach so that you can work toward them. How can you find just the right level of challenge? You can't, at first. Once you gain some experience in college, however, you'll become much better at knowing what you can achieve. Until then, you need to revise your goals as you gather more information about your skills and your performance. Of course, you could change your goals, raise them or lower them, at almost any time during the semester. However, the best time to review your "grade" goals is after the first exam. If you decided to work for a B in algebra but got a high A on the first exam, you should revise your goal upward. Your first exam demonstrated that you're capable of doing A work and consequently capable of getting an A in algebra.

Many students continue to improve in courses after the first exam, so you need to review your goals again after the second, third, or even fourth exam. In general, you should sit down and really think about where you are and where you want to be after the first round of exams, after midterms, and about 2 weeks before final exams.

SUMMARY

Setting goals helps motivate you to attend class regularly, keep up with your day-to-day assignments, and complete long-term projects on time. Writing goal statements that are self-chosen, moderately challenging, realistic, measurable, specific, and positive will help you accomplish the goals that you set this semester. Setting priorities is also important to your success because you'll need to find the right balance between your academic and personal goals. Use the Five-Step Approach to setting goals in order to realistically set grade goals for each of your courses this semester. Developing action plans and making academics your top priority, especially for the first three weeks of the semester, will get you off to a good start. Setting and writing down goals lets you know where you're going, gives you the motivation to get there, and allows you to look back to see whether you got there.

Activities

1. Write several paragraphs in which you describe your life 5 years from now. Include as many details as you can. How will your course work this semester help you achieve your long-term goals?

2. Make a list of ten goals that you would like to accomplish this semester. Then list ten goals that you would like to accomplish tomorrow. Label each of the goals as an academic (A) or personal (P) goal. Do you have an overabundance of personal goals? Were your first three goals on each list academic or personal goals? How would you change your lists so that your academic goals have top priority?

3. Go the the *Orientation to College Learning* Web site (http://info.wadsworth.com/vanblerkom04) and download one copy of Activity 2-2 from the Activities Packet for each of your classes. Use the Five-Step Approach to set goals for all of your courses.

4. During the first 5 minutes of the class, make a list of five to ten goals that you plan to accomplish this week. Then share your list with a group of your classmates. As each student's list of goals is reviewed, identify the type of goal (work, personal, or study) and decide how well it's formulated according to the six characteristics of good goal statements. Make suggestions for changing some of the goal statements to make them more positive, realistic, measurable, and specific.

5. Look at the list of short-term goals that you wrote in Activity 2 or 4. Choose one personal goal and one academic goal and develop action plans for each goal. Exchange your plan with one of your classmates. What changes would you suggest to make your partner's action plan more effective?

6. Make a list of the obstacles that you have encountered in college (or think you may encounter). Then make a list of the resources that are available to you at your college or through your work and home life. Match each resource to at least one obstacle on your list. Choose one obstacle (and list of resources) and describe how you could use the resources to overcome that obstacle.

7. Use the Internet to locate information about a career in which you are interested. If you haven't decided on a career yet, check out several that you've been thinking about. Use a search engine such as Google (www.google.com) to locate at least five different sources of information about your future career. What did you find? What specific information was surprising to you? How recent was the information you located? Did you find a listing for jobs in your career as part of your search? Be prepared to describe how you found the information.

8. If you're using InfoTrac College Edition, do a subject search for additional information on goal setting. Type the word *goal* in the search box. Use the help button if you need more information on how to do a subject search. View the periodicals listed under the heading *goal setting*. Scan down the list of articles until you locate one that looks interesting to you (you may need to go to the "next page" to find a good one). Begin to view articles by clicking on the view link. With InfoTrac College Edition, you get the entire article rather than just a library citation, so skim the article to see if you find it useful. When you've explored a few, make a list of three new strategies that you plan to use this week. Be prepared to share them with the class.

9. Think of three examples of how you've applied what you learned in this chapter. Choose one strategy and describe how you applied it to your other course work using the Journal Entry Form that's located on the *Orientation to College Learning* Web site. Consider the following questions as you complete your entry. Why did you use this strategy? What did you do? How did it work? How did it affect your performance on the task? How did this approach compare to your previous approach? What changes would you make the next time you use this strategy?

10. Now that you've completed Chapter 2, take a few minutes to repeat the "Where Are You Now?" activity, located on the *Orientation to College Learning* Web site. What changes did you make as a result of reading this chapter? How are you planning to apply what you've learned in this chapter?

Review Questions

Terms You Should Know:

Academic goals	Goals	Personal goals
Action plans	Long-term goals	Short-term goals
Action tasks	Measurable goals	Study goals

Completion: Fill in the blank to complete each of the following statements.

1. Goals should be _____ challenging.

2. You should avoid words like _____ and _____ in your goal statements.

3. The third step in setting goals is to list your _____.

4. _____ _____ help students break long-term goals down into individual steps.

5. When you have clear, _____ goals, you are more likely to persevere when a task becomes difficult.

Multiple Choice: Circle the letter of the best answer for each of the following questions. Be sure to underline key words and eliminate wrong answers.

6. The goal statement, "I will earn an A or B in Biology" should be revised because it is not:
   A. specific.
   B. measurable.
   C. realistic.
   D. positive.

7. Why should you revise your goals?
   A. You may have set your goals too low.
   B. You may have set your goals too high.
   C. After the first exam, you'll have a more accurate picture of your performance.
   D. All of the above are good reasons.

Short Answer-Essay: On a separate sheet, answer each of the following questions.

8. What are four main reasons that setting goals improves performance?

9. Why should students make academics their top priority for the first 3 weeks of the semester?

10. Why should students use the Five-Step Approach to setting goals?

Chapter 3

TIME MANAGEMENT

"After my first week of school I honestly thought I'd never be able to juggle all of my responsibilities both at work and at home—not to mention keeping up with the homework. However, after actually doing the fixed commitment calendar and identifying just when I had to do what, and then putting my assignment deadlines in writing on a calendar, it didn't seem so overwhelming. I was able to see that I had time for it all and it wasn't going to crash in on me all at once. . . . I like the organization this brings to my somewhat chaotic life."

Dawn Davis
Student

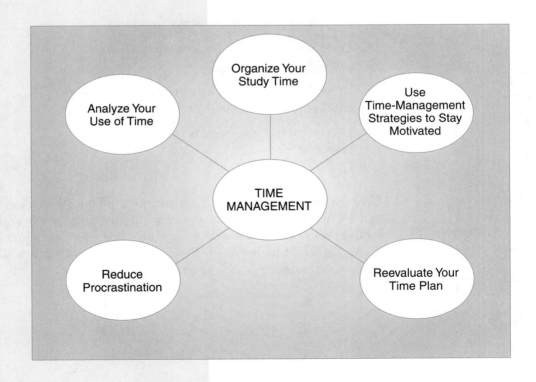

Where Are You Now?

Take a few minutes to answer *yes* or *no* to the following questions.

	YES	NO
1. Have you estimated how many hours you need to study this semester?	_____	_____
2. Do you tend to complete your assignments on time?	_____	_____
3. Have you estimated how long it takes you to read 10 pages in each of your textbooks?	_____	_____
4. Do you begin working on long-term assignments early in the semester?	_____	_____
5. Do you make lists of things to do in your head rather than on paper?	_____	_____
6. Do you find that you go out even when you know you should be studying?	_____	_____
7. Do you schedule time to study for exams?	_____	_____
8. Are you working at a job more than 20 hours a week?	_____	_____
9. Do you know exactly what you are going to work on when you sit down to study?	_____	_____
10. Do you do the assignments from your favorite class first?	_____	_____

TOTAL POINTS _____

Give yourself 1 point for each *yes* answer to all questions except 5, 6, 8 and 10, and 1 point for each *no* answer to questions 5, 6, 8, and 10. Now total up your points. A low score indicates that you need some help in managing your time now. A high score indicates that you are already using many good time-management techniques.

ANALYZE YOUR USE OF TIME

You can establish a good time plan once you know how you actually spend your time. Identifying how much time you have available for study and how much time you need for study can help you decide whether or not you should make any changes in your current time plan.

WHY IS TIME MANAGEMENT IMPORTANT?

Time management is the way you regulate or schedule your time. You can make more efficient use of your study time and complete your work in less time by using good time-management skills. The key to successful time management is allowing enough time to complete your work while still finding time to complete all of your other responsibilities. If you have additional time, you can take advantage of the other opportunities for growth and development that occur in college. Attending concerts, getting together with friends and family, and going to conferences or rallies are important parts of the college experience. However, these activities can be enjoyed more fully when you know that you have your course work done. Learning good time-management techniques can help keep you motivated to accomplish the goals that you set for yourself in Chapter 2.

In high school, your study time was fairly well defined or structured. In college, though, you won't find that kind of structure. You may need to use time-management strategies to balance school and work responsibilities.

Unlike high school students who are in class for almost 35 hours a week, most college students are in class for only 12 to 15 hours a week. To a college freshman, this seems like a breeze. However, in college, *most of your work must be completed outside of class*. And, even though you may not want to admit it, you can't get all that work done in just a few hours every evening. To achieve your goals, you also need to make use of your available daytime hours for study.

Good time-management skills can actually save you time. A few minutes each week spent on planning can make a real difference in how your study time is organized and spent. Once you learn good time-management skills, you may be surprised to find that you can do all the things you want to do. You may find that for the first time, you're in control of your life. The first rule of good time management is: *Don't let time manage you; you must learn, instead, to manage your time.*

HOW DO YOU MANAGE YOUR TIME NOW?

The first step in learning better time management is to evaluate how you actually use your time now. You can find out a lot about your own time use by writing down how you actually spend your time.

Keep a Time Diary

Although most students think that they spend enough time on academic tasks, many of them don't. By keeping a time diary, you'll be able to see how much or how little time you're actually spending. A *time diary* is a record of what you do each hour of the day for 1 week. To create your own time diary, just write down what you did in the morning at lunchtime, what you did in the afternoon at dinnertime, and what you did in the evening at bedtime. Some students prefer to carry an index card to record their activities and then copy them on to the time diary (available on the *Orientation to College Learning* Web site) at a later time. If you wait until the end of the day, you may have trouble remembering what you did. Split hours by drawing a diagonal line, but don't worry about 5- or 10-minute activities.

You may find it helpful to color code your time diary. Highlight all of your academic tasks (classes, meetings with professors or tutors, and study time) in one color, your sleep hours in another, and the rest of your life (work, social time, meals, and so on) in a third. A quick glance can tell you a lot about how effectively you're using your time now. To get a more accurate picture, create a time-use chart (Figure 3.1) to count the number of hours you used for each of the various activities. You'll need to modify the categories depending on your own activities.

If you're a full-time student, you should divide your total hours into three overall categories. You should spend about 56 hours a week sleeping (one-third of your time), about 56 hours for academics (classes, study time, tutoring, review sessions, and meetings with your TA's, professors, or advisor), and 56 hours for the rest of your life. If you're working full-time and attending college on a full-time basis, you won't have much time left over for many social activities or home responsibilities. Looking realistically at how you're using your time *now* can help you make some necessary changes to be more successful in college.

Complete a Prospective-Retrospective Calendar

Learning to manage your time effectively also depends on how well you can stick to a schedule. A *Prospective-Retrospective Calendar* allows you to compare what you *plan* to do on a given day *(prospective)* with what you *actually* do *(retrospective)*. What you do during each hour of the day is not important here. Instead, the key is how well you stick to your plan.

FIGURE 3.1

• • • • • • • • • • • • • •

Time-Use Chart

	Sleep	Meals	Class	Study	TV	Work	Internet	Social time	Commute	Get ready	Total hours
Monday											
Tuesday											
Wednesday											
Thursday											
Friday											
Saturday											
Sunday											
Total Hours											(Should total 168 hours)

	Sleep	Academics	The rest of my life
	☐	☐	☐

Note: A full-size version of this form is available on the *Orientation to College Learning* book-specific Web site.

Just setting up a plan for each hour of the day often provides sufficient motivation for completing it. Some students who try this activity are surprised to find that they faithfully follow their time plans. They are motivated to do everything that they planned to do. Many report that this was the first time they ever got all of their work done. Other students find that they have a great deal of difficulty staying on a schedule. Their most common problem involves getting study assignments done as planned.

IDENTIFY TIME AVAILABLE FOR STUDY

Identifying how much time you have available for study is the next step in setting up a good time plan. This involves looking at how much of your time is committed to other activities and also how much time you, as an individual, need to complete your work.

To establish how much of your time is committed to other activities, you should complete a *Fixed Commitment Calendar.*[1] What are fixed commitments? If you said classes, work hours, or even mealtimes, you were right. *Fixed commitments* are things you do the same time every day or every week. When completing your calendar, you should first write in your classes. You also should write in hours when you're asleep (normal sleep hours, not naps), mealtimes (setting regular times for meals helps you stay on a schedule), and work hours. If your work hours vary, don't write them in yet; we'll talk more about study and work later in this section. If you're involved in clubs, organizations, or sports, you may need to include additional hours for regularly scheduled meetings (same time each week) or practices and games. If you have family responsibilities such as dropping off or picking up your children at school or day care (or other regularly scheduled tasks), write them in, too. If you know that you'll be socializing on most Friday and Saturday evenings, you should write in those times even though your plans aren't definite. If you plan to sleep in or attend religious services Saturday or Sunday morning, include those hours as well.

After you've written in all the regularly committed hours, you should begin to see some patterns in your uncommitted time. You may have some very short blocks of time between classes, some 2- or 3-hour blocks in the morning or afternoon, and some longer blocks in the evenings and on weekends. Think of these time blocks as time *available* for study rather than free time. You also may notice that you have a lot of time to study on certain days but very little on others. All this information will be useful as you begin to schedule your study time.

After determining your available study time, trace around the perimeter of each time block (see the sample in Figure 3.2). Use a brightly colored marker to outline each time block. Being able to see at a glance the hours when you have time to study can be very helpful when scheduling study time.

If your work schedule changes each week, this calendar is even more important for you. Before you put your work hours on the schedule, make a photocopy of the calendar for each week of the semester. As you get your work schedule each week, go through and write in your hours. This will save you a lot of time because you won't have to start from scratch each week.

As a final step in preparing your Fixed Commitment Calendar, count the number of hours you have available for study. If you're not working, you may find that you have 50 to 70 hours available for study. Don't worry—you won't

---

[1]Adapted from Time Analysis Worksheet in Nancy V. Wood, *Reading and Study Skills*, 3d ed. (New York: Holt, Rinehart & Winston, 1986), pp. 18–20.

FIGURE 3.2

Greg's Fixed Commitment Calendar

	Monday	Tuesday	Wednesday	Thursday	Friday	Saturday	Sunday
7:00 A.M.	sleep	sleep	sleep	sleep	sleep	sleep	sleep
8:00 A.M.	shower/dress/eat	shower/dress/eat	shower/dress/eat	shower/dress/eat	shower/dress/eat	sleep	sleep
9:00 A.M.	Algebra class	lift weights	Algebra class	lift weights	Algebra class	sleep	sleep
10:00 A.M.	lift weights	lift weights		lift weights	lift weights	shower/dress	shower/dress
11:00 A.M.	English class	History class	English class	History class	English class	eat	eat
12:00 P.M.		eat		eat		work	watch football
1:00 P.M.	eat		eat		eat	work	watch football
2:00 P.M.	Sociology class		Sociology class		Sociology class	work	watch football
3:00 P.M.						work	watch football
4:00 P.M.	practice	practice	practice	practice	practice	work	watch football
5:00 P.M.	practice	practice	practice	practice	practice		work
6:00 P.M.	eat	eat	eat	eat	eat	eat	work
7:00 P.M.							work
8:00 P.M.					out	out	work
9:00 P.M.					out	out	work
10:00 P.M.					out	out	
11:00 P.M.	TV	TV	TV	TV	out	out	
12:00 A.M.	sleep	sleep	sleep	sleep	out	out	sleep
1:00 A.M.	sleep	sleep	sleep	sleep	out	out	sleep
2:00 A.M.	sleep	sleep	sleep	sleep	sleep	sleep	sleep

Hours Available for Study __34__   Hours Needed for Study __32__ need all of them for study. If you're working, however, this number may be substantially smaller, depending on the number of hours that you work each week.

Greg (see Figure 3.2) has only 34 hours available for study. He's working 10 hours a week and is participating in sports. He spends 1 or 2 hours a day lifting weights and another 2 hours a day practicing. To complete his assignments, Greg will have to make efficient use of his time.

Rayna's schedule (see Figure 3.3) is even tighter because she works full time and attends college three evenings a week. She has very little study time available during the week and spends most of the weekend completing her study tasks.

IDENTIFY TIME NEEDED FOR STUDY

Knowing how much time you have available for study is useless until you identify how much time you need for study. Formulas, such as those that allot 1 hour of outside study time for every hour in class or 2 hours of outside work for every hour in class, are designed to simplify the task of determining how much time you need for study. Some educators believe students need 2 hours of study time for each hour that they are in class. So, a student who is taking 15 credits would need 30 hours of study time per week. However, this figure is based on the *average* number of hours students study. Remember, too, that the average grade students earn is a C. To find out how much time you need to study, you need to consider a number of other factors.

Consider Your Credit Load

The first indicator of how much time you really need for study is your credit load. If you're taking 15 credits, you should begin with a 2 to 1 ratio (2 hours of study time for every hour in class). Remember that this is a *minimum* and probably will change when you consider the other factors—the goals you have set, how quickly or slowly you work, and the difficulty of your courses.

Consider the Difficulty Level of Your Classes

You may need to increase your study hours if you're taking very difficult classes. Certain classes at every school seem to have a reputation for being "killer" classes. If you're enrolled in a "killer" class, you may have to increase your study ratio to 3 to 1 (three hours of outside work for every hour in class) or even 4 to 1. Even if you're not taking a "killer" course this semester, you may find that one particular class is especially difficult for you. Calculus can be a tough course if you haven't used your math skills for a few years. If you're taking a course that is especially demanding, you should allow 3 or 4 hours of outside work for every hour that you're in class.

FIGURE 3.3

Rayna's Fixed Commitment Calendar

	Monday	Tuesday	Wednesday	Thursday	Friday	Saturday	Sunday
5:00 A.M.	shower/ dress	shower/ dress	shower/ dress	shower/ dress	shower/ dress	sleep	sleep
6:00 A.M.	breakfast/ drive	breakfast/ drive	breakfast/ drive	breakfast/ drive	breakfast/ drive	sleep	sleep
7:00 A.M.	work	work	work	work	work	sleep	sleep
8:00 A.M.	work	work	work	work	work	sleep	sleep
9:00 A.M.	work	work break	work break	work break	work break	shower/ dress	sleep
10:00 A.M.	break work	work	work	work	work	breakfast / clean apartment	shower/ dress / breakfast
11:00 A.M.	work	work	work	work	work		
12:00 P.M.	work lunch	work lunch	work lunch	work lunch	work lunch		
1:00 P.M.	work	work	work	work	work		
2:00 P.M.	work	work	work	work	work		buy groceries
3:00 P.M.	work	work	work	work	work	lunch	lunch
4:00 P.M.	drive home	drive home	drive home	drive home	drive home		
5:00 P.M.	drive	drive	drive				
6:00 P.M.	Biology	Anthropology	Study Skills		.		
7:00 P.M.	Biology	Anthropology	Study Skills	go to laundromat			
8:00 P.M.	Biology	Anthropology	Study Skills	go to laundromat	out to dinner		dinner
9:00 P.M.	drive home/ dinner	drive home/ dinner	drive home/ dinner	dinner	out to dinner	dinner	
10:00 P.M.					out to dinner	dancing	sleep
11:00 P.M.	sleep	sleep	sleep	sleep	sleep	dancing	sleep
12:00 A.M.	sleep	sleep	sleep	sleep	sleep	dancing	sleep
1:00 A.M.	sleep	sleep	sleep	sleep	sleep	dancing	sleep
2:00 A.M.	sleep	sleep	sleep	sleep	sleep	sleep	sleep

Hours Available for Study _28½_   Hours Needed for Study _21_

Consider Your Goals

You may also need to increase your study time if you want to get As or Bs in one or more of your courses. Remember, average students study only 2 hours outside of class for every hour in class and get average (C) grades. You'll have to spend more time on your course work to earn high grades. This may involve editing your lecture notes (see Chapter 6), taking text notes as a weekly review (see Chapter 9), and studying more actively for quizzes and exams (see Chapter 10). You may need to spend more time on your assignments to ensure that they reflect your best effort. Some students also work with tutors or form a study group to maximize their grades. All these activities take additional time.

Learn How Long It Takes to Do Your Assignments

You also can learn to judge how much time you need for study by estimating how long it takes you to do individual assignments. Some students read, do math, or write papers faster than others. Time yourself the next time you read one of your textbooks. Finding out how long it takes to read 10 pages in each of your texts will help you plan more accurately. You can also time yourself as you complete math assignments and writing assignments or as you edit and review your notes. When you know how long it takes to do the routine work, you'll be able to accurately determine how much time you need for study.

Consider Long-Term Assignments

Many students forget to include weekly study time for long-term assignments. You need to allow time to study for exams, prepare term papers, and complete semester projects. Some students expect the regular assignment load to disappear when test or paper deadlines roll around. Unfortunately, this doesn't happen. If you don't adjust your study schedule for these long-range assignments, you may find that you have to "steal" time from your regular work in order to prepare for them. As a result, you may fall behind in everything else.

Monitor Your Current Study Time

One way to get a better estimate of how much time you actually need for study is by monitoring your current study time. By keeping track of how many hours you actually study (read, take notes, edit lecture notes, do math or writing assignments, and so on) during a typical week, you can evaluate the accuracy of your estimate of study time needed. You can also repeat the experiment during a week that is not so typical. Choose a week in which you have one or more exams and a paper or project due.

You may also find it helpful to keep a study log. A *study log* is a calendar where you write in the number of hours you spend doing assignments and studying for each of your courses. Use the chart available on the Web site. By keeping track of exactly how many hours you spend each day (and each week) on each of your courses, you can monitor your time use. You may find that you don't spend enough total time studying during the week or that you don't spend enough time on one class. You may also notice that on some days you spend a lot of time on academic tasks and very little time on other days. Look for patterns that will help you correct any problems early in the semester. Compare the total hours for each of your classes to the time goals that you set when you completed the study ratio chart. Like some of my students, you may find that keeping a study log will help you accurately evaluate your study time and motivate you to put more time into your work.

ESTABLISH A NEW TIME PLAN

If you found that you need more time to complete your work than you actually have, you need to modify your time plan. Basically, you have two options. One is to make more time for study, and the other is to reduce the amount of time that you need for study.

One way to reduce the amount of time that you need for study is to consider reducing your credit load. If this is your first semester in college, you should take 12 to 14 credits only. If you've been out of school for a while, you may find that taking only one or two classes (three to six credits) is a good way to begin. Earning good grades the first semester is much more important than earning a lot of credits. If you're working full time, you may have to take a lighter load as well. After all, what's the point of working so hard to pay for college if you can't find enough time to do your best?

If you absolutely can't reduce your credit load, then you need to reduce some of your fixed commitments and make more time for study. If you're attending school full time, you may find it difficult to work more than 20 hours a week. Certainly, some people can go to school full time and work full time, but many of them report that they don't have time for *anything* else (even meals or sleep).

Extracurricular activities can take a lot of time. Although it's important for students to be involved in college experiences outside the classroom, some students go too far. If you're always running off to some meeting, practice, or activity and don't have enough time to study, you need to rethink your level of involvement in extracurricular activities. You don't have to eliminate all activities; instead, be selective and choose one or two that you really enjoy. Let the others go for another semester.

ORGANIZE YOUR STUDY TIME

Once you've set up a time plan that allows you enough time to complete all your work, you need to learn how to organize your time so that it can be used efficiently. By learning to plan and schedule your study time, you can begin to take control of your time.

CREATE A SEMESTER CALENDAR

One of the best ways to organize your study time is to make a semester calendar. A *semester calendar* includes all of your assignments, quizzes, and exams. Seeing what you have to do for each day of the semester is the first step in planning your study time.

The easiest way to prepare a semester calendar is to use a blank block calendar similar to the one in Figure 3.4. Write in the name of the month, and number the

FIGURE 3.4

• • • • • • • • • • • • • • • •

Sample Semester Calendar for September

Month _____ September _____

Sunday	Monday	Tuesday	Wednesday	Thursday	Friday	Saturday
2	3	4 H - Ch 1 SS - Ch 1	5 A - 1.1 & 1.2 E - 1-35 Journal	6 H - Ch 2 SS - Ch 2	7 A - 1.3 & 1.4 E - 38-52 Journal Soc - Ch 1 (2-24)	8
9	10 A - 1.5 & 1.6 E - Experience essay-draft	11 H - Ch 3	12 A - 2.1 & 2.2 Soc - Ch 2 (26-48)	13 SS - Goal statements	14 A - 2.3 & 2.4 E - Experience essay	15
16	17 A - 2.5 & 2.6 E - 53-56 Soc - Ch 3 (52-74)	18 H - Ch 4 SS - Ch 3 To Do lists	19 A - 3.1 & 3.2 E - Observation essay-draft	20 SS - Ch 4 & H.O. Calendars due	21 A - 3.3 & 3.4 E - Observation essay due	22
23	24 A - 3.5 & 3.6 SOC-EXAM 1	25 H - Ch 5 SS - Ch 5 notes due	26 A - 4.1 & 4.2 Soc - Ch 4 (75-103)	27	28 A - 4.3 & 4.4 E - 65-81	29
30						

A = College Algebra H = Western Civilization SS = Study Skills
E = English Composition Soc = Sociology

days of the month. Next, pull out your course syllabi. Write all your assignments on your calendar. (You may have reading assignments, math exercises, and an English paper all due on the same day.) If some of your professors don't give you a day-to-day syllabus, you'll need to add assignments to your calendar as you learn of them. You may find it helpful to put the assignments for each separate course in a different color or list them all in black ink and then use colored markers to differentiate each subject. By color coding your assignments, you can quickly identify the work that you have to do each day. Make exams stand out on your calendar by writing them in large capital letters and putting a box around them.

After you've completed your calendars for each month of the semester, post them where you can see them easily—for example, on your refrigerator or bulletin board—and make sure that you're able to see 2 months at any one time. There's nothing more frustrating than turning the page on your calendar too late and realizing that you missed an important event. This is true for assignments and exams, too. Look at the sample calendars in Figures 3.4 and 3.5. The last week of September looks like a pretty easy week—after the Sociology exam on Monday.

FIGURE 3.5

Sample Semester Calendar for October

Month _____ *October* _____

Sunday	Monday	Tuesday	Wednesday	Thursday	Friday	Saturday
	1 A - 4.5 & 4.6.6 E - Exposition essay-draft	**2** H - EXAM 1 SS - Text marking due	**3** A - EXAM 1 E - Revision Soc - Ch 5 (105-130)	**4** H - Ch 6 SS - EXAM 1	**5** A - 5.1 & 5.2 E - Exposition essay due	**6**
7	**8** A - 5.3 & 5.4 E - 82-111 Soc - Ch 7 (162-189)	**9** H - Ch 7 SS - Ch 9 text notes	**10** A - 5.5 & 5.6 E - Revision due	**11** SS - Predicted questions	**12** A - 6.1 & 6.2	**13**
14	**15** A - 6.3 & 6.4 E - Portfolio due	**16** H - Ch 8 SS - Ch 6 & H.O.	**17** A - 6.5 & 6.6 Soc - Ch 8 (191-240)	**18** SS - Ch 7	**19** A - 7.1 & 7.2 E - 112-125	**20**
21	**22** A - 7.3 & 7.4 E - Definition essay-draft SOC - EXAM II	**23** H - Ch 9 SS - Ch 10	**24** A -7.5 & 7.6 E - 127-140	**25** H - Ch 10 SS - Study plan due	**26** A - EXAM II E - Definition essay due Soc - Ch 11 (278-310)	**27**
28	**29** A - 8.1 & 8.2 E - Argument essay due	**30** H - EXAM II SS - EXAM II	**31** A -8.3 & 8.4 E - 141-162			

A = College Algebra   H = Western Civilization   SS = Study Skills
E = English Composition   Soc = Sociology

There is a little reading to do, but the workload definitely seems to be on the light side. If this were your calendar, you might think that you could take it easy for a week. Now look at the first week of October. You have exams in History, Algebra, and Study Skills, three papers due for English, and two chapters of reading. If you had waited until the beginning of October to turn the page of your calendar, it would have been too late to prepare for your exams and complete your papers.

PREPARE WEEKLY TASK LISTS

After you've completed your semester calendar, you should begin to think about identifying your study tasks and planning when to do them. Each assignment that you put on your calendar represents a study task that must be completed. One way to plan your study time is to prepare *weekly task lists*. Just list all of the assignments (reading, math, writing, exams, and so on) due that week. It's a good idea to set aside 1 hour a week to use for planning. Remember to look ahead for exams or long-range assignments and to include these tasks in your plan. You can list your assignments for the week in the order that they are due or by the course; either way is fine. The important thing is to learn to plan ahead.

USE DAILY "TO DO" LISTS

After you decide what you need to do for the week, you need to begin to plan what you're going to do each day. A *"To Do" list* is a list of the tasks that you want to complete each day. Break down some of the tasks from your weekly task list. You might decide to read your History assignment over the next 2 days or work on writing your English essay for 1 hour every day during the week. (You may want to refer to the section in Chapter 2 on how to write good study goals.)

Putting your personal goals on the list is important, too. This further reinforces your commitment to put all your plans in writing. In addition, writing your personal goals on your "To Do" list will help you stay more organized. The more organized you are in completing your personal goals, the more time you'll have to complete your academic goals.

Making "To Do" lists can become habit forming, so by all means get started immediately. Don't worry if you don't accomplish everything on your list; few people do everything they set out to do every day. Just move the one or two tasks that were left uncompleted to the top of the list for the next day. Remember, though: It's important to plan realistically. A pattern of planning too much to do and then moving half of your tasks to the next day can lead to procrastination.

Consider prioritizing some of your tasks. Use numbers, a star, or another symbol to indicate that certain tasks need to be done first. Look at the "To Do" lists in Figure 3.6. In the first example, Jean mixed study goals and personal goals together. As you might expect, the personal goals were completed, and the study goals were left undone. Put your academic goals at the top of the page and your personal goals at the bottom. By putting your study goals first, you're reinforcing your commitment to academics. By setting priorities, Robin was able to complete all of her study tasks before beginning her personal goals (Figure 3.6).

Many students use professional planners (available in college bookstores or office supply stores) to keep track of assignments and personal goals. Many planners are designed with space for hour-by-hour planning, blocks for listing

FIGURE 3.6

• • • • • • • • • • • • • • • •

Sample "To-Do" Lists

JEAN'S "TO DO" LIST

DAY _____ Wednesday _____

Study Goals:

✓1   Go to student aid office

✓2   Do laundry

7   Final draft Engl paper

✓6   Go copy Fr tape Ch 3

✓3   Get card for Grandma B-day

11   Make to do list for tomorrow

5   Study Ch 2 Fr

✓8   Read Art pp 53-63

9   Do Alg Ch 2-5

✓4   Dentist Appt. 2:30

✓10   Meet Tom 5:30

Personal Goals:

☐ _____

☐ _____

☐ _____

☐ _____

ROBIN'S "TO DO" LIST

DAY _____ THURSDAY _____

Study Goals:

✓2   MAKE COPY OF SPEECH OUTLINE

✓3   PRACTICE SPEECH

✓4   READ PP. 135-145 IN BLACK LIT

✓1   READ ESSAY 2 IN POL SCI

✓8   DO FEB. CALENDAR

✓6   READ PP. 146-156 IN BLACK LIT

✓5   READ 10 PPS. OF CH. 1 POL SCI

✓7   READ PP. 163-173 IN SS

✓9   DO "THINGS TO DO" FOR TOMORROW

☐ _____

☐ _____

Personal Goals:

✓10   WRITE LETTER HOME

✓11   CHECK MAIL

✓12   GO TO BASKETBALL GAME

13   CLEAN ROOM

tasks due each week, and monthly calendars. Using a professional planner can help you organize all your study, work, and personal goals in one place. Remember: It doesn't matter what kind of planner you use; the important thing is to plan ahead and write down what you plan to accomplish each day.

SET UP YOUR STUDY SCHEDULE

To make the best use of your study time, you should begin to plan weekly or daily what you're going to do and when. Now that you know how long it takes to read 10 pages in each of your textbooks, you can easily schedule all your reading assignments. You also should have a pretty good estimate of how long it will take to complete your writing, math, and study assignments. All these factors affect how efficiently you use your study time and how effectively you complete your assignments.

Assign Tasks to Available Study Time

To set up your study schedule, you need to refer to your Fixed Commitment Calendar to assign specific tasks to your available study time. If you look back at Greg's Fixed Commitment Calendar in Figure 3.2, you'll notice that Greg has three 1-hour time blocks and a 4-hour time block on Wednesdays. Greg prefers to do his Algebra homework right after class when the information is still fresh. If he has a 30-page chapter of History to read, for example, he could read the first 10 pages before lunch, the next 10 pages right after class, and the last 10 pages from 7:00 to 8:00. Of course, Greg could have begun reading his History on Tuesday, too. Greg could then use his longer time block in the evening to work on an upcoming English paper. Assigning specific tasks to specific blocks of study time can help you complete your work on time.

Use 1-Hour Time Blocks

Many students ignore 1-hour blocks of time because they think that 1 hour isn't long enough to really accomplish anything. In fact, 1-hour blocks are the most important study blocks that you have. During a 1-hour block of time, you can get a good start on a math assignment, complete a "chunk" of a reading assignment, complete a short writing assignment, or even review or expand on your lecture notes. If you've planned ahead, you'll find you can get a lot done in these short periods of time.

Use Your Daytime Study Hours

When you're planning your study schedule, don't forget to use your daytime study hours. In high school you may have been able to get all your homework done during the evening, but there aren't enough evening hours to complete all your study assignments in college. Look back at Greg's Fixed Commitment Calendar in Figure 3.2. Greg needed a minimum of 32 hours of study time per week to complete his assignments. If he used only his evening hours, he would be 12 hours short of his minimum. The 14 hours that Greg has available during the day are necessary for him to do his work. By starting your study tasks early in the day, you increase your chances of completing them.

WORK AHEAD

To be in control of your time, learn to work ahead on your assignments. You'll find college much less stressful if you stop doing Tuesday's assignments on Monday. Get into the habit of doing the work due for Tuesday on Sunday or even on Friday. Always being a little ahead of the game will give you a feeling of security. If something comes up (and something always does, at just the wrong time), you'll still be prepared for class the next morning. There's no worse feeling than walking into class unprepared. It's incredible how professors always seem to call on you or give a quiz the one time that you didn't do the reading.

You should work ahead on long-range assignments, too. Schedule 1 to 2 hours each week to work on a term paper or project. By starting early in the semester, you can easily complete your term paper and still keep up with your regular assignments. Develop a list of tasks for your paper or project and decide when you'll work on each task. Putting up a time line across the top of your bulletin board also may motivate you to work on completing your project.

USE TIME-MANAGEMENT STRATEGIES TO STAY MOTIVATED

Organizing your work and scheduling your time can make a huge difference in how much time it takes to do your work. However, just planning to read 20 pages at 2:00 P.M. is no guarantee that you'll get it done. Schedules are designed to organize your use of time, but they aren't designed to make you do the work. *You* have to do that.

One thing that can make a difference in whether you accomplish your goals is your level of motivation. You can keep your motivation high by using some specific techniques.

STUDY IN 1-HOUR BLOCKS

One effective strategy for keeping yourself motivated is to study in 60-minute time blocks. As you schedule your study tasks, break them down so that they can be accomplished in 1-hour blocks of time. Then plan to read, do problems, write, or study for 50 minutes. If you find that you can't concentrate on your work for the entire 50 minutes, work for 30 minutes and then take a 5-minute break.

TAKE BREAKS

After each study block of 50 minutes, you should plan a 10-minute break. Be realistic about the kind of activity that you plan for a study break. Taking a 10-minute nap just will not work, and going out to play a quick game of basketball inevitably will lead to a longer game of basketball. What can you do in 10 minutes? You can grab a snack, check your e-mail, check on your kids, throw a load of laundry in the washer, or make a phone call. (Resist the temptation to call a good friend to chat—you won't be able to hang up in 10 minutes.) Doing aerobics or just stretching is also a great activity for a break between study periods.

TACKLE DIFFICULT ASSIGNMENTS FIRST

Do the assignments for the course you dislike first and get them out of the way. You can easily complete the assignments for your favorite classes late in the day, even when you're feeling tired. Unfortunately, that usually isn't true for those more difficult assignments. If you leave them until the wee hours of the morning, you may find instead that you don't do them at all.

Also, if you do the assignments that you like the most first, you have nothing to look forward to. It's kind of like eating dessert before you eat your meal. The best part is already over, and the rest is somewhat disappointing. You also may find that if you leave the more difficult tasks for the end of the day, you worry about them as you work on other tasks. A difficult assignment can feel like a heavy weight hanging over your head. Doing your least favorite or most difficult assignments first and your easiest or favorite assignments last will help you stay motivated throughout the day.

SWITCH SUBJECTS

Another good strategy for maintaining your motivation to study is to switch subjects. By alternating between reading psychology and working algebra problems, you can get more done without becoming bored and tired. If you have a long

MORE TIME-MANAGEMENT TIPS

DEVELOP A SCHEDULE. Set up a schedule for both studying and completing your other responsibilities. Put your schedule in writing and stick to it. You may need to explain to your friends or parents (or your children) that you need more time to study now that you're in college and won't be able to spend as much time going out or doing household chores as you did before.

POST YOUR STUDY SCHEDULE. Put your list of study tasks on the bulletin board or on the refrigerator each week so that everyone in your family knows what you need to accomplish that week. This will help keep you more organized and let your family know what you need to do.

MAKE USE OF SMALL BLOCKS OF TIME. Use time between classes to get started on an assignment, edit notes, or review for a quiz. Instead of waiting for large blocks of time to do your work, break down your tasks and work on smaller portions of the assignment during 15-, 30-, or even 45-minute time blocks throughout the day.

STUDY DURING BREAKS AT WORK. You'd be surprised at how much schoolwork you can do during breaks over a 1-week period. You could read 5 pages of a chapter during lunch. You could review your word cards (flash cards for technical terminology) during a 15-minute break. You could even mentally review or quiz yourself on the material for an exam during a slow time at work.

PLAN TIME WITH YOUR FAMILY. Set aside time to spend with your family or friends each day or each week. Make this a regular part of your time-management schedule. During "slow" weeks or term breaks, plan special activities as a way of saying thank you for their support, patience, and help during the busier weeks.

DELEGATE SOME HOUSEHOLD TASKS. Unless you aren't planning to sleep, eat, or ever relax, you won't have time to do all your household chores when you're going to school. Do what you *have* to do and leave the rest for a slow week, day off, or even until term break. Ask your family to help out by doing some of the cooking, cleaning, or laundry. If each member of the family accepts just one task, you'll be amazed at the time you gain.

COOK AHEAD AND FREEZE MAIN COURSES. Instead of making one meat loaf for dinner tonight, make two and freeze one for the next week. You can also cook ahead during "light" weeks of the semester or during term breaks. Having dinner ready to pop in the microwave can be a real time-saver during busy weeks.

LEARN TO SAY NO. Believe it or not, I was a Girl Scout leader my first year in graduate school. As a mother, it was a great decision. As a returning student, it was a disaster. While you're attending college, you won't have time for many outside activities. When you do say no, explain that when you complete your education, you'll be happy to help out.

time block available for study (for instance, from 6:00 to 11:00), you should switch subjects every hour. Occasionally, you'll find that you're really progressing on an assignment and, after the 10-minute break, want to continue working on it. In such cases, you should do so. However, most students find that after an hour they're only too willing to work on something else for a while.

BREAK TASKS DOWN

You may find that breaking down your tasks into manageable units will help you accomplish your goals. Which would you rather read, a 50-page chapter or a 10-page chapter? Most people would agree that a 10-page chapter sounds much more appealing. If you have long reading assignments, break them down on your "To Do" list. You could divide that 50-page chapter into 5 separate tasks. It may make your list a little longer, but it also will allow you to shorten it more rapidly. Once you complete the first 10-page chunk of reading, you'll feel a sense of accomplishment and be motivated to read the next ten pages. Many of my students find that breaking down tasks reduces their tendency to procrastinate—perhaps you will, too.

PLAN REWARDS

In many ways, your 10-minute study break is a reward for having completed one block of study tasks. These short breaks, however, aren't always enough of a reward to keep you motivated. It's a good idea to get into the habit of rewarding yourself for completing difficult tasks or for completing all your work on a particular day. *Rewards* are whatever you plan to do that will help keep you working when you want to stop. Students use many kinds of rewards to stay motivated. Ordering a pizza after finishing a tough assignment works for some students. Others work hard to complete their studying in time to watch a favorite television show. If you know that you want to watch "Monday Night Football," plan your work on Sunday and Monday so that you can be finished in time; then you'll be able to sit back and watch the game without feeling guilty. Going to a party or watching your favorite "soap" each day also can be used as a reward for completing one or two specific study goals. Using rewards can help keep you motivated to do your work.

REEVALUATE YOUR TIME PLAN

After you've used your time plan for a while, you may find that it's not working well for you. You may need more time for long-range assignments, or you may discover you need more time available for study than you thought. It's important to take a look periodically at how you're using your time during the semester.

A good time to reevaluate your time plan is after the fourth week of the semester; that's when the first round of exams usually occurs. One good way to determine whether you're putting in enough time studying is to consider the grades you received on your first set of exams. If your grades are in line with the goals you set, then your time plan is probably working effectively for you. You also can judge whether you're using your time efficiently by looking back at some of your calendars and "To Do" lists. Have you been accomplishing the study goals that you set each day? Are you moving many tasks to the next day? Are you leaving work undone? Did you have time to prepare adequately for your exams? By answering these questions, you can determine whether you need to change your time plan.

The second point at which you should evaluate your time plan is after midterm exams. By this time in the semester, you should be able to determine quite accurately which parts of your time plan work and which don't. This is the best time to make some changes that will help you improve your grades. Finally, you also should rethink your time plan about 2 weeks before final exams. We'll talk more about this in Chapter 14.

REDUCE PROCRASTINATION

Procrastination, putting things off, is a common behavior pattern for many students. It's often the result of not wanting to start a task that seems difficult or time-consuming. Unfortunately, procrastination can become a habit. The more you avoid a task, the more daunting it becomes; the more you tend to dwell on the negative aspects of a task, the more it's blown all out of proportion. After a while you may feel that you can't ever complete the task because you don't have the time to finish it.

MAIN CAUSES OF PROCRASTINATION

According to Albert Ellis and William Knaus, the three main causes of procrastination are "self-downing," low frustration tolerance, and hostility.[2] *Self-downing* refers to putting yourself down—telling yourself you can't do it or

---

[2]Albert Ellis and William J. Knaus, *Overcoming Procrastination* (New York: Signet, 1977), p. 16.

you're not smart enough. When you don't complete tasks successfully or on time, you may begin to doubt your ability to succeed. If you set unrealistic goals such as planning to study the entire weekend or getting an A in every class, you may begin to worry about whether you can really achieve them. This can result in procrastination or avoidance caused by self-downing.

A second cause of procrastination is low frustration tolerance. If you're easily frustrated and tend to give up or have trouble starting on a task when it appears to be difficult or too time consuming, you may be experiencing *low frustration tolerance.* You may be thinking, "It's too hard." Writing a 20-page term paper for your Political Science class, for example, may be extremely difficult for you. The task may appear to be too difficult or require too much of your time, and just thinking about it may become a very unpleasant experience. Your low tolerance for frustration may lead you to put off this difficult task and do something else instead. The next time you decide to work on the paper, you may experience even more feelings of anxiety and panic because you have even less time available to complete the paper. If this pattern persists, you eventually may feel that you can't possibly complete the paper on time and decide not to do it at all.

Ellis and Knaus's third cause of procrastination is *hostility* toward others. You may put off doing that term paper because of your anger toward your professor. Comments like "He just expects too much of our class" or "She didn't even assign us that paper until 2 weeks before the end of the semester" or "That assignment is so unfair" are indicative of angry feelings toward your instructors. If you're angry at one of your instructors for giving you a difficult assignment, because you received a poor test grade, or for embarrassing you in class, you may find it unpleasant to work on the assignment for that class. Your angry feelings can in fact increase your feelings of frustration about the task. Together, these feelings lead to procrastination.

OTHER REASONS WHY STUDENTS PROCRASTINATE

Some students put off studying for exams until it's almost too late. Have you ever done that? You may be procrastinating for another reason—to protect yourself from feelings of inadequacy. By not studying well enough, you can protect your ego because you can blame your failure on your lack of preparation rather than on your lack of ability. For example, you might say, "Well, if I had studied, I would have gotten a B, but I just didn't have time." In this way you tell yourself that you *could* have done a good job if you had chosen to.

Procrastination also can be the result of poor time management. Not planning ahead for long-range assignments leaves some students in a time crunch when they realize that a paper or project deadline is approaching. Instead of having 6 to 8 weeks to prepare a term paper, procrastinators may find themselves with 1 week or less to complete it. Of course, this often leads to panic and poor performance.

Procrastination can become a habit, a way of life, for some students. Procrastination leads to more procrastination. Once you start to put work off, things pile up. As your workload grows, it becomes even more difficult to get it all done. Knowing you're weeks behind in one class can be so overwhelming that you can't even think about trying to catch up.

Another reason students procrastinate is lack of motivation; they sometimes just can't get motivated to start a particular assignment. This may be the result of poor performance in the course to date or poor performance on similar tasks. A student who has a low grade in a class after midterm may find it difficult to get excited about a group project that is due in 2 weeks. If you feel that a course or an assignment is irrelevant or has little meaning, you also may find it difficult to become motivated.

Finally, some students procrastinate because they're waiting for the *perfect* time, place, or mood to do the assignment. Without realizing it, they fall into the procrastination trap.

STRATEGIES FOR OVERCOMING PROCRASTINATION

Because so many people have problems with procrastination, many books, articles, and Web sites are devoted to the topic. They include hundreds of suggestions for dealing with procrastination. Below, you'll find a number of strategies and techniques that will help you overcome procrastination related to your academic work.

The best way to overcome procrastination is to simply get started—to take action. When you decide to work on your term paper or math assignment, don't think about why you should or shouldn't do it—just start it. Do anything. Take out paper and write anything. Tell yourself you only have to work for 5 to 10 minutes. At the end of that time, you can decide whether you want to work for another 10 minutes. Make sure you know what you're expected to do, too. Check with your professor or a classmate. It's hard to get started when you really aren't sure what you're expected to do. Then start with the easiest part of the task or the smallest part (remember, breaking tasks down makes them seem less difficult to accomplish). Once you get started, you're likely to continue. A number of other strategies that can help you overcome procrastination problems are shown in Figure 3.7.

FIGURE 3.7

• • • • • • • • • •

Strategies to Reduce Procrastination

- **Set realistic goals.** If you set realistic expectations for yourself, you're more likely to accomplish your goals and increase your self-efficacy.

- **Avoid overscheduling.** Monitor how long it takes to do each of your assignments. Then plan to do only what you actually have time to do, so you won't have long lists of tasks to carry over to the next day.

- **Create "To Do" lists.** Putting your tasks in writing helps you see exactly what you need to accomplish and strengthens your commitment to do your work.

- **Set priorities.** Prioritize each of your tasks so that you can complete the most important ones first.

- **Recognize that not all tasks are easy.** You'll have to do some assignments that are difficult or time-consuming. If you can accept that fact, that in itself will help you approach them more willingly.

- **Recognize that all courses are relevant.** Although not all of your classes can be in your major, all of them can help prepare you for the future. A college education will help prepare you for a career, but it is also your opportunity to become an educated person (something that will serve you well in any career).

- **Use positive self-talk.** Tell yourself that you can complete the task, that you want to do it, and that you can be successful. Don't tell yourself that it's too hard, too big, or that it's a waste of time. Making excuses for not working leads to procrastination; using positive self-talk helps you get started now.

- **Identify escapist techniques.** By figuring out your escapist techniques—the things you do to keep from doing your work—you can stop procrastinating. You may not even be aware that you use television, e-mail, or cleaning to avoid doing your assignments.

SUMMARY

Good time-management strategies are crucial to your college success. Monitoring how you use your time now is the first step to achieving good time management. Keeping a time diary will help you get a better picture of any time-use problems that you have. Complete a Fixed Commitment Calendar to see how much time you actually have available for study tasks. Then set up an assignment calendar so that you get a semester view of your workload and important due dates for each of your courses. Preparing weekly task lists and daily "To Do" lists will keep you organized and up to date with your work. Make academics your number one priority when you decide how to use your *free* time. Taking breaks, switching subjects, and planning rewards are just a few of the strategies that will keep you motivated and on schedule. Many students fall into the procrastination trap. Understanding the real reasons for procrastination will help you learn why you may procrastinate in certain situations. By identifying your escapist techniques and making a decision to use more effective strategies, you can overcome this problem. Breaking down tasks, starting with the easiest part of the assignment, and setting specific goals are all good strategies for breaking the procrastination cycle. If you use good time-management techniques, you can stay up-to-date on your course assignments, have time for relaxation and other responsiblilities, and eliminate the stress and panic that often result from not getting your work done.

Activities

1. Complete a time diary for 1 week. Exchange diaries with a classmate and analyze each other's use of time. Count the total hours spent in class, working, eating, sleeping, commuting, completing personal tasks, studying, watching television, socializing, and so on. Compare the hours spent in class to those spent studying. What ratio did your classmate use? Discuss this and any other patterns of time use that you notice. Share any suggestions you have for improving your partner's time plan.

2. Complete the Fixed Commitment Calendar (available on the *Orientation to College Learning* Web site). Calculate the time you have available for study and compare it with the time you need for study. Do you need to make any changes in your time plan?

3. Purchase a blank monthly calendar or download copies from the *Orientation to College Learning* Web site. Write in the months and dates for the entire semester. Then use your course syllabi to list all of your assignments on the calendar.

4. Use the study log on the Web site to keep track of how much time you spend studying every day for the next week. (Be sure to include weekends.) List each of your classes. How closely does this total match your estimated time needed for study? What patterns did you notice? Did you complete all of your work?

5. Make a list of your study goals for tomorrow. Don't forget to break long assignments down into manageable units. Then refer to your Fixed Commitment Calendar and schedule your assignments into appropriate time blocks. Take your plan to class and discuss it with a group of your classmates. Did anyone have suggestions to improve your schedule?

6. Go to the *Orientation to College Learning* book-specific Web site and follow the link in Chapter 3 to the University of Texas Procrastination Quotient online evaluation tool. After answering each of the questions, score your responses.

7. On a separate sheet of paper, create a chart using the following headings. Jot down all of the escapist techniques that you use in a 1-week period to keep from doing your work. What can you do to keep from repeating these avoidance patterns?

DATE	ASSIGNMENT OR STUDY TASK	WHAT DID I DO TO ESCAPE?	WHY DID I WANT TO ESCAPE?	WHAT STRATEGIES CAN I USE TO KEEP FROM TRYING TO ESCAPE MY WORK

8. If you're using the InfoTrac College Edition, read the directions for doing a PowerTrac search, click on the search entry box, and do a key word search on the topic of *time management*. Experiment with several combinations of terms using the *and, not,* and *or* logical operators. You can learn more about how to use logical operators by following the link that appeared on the Searching PowerTrac screen. If you get thousands of hits (articles containing the key words), you need to narrow the search more. Try using *time management* and *procrastination* this time. With a few hits this time, click on the view button to explore what you found. Locate at least one article that includes information about coping with procrastination and share it with the class.

9. Think of three examples of how you've applied what you learned in this chapter. Choose one strategy and describe how you applied it to your other course work using the Journal Entry Form that is located on the *Orientation to College Learning* Web site. Consider the following questions as you complete your entry. Why did you use this strategy? What did you do? How did it work? How did it affect your performance on the task? How did this approach compare with your previous approach? What changes would you make the next time you use this strategy?

10. Now that you've completed Chapter 3, take a few minutes to repeat the "Where Are You Now?" activity, located on the *Orientation to College Learning* Web site. What changes did you make as a result of reading this chapter? How are you planning to apply what you've learned in this chapter?

Review Questions

Terms You Should Know:

Escapist techniques	Prospective	Study log
Fixed commitment	Retrospective	Time diary
Fixed commitment calendar	Rewards	Time management
Hostility	Self-downing	"To Do" list
Low frustration tolerance	Semester calendar	Weekly task lists
Procrastination		

Completion: Fill in the blank to complete each of the following statements.

1. The first step in good time management is _____ how you use your time now.

2. You need to spend almost one- _____ of your time each week on academic tasks if you are a full-time student.

3. The average student spends about _____ hours outside of class for every hour in class to complete assignments.

4. Completing a _____ calendar will help you determine how well you can stick to a schedule.

5. The best way to overcome problems with procrastination is simply to

   _____ _____.

Multiple Choice: Circle the letter of the best answer for each of the following questions. Be sure to underline key words and eliminate wrong answers.

6. You can determine your time available for study by completing a:
   A. time diary.
   B. fixed commitment calendar.
   C. semester calendar.
   D. prospective-retrospective calendar.

7. Which of the following is <u>not</u> one of the main causes of procrastination?
   A. Self-downing
   B. Low frustration tolerance
   C. Feelings of inadequacy
   D. Hostility

Short Answer–Essay: On a separate sheet, answer each of the following questions.

8. What are the five factors that influence how much time you need for study?

9. How can time-management strategies keep you motivated?

10. What are five strategies that students can use to overcome problems with procrastination?

Chapter 4

IMPROVING CONCENTRATION

"I think I have the ability to concentrate better now than I used to. Before, I used to always drift off while studying, but now when I start to, I catch myself. I can stay focused, and I am able to maintain my concentration much better. I have learned many new techniques for improving concentration, which I have put to use. I believe that when I am able to concentrate on my work, I also study much better."

Martin Ng
Student

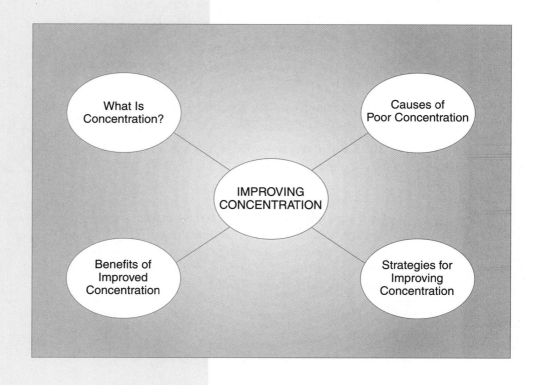

Where Are You Now?

Take a few minutes to answer *yes* or *no* to the following questions.

	YES	NO
1. Do you have trouble getting back into your work after you've been interrupted?	____	____
2. Do you read and study in a noisy, cluttered room?	____	____
3. Do you find that even though you schedule study time, you don't actually accomplish very much?	____	____
4. Do you use any strategies to help increase your ability to concentrate?	____	____
5. Can you concentrate on your work even if the subject doesn't interest you?	____	____
6. Do you use your preferred learning style when completing assignments?	____	____
7. Do you tend to think about personal plans or problems when you're reading and studying?	____	____
8. Do you find that when you finish reading your textbook assignment, you don't really remember what you read?	____	____
9. Do you get totally engrossed in the material when you read and study?	____	____
10. Do you daydream a lot when you're listening to lectures?	____	____
TOTAL POINTS		____

Give yourself 1 point for each *yes* answer to questions 4, 5, 6, and 9, and 1 point for each *no* answer to questions 1, 2, 3, 7, 8, and 10. Now total up your points. A low score indicates that you need some help improving your concentration. A high score indicates that you're already using many good concentration strategies.

WHAT IS CONCENTRATION?

Concentration is focusing your attention on what you're doing. Concentration is important in just about anything you do, but in this chapter we'll focus on improving concentration during reading, listening, and studying. It's hard to describe what concentration is, but it's easy to explain what it isn't. Consider the following example. If you're reading a chapter in your sociology text, you're concentrating on it only as long as you're thinking of nothing else. As soon as you think about how many pages you have left to read, what time you're going to eat dinner, or what the professor will discuss in class, you're experiencing a lack of concentration. If you think about the fact that you *should* be concentrating on the assignment, that means you have in fact lost your concentration. Let's look at another example. If, during a lecture class, you become interested in the conversation going on in the row behind you, you've lost your concentration. You may even find that you've missed several new points that your professor just introduced.

Being distracted interferes with your ability to attend to or focus on the task at hand. In each of the above examples, you were actually concentrating on something. The problem is that you were concentrating on something other than the lecture or the reading material—you were concentrating on the distractions.

Difficulty with concentration is a common problem for college students. Every semester, I ask students to look over the syllabus and mark the three topics that they think will help them the most. Improving concentration is one of the most common choices.

THE THREE LEVELS OF CONCENTRATION

As you read your text assignment, ask someone to time you for about 20 minutes. Each time you think of something else or even look up from your reading, put a check mark in the margin of your book. You may have found that you were not always concentrating at the same level. At some points during the 20-minute period, you may have noticed that you were more focused on the material than at other times. Look back at the check marks you made in your book. Were more of them located in the early pages of the assignment? Why does this happen?

To understand why students are less distracted toward the end of a 20-minute reading period, let's take a better look at how concentration works. Anne Bradley has divided concentration into three levels: light, moderate, and deep.[1] Look at the diagram in Figure 4.1.

---

[1]Adapted from Anne Bradley, *Take Note of College Study Skills* (Glenview, IL: Scott, Foresman, 1983), pp. 41–42.

FIGURE 4.1

● ● ● ● ● ● ● ● ●

The Concentration Cycle

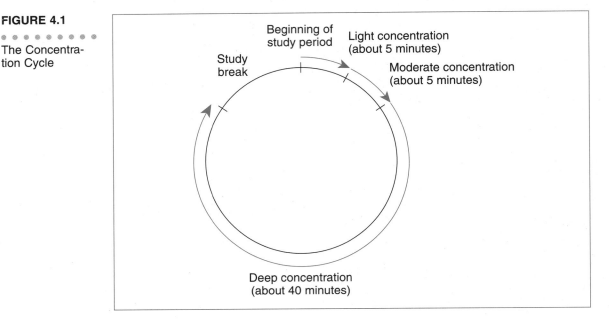

Light Concentration

When you first sit down to read or study, you're in a state of *light concentration.* This stage of concentration continues for about the first 5 minutes of study. At this point, you're just getting settled into your reading, listening, or studying. Students in light concentration can be seen wiggling around in their chairs, twisting their hair, or pulling out study supplies. When you're in light concentration, you're easily distracted. You may hear people talking down the hall, notice other students walking into the room, be annoyed by any noise occurring around you, or find yourself thinking about other things. You don't accomplish much during this stage, and very little learning actually occurs.

Moderate Concentration

During the next 5 minutes or so, you move into *moderate concentration.* At this point you begin to pay attention to the material that you're reading, hearing, or studying. You may find that you're actually getting interested in the lecture or text material. In this stage you'll probably find that you're not as easily distracted. Although you may lose your concentration if someone talks directly to you, you may not notice the voices of people talking down the hall or even someone coughing in the same room. Some learning occurs in this stage.

Deep Concentration

Once you move into *deep concentration,* you aren't thinking about anything except what you're hearing, writing, or reading. At this point, you're totally en-

FIGURE 4.2

• • • • • • • • •

Study Sessions
and Levels of
Concentration

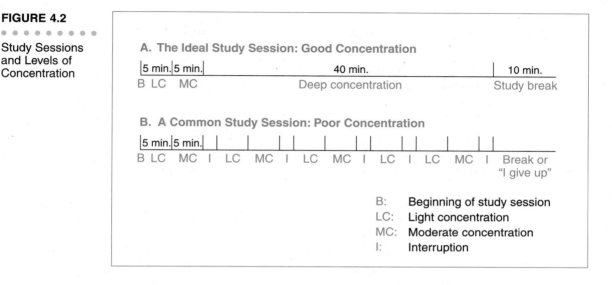

A. The Ideal Study Session: Good Concentration

| 5 min. | 5 min. | 40 min. | 10 min. |
| B LC | MC | Deep concentration | Study break |

B. A Common Study Session: Poor Concentration

| 5 min. | 5 min. | | | | | | | | | | | | | |
| B LC | MC | I | LC | MC | I | LC | MC | I | LC | I | LC | MC | I | Break or "I give up" |

B: Beginning of study session
LC: Light concentration
MC: Moderate concentration
I: Interruption

grossed in the material. Have you ever jumped when someone came up behind you and touched your arm? Because you were in deep concentration, you may not have even noticed that person enter the room or call your name. When you're in deep concentration, you're not aware of the clock ticking, the door opening, or the things that you normally would find rather distracting. It's at this stage in the concentration cycle that you're working most effectively. You learn the most and can complete more work in less time in deep concentration.

THE CONCENTRATION CYCLE

You may be thinking that it sounds fairly easy to reach a high level of concentration—that after an initial 10 minutes or so, you can expect to remain at a level of deep concentration. Unfortunately, this is not the way it really works for many students. Instead, they move in and out of the three stages of concentration.

Look at the diagram of the ideal study session in Figure 4.2A. In this situation, you would be able to work in deep concentration for 40 minutes during a 50-minute study session. You can learn the most during this type of study session because when you're in deep concentration, you're working at your highest level of comprehension and learning.

Unfortunately, some students never get into deep concentration. They move back and forth between light and moderate concentration because they're distracted constantly (Figure 4.2B). Every time you're distracted, you move back to the stage of light concentration. If your roommate asks if she can borrow your navy sweater and you respond, you've experienced a distraction.

If you stop to check how many more pages you still have to read, you've been distracted. If you look up when someone walks past you in the library, you've been distracted. If a family member asks you a question, you've been distracted. Each time you're interrupted while you're listening to a lecture, working on a homework assignment, or studying for a test, you move out of deep concentration.

You may find it doesn't take you quite as long to get interested in the material on your second or third try. However, you'll still have to move through the "warming up" stages again before you can reach a state of deep concentration. If you tend to study in places where you're interrupted a lot, your study session may more closely resemble the concentration cycle in Figure 4.2B. Without strategies that will improve your ability to concentrate, you may have difficulty concentrating on a lecture, or you may spend a lot of time reading or studying yet accomplish very little.

You may also find that your ability to concentrate varies from text to text (what you study), place to place (where you study), and time to time (when you study). You may have to use more active strategies or different strategies in order to increase your ability to concentrate when you're working on material that doesn't interest you, in noisy or distracting study areas, or even at different times of the day.

CONCENTRATION COMPONENTS

Most students have concentration problems, but not all students actually have the same problems concentrating. Concentration involves three basic components: the ability to focus at will, the ability to sustain focus over a period of time, and the ability to limit focus to one task at a time.[2]

The Ability to Focus at Will

Have you ever noticed that you have difficulty concentrating when the professor begins to lecture? You may find yourself looking around the room, pulling out your notebook and pen, or even thinking about whether you'll get out of class early. If you have trouble focusing your attention on the lecture, you may have difficulty *focusing at will*, being able to turn your attention to the task of listening to a lecture at the moment the professor begins to speak.

Why can some students concentrate immediately while others find it difficult to focus their attention? Many students have developed techniques to

---

[2]Becky Patterson, *Concentration: Strategies for Attaining Focus* (Dubuque, IA: Kendall Hunt, 1993).

focus their attention on the task. Have you ever competed in a sporting event? Picture yourself at that critical moment when you're about to "make your move." Do you go through a ritual designed to calm yourself, to focus your attention, to remove all other distractions? Ball players, bowlers, tennis players, and runners (just to name a few) all have strategies for focusing their attention just as they shoot a foul shot, attempt a difficult split, serve, or begin a race. Of course, listening to a lecture, writing a paper, and reading a text chapter aren't exactly the same as sporting events, but you can use the same techniques to focus your attention.

Many students use self-talk to focus at will. You may say things like: pay attention; okay, I need to do this; let's get going now! However, creating a verbal prompt is only one way to help you focus at will. Other students find that creating physical prompts are just as effective. Sitting down in your seat and pulling out your notebook and pen may be enough to focus your attention. Some students can instantly begin to concentrate when they sit down at a table or desk, pick up a special pen or highlighter, or put on a special hat or study slippers. Anything that you associate with concentrating on your work can help you learn to focus at will.

Sustaining Your Focus Over a Period of Time

Although learning to focus your concentration immediately is important, it's also important to *sustain your focus.* As you learned in the previous section on the concentration cycle, this is not always as easy as it sounds. Some students have difficulty maintaining their concentration no matter what the task. Other students, however, can concentrate for long periods of time when reading their text assignments, but are constantly distracted when doing their math and vice versa. What makes the difference? The difficulty level of the task, the student's interest in the material, and the student's level of motivation all could be factors. In the next two sections, you'll learn more about the causes of poor concentration and some suggestions for improving concentration. Many of the strategies described will help you sustain your concentration for a longer period of time.

Limiting Your Focus to One Task at a Time

The final component of concentration is *limiting your focus* to one task at a time. You need to learn to focus your attention on one page in your text (without looking over at the English paper you must do for tomorrow), one math problem (without thinking about how many others are on the page), or studying for one quiz (without thinking about the other two you have this week). Many of the strategies that involve creating a good study environment can help you avoid distractions around you. The strategies that you learned for setting goals and establishing priorities will also help you focus on one task at a time.

CAUSES OF POOR CONCENTRATION

The two main causes of poor concentration are external and internal distractions. A *distraction* is anything that diverts your focus (attention) from the task at hand. *External distractions* include things like noise, an uncomfortable study area, and, of course, other people. If you try to study in a noisy place, you may find that you're constantly distracted and interrupted. Dorm rooms and the kitchen table at home are not always good places to do your work. The phone rings, people stop by, and TVs and stereos are on all the time.

Although you can walk away from noisy study areas, you can't escape internal distractions; they go with you wherever you go. *Internal distractions* are things that you think about or worry about. Common internal distractions are anxiety caused by a certain course, the feeling that study won't help, worry over personal problems, indecision about what to do next, and so on. Many students even worry about the fact that they can't concentrate, and *that* worry interferes further with their ability to concentrate on their work.

Although it's easy to blame all concentration problems on internal and external distractions, the real causes of most concentration problems are lack of attention, lack of interest, and lack of motivation. By identifying the real reason for your concentration problems, you'll be able to select the appropriate strategy to overcome each of your concentration problems.[3]

The internal and external distractions that were discussed earlier often stem from a lack of attention to the task at hand. When you find yourself thinking of other things, staring out the window, or being distracted by noises around you, you may not be focusing your attention. You may be having difficulty focusing your attention at will, sustaining your attention, or limiting your attention to only one thing.

You've probably already found that it's easy to concentrate when you're interested in what you're doing. Do you find that you can concentrate well in some lecture classes but not in others? Is it easy to stay involved in your reading in some texts but not in others? If you answered yes to either of these questions, your level of interest in the course or in the material may be the reason for your concentration success in one course and difficulty in the other. Without a high level of interest, it's easy to lose concentration, especially when you're surrounded by distractions.

Lack of motivation is another cause of poor concentration. If you really don't care about getting a college degree, it's hard to go to class, read your text assignments, take lecture notes, and prepare for exams. If you don't see the relevance of the course or the assignment, it's hard to exert the effort to do it well.

---

[3]Based on ideas from "AIM to Listen," from *The Secretary* magazine, reprinted in *Communication Briefings*, 1991.

If you don't really care about making the grade, it's going to be very difficult to concentrate on your work. If you ever find yourself asking, "Why am I even trying to do this assignment?" "Why am I sitting in this class?" or "Why am I in college?" you may have a motivation problem. To improve your ability to concentrate, you need to be motivated to succeed.

CONCENTRATION PROBLEMS DURING LECTURE CLASSES

Many students experience problems with concentration when they're trying to listen and learn in class. Do you ever have trouble concentrating on the lecture your professor is presenting? What gets in your way? One of the more common problems is distractions caused by other students. It's hard to concentrate on what the professor is saying when the person sitting next to you is constantly talking to you or to someone near you. Even a conversation two or three rows behind you can interfere with your ability to stay focused on the lecture. Noises outside the lecture room also can be distracting and can interfere with your ability to stay focused.

Internal distractions are another cause of difficulty during lecture classes. Worrying about personal problems and thinking about what you have to do after class are common internal distractions. Feeling hungry or tired is another common internal distraction.

A number of students indicate that they can't concentrate on a lecture if they're not actively involved in the class; they have difficulty playing the role of a passive observer. Other students complain that it's impossible to stay involved and focused on a lecture when the professor always mumbles or speaks in a quiet voice. Still others have problems when the professor doesn't ask questions or interact with students during the lecture.

Finally, some students have concentration problems during lecture classes because of their attitude toward the class or the material. Many students have more trouble concentrating when they place a low value on the material or the course. Moreover, they experience more difficulty paying attention to the lecture when the topic is uninteresting or difficult to understand. In situations like this, some students begin to daydream or even doze off.

CONCENTRATION PROBLEMS WHEN
YOU READ YOUR TEXT

Many students have difficulty concentrating when they read textbook assignments. Unlike lecture classes, where the professor may help keep you focused by varying his or her tone of voice or by asking questions, you alone are responsible for concentrating on your reading assignments. Do you have trouble concentrating when you read some or all of your text assignments? If you think that you're the only student with this problem, you're wrong. Many students indicate that they have more trouble concentrating when they read than at any other time.

External distractions such as a cluttered or uncomfortable study environment, noise, and other people are common causes of poor concentration when reading. How many times this week were you interrupted as you tried to read your text assignment? Many students need complete silence in order to concentrate on reading assignments. If you live in a dormitory, finding a quiet study place can be quite a problem. However, students who live at home find that a family can be just as distracting.

The time of day that you tackle your reading assignments also can affect your ability to concentrate. If you try to do your reading late at night, you may experience more difficulty staying focused because you're tired. Concentration requires effort, and it's harder to make that effort when you're tired. Have you noticed that it's more difficult to concentrate on the road when you're driving late at night and feel tired? For the same reason, many students have more difficulty maintaining their concentration when they try to read for long periods of time without a break.

Although most students indicate that their problems with concentration stem from external distractions or from internal distractions such as the interest they have in the material or the value they place on the course, other internal distractions can also be a factor. Personal problems, concerns about grades or progress in the course, and fear of not knowing the answer or how to do the problems in class can all interfere with a student's ability to focus on the material. Many students find that when they have difficulty concentrating (for any of the above reasons), they tend to think about other things. Sometimes they worry about both academic and personal problems. At other times, they tend to use escapist techniques and daydream about something that they would rather be doing—something that would be a lot more interesting or a lot more fun than reading a textbook.

CONCENTRATION PROBLEMS WHEN YOU STUDY FOR EXAMS

Some students have a lot of trouble concentrating when they're preparing for exams. Aside from the usual external distractions, they often experience special problems. Some students may not be as motivated to focus on the task of test preparation early in the semester because they don't put as much value on the first exam. It's more difficult to concentrate when you're studying for a test on which you place little value. Other students get distracted when they study because the material is difficult or uninteresting. Some students have concentration problems because studying is not a specific assignment like "reading pages 186 to 201." Any time your goals are vague or you're not sure what to do, it's more difficult to stay focused.

A common complaint from students is that they get tired of studying and begin to think of other things. Some think about things they would rather be doing or things that their friends, who don't have exams, are doing. Worrying about what the test will be like, what questions will be on it, and how well you will do are all common internal distractions.

Another problem that leads to poor concentration when preparing for exams is passive study techniques. Most students still study for college exams by simply reading over the text and lecture material. What could be more boring?

Procrastination can also lead to poor concentration. When you leave your test preparation to the last minute, you may feel overwhelmed by having too much to learn in too little time. In situations like this, students generally try to cram for the exam, which often results in passive study and increased worry about the results.

STRATEGIES FOR IMPROVING CONCENTRATION

By now you probably realize that problems with concentration are fairly common for college students. Although it may make you feel better to know you aren't the only person in the world who can't concentrate, it doesn't help you correct the problem. Many students indicate that they have few, if any, strategies for improving their concentration; they have a problem concentrating, but they don't know how to correct it. You can improve your ability to concentrate by using motivational and organizational strategies, by creating a good learning environment, by dealing promptly with internal distractions, by using active learning strategies, by monitoring your concentration, and by matching your learning style to the task.

USE MOTIVATIONAL AND ORGANIZATIONAL STRATEGIES

You can improve your concentration by using many of the motivational and organizational strategies that you learned in Chapters 1, 2, and 3. Several of the most helpful strategies are having a positive attitude, setting goals, and scheduling your assignments.

Develop a Positive Attitude Toward Your Work

Having a positive attitude toward your assignments is critical to focusing at will—concentrating on the task the minute you begin to work. First, you must *want* to do the assignment. You need to see the relevance, value, and importance of the task. If you aren't interested in completing the task, you'll also have difficulty concentrating. You need to find ways to make the material more interesting—you *can* generate interest. Second, you must believe that you *can* do the assignment. You need to have confidence in your ability to successfully complete the task. If you have self doubts or feelings of anger or frustration about the task, they'll interfere with your concentration. Having a positive attitude will help you focus as you begin to study and will help sustain your focus as you work.

Use Goal-Setting Strategies

Setting clear, specific goals can also help you achieve better concentration. If you know exactly what you want to accomplish when you begin an assignment, you'll be able to limit your focus to the task at hand. Setting learning goals can help you determine what you need to learn or accomplish during a specific study session. It's equally important to know exactly what you need to do to complete the assignment—you need to understand what the professor expects from you and what the grading criteria will be. If you aren't sure about how to do the assignment, check with a classmate or the professor. If you don't, you may find that you'll have problems concentrating on the task because you'll be worrying about whether you're doing it correctly. Having a clear purpose in mind can help you limit distractions as you complete your work.

Use Time-Management Strategies

Almost any of the time-management strategies that you learned in Chapter 3 will help you improve your concentration. Using "To Do" lists and planning calendars are critical to good concentration. One of the most common internal distractions among college students is the worry that they won't get their work done. Many students report that they're constantly thinking of other assignments when they try to concentrate on their work. Do you? If you develop a study schedule each day and assign each of your study tasks to available study time, you won't have to worry about getting your work done. You'll be able to focus completely on each task as you work on it, knowing that you have already scheduled all of the others. By organizing your study time you can better focus your attention on one task at a time.

CREATE A POSITIVE LEARNING ENVIRONMENT

You can dramatically improve your ability to concentrate by creating a positive learning environment. The first step is to control external distractions, and the best way to control external distractions is simply to eliminate them.

Strategies for Lecture Classes

In lecture classes, you can avoid most external distractions by moving to the front of the room. Fortunately, most students who chat during class tend to sit in the back. However, you still occasionally may find yourself sitting near some noisy students. If the students sitting near you keep you from concentrating on the lecture, get up and move! You also can be distracted by things going on around you. If you find yourself looking out the window or watching what goes on in the hall, find a seat where you can't see out the window or the door. Make the professor the center of your line of vision.

Strategies for Your Study Environment

Although it's fairly easy to find a new seat during lecture classes, it's not so easy to find a new place to study when you can't concentrate. If you live in a dormitory or if you live at home, you're surrounded by noise. Some students stay in their rooms or work at the kitchen table even when they can't concentrate, almost out of stubbornness. "It's my room and I should be able to work there" is a commonly heard statement. But if you've tried unsuccessfully to eliminate the distractions in your study area and you still can't concentrate on your work, you have only one other option. You need to find somewhere else to study. It may not seem fair that you have to gather up all your materials and go somewhere else, but if you can't change your study environment, you have to find a new one. If you force yourself to continue working in a noisy study area, you probably won't be able to accomplish very much and you may become even more frustrated.

Finding a good place to read and study may require some experimentation. Try working in different places at different times of the day to see which study area works best for you. The library, study rooms, and empty classrooms are usually good study areas. If you're living at home, you may find that setting up a table or desk in the basement or the attic is the only way you can avoid constant interruptions. Once you find a good place to work, establish a regular routine. Studying in the same place at the same time each day helps you get down to work. It may even help to use special objects that you associate with study. By sitting in a special chair, wearing your "study" slippers, or even using a special pen or clipboard, you'll help yourself get into a study mode, and this will help you improve your concentration. The Tip Block includes some additional suggestions for creating a better study environment.

DEAL WITH INTERNAL DISTRACTIONS

Once you set up a quiet study environment, you should see a big difference in your ability to concentrate. However, just eliminating external distractions

TEN TIPS FOR SETTING UP A GOOD STUDY ENVIRONMENT

FIND A QUIET STUDY SPACE. Find a place to study that's away from the "center" of dormitory or household activities. It's almost impossible to concentrate if you're surrounded by distractions. A card table in the basement may not look pretty, but the quiet will make up for it. If you can't study at home, try the library or a quiet study room.

LIMIT YOUR DISTRACTIONS. Put your desk against the wall and remove all photos, mementos, and decorations. When you look up from your work, you won't be distracted by reminders of your friends or family or other responsibilities.

USE YOUR DESK FOR STUDYING ONLY. If you use your desk only for studying, you'll automatically think about studying when you sit down.

STUDY IN A COMFORTABLE CHAIR. Sitting in a chair that is *too* comfortable, though, may lead to passive reading. Completing assignments is hard work, so you need to study in a semitense position.

NEVER STUDY LYING DOWN IN BED. You'll have trouble concentrating and may get so comfortable that you fall asleep.

SCREEN YOUR PHONE CALLS. If you're constantly interrupted by phone calls, take the phone off the hook or let an answering machine screen your calls.

TURN OFF THE TELEVISION, STEREO, AND RADIO. If you need some sound to serve as a "white noise" to block out the other noises around you, use soft, familiar music. Save that new CD as a reward for completing your work.

DO YOUR WORK WHEN YOUR HOUSE IS QUIET. Study when family members are asleep or out. Schedule study hours before your children get up and after they go to bed. If you get home from work or school an hour before they do, use that time to do course work.

CONSIDER STUDYING AT SCHOOL. If you can't concentrate at home, you may have to do your work at school, before or after class. You can often find an empty classroom, quiet corner in the library, or study area in the student union. Compare your distractions when studying on campus and at home.

GET HELP WHEN YOU NEED IT. Ask a family member or friend to stay with your children when you're trying to study for exams or complete major assignments. If necessary, hire a sitter or a mother's helper to entertain or care for your children.

doesn't guarantee that you'll be able to focus on your work. Many students find that after they eliminate the external noises around them, they notice the internal "noises" even more. Although you can't really eliminate internal distractions, you can take steps to keep them from interfering with your work.

Deal with Competing Activities

No matter how focused you are when studying, it's not unusual to think about other things. If you think of something that you want or need to do or if you come up with an idea for another assignment, jot it down or plan a time to do it, and then continue with your work. The key is to minimize the distraction—to keep it as short as possible. Then you can move back to deep concentration more quickly. If you don't write it down, you'll probably continue thinking about it or even begin to worry that you may forget it. In either case, you'll be concentrating more on the internal distraction than on your assignment.

Deal with Academic Problems

Worrying about academic problems is a common internal distraction. Instead of worrying, do something! Go see your professor and share your concerns about the course. Get a tutor or have a talk with yourself about what you need to do to meet your goals. Remind yourself that getting down to work and doing your best are steps in the right direction. Then, if you still don't understand the material or can't do the problems, ask for help. Remember, it's easier to block out internal distractions when you have confidence in yourself as a student. You'll gain this confidence by learning that you can be successful in college, not by worrying about it.

Deal with Personal Problems

Personal worries and concerns are common internal distractions. Many students allow an argument with a boyfriend or girlfriend or family problems to interfere with their concentration. Make a decision to do something about your problem as soon as you complete your work. Write down exactly what you plan to do and return immediately to your study tasks. Calling a friend and talking honestly about your problem or scheduling an appointment at your campus counseling center are good strategies for dealing with personal problems. Some students find that writing about whatever is bothering them in a journal or talking it out with friends helps them experience a feeling of closure about the problem.

USE ACTIVE LEARNING STRATEGIES

One of the best ways to keep external and internal distractions from interfering with your concentration is to become more involved in the lecture, the text, or your test preparation. You can generate this high level of involvement by using active learning strategies.

You may have noticed that you concentrate better when you do math problems and grammar exercises or complete a study guide for your Psychology textbook. Why does this happen? One possible reason is that you like those classes or assignments more than some of your other classes. However, another reason may be that you need to use active learning strategies to complete those tasks. Solving problems, correcting grammatical errors in sentences, and looking for answers to study guide questions are all active strategies that get you involved in and help you focus your attention on each of the tasks.

Strategies for Lecture Classes

Taking notes during lecture classes helps you focus on what the professor is saying. If you know that you're going to have to write something, you'll be more motivated to pay attention. Many students actually find that lecture classes become more interesting and go much faster when they take notes. Because they are actively involved, they have reached a state of deep concentration.

Many students have trouble concentrating during lecture classes simply because they're not actively involved in what's going on in the class. Asking questions, predicting what the professor will say next, and taking notes are all ways of becoming more involved during lecture classes. (You'll learn about these strategies in Chapter 6.) Becoming a more active participant in class is one of the keys to eliminating internal and external distractions and increasing concentration.

You may also find that you can increase your concentration in lecture classes by sitting directly in your professor's line of vision. You're more likely to pay attention if you feel as if you're on the spot. It's pretty hard to fall asleep or look out the window when your professor is standing right in front of you. If you focus your attention on the professor and keep him or her directly in your line of vision, you'll be able to block out distractions more easily, too.

Strategies for Reading Text Assignments

Becoming an active reader will significantly improve your ability to concentrate when you read your textbook assignments. Reading with your eyes but not your brain leads to daydreaming and other concentration problems. Have you ever read a paragraph or even an entire page of text and then realized that you had no idea what you had just read? Even though your eyes did "look at the words," your mind was somewhere else. Using a reading/study system, previewing, highlighting, and taking notes are all active strategies that can improve your concentration. You can also increase your concentration by creating word cards as you read your assignment. Becoming familiar with the technical terminology can help you understand your reading assignment more easily. Predicting quiz questions in the margin also helps you focus on the important information in the text. We'll talk more about all of these strategies in Chapters 7, 8, and 9.

Strategies for Test Preparation

How can you maintain your concentration as you prepare for exams? Jennifer sums it up pretty well: "When studying for a test, I'm active. I don't just reread my notes and the chapter. I write down what I need to know from the text and then I rewrite my notes." Just reading over the textbook and your lecture notes isn't a very effective way to improve your concentration when you study. You need to increase your involvement with the material. When you prepare for an exam, dig through the material, looking for important information. Taking notes, developing study sheets, and creating graphic displays will help you become totally engrossed in the material. Reciting the key information out loud and doing some self-testing are just two of many rehearsal strategies that also can help you learn. We'll talk more about them in Chapters 5 and 10. For now, however, remember that the more actively involved you are in studying the material, the easier it'll be to maintain your concentration.

You can also increase your concentration by using motivational strategies. Jennifer motivates herself to study by thinking about getting a good grade. She says, "You just need to make the decision that you want to succeed." Taking breaks, switching subjects, and planning rewards are helpful in increasing your motivation, and they also can help increase your concentration. It's much harder to stay focused on your work when you become tired or bored. When you just can't concentrate anymore, stop and take a break. Then switch to a different subject to eliminate feelings of boredom and frustration. Setting deadlines and limiting the amount of time that you allow for each of your study tasks also can motivate you to use your time more effectively. Deadlines make you feel rushed, so you actually force yourself to concentrate better (unless you've left yourself too little time—in that case, your anxiety will only increase).

MATCH YOUR LEARNING STYLE TO THE TASK

You learned in Chapter 1 that you can maximize your time and effort by working in your preferred learning style or using the learning style that best suits the task you need to complete. You may have also discovered that matching your learning style to the task helps you improve your concentration, too. If you learn best in the morning, you'll also find it easier to concentrate in the morning. If you tend to work best with quiet music playing in the background, you may discover that music helps you concentrate by blocking out other noises that might actually distract you. Approaching a task from your preferred style results in a better fit or match—studying feels right. However, using a style that's inappropriate to the task or to the material you want to learn (even if it's the style you prefer) can itself become distracting and interfere with your ability to concentrate. When you use the appropriate learning style for each task during a study session, you'll probably be less distracted and move into deep concentration more easily.

MONITOR YOUR CONCENTRATION

Monitoring how often you lose your concentration can be very helpful in learning how to improve your concentration. Put a check mark or write the time in the margin of your book or your lecture notes every time you're distracted. At the end of your class or study session, count the number of interruptions. Make a commitment to reduce that number the next time you read or go to your lecture. In a few weeks, you may find that your ability to concentrate improves dramatically.

   When you notice that you're daydreaming or thinking about other things, try to figure out what actually triggered your loss in concentration. If you can pinpoint the cause of your distraction, you're only one step away from the solution. Hold yourself accountable for your lapses in concentration—find a way to overcome them. Remember, you can improve your ability to concentrate, but it is you who must take the responsibility for doing so.

PEANUTS reprinted by permission of Newspaper Enterprise Association, Inc.

BENEFITS OF IMPROVED CONCENTRATION

There are many benefits to improved concentration. One of the most obvious is that you'll be able to make better use of your time. You'll find that when you spend the majority of your time in deep concentration, you get more done during a study session. In addition, because you're operating in deep concentration for a longer period of time, you'll gain a better understanding of what you have read. It stands to reason that if you spend most of your time focused on the course material, you'll understand it better than if you're constantly alternating between the material and other things.

Improved concentration during lecture classes can help you take better lecture notes. If you're focused on the information your professor is presenting rather than on other people or personal plans, you'll be able to take better notes. In addition, you may find that you become more involved in the lecture and gain a better understanding of the material. You'll be able to form connections between the material being presented and the material you already know. This helps you learn and understand what you're hearing.

You may also notice that once you set up a better study environment, you're better able to prepare for quizzes and exams. Working in a quiet, nondistracting study area can have a positive effect on what you study and learn. Using active study strategies will not only improve your concentration but also your mastery of the material. After concentrating on your studies for 1 or 2 hours, you'll be pleased by what you were able to accomplish. You may even experience increased self-confidence and higher self-esteem.

SUMMARY

Most college students have problems with concentration. Unfortunately, if you're focusing on the conversations going on out in the hall, instead of on your professor's lecture, you're concentrating on the wrong thing. During an ideal study session, students move from light, to moderate, to deep concentration—the level where most learning occurs. During a typical study session, however, students move in and out of these stages of concentration because of interruptions or distractions. Some students never even reach deep concentration.

The main causes of poor concentration are external and internal distractions. By monitoring your distractions, you can hold yourself more accountable during lecture classes, as you do your day-to-day assignments, and when you prepare for exams. Avoiding common distractions and using active study strategies can help you increase your concentration. Creating a positive learning environment is critical to good concentration. It's easy to blame all concentration problems on a noisy room or a cluttered desk, but many times the real culprits are lack of attention, lack of interest, and lack of motivation. By analyzing the real cause of your external and internal distractions, you may be able to identify the real cause of your concentration problems. If you focus your attention, increase your interest, and improve your motivation, your ability to concentrate will improve. If you find that you're putting a lot of time into your studies but not getting much accomplished, you may have a concentration problem. You can learn more and do it in less time when you're working in deep concentration.

Activities

1. Draw a time line to evaluate your last 50-minute study session. Plot the interruptions that you experienced and how much time you spent in each of the three levels of concentration. What did you discover?

2. Review Emily's list of distractions from a 1-hour study session, available on the *Orientation to College Learning* Web site. Label each distraction as external or internal and personal or academic. Then jot down a suggestion for how Emily should have dealt with the distraction. Discuss your responses in a group or with the other members of your class. What would you have done if this were your study session? Note: Emily read four pages of her Biology text in 1 hour during this study session.

3. Choose one of your texts and read a section that you haven't already read. After you finish reading, make a list of the distractions you experienced. Repeat the task using another text or at different time of day. What differences do you notice in your lists or in your ability to concentrate on the two reading assignments?

4. Go to the *Orientation to College Learning* Web site (http://info.wadsworth.com/vanblerkom04) and download one copy of Activity 4–3, 4–4, or 4–5 from the Activities Packet. What advice would you give to each of the students? Compare your responses with those of others in your group.

5. On a separate sheet of paper, create a chart using the following headings. Record up to 10 of the concentration problems that you encounter over a 1-week period. Include one or more strategies that you used or should have used to improve your concentration.

DATE	STUDY TASK	CONCENTRATION PROBLEM	CAUSE	STRATEGY

6. Go to google.com and type in "concentration tips." Select three or four of the Web sites and check them out. Copy the five best concentration tips that you locate onto 5 separate index cards. Put the address for the Web site on the back of each. Exchange cards with other members of your class or study group and generate a list of the 10 best Internet

concentration tips. Which ones do you already use? Which do you plan to use? Why?

7. If you're using InfoTrac College Edition, access it and do a subject search for articles related to concentration. View the articles under the heading Attention. Although you won't find a huge number on this topic, there are several that will provide you with additional information and new perspectives on how some researchers look at concentration and learning. Locate one article and read it. Print both the article and the list of references and go to the library and locate one additional article from the list of references or request it through interlibrary loan. (InfoTrac College Edition can help you locate library references on various topics if you note the references used in recent articles.) Write a paragraph or two describing what you learned about how to improve your concentration.

8. Write three concentration problems that you experienced during the past week on each of three index cards. Put the last four digits of your Social Security number at the top right corner of the back of the card (do not use your name). After the cards are shuffled and distributed to various groups within the class, discuss each of the problems assigned to your group. Discuss possible solutions to the problem and write several of the best on the back of the card. Select one or two of the most common (or most interesting) to describe to the class. At the end of the class period, each student can claim his or her card (by Social Security number) and make use of the suggestions that were offered.

9. Think of three examples of how you've applied what you learned in this chapter. Choose one strategy and describe how you applied it to your other course work using the Journal Entry Form that is located on the *Orientation to College Learning* Web site. Consider the following questions as you complete your entry. Why did you use this strategy? What did you do? How did it work? How did it affect your performance on the task? How did this approach compare with your previous approach? What changes would you make the next time you use this strategy?

10. Now that you've completed Chapter 4, take a few minutes to repeat the "Where Are You Now?" activity, located on the *Orientation to College Learning* Web site. What changes did you make as a result of reading this chapter? How are you planning to apply what you've learned in this chapter?

Review Questions

Terms You Should Know:

Concentration	Focusing at will	Moderate concentration
Deep concentration	Internal distraction	Sustaining your focus
Distraction	Light concentration	
External distraction	Limiting your focus	

Completion: Fill in the blank to complete each of the following statements.

1. _____ college freshmen experience concentration problems.

2. Some students never get into _____ concentration.

3. Use _____ study strategies to improve your concentration when studying for exams.

4. Both _____ and _____ distractions affect your ability to concentrate during lectures.

5. Having difficulty concentrating at the beginning of a task is referred to as a problem focusing at _____.

Multiple Choice: Circle the letter of the best answer for each of the following questions. Be sure to underline key words and eliminate wrong answers.

6. Which of the following is <u>not</u> one of the real causes of poor concentration?
   A. Lack of interest
   B. Lack of attention
   C. Lack of motivation
   D. Lack of self-efficacy

7. You can reduce your distractions by:
   A. studying in an empty classroom.
   B. using your desk only for study.
   C. screening your phone calls.
   D. all of the above are good strategies.

Short Answer–Essay: On a separate sheet, answer each of the following questions.

8. Describe the characteristics of each of the three stages of the concentration cycle.

9. How should students overcome problems with internal and external distractions?

10. How will improving your concentration benefit you in college?

Chapter 5

IMPROVING MEMORY

"It is much easier to memorize when you use acronyms. I've used acronyms for as long as I can remember, starting with "ROY G BIV [the color spectrum: red, orange, yellow, green, blue, indigo, violet]. I even remember memorizing the presidents by taking their last initials and making a group of phrases out of them to remember. I find doing these types of activities really helps, and it seems the more ridiculous the mnemonic, the easier it is to remember—especially when I'm experiencing test anxiety. Also, overlearning and spaced study have really been paying off for me by helping to reduce forgetting."

Jen Perry
Student

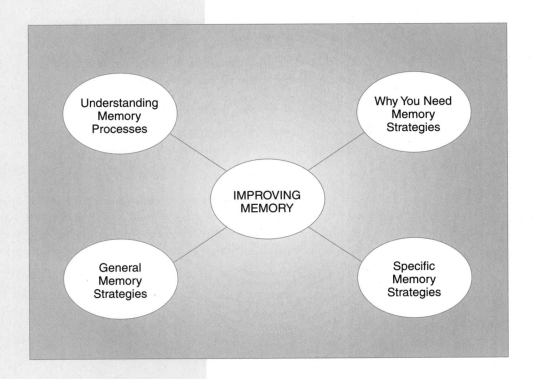

Where Are You Now?

Take a few minutes to answer *yes* or *no* to the following questions.

	YES	NO
1. Do you often know the answer to a question but find that you can't think of it?	_____	_____
2. Do you organize or group information to help you remember it?	_____	_____
3. After you study, do you go back and test yourself to monitor your learning?	_____	_____
4. Do you make up rhymes or words to help you remember some information?	_____	_____
5. Do you space your practice when reviewing information?	_____	_____
6. Do you try to memorize all the information that you need to know for an exam?	_____	_____
7. Do you often find that you get confused by closely related information?	_____	_____
8. Do you often forget a lot of the information that you studied by the time you take the test?	_____	_____
9. Is the TV or stereo on while you study?	_____	_____
10. Can you learn and remember information just by making up a rhyme, word, or other memory aid?	_____	_____

TOTAL POINTS   _____

Give yourself 1 point for each *yes* answer to questions 2, 3, 4, and 5 and 1 point for each *no* answer to questions 1, 6, 7, 8, 9, and 10. Now total up your points. A low score indicates that you need to improve your memory skills. A high score indicates that you're already using many good memory strategies.

UNDERSTANDING MEMORY PROCESSES

Doing well on exams requires an effective study plan, active study strategies, and a good memory. What you typically think of as learning involves storing information in your memory so that it will be available later when you need it. In this chapter, you'll gain a better understanding of how information is stored in memory. This will help you understand why many of the exam-preparation strategies that are described in Chapter 10 will help you learn and retain course material. "Having a good memory" involves both putting information into memory and getting it back out—both storage and retrieval. Can you recall a time when you thought you had studied a particular topic well enough that you knew it for the exam, only to find that you couldn't remember the information during the test? Perhaps you never really got the information into your long-term memory, or perhaps you simply were unable to recall it when you needed to. Why do we forget? How do we learn? Many students really don't understand how memory works. Do you? Learning about how we store and retrieve information will help you understand why some study strategies work and others don't. Over the years, psychologists have tried to develop theories to explain how memory works. One of the most useful of these is the Information Processing Model.

INFORMATION PROCESSING MODEL

The *Information Processing Model* suggests that memory is complex and consists of various processes and stages. For example, there are at least three types of memory: sensory memory, short-term memory (STM), and long-term memory (LTM). In addition, there are three important memory processes: encoding, storage, and retrieval. Figure 5.1, which was adapted from a model developed by Bourne, Dominowski, Loftus, and Healy,[1] shows the three types of memory (represented as boxes) and the memory processes (represented as arrows).

To learn and remember, we must encode, store, and retrieve information. The first step in this process is *encoding*—interpreting information in a meaningful way. Suppose you want to remember what a cloud looks like. Clouds are amorphous (without a definite shape) and lack any clear structure. You might find it difficult to remember exactly how a cloud looks after observing it briefly. However, if you notice that the cloud looks somewhat like an elephant, you'll be better able to remember its shape later simply by picturing an elephant. To be remembered, information must be encoded; it must be interpreted in a meaningful

---

[1] L. E. Bourne, R. L. Dominowski, E. F. Loftus, and A. F. Healy, *Cognitive Processes*, 2d. ed. (Englewood Cliffs, NJ: Prentice Hall, 1986).

FIGURE 5.1

• • • • • • • • •

Information Processing Model

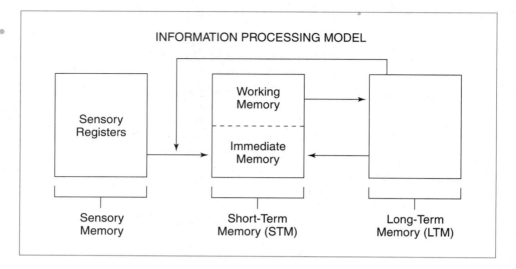

way. The second step in the memory process, *storage,* involves working on (for example, repeating and organizing) information so that it can be placed into LTM. Information doesn't automatically move into LTM unless we work to store it there. Much of what we think of as studying involves storage processes. The third step, *retrieval,* involves getting information out of LTM. As you'll see, retrieving a memory is very much like going into your basement to find the badminton set that you know is there, somewhere—you may have to hunt for a while, but eventually you'll find a clue that will lead you to it.

Sensory Memory

You probably have heard about short-term and long-term memory. However, *sensory memory,* also known as the *sensory registers,* may be new to you. Essentially, our senses (vision, hearing, smell, taste, and touch) are always very busy. We hear, see, smell, taste, and touch hundreds of stimuli each moment. Most of these stimuli are unimportant and are therefore quickly. forgotten. However, some stimuli are important to us and worth remembering.

At one time scientists believed that we remembered, somewhere in our brain, everything that we ever saw, heard, smelled, tasted, or touched. We now realize that such a feat would be nearly impossible; our memories quickly would fill up with billions upon billions of bits of useless information. Instead, we remember only those stimuli that we decide are important, those to which we *attend.* Unless we pay attention to stimuli, they are quickly forgotten. We choose those stimuli to which we attend, and we choose to ignore others.

When we see something, even if only for a split second, we hold onto an "afterimage" of the stimulus for between ½ and 1 second. Although 1 second isn't a very long time, it gives our memory system plenty of time to decide whether the material is important and whether we want to remember it and to pick out details. This visual process is known as *iconic memory*.

There also is a sensory register for hearing known as *echoic memory*. After hearing a sound, we hold onto an afterimage, or "echo," of that sound for between 2 and 4 seconds. Again, this gives our memory system enough time to decide whether we need to remember the stimulus and to pick out details.

Short-Term Memory

Once we decide to remember material, we immediately have to move it into short-term memory. However, for us to do this, the material must be encoded. Encoding, as you know, involves making information meaningful, making sense out of it. Short-term memory, has two components: immediate memory and working memory. *Immediate memory* is related to the concept of consciousness. Whatever we currently are thinking about is in our immediate memory. Think of your immediate memory as being similar to a small desk. In a 2-hour study session you may work on several tasks at your desk. However, because your desk is very small, you can place only a limited amount of material on it at any one time. If you want to work on something new, you need to move aside the material on which you were just working. Immediate memory is similar to this because you can remember only the material that is "sitting on your desk" at any one time. Because immediate memory is very limited, we typically can retain only about seven (plus or minus two) chunks of information on our "desk." Furthermore, without continual rehearsal, those seven chunks can stay on the "desk" for only 20 to 30 seconds before they slip away.

To hold on to information and get it into your long-term memory, you must first move the material into the other part of your short-term memory, the *working memory*. This part of the memory system is aptly named because you really have to "work" on the material to make it meaningful, memorable, and easy to remember. You can use a variety of strategies to move information from your working memory into your LTM, but all have one thing in common. The harder you work on the material, the greater the probability that you'll put the material into LTM in a place where you can find it again.

The strategies that we use in our working memory all are geared toward making material more memorable. Some strategies require us to organize material in a way that's logical for each of us, whereas other strategies require us to make material meaningful, to relate it to ideas we already remember well.[2] In the remainder of this chapter and in later chapters, you'll learn many new strategies that you can use in working memory.

---

[2]C. F. Weinstein and R. F. Mayer, "The Teaching of Learning Strategies," in M. C. Wittrock, ed., *Handbook of Research on Teaching* (New York: Macmillan, 1986).

Long-Term Memory

Once material has been processed in working memory, it can be moved into long-term memory. What's so remarkable about LTM is that it has an almost unlimited capacity. In fact, the more we learn, the more capacity for learning we appear to have. Building long-term memories appears to provide a structure for adding new memories. LTM also is remarkable because we appear to hold on to most of our memories indefinitely.

Long-term memory is like a warehouse full of filing cabinets. The cabinets in the warehouse and the material within the cabinets are arranged in a logical order; each cabinet drawer is labeled, and there are dividers within each drawer. Materials (memories) are placed in specific folders, in specific sections, in specific drawers, in specific file cabinets, in specific sections of the warehouse. However, the warehouse (your LTM) is enormous. Unless the material is carefully classified and placed in the correct file, it can easily be misfiled. Once material is misfiled, or just poorly classified and filed, it's much more difficult to retrieve. Only when we really work to appropriately classify and store information are we able to retrieve it easily.

RETRIEVAL AND FORGETTING

If we can hold on to memories indefinitely, why do we forget? As you might guess, there are a number of reasons for forgetting, some of which are related to retrieval. At times, we think that we've forgotten information, but in fact we never really got it into LTM at all. Either we worked on it too little to store it or we did such a poor job of organizing it that, although it is in LTM, it's in a form that's unrecognizable and unusable.

Many memories are available to us in our long-term memory; however, they aren't readily accessible. To access a memory, we need to know how to find it. Many times we need a key term, or what psychologists call a *cue,* a hook or link to the information, to unlock the memory. Memories that we use frequently typically are stored with a number of cues, thus making them easier to remember. However, at times we store memories with only one or two cues. Unless we use those cues, we can't retrieve those memories. Clearly, the more ways we devise for material to be remembered, the more cues we develop that make the material more accessible to us. For example, creating study sheets (see Chapter 10) with specific headings helps integrate the material better than just learning lists of facts, details, and definitions in isolation because more associations (more cues) are formed with the material.

Other processes also affect retrieval. For example, organization affects retrieval. Memories that are well organized are easier to retrieve than material that isn't well organized. Anxiety also affects retrieval. When we're anxious, it's more difficult to recall cues and retrieve important information because anxiety affects our ability to focus and concentrate. Many of us have had the experience of being unable to retrieve a memory during an examination and then remembering the material once the exam is over and our anxiety is reduced.

Interference theory, another memory model, also is important to the concept of forgetting. Interference theory states that memories can interfere with one another during the retrieval process. Over the years we tend to learn many things that are similar to one another. Unless we make each of these memories distinctive, there's a strong likelihood that one memory will interfere with another. It's well worth the effort to develop some unique cues that will help make each memory distinctive.

Due to a combination of failing to store information properly in long-term memory, using too few cues, and interference, we tend to forget newly learned material rapidly if we don't continue to rehearse it. The remainder of this chapter will discuss strategies you can use to improve your memory.

WHY YOU NEED MEMORY STRATEGIES

Now that you understand how information is encoded, stored, and retrieved, you may wonder why you need to learn specific strategies to aid your memory. According to Donald Norman, "To remember is to have managed three things successfully: the acquisition, retention, and retrieval of information. Failure to remember means failure at managing one of those steps."[3] To perform well in college courses, you need to use strategies that aid the acquisition, retention, and retrieval of the information that you want to learn. In college, learning to get information out of memory is just as important as learning to put that information into memory.

Let's try an experiment to find out what kinds of strategies you already use. Can you name all fifty states? Write down the first ten that you can remember in the margin of your text, then read the remainder of this page.

How did you remember the states that you wrote down? What method did you use to remember them? Look at the first couple of states that you wrote down. Do they follow some type of order? Some students use alphabetical order to list the states. Is that what you did? Others use a geographic order like Maine, New Hampshire, Vermont or Washington, Oregon, California. Although these are the two most common ways that students tend to remember the states,

---

[3]D. A. Norman, *Learning and Memory* (New York: Freeman, 1982), p. 2.

many students use other strategies. How you remembered the states really isn't important. The important thing is that you used some strategy to recall information that you probably learned many years ago.

If you learned the states in alphabetical order, it's easier for you to retrieve that information alphabetically than geographically. On the other hand, if you learned the information geographically, by doing maps or by travel, you may find it difficult to list the states alphabetically. From this exercise, you should have learned that the method you use to organize information during study will in some way determine how effectively you can retrieve that information. In addition, the more associations you develop for particular information, the easier it'll be to retrieve. In this section, you'll learn some general and specific strategies that will help improve your ability to learn and retrieve information.

GENERAL MEMORY STRATEGIES

The following general strategies can help you acquire, retain, and retrieve course information.

SPACED PRACTICE

There are many benefits to using spaced practice instead of massed practice. *Massed practice,* like cramming, involves studying all the material at one time. *Spaced practice,* on the other hand, involves spacing your study time over a longer period, with breaks between practice sessions. Studying for short periods of time, such as one 50-minute session, prevents boredom, helps avoid fatigue, and improves motivation. If you space out your study over a period of days, you gain additional benefits. First of all, you delay forgetting. As pointed out earlier, even when you think you've learned the information, some information usually is "forgotten." By reviewing the same material the next day, you have a chance to find out what you've forgotten and work on it again. In addition, you benefit by reviewing and reinforcing the information that you previously studied. By spacing out your learning, you can delay or prevent some of the forgetting that would occur before an exam.

Spaced practice, or distributed practice—as it is also known—allows time for the information to consolidate or jell in long-term memory. During *consolidation,* information is organized and stored in LTM. If you try to shove too much information into memory at one time, you won't be able to retrieve very much of it. One explanation for this is that the longer you study, the more inhi-

bitions you develop (feeling tired, bored, and so on) that decrease your effi-
ciency for storing the material in LTM. With massed practice, you may get to
the point where you're just looking over the material rather than "working on it"
to learn it.

Another problem that may occur with massed practice is that you don't organize the information well enough to store it in a way that you can find it again
in your LTM storehouse. Allowing breaks between learning sessions gives you
time to think about what you've been studying and to structure or organize it according to what you already know about the topic.

BREAKING DOWN TASKS

By spacing out your learning, you can also focus your study. Instead of trying to
learn all of the material for your exam at one time (cramming), study only one
or two chapters (and the accompanying lecture material) each day. When you
study small chunks of material at one time, you can do a better job of getting it
into LTM. It's easier to stay focused and actively involved in your learning when
you don't feel as if you have to learn it all at one time. You'll be more willing to
take the time to create study sheets, create word and question cards, or recite or
self-test yourself on the material. By breaking down study tasks and organizing
and storing small units of material, you increase the likelihood that you'll efficiently and effectively store the material in your LTM.

REPETITION

Spaced learning also works because it involves repeating the material. Each time
you write or recite the same information (especially if you do it in a slightly different way), you strengthen your memory of it. An early theory of how memory
works described traces or pathways in the brain. Although developing a memory really is not like wearing a path in the brain, you may find that this analogy
helps you understand how learning and retrieval occur. Each time you work on
the material (by writing, reciting, or even thinking about it), you strengthen the
path to the material in LTM. Here's another way to look at it. Imagine that each
time you practice the same piece of information, you open a particular file in one
of the drawers of your LTM filing cabinet. The more times that you open that
same drawer and pull out that same file, the easier it is to do it the next time;
you know just where to go in LTM and exactly where in the filing cabinet to look.
Repetition, especially spaced over several hours or days, can help you
strengthen and maintain your memory of important material.

The Wizard of Id

Reprinted by permission of Johnny Hart and Creators Syndicate, Inc

OVERLEARNING

Overlearning is an important strategy for test preparation. *Overlearning* involves continuing to work on material even after it's learned. This practice is very helpful in improving your memory. Each time you review the material, you reduce forgetting and strengthen the path to your LTM. Overlearning may provide additional benefits. It may lead you to review the material in other ways so you may form different cues for, or associations with, the material. You may even find that as you continue to work on the material, you gain a better understanding of it.

Overlearning also can help you cope with test anxiety, which interferes with your ability to retrieve information from LTM. If you're worrying about an exam, you may have difficulty identifying or remembering the cues that you need to locate the information that you stored. Overlearned material is less susceptible to the debilitating effects of anxiety because it's so firmly embedded in LTM. You can count on overlearned information to help you get started during the exam. Answering questions that cover overlearned information is a good way to use your test time efficiently until you calm down.

SPECIFIC MEMORY STRATEGIES

Besides the general strategies described earlier, many specific learning strategies are effective in developing your memory processes. Weinstein and Mayer describe five groups of learning strategies: rehearsal strategies, elaboration strategies, organizational strategies, comprehension monitoring strategies, and affective and motivational strategies.[4] Each category includes a variety of learning strategies that can be used to improve the various memory processes. Let's look at some of them.

---

[4]Weinstein and Mayer.

REHEARSAL STRATEGIES

Rehearsal strategies involve repeating the material until it's learned. How did you study your spelling and vocabulary word lists in elementary school and junior high? If you wrote them ten times or recited them over and over again, you were using low-level rehearsal strategies. You may have studied for many of your high school exams by simply reading over the material two or three times until you felt that you knew it. Here again, you were using low-level rehearsal strategies. Although these rehearsal strategies are quite effective for learning simple lists or remembering easy-to-recall information, they are not as well suited to some of the more complex learning tasks that you need to use for college classes.

High-level rehearsal strategies such as outlining, predicting quiz questions, and creating charts and concept maps all help you rehearse the information (you're still going over it) as you organize and condense it for later review. When you use higher-level rehearsal strategies, you're working on the material—you may be adding information that you already know, organizing the material in a way that's more memorable to you, creating additional cues to help you locate and recall the material in long-term memory. In Chapter 9, you'll learn note-taking strategies that will aid your learning. If you make up questions in the margin of your text, you'll use high-level rehearsal strategies. To make up even one question, you probably have to reread, write, or think about the material four times—providing you with a significant amount of rehearsal. You're also using high-level rehearsal strategies when you recite information from question cards or recall columns, explain information in your own words, answer review questions, or take self-tests.

In Chapter 10, you'll learn other high-level rehearsal strategies, such as creating study sheets and making self-tests. Just about any strategy that you use to prepare for a quiz or test involves rehearsal. The key, though, to effective rehearsal is combining your review of the material with one or more of the organizational, elaboration, comprehension monitoring, or motivational strategies that are presented in the remainder of the chapter.

ELABORATION STRATEGIES

Elaboration strategies involve expanding on the information, forming associations, or determining how new information relates to what you already know. Paraphrasing, summarizing, explaining, answering questions, forming mental images, and using mnemonics ("ni-mon-iks") are all elaboration strategies. Effective note taking requires you to embellish or refine what the professor or the author has said. When you take notes in your own words and add comments or make connections, you're using an elaboration strategy. One of the chief advantages of elaboration strategies is that they help you create more associations with the material to be learned, thereby providing you with more routes for getting to the information during retrieval. Explaining the material out loud, creating questions in the margin, and making maps also are examples of elaboration strategies that you'll learn to use in later chapters.

Mnemonic devices or techniques often are referred to as memory tricks. However, many of these techniques aren't tricks at all. They are, instead, techniques that can help you remember things when you can't seem to remember them any other way. Did you ever tie a string around your finger to remind yourself to do something? If so, you may have had the same problem I had: I noticed the string and remembered that I had to do something, but I still couldn't remember what that something was. The advantage of mnemonic devices is that they form an *association* with the material, so if you remember the mnemonic, you remember the material. Mnemonics provide an organizational framework or structure for remembering information that may not appear to have a structure of its own.

This brings up a very important point. Mnemonic devices are aids to retrieval, but they do <u>not</u> guarantee that you will learn the material. You can't just decide that you're going to remember Weinstein and Mayer's five categories of learning strategies by remembering the word REOCA (<u>R</u>ehearsal, <u>E</u>laboration, <u>O</u>rganizational, <u>C</u>omprehension, <u>A</u>ffective). Before you can use "REOCA" to help you list or discuss these strategies, you have to practice the connection between the mnemonic and the information to be learned. Although this section focuses on the use of mnemonics, it's important to remember that you must use the other high-level rehearsal strategies to learn the information in the first place. You can then use mnemonics to retrieve what you have learned.

According to Kenneth Higbee, "A mnemonic system may help you in at least three ways when you're trying to find items in your memory: (1) It will give you a place to start your search, a way to locate the first item. (2) It will give you a way of proceeding systematically from one item to the next. (3) It will let you know when your recall is finished, when you have reached the last item."[5] You'll learn more about how to make those connections and use mnemonics as retrieval aids as you examine the use of associations, acronyms, acrostics, and imagery.

Associations

Forming associations is always important when you're trying to remember something. We use this technique every day.

When I was in eighth grade, we were studying longitude and latitude in geography class. Every day for a week, we had a quiz, and I kept getting longitude and latitude confused. I went home and almost cried because I was so frustrated and embarrassed that I couldn't keep them straight in my mind. I stared and stared at those words until suddenly I figured out what to do. I told myself, when

---

[5]K. Higbee, *Your Memory: How It Works and How to Improve It* (Englewood Cliffs, NJ: Prentice Hall, 1977), p. 78.

you see that *n* in longitude it will remind you of the word *north*. Therefore, it will be easy to remember that longitude lines go from north to south. It worked; I got them all right on the next quiz, and the next, and on the exam.

When I tell this story in class, some of my students laugh because it seems silly to them that anyone could get longitude and latitude confused. However, some of us do get confused about things that may seem simple to others. It's very easy to become confused by closely related information. Mnemonics helps you *know* for sure which choice is the correct one.

Acronyms, or Catchwords

Acronyms are "words" that are made up of the first letters of other words. Acronyms are so commonly used today that most of us don't even realize that some aren't real words. SCUBA, NASA, FBI, and COD are all quite familiar. We don't even think of them as standing for self-contained underwater breathing apparatus, National Aeronautics and Space Administration, Federal Bureau of Investigation, and cash on delivery; they all are well understood in their abbreviated form.

John Langan used the term *catchword* to describe an acronym.[6] In a sense, acronyms do help us catch or hold on to the information that we have learned. *Catchwords,* or acronyms, can be real words or nonsense words designed to aid recall. You probably can name all of the colors in the spectrum because someone taught you to use the catchword "ROY G. BIV" (red, orange, yellow, green, blue, indigo, violet). "REOCA" also is an example of a catchword; each letter stands for the first letter in a list of other words. Can you say them now? Try it.

How to Create Catchwords

Catchwords are useful for remembering lists of information. Look at the five general principles of nonverbal communication listed below. Try to create a catchword to remember them.

1. Nonverbal communication is multichanneled.

2. Nonverbal communication conveys emotions.

3. Nonverbal communication is ambiguous.

4. Nonverbal communication may contradict verbal messages.

5. Nonverbal communication is culture-bound.[7]

To make an acronym or catchword, you first have to identify a key word in each statement. Go back and underline the following words: *multichanneled, emotions, ambiguous, contradict,* and *culture-bound.* These words should work well as hooks

---

[6]J. Langan, *Reading and Study Skills*, 4th ed. (New York: McGraw-Hill, 1989), p. 207.
[7]From W. Weiten and M. A. Lloyd, *Psychology Applied to Modern Life,* 6th ed. (Belmont, CA: Wadsworth, 2000), p. 189. Used with permission.

or tags to help you remember the entire list of principles. Next, list (or underline) the first letter of each word: M, E, A, C, C. "MEACC" doesn't sound as though it will be very memorable, but by simply rearranging the letters you could form the catchword "MECCA" or "CAMEC." Both of these are fairly easy to recall.

Your work is not done, though. Can you list the five general principles of nonverbal communication? Just creating the catchword does not mean that you've learned the material. To strengthen the associations and learn the material, you need to practice connecting the catchword to the key word and then the key word to the entire phrase. Reciting or writing will help you form the connections. If I were going to use the catchword "MECCA," I would rehearse the information this way: "M" stands for "multichanneled," and "multichanneled" stands for "nonverbal communication is multichanneled." "E" stands for "emotions," and "emotions" stands for "nonverbal communication conveys emotions" (and so on). You may need to practice this connection several times. Of course, you still have to be sure that you understand what the terms *multichanneled* and *emotions* mean in this context. Students who say that mnemonics don't work for them often think that simply constructing the mnemonic should firmly embed the information in long-term memory. Unfortunately, the mere construction of a word or phrase doesn't replace learning the information. Your catchword will help you retrieve the information from memory *only after the information is learned.* Take a look at how some students used catchwords to remember course material (Figure 5.2).

Acrostics, or Catchphrases

Acrostics, or catchphrases as Langan called them, are phrases or sentences that are made up of words beginning with the first letters of other words. Just as the catchword "FACE" helped most of us remember the names of the spaces in music class, the catchphrase "Every Good Boy Does Fine" worked to recall the names of the lines. Did you remember learning "My Very Educated Mother Just Served Us Nine Pies" to remember the nine planets in order? If you did, you used an acrostic, or catchphrase, to remember the information. Catchphrases worked in junior high, and they can work in college, too. The difference, though, is that you need to create your own catchphrases in college to help you remember the information that you want to learn for your exams.

When to Use Catchphrases

Catchphrases are especially useful if you have to remember the information in a special order or if you can't form an easy-to-remember word from the letters available to you (for instance, you may have all consonants but no vowels). You can create catchphrases to recall all kinds of course material. Remembering lists of names, steps in a process, causes and effects, and key points for essay answers are just a few ways that students use catchphrases.

FIGURE 5.2

• • • • • • • • •

Student Examples of Catchwords

Swinburne's and Aquinas's Views

Swinburne—SWOMP   Aquinas—ICON

S   simultaneously   I   immutable

W   within time   C   continuum

O   own actions   O   omniscient

M   mutable   N   not in time

P   personable

Kwan's Catchwords

FASCISM

1. <u>A</u>uthoritarian governments
2. <u>M</u>asses are incapable of governing themselves (democratically)
3. <u>S</u>tate terrorism is used
4. <u>H</u>ierarchically structured organic society
5. <u>E</u>lites govern

A M S H E = SHAME

Heather's Catchword

Four Stages of Food Processing

1. <u>I</u>ngestion—eating
2. <u>D</u>igestion—breaking down food
3. <u>A</u>bsorption—cells absorb nutrients
4. <u>E</u>limination—undigested wastes removed

I D A E = IDEA (extra association: Eating is a good IDEA)

Cheri's Catchword

How to Create Catchphrases

You can create catchphrases in much the same way you created catchwords. If you had to learn the five principles of nonverbal behavior in order, you might find that "Mary Ellen Answered Conrad Curtly," is more memorable than "MEACC." This example can provide us with some additional tips for creating acrostics, or catchphrases. You may have noticed that in the example ("Mary Ellen Answered Conrad Curtly"), the two *c* words have the same second letters (the vowels *o* and *u*) as the original key words (*contradict* and *culture-bound*). When you have two key words that start with the same letter, it's helpful to use the second letter to show which one comes first. You may also find that making your mnemonic sentences outrageous, silly, or humorous help you remember them. We tend to remember funny or outrageous catchphrases better than dull and boring ones.

Whenever you're using catchphrases to help you learn and remember text material, consider the following five rules:

1. Select a key word to represent each piece of information.

2. Underline or write down the first letter of each key word.

3. Form a catchphrase from words beginning with the first letter of each word.

4. Practice associating the words in your catchphrase to the key words and then the key words to the actual information that you need to know.

5. Use the mnemonic to test your memory for the original information.

After a little practice, you'll find that you can use catchphrases to help you recall information for many of your college courses. Figure 5.3 includes several examples of acrostics, or catchphrases, that students used when preparing for essay exams.

Imagery

You can also create visual images related to your catchphrases. These additional cues can aid your memory. However, you can create visual images to remember course material without writing catchwords or catchphrases. Semantic, hierarchical, and line maps (described in Chapter 9) all can be used to present a visual display of material that you need to remember. After developing and practicing a map, you may be able to recall much of the information by visualizing the map itself.

You also can paint visual pictures in your mind to remember information. If you were studying the Boston Tea Party, for example, you could remember many of the details about this historic event just by visualizing what happened. By incorporating names, places, dates, and so on in your visual image, you can recall a great deal of information about your topic.

Another mnemonic device that uses imagery is known as the method of place or the *method of loci* ("lo-sigh," meaning locations). Let's say that you have to present a speech about healthy eating habits in one of your classes and that your speech consists of seven main ideas. You simply imagine yourself taking a very familiar walk. As you pass the first familiar landmark on that walk, you develop an image that somehow connects that familiar landmark to the first point in your speech. (For example, the image of a tree with a nest of baby birds could help you remember that you have to begin providing healthy foods when children are young.) You continue in this manner until

FIGURE 5.3

• • • • • • • • •

Student Examples of Catchphrases

> ### Four Classes of Heterotrophic Organisms
>
> Carnivores—animal eaters
> Herbivores—plant eaters
> Omnivores—animal and plant eaters
> Decomposers—eat decaying organisms
>
> **"Can Henry Omit Dents"**
>
> Terri's Catchphrase
>
> ### Five Building Blocks of Structure
>
> 1. Job design
> 2. Departmentalization
> 3. Coordinating mechanisms
> 4. Span of management
> 5. Delegation
>
> **"Jeff is depressed about coming to see David"**
>
> Todd's Catchphrase
>
> ### FOUR KINDS OF LOVE
>
> 1. Passionate love   3. Fatuous love
> 2. Compassionate love   4. Consummate love
>
> **Peggy counted four chickens**   Peggy's Catchphrase
> **Playing cards for cash**   Mathew's Catchphrase

you've developed an image connecting each point in your speech to a landmark. Then, when it's time to present the speech, you simply imagine that you're taking that familiar walk. As you pass each landmark, you should be able to recall the next point in your speech.

ORGANIZATIONAL STRATEGIES

Organizational strategies allow you to organize the information to make it easier to learn and recall. Tasks such as listing, ordering, grouping, outlining, mapping, and diagramming are all examples of organizational strategies. In each of these activities, you structure the material that is to be mastered. With outlining or mapping, for example, you organize the material in a way that shows how each component is related to the others. In Chapter 9, you'll learn to use both outlining and mapping techniques. One of the advantages of organizational strategies is that by structuring the material, you provide yourself with new ways to remember many of the details. If you can remember the structure—the main headings of the outline or the web strands of your map, for example—you'll be able to remember many of the details.

Look at the following list of words for 60 seconds; then cover it with your hand or a piece of paper and try to write the words in the margin.

Newspaper, pencil, bus, automobile, book, pen, boat, magazine, comic book, chalk, crayon, train

You may have found that it was difficult to remember all twelve of the items. Do you know why? Earlier you learned about the capacity of short-term memory. If you recall, you can remember only about seven pieces of information at one time. You can, however, increase this capacity by chunking (grouping) the information. You probably will be able to remember all 12 items if you group them as follows:

THINGS YOU READ	THINGS YOU WRITE WITH	THINGS YOU RIDE IN
newspaper	pencil	bus
book	pen	automobile
magazine	chalk	boat
comic book	crayon	train

With this grouping, you have 3 pieces or chunks of information to remember instead of 12. It's easy to remember three things, right? You also can remember the four items in each category quite easily because the headings help trigger your memory. Now look at the three groups for 60 seconds and try to write down as many of the items as you can in the margin.

Organize Material by Grouping

You can improve your ability to learn and recall a large amount of material by grouping or chunking it. However, you should follow some basic guidelines when setting up your groups. First, never set up more than seven groups. Why? If you make up 10 or 15 groups, you won't be able to remember all the group headings. For the same reason, limit the number of items in each group to seven. Second, be sure you use a simple system. If your plan for remembering the information is extremely complex, you won't be able to remember it (the plan), and then you won't be able to remember the information itself. Third, you can't learn the information just by looking at it. You need to write or recite the lists and then test yourself. Finally, there's a tendency to forget the items in the middle of the list more quickly than those that are first or last. Did you have that problem earlier? You can avoid this problem by practicing the items in different orders or by using some of the elaboration strategies previously described. Remember, the more organized the information is when you put it into LTM, the more easily you'll be able to retrieve it later.

Before her exam in Computer Literacy, Heather organized the information on the five different programming languages by using the informal outline and catchphrases in Figure 5.4. She pulled the important information out of her text and notes and structured it in such a way that she could learn and remember it. Then she created catchphrases to prompt her memory. Her first sentence, "Corey Finds Bobby Playing Alone," provides hooks for the five programming languages. The other five sentences are designed to help her remember the details about each language. By organizing the information and practicing the connections between the catchphrases and the material she wanted to learn, Heather created a mechanism to recall the information.

COMPREHENSION MONITORING STRATEGIES

Comprehension monitoring strategies allow us to keep tabs on our learning. They help us monitor our progress in mastering the material and allow us to evaluate the effectiveness of the strategies that we use to gain that mastery. Setting goals and then assessing your progress, reciting from recall columns or question cards, taking self-tests, replicating study sheets, and even just asking yourself whether you understand something are all examples of comprehension monitoring strategies.

All these activities involve *metacognition*—the ability to think about and control one's learning.[8] Metacognition involves three types of awareness on the part of the learner. First, students must learn *task awareness*—they must learn to identify what information they have to study and learn in a particular situation. Second, students must learn *strategy awareness*—they need to determine which strategy will be most effective for learning specific information, for preparing for different types of exams, and for using with different types of course material. Finally, students must learn *performance awareness*—they must learn to determine whether they have mastered the material that they previously identified as important, and how well it has been learned.[9]

---

[8]L. Baker and A. L. Brown, "Metacognitive Skills and Reading," in P. D. Pearson, ed., *Handbook of Reading Research* (New York: Longman, 1984).

[9]S. E. Wade and R. E. Reynolds, "Developing Metacognitive Awareness," *Journal of Reading*, 33 (1989): 6–14.

FIGURE 5.4

• • • • • • • • •

Heather's Informal Outline (with Catchphrases)

Computer Programming Languages	
Corey	1. COBOL — Corey
	— widely accepted — wins
	— English statements, business applications — every
	— processes, records, produces — program
Finds	2. FORTRAN — Fanny
	— solve science, math, engineer problems — Smith
	— programming — plays
	— widespread use, science – engineer — walleyball
	communities — Saturdays
	— solve problems
Bobby	3. BASIC — Bobby
	— teaching tool — tells
	— easiest — everyone
	— programming language — Pat
	— Apple, IBM — ate
	— data structure – FORTRAN — dirt.
Playing	4. PASCAL — Pat
	— preferred teaching language — prefers
	— teaching tool — tulips
Alone	5. ADA language — All
	— general purpose — girls
	— most advantages — must
	— structures – PASCAL — stay
	— strong type — strong.

When to Use Comprehension Monitoring Strategies

Comprehension monitoring strategies help us determine when learning or understanding breaks down. For example, you may find, as you read and take notes on one of your textbooks, that you can't figure out how to formulate questions about the information under one of the headings. At that point, you should realize that you did not comprehend or understand that section of the text.

TIP   MORE TIPS FOR IMPROVING YOUR MEMORY

DON'T ASSUME THAT YOU WILL REMEMBER. Many students think they'll remember everything that they read in their textbooks and hear in their class lectures. However, even if it worked for you in high school, it won't in college because college tests are spaced further apart, allowing us to forget much of the information. Take good class notes and highlight or take notes as you read and then work hard to learn the information.

REVIEW REGULARLY. Review your text and lecture information on a daily or weekly basis to keep the information fresh in your memory. Doing an end-of-week review also allows you to integrate text and lecture material and organize it in long-term memory.

ORGANIZE THE INFORMATION LOGICALLY. The more logically you organize the information you need to remember, the easier it'll be to learn it and retrieve it from memory. Restructuring the information so that it's more meaningful to you aids your memory of it.

FORM ASSOCIATIONS TO INCREASE MEMORY CUES. Don't study information in isolation. It's very difficult to recall information when you learn it as an isolated piece of information. By developing study sheets, explaining the material, or making maps, you form associations with and among the material that add a variety of cues that will help you remember it for an exam.

ORGANIZE THE INFORMATION IN YOUR STUDY SHEETS. The more organized the information is when you put it into long-term memory, the more easily you'll be able to find it when you're taking an exam. Creating titles, headings, and main points in your study sheets helps you organize the information and provides you with cues to aid retrieval.

USE YOUR OWN EXPERTISE TO AID MEMORY. When information is meaningful, it's easier to remember. Think of how what you're learning connects with your own life and work experiences. Create examples from your own experiences to help you remember the information you're learning in your college classes.

USE RHYMES, STORIES, OR SONGS TO HELP YOU REMEMBER. If you're good at writing or remembering songs, rhymes, or stories, use those methods to help improve your memory. Words that rhyme, the details of a story, or even the melody of a song add additional cues that may help you remember information for your exam.

MONITOR YOUR MEMORY. Many students are frustrated when they can't remember information during an exam. If this has happened to you, you may not have *learned* the information (at least not at the recall level). Check your memory of the information before the exam by self-testing on paper or by reciting. If you can't say the answer out loud without peeking, you don't really know it.

When you use self-testing activities, you're monitoring your learning. If you find that you don't really know the information as well as you thought you did, you can review it again. Self-testing also allows you to practice retrieving the information from LTM in a testlike situation. Some students become frustrated when they take exams because they spend hours and hours studying but can't seem to recall the information during the exam. Although they may have worked on acquisition and retention, they probably didn't spend much time working on retrieval of the information. Each time you self-test, you practice getting the information back out of memory. This provides you with an opportunity to practice the cues and strategies that you intend to use during the exam and to monitor their effectiveness.

Comprehension monitoring strategies also help us examine and evaluate the strategies that we're using to acquire, retain, and retrieve information. By taking a self-test, for example, you may discover that you don't really know as much as you thought you did about a particular section of the text and lecture material. Again, your discovery that you haven't learned that material provides you with some feedback on your progress in preparing for an exam. However, it also may allow you to evaluate the strategy that you originally used to "learn" that material. You may realize, for example, that just reading over the material was not very effective for getting it into LTM or that just reciting the information from your notes did not prepare you to write an essay about it. Once you determine that your study strategies aren't effective, you can modify the way you study and select more effective strategies to use.

AFFECTIVE AND MOTIVATIONAL STRATEGIES

Affective and motivational strategies are strategies that relate to your attitude, interest, and motivation toward learning. They can influence how effectively you learn and remember information. Many of the strategies that you used for setting goals, managing time, and improving concentration are examples of affective and motivational strategies. These strategies help prepare us mentally for studying and create a positive learning environment. Setting realistic, moderately challenging goals helps get you motivated to study and learn. Using "To Do" lists, planning rewards, and taking breaks are just a few of the motivational strategies that you probably are using on a regular basis. They help you keep up with your daily assignments and give you a sense of accomplishment at the end of the day.

Your attitude about learning the material can influence how well you will attend to it, organize it, and store it. If you're trying to prepare for an exam, it's important that you feel interested in the material and motivated to learn and remember. Establishing a purpose for studying, seeing the relevance of the course, and using active learning strategies can all help increase your motivation. If you think studying won't help, you won't be very motivated to study. In Chapter 10, you'll learn a number of active learning strategies that will help you learn and remember the material. Using strategies that are both effective and interesting can make learning fun. Many students actually enjoy studying for a test using these strategies because they end each study session feeling good about what they have accomplished.

Monitoring your learning also can be an effective motivational device. If you test your learning by covering the material and trying to recite the information, you'll be able to evaluate your storage and retrieval processes. You also can accomplish this by reciting from a recall column, taking self-tests, reproducing maps or charts, and so on. One advantage of reciting is that it allows you to test your memory. If you're able to remember the information that you're reviewing, you feel good—you know you're learning. Successful recitations motivate you to continue to study and to continue to use that learning strategy because it worked. Changing to a different learning strategy or studying for a longer period of time may be necessary to successfully store the "missed" information in LTM. When you know that you know the important information for a test, you develop more confidence in yourself as a student, and this can affect your performance on the exam.

In Chapter 10, you'll also learn to use the Five-Day Study Plan. This plan helps you select, organize, and schedule your exam preparation tasks. The Five-Day Study Plan includes many affective and motivational strategies. You'll know each day exactly what you need to accomplish and can check off your completion of each task. The Five-Day Study Plan also incorporates active learning strategies that make studying effective and interesting and provides you with numerous opportunities to monitor your learning. If you're still having difficulty recalling information during an exam, you may need to change the way you're studying. Try using the Five-Day Study Plan—you may find that using it significantly improves your exam performance.

Your state of mind during the exam also affects how well you're able to retrieve the information. If you experience test anxiety, you may not be able to concentrate on the exam questions. You may find that you're so upset that you can't think of the answers. Knowing you're well prepared for an exam reduces and, in some cases, eliminates feelings of test anxiety. Most test anxiety stems from not knowing the material well enough or not being sure that you know the material well enough. You'll learn more about how to cope with test anxiety in Chapter 11. Spacing your study, using active learning strategies, and practicing retrieval all help you prepare well for the exam. If you begin the exam with positive feelings about your preparation and expect to do well, you can increase your probability for success.

SUMMARY

Learning how information is stored and retrieved in the human brain—learning how memory works—may help you better understand why you need to be actively involved with your course material as you complete day-to-day assignments and prepare for exams. To learn anything, we must encode it—make it meaningful. At that point, we must rehearse the material in some way to move it from short-term to long-term memory. The more organized the information is as we store it, the more easily we'll be able to locate it later—retrieve it. By working on the material in different ways, we can form many associations or cues to help us retrieve the information when we need it. However, interference, anxiety, and passive study can all lead to poor retrieval and what we call forgetting.

Learning to use general and specific memory strategies can help you improve your ability to encode, store, and retrieve information. Strategies such as spaced practice, breaking down tasks, repetition, and overlearning—the basic components of the Five-Day Study Plan—are the cornerstones of improving your memory. Specific memory strategies can also be used effectively to increase your ability to store and retrieve information. Rehearsal strategies help you store course information in long-term memory. Elaboration strategies such as forming associations, creating acronyms and acrostics, and using visual imagery are mnemonic devices that can help you more easily retrieve the information that you've already learned. These strategies work, however, only after you identify and practice the associations between the key information and the device you create to remember it. You can also improve your memory by using organizational strategies like grouping, outlining, mapping, and charting. Through comprehension monitoring strategies such as recitation, self-testing, and evaluating your progress in learning, you can keep tabs on how well you're learning the material and how effective your strategies are. As you've probably discovered, many of these strategies work best when you use them together. Affective and motivational strategies help keep you on task, encourage you to work hard, and reward you when your efforts pay off. A good memory is not something most people are born with, but anyone can develop a good memory by working hard and becoming a strategic learner.

Activities

1. Go to the *Orientation to College Learning* book-specific Web site and follow the link in Chapter 5 to the QueenDom.com Web site to take a visual memory test. Then take the Short-Term Memory Test by clicking on the University of Washington link. Be prepared to discuss the results.

2. After you read and mark the text selection "Defining Global Media Systems," available on the *Orientation to College Learning* Web site, organize the information that you need to learn. Group, outline, or map the information to make it more meaningful. Then devise a strategy for remembering the main points that you included. Compare your organizational structure and any mnemonics you create with those of your group. Describe the processes you used.

3. As you prepare for your next exam, use work or home experiences to help you remember some of the information that you need to know. List at least three things that you need to know for your exam and describe the "life experience" mnemonic that you developed. Try creating a story about the information, a catchphrase about someone from work, an association with something you already know, or all three.

4. Go the the *Orientation to College Learning* Web site and download one copy of Activity 5-4 from the Activities Packet. Create catchphrases for each of the examples listed. Compare your catchphrases to those developed by the other members in your group.

5. Choose a chapter or part of a chapter in one of your textbooks, select the material that you think you need to learn for an exam, and organize it on a separate sheet of paper. Then determine how you could learn the material. Then work on it until you think you know it. Finally, test yourself to monitor your learning. Write a paragraph or two describing the process that you used to learn the material and how you decided to monitor your learning. Describe your results.

6. List at least five affective and motivational strategies that you used during the past week. How did they help you improve your memory? Which was the most effective? Why?

7. Using the Internet, locate additional information on how to improve your memory. Follow any links that you find as you search for the new strategies or suggestions. Make a list of the top five sites that you found and share them with the other members of your class. Annotate each site, listing the Internet address, a brief description of the information that was available, any links that proved to be helpful, and several new strategies that you found. What was the most successful strategy that you used during your search?

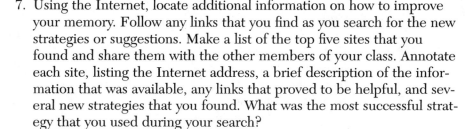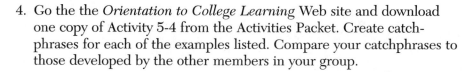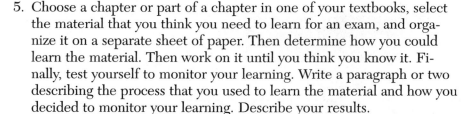

8. If you're using InfoTrac College Edition, find an article that contains information on memory techniques. Print the article and make a list of the key points for two topics presented in the article. Then develop at

least two mnemonics that will help you remember the key points in the article. Share the information with other members of your class.

9. Think of three examples of how you've applied what you learned in this chapter. Choose one strategy and describe how you applied it to your other course work using the Journal Entry Form that is located on the *Orientation to College Learning* Web site. Consider the following questions as you complete your entry. Why did you use this strategy? What did you do? How did it work? How did it affect your performance on the task? How did this approach compare with your previous approach? What changes would you make the next time you use this strategy?

10. Now that you've completed Chapter 5, take a few minutes to repeat the "Where Are You Now?" activity, located on the *Orientation to College Learning* Web site. What changes did you make as a result of reading this chapter? How are you planning to apply what you've learned in this chapter?

Review Questions

Terms You Should Know:

Acronyms
Acrostics
Affective and motivational strategies
Comprehension monitoring strategies
Consolidation
Cue
Echoic memory
Elaboration strategies
Encoding
Iconic memory
Immediate memory
Information Processing Model
Massed practice

Metacognition
Method of loci
Mnemonic devices
Organizational strategies
Overlearning
Rehearsal strategies
Retrieval
Sensory memory
Sensory registers
Spaced practice
Storage
Working memory

Completion: Fill in the blank to complete each of the following statements.

1. _____ memory is very susceptible to interference.

2. If information is well _____, it is easier to learn and recall.

3. Another term for spaced practice is _____ practice.

4. Mnemonic devices are designed to aid _____, not _____.

5. _____-level rehearsal strategies are more effective in getting information into long-term memory.

Multiple Choice: Circle the letter of the best answer for each of the following questions. Be sure to underline key words and eliminate wrong answers.

6. _____ occurs when we make things meaningful.
   A. Encoding
   B. Storage
   C. Retrieval
   D. Memory

7. Which of the following is not an advantage of overlearning?
   A. It helps you organize the information you need to learn.
   B. It reduces test anxiety.
   C. It prevents forgetting.
   D. It helps you understand the material better.

Short Answer–Essay: On a separate sheet, answer each of the following questions.

8. Compare and contrast short-term and long-term memory.

9. Why do some students have difficulty retrieving information? What should they do differently?

10. Describe Weinstein and Mayer's Five Groups of Learning Strategies.

Chapter 6

TAKING LECTURE NOTES

"The new strategies for taking lecture notes really do work. They make the class time move faster, and at the end when I leave, I really feel that I learned something instead of just spending 50 minutes deciding what to pack for spring break. Good lecture notes come in handy when it comes to study for tests, too. Paying attention in class is so much easier when I take notes."

Nicole Modechi
Student

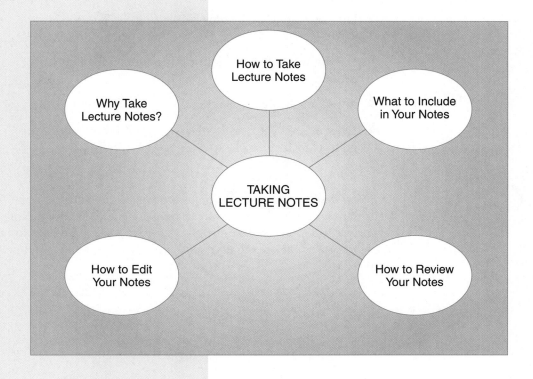

Where Are You Now?

Take a few minutes to answer *yes* or *no* to the following questions.

	YES	NO
1. Do you review and edit your notes within 24 hours after each of your classes?	____	____
2. Do you try to write down exactly what your professor says in class?	____	____
3. Do you separate the main points from supporting information in your notes?	____	____
4. Are you able to read and understand your notes when you study for your exam?	____	____
5. Do you sometimes find that your notes don't make sense when you review them before an exam?	____	____
6. Do you tend to write down only important or key words when you take notes?	____	____
7. Do you review your notes by reciting them out loud?	____	____
8. Do you tend to miss a lot of information when you take notes?	____	____
9. Are you actively involved in the lecture?	____	____
10. Do you read your textbook assignment before you go to your lecture class?	____	____
TOTAL POINTS		____

Give yourself 1 point for each *yes* answer to questions 1, 3, 4, 7, 9, and 10 and 1 point for each *no* answer to questions 2, 5, 6, and 8. Now total up your points. A low score indicates that you need some help in note taking. A high score indicates that you are already using many good note-taking strategies.

WHY TAKE LECTURE NOTES?

Other than attending class every day, taking good lecture notes is probably the single most important activity for college students. Taking notes during college lectures is a difficult task for most entering college students because little or no real practice in note taking occurred when they were in high school. There, note taking involved copying the information off the chalkboard as the teacher talked and wrote. In college, however, most professors don't do the job of note taking for you. Instead, you must listen, select the appropriate information, paraphrase it, condense it, and then write it down with few (if any) clues from the professor. Developing good note-taking skills takes both time and practice. Taking lecture notes promotes active listening; provides an accurate record of information; provides an opportunity to interpret, condense, and organize the information; and provides an opportunity for repetition of the material.

PROMOTES ACTIVE LISTENING

Taking notes in class promotes active listening by helping you concentrate on the lecture. Have you ever sat in class and realized that you had no idea what the professor just said? This is a very common experience for many students. Even though everyone gets distracted once in a while, it becomes a real problem if you daydream so much that you miss what your professor is saying. By taking notes, you can improve your concentration because you're focusing your attention on what's being said; you have a purpose—listening for the next point that the professor will make so that you can write it down.

Some students find sitting in lecture classes very boring; they prefer classes where they're more actively involved in the learning experience. Taking notes, however, is a very active process. You can generate a high level of involvement in your own learning by taking notes. Note taking involves more than just writing down what the instructor is saying. It includes thinking about what's been said, determining what's important, recognizing how different points relate to others, anticipating what will be said next, putting the information into your own words, and organizing the information in your notes. The process of taking good lecture notes can help you become both an active listener and an active participant in your classes.

PROVIDES AN ACCURATE RECORD OF INFORMATION

The most important reason for taking notes is to get an accurate record of the information that was presented in class. Taking notes can actually help you learn and remember the information. Even if you learn some of the information during the lecture class, there's no guarantee that you'll remember it by the time you take your exam. In college, exams are given after four, seven, or even fifteen weeks; you won't remember all the lecture material by the time you take a test. Research studies indicate that without rehearsal, you may forget 50 percent of what you hear in a lecture within 24 hours and 80 percent in just 2 weeks.[1] In fact, you may forget 95 percent within 1 month. This comes as a big shock to most college students; however, it explains why some students have difficulty on exams. If you don't leave a lecture class with a good set of notes, an accurate record of information, you won't have the opportunity to review that material again before the exam. You can't just rely on your memory of the lecture; you need your notes, too! Why? In many classes the majority of the exam questions come from the lecture material. Without a good set of notes, you won't be able to prepare for the exam.

MAKES YOU RESTRUCTURE THE INFORMATION

Taking lecture notes forces you to interpret, condense, and organize the information that's presented. You've probably already discovered that you can't write as fast as your professor speaks. If you were able to do so, you could simply jot down the lecture word for word with little thought, and, as a result, you wouldn't really learn very much. In many ways it's probably better that you can't. Because you have to condense the information, you have to think about each sentence and interpret it—often putting the information into your own words. As you write down the information in a condensed form, you also are forced to create a system of organization that separates the main and supporting points. These processes make note taking very active and help you understand and learn the information during the lecture. They also provide you with a record of the important information in a format that's more useful for later study.

PROVIDES ADDITIONAL REPETITION

Taking lecture notes also provides you with repetition on the material. By writing down the important information, you are, in fact, reviewing it several times. To take notes, you must actually work on the material (think about it). You need

---

[1]H. Spitzer, "Studies in Retention," *Journal of Educational Psychology* 30 (1939): 641–656.

to listen to each sentence the professor states, evaluate its importance, interpret its meaning, condense it into a meaningful phrase, organize it under a heading or subheading, and finally write it down. You may find that you think about the material again as you go through the same process for the next sentence, too, because it may connect to the previous notes you took. In this way, you get a great deal of repetition on each point—something that may not occur were you simply listening to the lecture. Of course, as you edit (discussed later in the chapter) and review your notes, you'll get even more repetition.

HOW TO TAKE LECTURE NOTES

Learning to take notes effectively and efficiently takes time. You can begin to improve your note-taking skills rapidly, however, if you learn to use some basic strategies. One of the first things you need to do is learn to become an active listener. Although there's no one correct way to take notes, some methods or systems work better than others. In this section, you'll learn a number of basic strategies to help improve your note taking, as well as several options for form and format. Instead of just selecting one method to use, you may find it beneficial to try all the techniques and then decide which ones work best for you.

PREPARE BEFORE TAKING NOTES

Before you ever walk into a lecture class, you need to prepare to take notes. The best way to prepare for your note-taking activity is to read the text assignment before class. Much of the material that's presented in college lectures will be new to you. By reading the text assignment before the lecture, you build up some background about the topic. If you have some idea what the lecture is about, it will be easier for you to understand the presentation and take good notes. Reading before the lecture also will give you the opportunity to become familiar with the main topics or ideas that will be presented. You'll find it easier to identify main ideas and organize your notes as the professor delivers the lecture. Finally, you'll be somewhat familiar with key terms and names after reading the text. This will help you keep up with the lecturer and avoid making content errors in your notes. If you've been having difficulty understanding the lecture or taking notes, try reading your text assignment before the next lecture. Remember, you only get one chance to listen to the lecture, but you can read the text as many times as you want.

As you walk into the lecture classroom, get ready to take notes. If you sit near the front, you'll be able to see and hear better. You'll probably find that other interested and motivated students also tend to sit in the first few rows of the class. By avoiding the back of the room, you'll avoid those students who tend to chat and walk in late. While you're waiting for class to begin, review the notes that you took during the last class meeting. Many professors pick up where they left off in the last lecture. Your review will remind you of the main topics and the general organization of the lecture and will prepare you for the next point that will be made.

BECOME AN ACTIVE LISTENER

Although reading your text assignment helps you build some background for understanding the lecture, it doesn't guarantee that you'll take good notes. Researchers have discovered that we ignore, misunderstand, or forget about 75 percent of what we hear.[2] As you may have discovered earlier, note taking is an active process that involves paying attention to the information that the lecturer is presenting, interpreting it (so you can understand and remember it), condensing it, and writing it down in an organized manner. To achieve this goal, students must first become active and effective listeners.

Active Versus Passive Listening

Many students confuse hearing and listening. Our ears may receive sounds during a lecture, or we may listen by watching a sign language interpreter or real-time reporter, but that doesn't mean that we're listening—paying attention to and interpreting what we're hearing. As you learned in Chapter 5, we only remember a small proportion of the sounds that we hear because we don't attend to (pay attention to) most of them. *Hearing* is a passive process; it is *nonselective* and *involuntary. Listening,* on the other hand, is an active "process that involves receiving, attending to, and assigning meaning to aural [verbal] and visual [nonverbal] stimuli"[3] (material in brackets not in the original definition).

Characteristics of Active Listeners

Active listeners are physically and mentally focused on the lecture. They sit up straight, lean forward slightly (indicating interest), and make the lecturer the center of their attention by making eye contact or sitting directly in the lecturer's line of vision. Active listeners often sit near the front of the classroom to avoid external distractions. They eliminate internal distractions, too, by pushing other thoughts out and focusing all their attention on the information being presented. They are open minded and willing to listen to the lecture, putting aside their own

---

[2]Diane Bone, *The Business of Listening* (Los Altos, CA: Crisp Publications, 1988), p. 5.
[3]A. D. Wolvin and C. G. Coakley, *Listening,* 5th ed. (Dubuque, IA: Brown and Benchmark), 1996, p. 69.

biases. Students who are actively involved in the lecture ask questions, answer questions, and take notes. They evaluate what they're hearing and often consider how this information connects to their prior knowledge of the subject. Professors often can identify students who are actively involved in the lecture by their body language, too. They may nod or smile in agreement, look amazed or confused at times, and pull back or frown when they disagree with what's being said. Active listeners are physically, intellectually, and emotionally involved in the lecture.

Factors That Interfere with Effective Listening

Without realizing it, even the most dedicated students may at times be thwarted in their efforts to be active listeners. Both internal and external distractions can interfere with a student's ability to concentrate on the lecture. Not attending to the lecture can lead to uncertainty about what was said, difficulty understanding the information, or missed information. Many students also either stop listening or become less involved in the presentation when they're angry or offended by the speaker or the message. They react emotionally to the situation and blame the speaker and often stop paying attention to what he or she is saying as a way of retaliating. Some students become angry or closed minded when the lecturer discusses controversial material that's in direct opposition to their own personal point of view. Similarly, some students are "turned off" by language or gestures that they consider inappropriate. They allow their personal sense of propriety to interfere with their listening.

Strategies to Improve Your Listening Skills

Although there are many strategies for becoming an active listener, the following should help you increase your skills:

- Read the text assignment and review your last set of notes prior to the lecture.

- Decide that you want to listen.

- Focus your attention physically by sitting up and making eye contact with the speaker.

- Focus your attention mentally by eliminating or avoiding distractions.

- Listen with an open mind, setting aside your own biases.

- Control your emotional responses.

- Listen for the main points and related details and take notes.

- Monitor your listening. Check with the lecturer if you're unsure of some of the information.

- Hold yourself accountable for the material presented.

USE AN EFFECTIVE NOTE-TAKING SYSTEM

Dozens of systems have been developed to help students become effective note takers. Some of them are quite complex and provide explicit details on every step of the process. Unfortunately, a number of these systems involve so many steps and so much work that many students resort to their old methods or just don't take notes at all. Other systems are rather simple and provide only a few basic guidelines. For the new college student, they may not provide enough structure about how to get the information on paper.

The Cornell note-taking system (developed at Cornell University) includes an excellent format for setting up your notes. Use an 8½- by 11-inch notebook (I recommend a separate notebook for each class), so that you have enough space to take notes, create a recall column, and write a summary at the end of each page. A sample note page using the *Cornell system* is shown in Figure 6.1. To set up your page, use a ruler to create a new margin line that is 2½ inches from the edge or purchase a summary margin notebook available in some college bookstores. Most notebooks give you a 1-inch margin, which doesn't allow enough space to write recall questions that will help you prompt your memory as you review your notes (you'll learn more about this later in the chapter). At the end of each page, leave a 2-inch margin so that you can write a summary of the important points as you review your notes. In the large 6-inch space to the right of the margin, write down as much information about the lecture as you can. You can use a variety of methods to take your notes, but the outline, block, and modified-block styles have proven to be effective for most college lectures.

The Outline Method

Many students use the *outline method* to take notes in lecture classes. *Outlining* involves indenting each level of supporting details under the preceding heading, subheading, or detail. One of the reasons this style is so popular is that it's familiar to many students. Is this the style that you're using now? Some students use outlines because their professors provide them with some form of outline at the beginning of the lecture. Even the four- or five-point outline written on the board can set the pattern that you use for taking notes. Outlines work, however, only when the lecturer is well organized and proceeds in an orderly manner from main points to supporting points.

You can effectively use an outline style of note taking as long as you're careful not to fall into several traps. Don't get distracted by the "rules" of formal outlining. You may spend too much time thinking about how you should label or designate the next point in your notes. You could be thinking about whether you should write a "B" or a "2" in your notes instead of concentrating on the content of the lecture.

FIGURE 6.1

Cornell Note Page

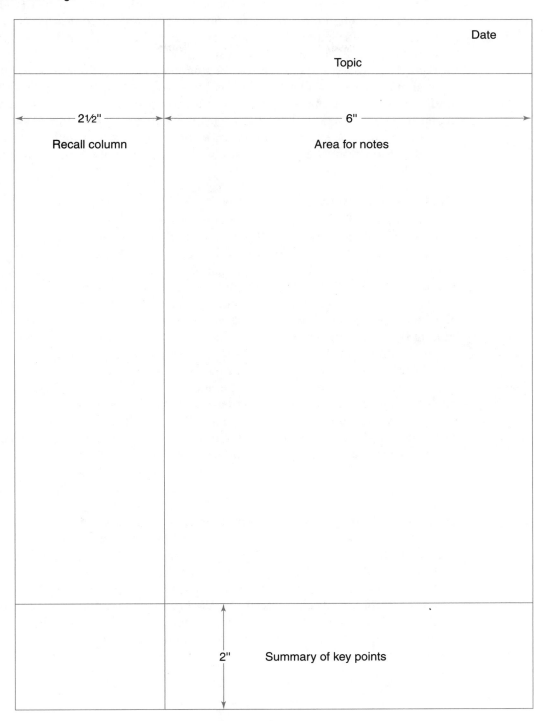

Too often, students equate outlining with just writing down key words. One-word outlines contain too little of the content of the lecture to provide an accurate record of information. You may not realize how little information you have in your notes until you look at another student's notes. Look at the sample notes in Figure 6.2, which were taken by two students in the same Economics class. Gary simply wrote down key words. His notes look well organized and effective until you compare them with the notes taken by Bryan. Bryan's notes contain much more information about the topics presented in the lecture. When it's time to prepare for exams, students with "one-word notes" simply don't have enough information from which to study. Which set of notes would you rather have before the exam?

The Block Method

The block style of note taking is another very simple system to learn. After noting the topic of the lecture and the date, write the first heading (main point the professor makes) (for example, "Depth Perception" or "What About Depth Perception?") starting at the left-hand margin of your notebook. Indent a few spaces on the next line and then begin to write your notes in block form. Listen for what the lecturer has to say about the heading and write down as many of the details as you can. *Block notes* are written continuously across the page, separating the details by dashes (—) or slashes (/). Demonstrating the block form, Figure 6.3 contains a set of notes from a lecture on Intellectual Development. The headings from the lecture stand out because they're next to the margin, whereas the details are clustered together in a block indented slightly under each heading. Remember, you don't have to write complete sentences just because your notes are shaped like a paragraph; you still want to concentrate on using *meaningful phrases*. By skipping a line or two between each main heading, you can organize your notes and leave room to add something later in the lecture.

The Modified-Block Method

Some students are uncomfortable putting all their notes in block form. If you like the idea of having all information grouped under a heading without showing various levels of support as in an outline, you may prefer to use a modified-block format. To use the *modified-block method*, you simply indent about ½-inch and list all related details straight down the page under each heading. You would take each of the details clustered under the heading, "Development of Perception" and list them individually, one statement per line (Figure 6.4). Having each detail on a separate line makes it easy to take notes, organize them, and review for the exam.

FIGURE 6.2

· · · · · · · · ·

Two Examples
from the Same
Economics
Lecture

1) ALL PEOPLE ACT "SELFISHLY"
    BUYING   PRODUCT (OUTPUTS)
    SELLING   FACTOR (INPUTS)
2) "MANY" BUYERS & SELLERS
    PRODUCT MARKETS: SELLERS
    MONOPOLY: 1 SELLER
    SUBSTITUTES - FOR SUCCESSFUL MARKET

Gary's Notes

Starting pts. for an economic system
  A. All people act selfishly (economically)
    Two Broad Types of Markets
      Product Markets (output) Market Activity
      Selfish
      Factor Market (input)
    1. Product Market
      Seller → firms (bus organ.) such as corporations
        → Maximize profits
      Consumers → buyers
        – Maximize utility
        – as prices increase, less is bought
    2. Factor Market
      Sellers – laborers, workers
        – maximize wages, minimize effort
      Buyers – firms (bus organ.)
        – maximize profits
  B. All markets structural – great #'s of buyers
    & sellers. Market is competitive – no single
    buyer or seller influences the outcome

Bryan's Notes

FIGURE 6.3
. . . .
Sample Block
Notes

Piaget – Intellectual Development   9/17

Development of Perception
   Knowledge of infants limited – 60s no visual or hearing ability –
   difficult to test – infants do have percep abilities at birth – even
   prenatally can hear

Vision
   visual acuity poor 20/600 at birth – see 20 ft what we see
   600 ft away – 1 mo – 20/150 = someone w glasses –
   12 mo – 20/20 – abilities improve as does abilities to use them
   newborns – only fixed focus 9" – same distance as mom to
   baby's eyes when fed – eye muscles weak – lack
   coordination = normal

Abilities at birth
   1. can see – follow bright light
   2. have preferences – exper infant in seat – 2 panels – objects on
      each – experimenter watch infant's pupils – see obj in eye - now
      peep board use TV camera to computer – Prefer complex pattern to simple –
      bk/w checkerboard over red board - most preferred at 2 mo –
      simple human face ☺ inborn pref for human face – smile first

Depth perception
   Born w it? 1st to look at it – Gibson 50s studied in young animals
   ex: 18 mo old & wife Eleanor visit to Grand Canyon
   Exper – Visual Cliff – plexiglass table – red/wh cloth – drape it
   under table so half looks solid – looks like half drops off
   ⌐ ‒ ‒ ‒ ‒ ‒ ‒ ‒ glass
Infant will crawl on solid side not along clear (open) side – By time they
   crawl or creep they perceive depth. Unsure if born w it.

The block and modified-block methods allow you to take notes efficiently and effectively because you have to concentrate on only two things: (1) writing down the main points (headings) and (2) writing down any details about them. You don't have to spend a lot of time trying to figure out where to place or how to label each new piece of information.

FIGURE 6.4

• • • • • • • • •

Sample Modified-
Block Notes

Piaget – Intellectual Development   9/17

Development of Perception
    Knowledge of infants limited
    60s no visual or hearing ability
    difficult to test
    infants do have percep abilities at birth
    even prenatally can hear

Vision
    visual acuity poor 20/600 at birth
    see 20 ft what we see 600 ft away
    1 mo   20/150 = someone w glasses
    12 mo 20/20
    abilities improve as does ability to use them
    only fixed focus 9"
    same distance as mom to baby's eyes when fed
    eye muscles weak
    lack coordination = normal

WHAT TO INCLUDE IN YOUR NOTES

Although some general rules will help you figure out what to include in your notes, there's no simple answer to the question "What should I write down?" Some students are so afraid that they will miss even one point during the lecture that they try to write down every word the professor says. This is both impractical and ineffective. You can't write as fast as your professor can talk. A good general rule is to treat a lecture class like a lab class. You should be an active participant during the entire period. The best thing to do is to take as many notes as you can in a well-organized format. As soon as you pick out the heading, listen carefully for any information that explains or expands upon it, and add that information to your notes. Have you ever caught yourself thinking, "I wonder if I should write that down?" Anytime you think about whether to write something down, go ahead and write it down. You may even find that your hand hurts at the end of the period; that's fine. *Remember: When in doubt, write it out.*

HEADINGS

Always note all *headings*—the main points—that are made during a lecture. You may find that sometimes you have no trouble at all identifying the main points, and other times you have a lot of trouble. Main points appear to be obvious during some lectures because the lecturer states them in an easily recognizable manner. Introductions such as: "The next thing we're going to talk about is . . . ," "Another reason is . . . ," "What about vision?" and "First of all, . . ." make main points easy to pick out. Listen during your next lecture and see how your professor introduces each main topic. If your professor puts an outline on the board, you may want to copy it into your notebook right away. However, as each main topic comes up during the actual lecture, write it down again in your notes.

DETAILS

After you write the heading in your notes, listen for all *details,* the points that support each heading the professor presents about that topic. Until you develop more sophisticated note-taking skills, you may want to rely on some of the following tips in deciding which details to include.

1. Details, facts, or explanations that expand or explain the main points that are mentioned.

2. Definitions, word for word, especially if your professor repeats them several times.

3. Enumerations or lists of things that are discussed.

4. Examples; you don't need to note all details for each example, but you do need to know to which general topic (heading) each example relates.

5. Anything that is written on the chalkboard, powerpoint slide, or on a transparency (on an overhead projector).

6. Anything that is repeated or spelled out.

7. Drawings, charts, or problems that are written on the board.

DISCUSSION CLASSES

Most students don't take notes during discussion classes or during those portions of a lecture class that are devoted to discussion. This is a big mistake.

Many professors prefer the discussion format when teaching. They could very easily just "tell" students the information, but they prefer to allow the information to emerge through a guided discussion. Even though the material is presented in a different format, however, the information often will still appear on tests.

You can easily take notes on a discussion. Instead of writing down the main heading, write down the question that is posed. Then jot down the various points that are made during the discussion. Remember, it's very important to indicate who made which point in the discussion. The easiest method is to simply write "P" in front of any statement made by the professor and "S" in front of any statement made by a student.

MATH AND SCIENCE CLASSES

Taking notes in math and science classes requires special strategies. The modified-block method probably will be more effective than the outline method because you'll need to include many problems and drawings that are written on the board. You may not think that you need to write down all problems that the professor puts on the board, but you should. Even more important, however, you need to write down what the professor says *about* the problems. Get into the habit of writing the name or type of problem first. Then copy down the problem and take notes on steps to follow, tricky areas, what to do first, and even why you should do it. Think of the explanations about a particular problem or model as minilectures. You may find it helpful to write the problem on the left side of the note page and anything the professor says about it directly across from each step. Listen carefully for the main points and the important details and put them in your notes.

POWERPOINT PRESENTATIONS

Many professors are now using PowerPoint presentations (which incorporate a series of "slides" containing main points, details, diagrams, and examples) to enhance their lectures. In addition to showing each "slide" on a large screen, many of them pass out a paper copy with space for notes to their students. However, there isn't enough room on these handouts to take notes. Instead, use it to organize your notes by copying the headings and subheadings into your notes as the professor refers to them. Leave space in your notes to tape in the "slides" showing diagrams or problems (make a note with the name for each) and continue getting down the details.

MORE TIPS FOR TAKING LECTURE NOTES

DON'T RELY ON YOUR MEMORY ALONE. Many students think they should be able to remember the information presented in a lecture if they pay careful attention. Unfortunately, we tend to forget rapidly. With 4 to 7 weeks between exams, taking notes is critical.

USE A FULL-SIZE NOTEBOOK. Use a separate 8½- by 11-inch notebook for each of your classes. Using smaller notebooks can unconsciously lead to writing fewer notes.

INCLUDE THE TOPIC IN YOUR NOTES. By including the topic, you're helping to organize your mind for listening and your notes for later review.

LEAVE SOME SPACE IN YOUR NOTES. By leaving a 2½-inch margin on the left side of the page, you'll be able to add recall words and questions when you edit your notes. Also, leave a line or two before you write each of your headings in case the professor adds information later in the lecture.

USE COMMON ABBREVIATIONS IN YOUR NOTES. By using some familiar abbreviations, you can get the information down more quickly. Don't use too many abbreviations, though, or you won't know what they mean.

SKIP A FEW SPACES IF YOU MISS INFORMATION. Skip a line or two and go on to the next point. If you miss a keyword, draw a line and keep going. Ask a classmate or the professor about the missing information after the lecture.

USE A TAPE RECORDER WITH A COUNTER. If you need to use a tape recorder at the beginning of the semester, get one with a counter on it. When you can't keep up with the lecturer and miss information, make a note of the location where the information occurred on the tape (the number on the counter) in the margin of your notebook and leave some space in your notes. Later, fast forward using the counter numbers to fill in the material you need.

PLAY TAPED LECTURES WHILE YOU COMMUTE. If you have a long commute to and from school, you may want to tape your lectures for your most difficult classes. Then you can play them while you drive or ride the bus or train. The additional review may help you improve your understanding of the material.

FIND A NOTE-TAKING "BUDDY." Many students have to miss class due to illness or emergencies. Set up a plan with one of your classmates to let you copy his or her notes in case you're absent. Exchange phone numbers or e-mail addresses to check on any upcoming assignments or scheduled exams.

DON'T LET OPPOSING OPINIONS TURN YOU OFF. Part of a professor's job is to present various viewpoints about a topic and generate class discussion. Sometimes that's done by purposely taking an opposing view. Discuss your own views in class if open discussion is provided. If not, share your views after class or during the professor's office hours. In any event, continue taking notes on the discussion.

HOW TO EDIT YOUR NOTES

Taking good lecture notes is only the first step in the note-taking process. After you leave the classroom, you need to *edit,* revise your notes to correct errors, clarify meaning, make additions, and improve organization. Editing is a fairly easy process once you know how to do it. Early in the semester you may spend a lot of time making corrections or additions to your notes. You may need to re-organize your notes or rewrite them to make them more useful. You'll soon benefit from these editing experiences, however, and your ability to take good notes will improve. You'll probably find that by the second half of the semester, you won't need to spend nearly as much time editing, and you can instead devote that time to more active review of your notes.

Editing your notes helps you become a better note taker because you get feedback on the quality of your notes. As you go through your notes to check for accuracy, fill in gaps in information, and improve the organization, you can see where you made mistakes. Editing can also help you be better pre-pared for exams. Because most test questions tend to come from lecture notes, it's important that you have a complete, accurate, and well-organized set of notes. Finally, editing provides you with an active review of all of the important information in both your text and notes. This additional repetition (which requires both critical thinking and an active restructuring of the ma-terial) helps you reinforce what you read and heard, leading to a better un-derstanding of the material.

Edit your lecture notes within 24 hours after the lecture. If you wait much longer, you won't remember the lecture well enough to make any nec-essary additions or corrections in your notes. Look back at your Fixed Com-mitment Calendar and set aside a certain time each day to edit and review your lecture notes. In as little as half an hour, you can turn "so-so" notes into excellent notes.

FILL IN THE GAPS

The first thing you should do is read through your notes and fill in any missing information that you can recall from memory. As you read your notes, the lec-ture will "come back" to you. You may be able to add a few words to further clar-ify a point, fill in additional details, or even add information that you didn't have time to record during the lecture. Look at Nikki's and Todd's edited notes in Fig-ures 6.5 and 6.6. Both Nikki and Todd added some additional information (shown in blue) after the lecture. Nikki also added a brief summary of the key information in the bottom margin of her notes.

FIGURE 6.5

Nikki's Revised
Notes for Life
Science

	1/22
What are decomposers?	**(3) Decomposers** *– heterotrophs* *– get nourishment from other organisms* **– do not have digestive tracts**
What are scavengers?	**(4) Scavengers** **– let something else kill organism** **– bacteria that break down dead tissue**
What are waste feeders?	**(5) Waste feeders** **– feed on dung, feces, undigested food** **– type of scavenger**
What do they feed on?	**– have digestive systems** **– eat food** *Ex: Egyptian scarab beetles*
What is detritus?	**detritus – miscellaneous organic material passing by** *– mixture of decaying organisms + dung w/partially digested food* *Land – mixes w/soil – earthworms/soil insects eat* *– May float or settle on bottom*
How do filter feeders eat?	**(6) Filter feeders** **– pass water thru comb-like feeders** **– take things floating in water** **– may use** *mouth parts, gills, special limbs*
	Four types of consumers are decomposers/scavengers, waste feeders, and filter feeders. Detritus is a mixture of decaying organisms + dung along with partially digested food.

You also can refer to your textbook to help fill in gaps in your notes. If you still feel your notes are incomplete, you may need to use a friend's notes to expand on the ones you took in class. If you taped the lecture, listen to the recording and fill in the information you weren't able to write down during the lecture.

FIGURE 6.6

• • • • • • • • • • • • • • •

Todd's Edited Notes for Accounting

What are corporations?	Corporations- legal entity having an existence separate and distinct from that of its owners
What rights does an artificial person have?	- Artificial person - same legal rights as a person
	- can be such, can sue
	- assets of corporation belong to a corporation itself,
Who owns the assets of a corporation?	not to stockholders.
What are 5 advantages of a corporation?	Why have a corporation? (Advantages)
	1. No personal liability for stockholders
	2. Ease of accumulating capital
	3. Ownership shares are readily transferable
	4. Continuous existence - lives on forever
	5. Professional management
What are the limits of risk for stockholders?	- amount of money stockholders risk is limited to the amount of their investment
What are the 3 disadvantages of a corporation?	Disadvantages of having a corporation
	1. Heavy taxation
	- tax twice, when they earn and pay income- double taxation
What is the role of the owner of a corp.?	2. Greater regulation
	3. Separation of ownership and control
	-guy who owns corporation doesn't run it
What is double taxation?	Double taxation - First taxing corporate income and then taxing distributions of that income to stockholders

CHECK FOR ACCURACY

As you go through your notes, you also need to check for accuracy. If you notice some incorrect information in your notes or if you're unsure of the accuracy of some points, check with the professor or a friend or use your textbook to verify whether the information is correct. If you find that some of your information is incorrect, change it. Some students lose points on exams because they have incorrect information in their notes. Even though they study for the exam, they still get questions wrong because they've been rehearsing inaccurate information.

CLARIFY MEANING

You may find that some of your notes are cryptic or hard to understand. To make your notes more readable and understandable, you may need to expand some abbreviations, finish some words, or correct spelling errors. If you use a lot of abbreviations or shortcuts in note taking, you should try to clarify some of them while you still know what words they represent. For example, if you wrote "priv" in your notes, you may want to add on "ileged" after class, because "priv" is not a common abbreviation and you may become confused about what you meant when you review your notes at a later time. It's not necessary, however, to go back and add on the tail ends of all words that you shortened or abbreviated. For example, the abbreviations "w" and "w/" are commonly used to stand for "with," so there would be no need to write out the word.

Frank and Ernest is reprinted by permission of Newspaper Enterprise Assn., Inc.

REWRITE TO IMPROVE ORGANIZATION

You may need to rewrite your notes in order to improve the organization of the information. If you took notes on a lecture that was poorly organized, your notes may be disorganized, too. Even though you may have an accurate record of the information, you may find it difficult to study. By reorganizing the information in your notes, you can clarify the relationship between the main points and the supporting details. You may need to add headings or make the headings that you have in your notes stand out. You can do that by writing the headings next to the margin and then indenting the subordinate points. You also may need to reorganize your notes in order to group together related information. If your professor tends to jump from point to point during the lecture, you may find that information on the same topic is scattered over several pages in your notes. As you rewrite your notes, group these points together under the appropriate heading. Reorganizing and editing your notes will make your notes more useful when you're ready to study for the exam.

Another way to organize your notes is by using concept maps, diagrams, charts, and matrixes to show the relationships between main points and supporting details. You may find that you can restructure some or all of the information from the lecture into a visual display that's easy to picture and recall for exams. Creating maps, diagrams, and charts is an active-editing process. You'll learn more about these strategies in later chapters, but if you think this is something you would like to try now, refer to Chapter 9 for some tips.

DEVELOP A RECALL COLUMN

Adding recall words or questions in the margin helps increase the value of your notes. *Recall words* are key words or phrases that help you recall the information in your notes. The process of making up these recall words forces you to identify the most important aspect of each statement and condense the information down to its essence. The recall words serve as cues to prompt your memory. Recall words have been added in the margin for the notes in Figure 6.7.

Writing *recall questions* is also an effective strategy for editing. After you identify a key point that you want to remember for your exam, develop a question to which that point is the answer. Be sure to write the question directly across from the "answer." Developing both broad and specific questions will help you learn the information in different ways. Of course, the more questions you write, the more effectively you can use them to study the information in your lecture notes. Questions have been added to the recall column for the notes in Figure 6.8. Refer also to Todd's and Nikki's notes (Figures 6.5 and 6.6), which both include recall questions in the margin. After reviewing both recall words and questions, try using them with your own notes. Then you can decide which method works best for you.

FIGURE 6.7

• • • • • • • • •

Example Using
Recall Words

	2/8
	Language Development
○	People who study Language
Linguists	Psycholinguists
	Linguists
	Characteristics of Language:
	1) Sounds
Phonemes	Phonemes (actual sounds)
	different languages use different phonemes – these
	different interpretations create accents
	Identified by:
3 Methods to	1. Manner – some words have hissing sounds
identify	2. Place – where in mouth a sound is made
phonemes	3. Voice – where sound is produced (area)
	ex: voice box
	can be voiced or unvoiced
	2) Structure
Morphemes	Morphemes (actual words)
○	smallest meaningful unit of language can be broken down:
2 components	1. Lexical – as the word appears
of morphemes	2. Grammatical – change by adding prefixes and suffixes
	Children learn words by imitation
Syntax	syntax – words we put together to make sense
	3) Meaning
Meaning is	meaning can be affected by:
affected by	1. Semantics – word meaning & the meaning of word
(5 pts)	combinations can be:
	1. Lexical – dictionary meaning
3 components	2. Referents – have reference to something
of semantics	3. Context – how words are used in sentences
	2. Pragmatics – study of how context affects meaning
	3. Situations can influence the context or meaning
	4. Intentions can influence the context or meaning
○	5. Need to adjust our language to different people
"Motherese"	ex: "Motherese" – way adults talk to children

FIGURE 6.8

. . . .

Example Using
Recall Questions

	Impact of Computers on Society 9/14
What are the three ways computers extend the mind and body?	Extends capacity of human body & mind — Thru imaging, robotics, processing, memory.
What is Feasibly Finite?	Extends the boundaries of "Feasibly Finite" — Limits of what we can do — Acceleration in the rate of change
Who wrote Future Shock?	— Alvin Toffler "Future Shock"
How do computers work with the global village?	The Global Village – Marshall McLuhan — Extends communication around globe — World conflict awareness – stock market – business & trade – advances in research
Explain "High Tech-High Touch" What are five ways computers bring us closer to others?	Emphasis on education in an info. age — "High tech – high touch" — John Naisbitt — tech brings us closer to others communication – medicine – retail – manufacturing – home shopping
What are some computing inequities?	Computing Inequities — women & minorities get less opportun to work w/computers.

What are some computing crimes?	Concepts & Crime
	— Theft
	   phone fraud – credit cards
	— privacy invasion
	— software piracy
	   hacking & cracking

HOW TO REVIEW YOUR NOTES

Reviewing your notes is the final step in the note-taking process. Even though editing your notes provides you with a review of the lecture material, reviewing daily, weekly, and before an exam all help you master the information in your notes and prepare for exams. After you edit your notes and complete the recall column, you're ready to review. You can't learn all the information in your notes just by editing or reading over them. You also need to study the information in your notes using more active methods. How you review your notes often determines how much of the information you learn.

WHEN AND WHY YOU SHOULD REVIEW

You need to review your lecture notes on a regular basis in order to store the information in your memory. Even though you may have an accurate record of the information presented, you still need to learn it. The best time to review and edit your notes is immediately after the lecture, when the material is still fresh in your mind. You also can review your notes when you're waiting for your next class to begin. You may want to set aside an hour or two each weekend to review the notes that you took in all of your classes during the week. If you've been reviewing daily, you'll need only to test your memory (using the recall column) during your weekly review. Reviewing your notes frequently during the semester will keep you actively involved in the learning process and will reduce the amount of time you need to study before exams.

HOW YOU SHOULD REVIEW

The best way to review your notes is to recite the information—to say it out loud. Just reading over your notes is a very passive activity. You may not really concentrate on the information at all. Reciting also helps because you may learn more by hearing information than just by seeing it. Use the recall columns that you created or the headings in your notes to test your memory of the information. This self-testing will let you know whether you really do know the information in your notes.

Recite from the Recall Column

When you think that you know the information in your notes, use the recall cues to test your memory of the main points and supporting details. Put your hand or a piece of paper over your notes so that you can see only the recall words or questions. Then recite the points that you made in your notes. If you can't say them out loud, you don't really know the material. Use this technique to review the information in your notes on a regular basis. You should perform this kind of active review immediately following the lecture, at the end of the week, and again before the exam.

Recite from the Headings

You also can review your notes by using the headings or topics to prompt your memory. After you review your notes by reciting them aloud, cover the information under each heading and try to recall all points relating to that topic. Try to explain or recite aloud all details you can remember about each of the main topics in your notes. Then check your notes to see whether you missed anything. If you study in a place where you can't recite out loud, you can accomplish the same thing by mumbling quietly to yourself or by writing out the information from memory. Repeat this process until you know all the information in your notes.

Talk About the Information with Others

Another way to study the information in your notes is simply to talk about it. Putting the information in your own words and explaining it to others is an excellent way to move it into long-term memory. Get together with your note-taking buddy or a study group to edit and review your notes. You can take turns discussing the information (be sure you do some of the explaining), predicting test questions, and quizzing each other on the information. More strategies to review your lecture notes can be found in Chapter 10.

SUMMARY

Taking good lecture notes in college is critical to your success because the primary mode of instruction for most college professors is the formal lecture. Without an accurate record of information from the lecture, you won't have good information to review before the exam. However, just taking notes doesn't mean that you took good notes. The two most important criteria in evaluating the quality of your notes are their content and their organization. You can improve your note-taking skills by reading the text chapter prior to the lecture. Not only will you pick up background information about the topic but you will also get a sense of how the information is organized. To take good notes, you have to be actively involved in the lecture; you need to be an active listener. Unless you focus your attention on the professor and get actively involved in the lecture, you may miss a great deal of information. Many students get caught up in fancy note-taking systems. Using a simple system such as the informal outline, block, or modified-block will help you focus on the lecture material. These systems involve writing down the main topic (the heading) and then jotting down any information the professor provides about that topic (the details).

After the lecture, edit your notes within 24 hours. Recopying your notes to clean them up or make them look nicer is often a waste of time. Unless you're actively involved in evaluating and restructuring your notes, you won't benefit from the editing process. Checking the accuracy of your notes, filling in gaps, creating recall columns, and improving the organization of your notes are all active editing processes. Then review your notes daily, weekly, and before the exam in order to retain the information. Passive studying, like reading over your notes, doesn't help much. Instead, study your notes by reciting out loud from the recall column or from the headings. Talk about the material, explain key points to a friend, or try to reconstruct the lecture from your headings or recall cues.

Activities

1. A good set of notes should stand up to the test of time. Try the following exercise several times during the semester. Be sure to test the notes from each of your classes. Go back to the notes that you took yesterday in one of your classes and read them. Do they make sense to you? Do you feel as though you're sitting in the lecture and hearing your professor talk about the topic? Now go back to the notes that you took at the beginning of the semester. Do they still make sense? Do you feel as though you understand and recall all the information from the lecture?

2. Go to the *Orientation to College Learning* Web site and download one copy of Activity 6–1 from the Activities Packet. Practice condensing the statements into meaningful phrases.

3. Go to the *Orientation to College Learning* Web site and take the listening test in Activity 6–3 from the Activities Packet. What kind of listener are you?

4. After the first exam, reread your lecture notes, looking for information that appeared on the exam. Did you find the answers to most of the questions? Did you find that the answers to many of the test questions were missing?

5. Make a copy of the lecture notes that you took earlier this week. Exchange your notes with another member of your group. Ask your classmate to explain the course information to you. How similar was this explanation to the original lecture? What information in your notes needs to be expanded or clarified? What changes would you make the next time you take notes?

6. Choose a set of lecture notes that you took within the last 24 hours. Edit them, making any necessary changes or corrections. Also, write down any additional information that you remember. If you know that you're missing specific information, refer to your text or to someone else's notes in order to complete your notes. Finally, add recall words or questions in the margin and then review your notes. Write a paragraph describing the changes that you made, the type of recall cues that you used, and the method of review that you found most effective.

7. Select a set of your notes for review. Recite the information in your notes in order to learn it. Then cover the supporting points with your hand and try to recite them using only the headings as cues. Work on one section until you know it; then go on to the next. Halfway through your notes, switch and use the recall questions to review. Which strategy worked best for you? Why?

8. Pretend you were preparing a lecture on a topic that you recently studied in one of your classes. If you're using InfoTrac College Edition, locate information on the topic. Since you're planning to locate information on a particular subject, do a subject search in PowerTrac. Change the index to *subject search* and type in your topic after the two-letter index abbreviation. For more information on how to use index abbreviations, use the Help Index on the bar at the top of your screen. Click on the View button to display the list of articles. Locate one or two articles to "write" your lecture. Instead, take notes on the material in an informal outline, block, or modified-block format. Be sure to include meaningful phrases so that you could deliver the lecture using only your notes.

9. Think of three examples of how you've applied what you learned in this chapter. Choose one strategy and describe how you applied it to your other course work using the Journal Entry Form that is located on the *Orientation to College Learning* Web site. Consider the following questions as you complete your entry. Why did you use this strategy? What did you do? How did it work? How did it affect your performance on the task? How did this approach compare with your previous approach? What changes would you make the next time you use this strategy?

10. Now that you've completed Chapter 6, take a few minutes to repeat the "Where Are You Now?" activity, located on the *Orientation to College Learning* Web site. What changes did you make as a result of reading this chapter? How are you planning to apply what you've learned in this chapter?

Review Questions

Terms You Should Know:

Active listener	Edit	Organization
Block method	Headings	Outline method
Content	Hearing	Recall questions
Cornell system	Listening	Recall words
Details	Modified-block method	

Completion: Fill in the blank to complete each of the following statements.

1. The most important reason to take lecture notes is to get a(n) _____ record of information.

2. _____ is an active, selective process.

3. Take notes in _____ _____; don't write whole sentences.

4. Writing cues in the _____ _____ provides you with an opportunity to test your memory of your notes.

5. You should edit your notes within _____ _____ of the lecture.

Multiple Choice: Circle the letter of the best answer for each of the following questions. Be sure to underline key words and eliminate wrong answers.

6. You can improve your listening skills in all of the following ways except:
   A. reading along in the text as the professor gives the lecture.
   B. deciding that you want to listen.
   C. controlling your emotional response.
   D. holding yourself accountable for the material presented.

7. Which of the following is not a way to edit your notes?
   A. Recopy your notes to improve the appearance.
   B. Rewrite your notes to fill in missing information.
   C. Rewrite your notes to improve the organization.
   D. Add a recall column to your notes.

Short Answer–Essay: On a separate sheet, answer each of the following questions.

8. What are the key features of the outline, block, and modified-block methods of taking notes?

9. How do students benefit from taking notes?

10. How should students review their lecture notes?

Chapter 7

READING YOUR TEXTBOOK

"Although it takes more time than some other methods, the S-RUN-R method helped me with my sociology reading. I actually finished the reading instead of closing the book after reading only a few paragraphs. Along with understanding and taking notes in my own words, I created a recall column next to my notes. Taking notes helped me pay more attention to what I had read, and it (note taking) also helped me grasp the material better."

Michelle Podraza
Student

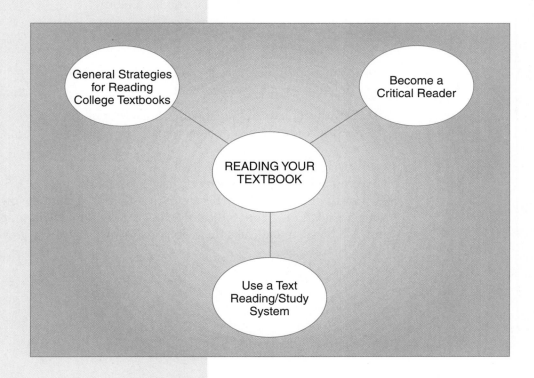

Where Are You Now?

Take a few minutes to answer *yes* or *no* to the following questions.

	YES	NO
1. Do you highlight or mark your textbook as you read?	_____	_____
2. Do you use a reading/study system when you read text material?	_____	_____
3. Do you preview a chapter before you begin to read it?	_____	_____
4. Do you usually try to read an entire chapter once you start?	_____	_____
5. Do you think about the quality of the evidence as you read your textbook?	_____	_____
6. Do you tend to read your text chapters again before the exam?	_____	_____
7. Do you generally pause at the end of each paragraph or page to think about what you have read?	_____	_____
8. Do you use different strategies to read more difficult text assignments?	_____	_____
9. Do you often forget what you have read when you complete a reading assignment?	_____	_____
10. Do you "talk to" (interact with) the author of the text as you are reading your assignment?	_____	_____
TOTAL POINTS	_____	

Give yourself 1 point for each *yes* answer to questions 1, 2, 3, 5, 7, 8, and 10 and 1 point for each *no* answer to questions 4, 6, and 9. Now total up your points. A low score indicates that you need some help in text reading. A high score indicates that you are already using many good text-reading strategies.

GENERAL STRATEGIES FOR READING COLLEGE TEXTBOOKS

Reading college textbooks is a different kind of reading from the reading you did in high school. College textbooks are more "idea dense" than most high school texts; that is, they contain many more facts and ideas per page. Not only is there much more information to learn, but also you may have much less time in which to read and learn it. You probably spent an entire school year covering only a part of your high school textbook; in college you may find that you're responsible for completing an entire text in only 10 to 15 weeks. In addition, college textbooks are written at a higher reading level than high school texts are. College textbooks also contain new, specialized, technical terminology. Unlike your high school textbooks, college texts also contain many more abstract ideas. They don't just seem harder—they are. This may be one of the reasons many students find that even though they read their textbooks, they don't understand what they read.

You can use a number of general strategies to improve your ability to read and comprehend college textbooks. Buying your textbooks early, previewing your texts, reading the chapter before the lecture, dividing the chapter into smaller portions, and monitoring your comprehension are just a few of the strategies that will help you get the most out of reading your texts. If you're already using some of these strategies, you know that they do help. If some of the strategies are new to you, experiment to see whether they're effective, too. The tips in the tip block will help you get off to the right start. Remember, you need a much more strategic approach to read and understand your college textbooks.

BUY YOUR TEXTBOOKS EARLY

You can get a head start on your reading for the next semester if you buy your textbooks during the current semester—before you leave campus for semester break. Even if you purchase only one or two of your texts, you can read the first two or three chapters during semester break. While other students are madly trying to get all their reading done during the first week or two of the new semester, you'll be able to devote time to some of your other classes. Reading ahead also will give you additional time to study for quizzes and nail down some As and Bs during those first few weeks.

TIPS FOR READING COLLEGE TEXTBOOKS

READ TEXTBOOKS DIFFERENTLY.
You can't read a college textbook the same way you read a novel or magazine article. You won't remember everything you read or even understand all of it after one quick reading. You may need to slow down or reread some portions of the chapter.

READ THE CHAPTER BEFORE THE LECTURE. As you learned in Chapter 6, reading the text chapter before the lecture will help you build background on the topic, learn the basic organizational structure of the material, and take better lecture notes.

BUILD ON PRIOR KNOWLEDGE.
Relate what you're reading to what you already know. By connecting the information in your textbook chapter to your own experiences and previous knowledge, you can improve your comprehension and memory of the material.

DIVIDE THE CHAPTER INTO READABLE CHUNKS. A 40-page chapter is probably best read in four chunks of 10 pages each. A 20-page chapter may be read in two chunks of ten or in three chunks of seven, seven, and six pages. Dividing the chapter into smaller reading segments increases your comprehension and actually decreases the time you spend reading the chapter.

PREVIEW THE CHAPTER BEFORE YOU READ. Read the title, introduction, headings, glance at charts and pictures, and read the summary. A 2- to 5-minute preview reduces the total time you spend reading and increases your comprehension.

USE A READING/STUDY SYSTEM.
Use a reading/study system such as P2R, SQ3R, or S-RUN-R, or develop your own system. Be sure you use one or more active strategies before you read the chapter, as you read the chapter, and after you read the chapter.

MARK THE TEXT OR TAKE NOTES AS YOU READ. Highlight, underline, or take notes at the end of each section. Wait until you finish reading the paragraph or a "headed" section before you begin to mark your text.

MONITOR YOUR COMPREHENSION. Stop to check your understanding of the material at regular intervals. Look for connections between topics and how the new information relates to your prior knowledge. Pause at the end of each paragraph and ask yourself if you understand what you're reading.

REVIEW WHAT YOU READ. After you complete your reading assignment, take five to ten minutes (or more) to review what you just read. Think about the main points that the author made in the chapter. Write recall questions or summarize the key information in the margin of the text.

PROMPT YOUR MEMORY. Use the headings of your textbook or your notes or use the recall words or questions to prompt your memory. Recite the information out loud or write it down.

PREVIEW YOUR TEXTBOOKS

As soon as you buy your textbooks, take a good look at them. You can learn a lot about your course and your textbook just by thumbing through the text. A quick look at the table of contents will give you a good idea of the topics you'll be discussing in the course. By looking at the headings in each chapter, you'll get a general idea of how each chapter is organized. By reading the preface or the "notes to the student," you may learn a little about how the author designed the text and how some topics relate to others. The end of your text may also include important study aids. Check to see whether there's an index, glossary, or answer key. The chapters may include lists of key vocabulary words that you should master, questions or problems, or even a sample test to check your understanding of key concepts. These study aids will help you monitor your comprehension of the text material and your mastery of the main and supporting points.

READ TEN PAGES AT A TIME

Which would you rather read, a 50-page chapter or a 10-page chapter? Most students say they'd much rather read a 10-page chapter. Did you? Take a look at the chapters in some of your textbooks. You may be surprised by how long they are. Fifty-page chapters are standard for many texts. Reading 50 pages at one time may not seem like a difficult task, but it is. One page of a college textbook may contain as many words as three pages of a novel. Have you ever sat and read 150 pages of a novel at one time? Not only are there more words on the page, but also the text may be difficult to read and understand. If you find that your attention begins to wander or you just aren't grasping the information anymore, you should stop reading and continue later.

Some students find that it takes them much longer to read the second half of the chapter than the first because, as they get tired or lose interest, their reading speed starts to slow. Time yourself as you read one of your chapters. Note the time at the end of each 10-page section. Did you read the earlier sections more quickly?

Using good time-management strategies can help you improve your textbook reading. Reading a chapter in chunks of 10 pages or even five pages at one sitting may help you maintain a faster reading speed and still have excellent comprehension. You also may find that when you're working on only 10 pages of text at one time, you feel more motivated to highlight or take notes as you read.

MONITOR YOUR COMPREHENSION

As you read your textbook, you should be aware not only of what you're reading but also of whether you understand what you're reading. You should pause frequently to reflect on what's being said. Too many students read their textbooks in a mechanical way. Their eyes see the words, but their minds are a million miles away. Comprehension monitoring will help you keep your mind on what you're reading. *Comprehension monitoring* refers to your own evaluation of whether or not you comprehend (understand) what you read. You can monitor your comprehension of the text material by stopping every so often (at the end of a paragraph, section, or page) and asking yourself what you just read and whether you understood it. When you realize that you don't understand what you've just read—when comprehension breaks down—you may find that you can correct the problem. The easiest thing to do is to read the sentence or the paragraph again (perhaps out loud if you're an auditory learner). Sometimes reading ahead or rereading the previous paragraph can provide more clarification. Looking up the definitions of unfamiliar vocabulary words can also help you gain a better understanding of the material. The reading/study systems discussed in this chapter will also help you monitor your comprehension and get more out of your reading.

BECOME A CRITICAL READER

What was the single most important thing that you learned in Chapter 6? To answer that question you need to determine the author's purpose for writing the chapter, identify the main and supporting points in the chapter, consider your purpose for reading the chapter, and evaluate the information that was presented. To choose the single most important point the author is making, you need to understand and think critically about each of the points in the chapter. After all, you must judge the value of each statement based on its own merits, your prior knowledge, and your purpose for reading.

WHAT IS CRITICAL READING?

Actually, it's difficult to define critical reading (perhaps because it's difficult to accurately describe what really happens when we read). However, most reading researchers agree that critical reading involves thinking critically as we read and after we read. This doesn't mean that you're expected to look for what's wrong with everything you read—you're not being critical in terms of finding fault. Instead, *critical reading* involves questioning, analyzing, and evaluating what you read. You use critical reading skills all the time. If you read labels of competing products when you go to the grocery store, you're using critical reading skills. If you read the course description guide before choosing your class schedule, you're using critical reading skills. When you skim several journal articles before choosing the one or two to use for a term paper or speech, you're using critical reading skills. In each case, you're thinking critically about the information as you read it and after you read it.

UNDERSTANDING CRITICAL READING SKILLS

To think critically about what you read, you must be able to comprehend, analyze, synthesize, apply, and evaluate the material. It's a process that requires you to be actively involved as you read each of your text assignments. You need to question as you read, monitor your comprehension, make connections and comparisons to other material or your own prior knowledge, and finally evaluate what you've read. To do all of these things, you must become an active participant in the reading process.

Comprehension

Because many college texts are so difficult, students don't always understand what they read. You need to *comprehend*—understand—what the individual words mean and how each group of words works together to create meaning within a sentence, paragraph, and headed section. The use of new, specialized, technical terminology is one of the most common causes of comprehension problems. You may be dealing with words you've never even seen before—you may not recognize some of the words, know how to pronounce them, or know what some words mean. Some words take on new or specialized meanings because of the way they're used in particular subject areas. Without understanding the words in the text, you can't understand the ideas and concepts that are presented. For this reason, it's important to look up words that you don't understand and gain some familiarity with the new terminology within the text. Making out word cards (see Chapter 10) or jotting a brief definition or synonym above a difficult word will help improve your comprehension. Without a clear understanding of the text material, you can't make judgments about its quality.

Application

You can gain a better understanding of your text material if you *apply* what you're reading to your own prior knowledge of the material or to your own life experiences. Many reading researchers agree that you can't think critically about written material if you don't have some prior knowledge or experiences with which to compare it. Many college texts are difficult because they contain abstract theories and concepts. Thinking about how the information can be applied to real-life situations can make it easier to understand. You may find that you can build prior knowledge by previewing your text material and by reading other books or articles on the same topic. Finally, you can increase your knowledge of the material by talking to others who have expertise in the area.

Analysis

To be a critical reader, you also must learn to analyze the information presented in the text. Learning to break the information into its component parts—*analysis*—will help you look more critically at the points made within your reading assignment. You need to identify the main points and their supporting details to better understand the relationships among and within the material. To understand the main points within the headed section, you have to consider how each of the reasons, facts, details, or examples supports the topic or main point being discussed. By identifying each component within the paragraph, you also can better evaluate the quality of the arguments the author is making. If you're currently marking your text, you're thinking about what's important as you read. In Chapter 8, you'll learn more about how to identify the main points and supporting points in your text material.

Synthesis

Your ability to organize and *synthesize*—pull information together from individual statements made in the paragraph (or headed section) into more general ideas or concepts—is critical to understanding what you read. You need to think about how each supporting point adds to the meaning of the main points in each paragraph and how the main points in each paragraph connect to form the key ideas presented in the text. By combining the smaller components within the text, you can gain a better understanding of the information or reach conclusions that aren't directly stated. This may involve adding to the prior knowledge you already have about the topic, modifying what you previously thought about the topic, or learning new information about the topic. Chapter 9 contains a number of strategies that help you learn to pull information together, using your own organizational system.

Evaluation

Critical reading also involves *evaluation*—judging the value of the information in the text. You need to think critically about what you read because not all material that you will read is accurate or presented in an objective way. Most textbooks are for the most part reliable sources of information, written and published by reputable authors and publishers. However, you'll also be expected to read many other types of material in many of your classes. You may read journal articles, research studies, critiques, essays, letters, and other original documents. As you begin to use the Internet to locate information, you need to be even more cautious in your acceptance of everything you read as factual and accurate. Anyone can put anything on the Internet. There are few, if any, regulatory agencies to monitor the accuracy or integrity of the information.

Considering the source of the information and the credibility of the author is only one part of critical reading, however. You must also judge the quality of the main and supporting points made in your reading material. Ask yourself if the facts, reasons, details, and examples really do support the author's conclusions. Think about whether there's enough evidence given to prove the point. Consider whether the evidence is *factual* (statements that can be verified as true or false) or only the *opinion* (statements that express feelings, attitudes, or beliefs) of the author. Watch for biased language (words used to sway you to believe one side of the argument) or *bias* in presenting only the evidence that supports one side of the issue. You may find that it's helpful to annotate your text as you read. Janet Maker recommends noting the author's point of view (position or stance on the topic) in the margin of the text and then listing each of the arguments or supporting points under it (across from its location in the text).[1] Jotting the supporting points in the margin helps you identify and evaluate the quality of the evidence.

To be a critical reader, you must also think about how the new information fits with what you learned in the lecture, another reading assignment, or through your own prior knowledge. You should also consider how well the information that you read accomplishes the author's purpose for writing and your purpose for reading.

USE A TEXT READING/STUDY SYSTEM

Dozens of reading/study systems have been developed to help students better understand what they read. Because they're all very similar, we'll discuss only three of them in this chapter. After you learn how to use each system, try it out, and then choose the one that works best for you. You may find that you like some parts of one and other parts of another. Mix and match as you see fit. You also may find that one reading/study system works well with one of your texts, but a different one is more helpful for another text. Using the appropriate reading/study system will help you get more out of the time you spend reading your textbooks.

---

[1] Janet Maker, "The ACT (Active Critical Thinking) Method of Teaching Critical and Study Reading," *Journal of College Reading and Learning* 27(2) (1996): 40–44.

THE P2R READING/STUDY SYSTEM

Many study skills instructors no longer teach students to use long, complicated reading/study systems. Although these systems do work, too many of their students don't use them because they simply take too much time. You can get more out of the time you spend reading your textbook by using an easy, three-step approach.

The *P2R* reading/study system is designed for textbooks that are from easy to average level in difficulty. Use P2R on the entire chapter or on 10-page chunks. First, preview the entire chapter. Next, read actively by highlighting or taking notes as you read. Finally, review using an active strategy such as reciting, answering review questions, or creating a recall column. If you're still just sitting back and reading over your text chapters, why not give P2R a try. Many of my students have found that it really increases their comprehension of the text material without adding much time to their reading.

Advantages of P2R

Previewing the chapter provides you with some background about topics in the chapter that may be new to you. Even a brief overview of the chapter can help you pick up some general information about the material. You may also gain some understanding of how the information is organized and presented. Both of these kinds of information can help you understand the text material better. Research studies have shown that previewing before reading can increase your comprehension of the textbook chapter by 10 to 20 percent.

Highlighting or note taking allows you to keep up with your class assignments, identify and mark the material that you will need to study further, and improve your ability to concentrate, which increases your comprehension. In recent years, there's been a great deal of discussion about the value of marking your textbook as you read. One view suggests that marking your textbook is a way to avoid learning the material as you read it. In some ways this is true. However, if you've already started college, you probably realize that you just don't have time to learn all of the material *well* the first time you read. The main reason for marking your text is to identify the important information and condense the text material so that you never have to read the entire chapter again. It's not unusual to have 300 pages of text to review for just one exam. Think about how long it would take to reread all of it. And remember, rereading the text does not ensure mastery of the material. You still have to learn the material for the exam.

Reviewing after you read each 10-page chunk helps you reinforce the important information. Without reviewing, you really can't be sure that you did understand the text material or that you can recall it for a quiz or class discussion. Reviewing provides you with an opportunity to move the information into long-term memory and test your learning. There are many ways to review text material. A few of the most common ones are described in the next section.

The Three Steps in P2R

Preview

You should always preview a chapter before you read it. A *preview* is a brief overview of a chapter done before reading it. Previewing takes very little time and effort—most students can do it in 2 to 5 minutes. The first thing to do is read the title of the chapter. Then read the introduction, outline, or structured overview (a visual display of key information) at the beginning of the chapter. If your text doesn't begin with an introduction, outline, or structured overview, read the first two paragraphs. As you turn the pages of the chapter, read the headings in bold print and glance at any pictures, tables, or graphs. Don't stop to read any of the text along the way. At the end of the chapter, read the summary or the last two paragraphs. If your text contains an extensive summary (a page or more in length), you may want to read only the first and last sentence of each of the paragraphs in the summary. If the chapter is extremely short or if you're reading a journal article or other short selection, you may find it helpful to read the first sentence of each paragraph.

Read Actively

The second step of the P2R system is to *read actively*—to do something while you read. One way you can become an active reader is by marking your text. After you've read a paragraph or headed section of text, pause to think about what you've read. Go back and use a highlighter to mark any material that you think you'll want to review again before the exam. By highlighting the text, you're actively involved in thinking about the material, and you're condensing what you'll need to review at a later time. Chapter 8 includes much more information on how to highlight.

Another way to read actively is to take notes. Taking notes on a text is a lot like taking notes on lectures. Write the heading in your notebook and then jot down the important details. You could also write recall questions or summary statements in the margin of the text. More information on how to take text notes is given in Chapter 9.

Review

After you complete a 10-page chunk of reading, you need to *review*—do something to reinforce the important information. There are a number of ways that you can review the text material, but here are four of the most common ones. First, you may want to summarize the key points that the author made. Write three or four statements that you think summarize the key points made in the reading selection. Second, you can recite the information. Using the headings as a guide, cover the page of text and recite the key information under each heading. You also may want to recite from the recall questions that you wrote in the margin of the text or from your notes. Third, you can do the test at the end of the chapter or any study guide material. Finally, you can review your text chapter by self-testing (predicting and answering questions that may be on a quiz or test). Don't try to use all of these strategies at the same time. Test them as you read assignments in several of your courses. Then choose the one that works best for you.

THE SQ3R READING/STUDY SYSTEM

SQ3R, developed by Francis Robinson in 1941, is one of the most widely taught reading/study systems.[2] Many students learn how to use SQ3R in junior high school, in senior high school, or even in college. Have you ever been taught how to use SQ3R? Did you ever use it? *SQ3R* is an acronym for *Survey, Question, Read, Recite,* and *Review.* By using these five steps when you read your college textbooks, you can overcome many of the difficulties you may encounter when dealing with hard-to-read and hard-to-understand material.

Some of the steps in the SQ3R system are similar to those in P2R. The main difference, however, is that the steps are performed on each "headed" section rather than on 10-page chunks or on whole chapters. As you'll see, this difference makes SQ3R a more time-consuming system. Because of this, you may want to save SQ3R for your more difficult textbooks. Although it takes a lot of time, many students find that it's very effective.

Advantages of SQ3R

One advantage of the SQ3R reading/study system is that it sets the stage for a great deal of interaction with the text material. As you go through the five steps, you're surveying the chapter to gain information about the topics presented, formulating questions about the material, reading to find the answers, reciting important information aloud, and, finally, reviewing again what you've read. By focusing on each "headed" section and going through all of the steps, you're breaking the task of reading an entire textbook chapter down into smaller units. If you have difficulty reading even 10 pages of text at one time, you may find SQ3R to be very helpful. Most students who use the five steps in the SQ3R system do report a greater understanding of the text material than they had before.

One of the greatest advantages of using the SQ3R system is that it allows for a great deal of repetition of the important information in the chapter. As you learned in Chapter 5, repetition is one of the key ingredients in learning. By going through all of the steps in the SQ3R system, you're repeating the key information in the chapter at least three or four times.

---

[2]The discussion of the five steps in the SQ3R process that follows was adapted from F. Robinson, *Effective Study*, 4th ed. (New York: Harper & Row, 1970), pp. 32–36.

Another advantage of SQ3R is that it has a built-in comprehension-monitoring system. When you stop to recite the answer to the question that you formulated, you're testing your understanding of the material that you read. This step in the SQ3R process keeps you on track as you read. Knowing that you must be accountable for what you have read can prevent the passive reading that so often characterizes text reading.

The Five Steps in SQ3R

Survey

Survey the chapter before you read it. Go through the chapter quickly, glance at the headings, and then read the final paragraph of the chapter in order to get a general idea of what the chapter is about and the main points that the author is making.

Question

Before you begin to read the first section in your chapter, turn the heading of the first section into a question. Then read to answer the question that you generated. How would you change the heading "Ego Defense Mechanisms" into a question? Actually, you could generate a number of different questions. One of the most typical (though not necessarily the best) is "What are ego defense mechanisms?" Formulating questions forces you to think about what you're about to read; it makes you try to predict what the author's main point will be.

Read

Read the text material under the heading in order to find the answer to the question that you generated. Turning the heading into a question helps you focus your reading. Reading the section to locate the answer to your question helps you get actively involved in the text material.

Recite

At the end of the first headed section, answer the question that you formulated. Recite the answer in your own words, without looking at the text. If you find that you're unable to recall a part or all of the answer, glance over the section again. Then jot down a brief answer in outline form on a piece of paper. Don't make any notes until you've read the entire section.

Review

After you've finished reading the entire chapter, look over the notes that you made to again familiarize yourself with the important information in the chapter. Check your memory by covering your notes and reciting the main points out loud. Then cover each main point in your notes and try to recite the subordinate points that you noted until you have reviewed each headed section. This review should take only about 5 minutes.

Adapting SQ3R

There are a number of ways that you can adapt or modify SQ3R to make it more effective and easy to use. First of all, you don't have to use SQ3R for all your reading assignments. Many students use SQ3R or a variation of it only for reading their most difficult textbooks. Try using SQ3R with an easy text and with a difficult-to-understand text. You'll probably discover that you really don't need to use SQ3R with your easy textbook, but you may discover that it does help improve your comprehension with your hard-to-understand text.

Because college texts contain so much information in each headed section, you need to modify the way you generate questions for each heading. If you simply ask "What are . . ." type of questions, you may be focusing only on the definition. Other important points would have been overlooked. You may find it more useful to generate broad questions such as "What do I need to know about ego defense mechanisms?" or "What's important about ego defense mechanisms?" Broad questions will lead you to read for *all* of the important information within the headed section.

Writing your question in the margin across from the heading and then noting the "answer" below it in the margin is also an effective modification. By *annotating* (adding explanatory notes) your text, you'll increase your level of involvement with the material and prepare your text for later review. More information on how to annotate your text is presented in Chapters 8 and 9.

Rather than just reciting the answer to the question that you formulated from the heading, cover the section of text and try to recite all the important information that it contained. By modifying the way you use SQ3R, you can still make it an effective and an efficient study tool, especially for reading very difficult textbooks.

THE S-RUN-R READING/STUDY SYSTEM

The SQ3R system has been adapted by many reading and study skills educators. Because of its simplicity, one variation that may be very useful for college students is the *S-RUN* (*S*urvey, *R*ead, *U*nderline, *N*otetaking) reading method designed by Nancy Bailey.[3] Bailey's students were reluctant to use SQ3R because it seemed like too much work; however, they used S-RUN with great success.

---

[3]Nancy Bailey, "S-RUN: Beyond SQ3R," *Journal of Reading* 32 (1988): 170.

The *S-RUN-R* reading/study system combines Bailey's system with a review step to better meet the needs of college students. Because you focus on the text one headed section at a time, S-RUN-R should be used with more difficult text material.

Advantages of S-RUN-R

The S-RUN-R reading/study system contains many of the strengths of SQ3R but also has been adapted so that it's more suitable for college text material. First, like SQ3R, S-RUN-R provides you with a great deal of repetition. You survey, read, mark, take notes on, and review all important information in the chapter. You get at least four repetitions on the important points in each headed section. This helps you better understand the information and learn it. Second, S-RUN-R also allows you to focus on one headed section at a time. This helps increase your comprehension because you don't move on to another section until you thoroughly understand the previous one. The S-RUN-R reading/study system also helps you focus on all important information in the headed section rather than on only one question and its answer. Finally, S-RUN-R provides you with a system that uses active strategies, which help increase your comprehension and at the same time condenses the material for later review. Many students have found that S-RUN-R is a very effective reading/study system. Try it and see if it works for you, too.

The Five Steps in S-RUN-R

Survey

The first step in the S-RUN-R reading/study system is to survey the entire chapter. Read the title, introduction, headings, subheadings, and summary (and glance at pictures, charts, and graphs). Like P2R and SQ3R, this survey provides a quick overview of the chapter, building background and interest. You should spend only about 2 (for short chapters) to 5 minutes (for longer chapters) completing the survey. If it's taking you longer, you're probably reading too much or stopping too long to look at the illustrations.

Read

Instead of formulating a question before reading a headed section, write the heading on a piece of notebook paper next to the left margin. Just copying the heading helps you pay more attention to it and may help focus your reading. Then read the section as you would any other text material, thinking critically about the material.

Underline

After you finish reading each paragraph, think about what was important in the paragraph and underline or highlight the important information. As you'll see in Chapter 8, highlighting takes much less time than underlining, so feel free to make the change. In the next chapter, you'll learn more about how to choose what to mark. For now, highlight the information that you think you would like to review for an exam.

Note Take

As soon as you complete all of the highlighting for the entire headed section, stop and turn back to your notebook page. Now take notes on the key information. Briefly summarize the underlined or highlighted information under the previously written heading. Skip to the next line in your notebook, indenting slightly, and write the notes using meaningful phrases as you do when taking lecture notes. Don't just copy what you highlighted; try to put the information into your own words. You'll increase your comprehension even more. Continue jotting down each heading, reading, underlining (or highlighting), and taking notes for each remaining headed section.

Review

When you've completed the entire chapter, review to reinforce the important information. You can recite the key information that you wrote under each heading. Doing the end-of-chapter questions (if there are any) may also help you review the key information in the chapter. Some students find that predicting questions and creating self-tests helps them identify and practice the main points in the chapter. You may also create a recall column in your textbook or for your text notes. Writing recall questions in the margin can help you prompt your memory of the key points you underlined (or highlighted) or included in your text notes. You can use the review step to simply get more repetition on the material or to actually check your understanding or memory of it. Writing questions in the margin of your textbook or notebook provides you with repetition on the material, but actually self-testing with those questions will let you know whether or not you really have learned the material.

Adapting S-RUN-R

As with any of the reading/study systems, S-RUN-R can be adapted or modified to better fit your needs or those of the text you're using. You may find that you still want to read your chapter in 10-page chunks. If that's the case, you should do a quick review after you complete each chunk of the chapter and then choose a different strategy to review when you complete the entire chapter. You can also modify S-RUN-R by taking your notes in the margin of your textbook (if it's large enough) or by writing your notes on a narrow strip of paper (similar to the size of a bookmark) that you can insert in each page to take the place of the wide margin. A number of office supply stores sell note pads that are about this size.

SUMMARY

College textbooks are different from high school textbooks. They're generally written at a higher reading level and are longer and more idea dense. They don't just seem harder—they are! Using good time-management strategies can help you keep up with your reading assignments, which may total 200 or 300 pages per week. To understand what you're reading, you need to use some type of text-reading strategy before you read, as you read, and after you read. It's also important to monitor your comprehension while you're reading your textbooks. Learning to be a critical reader will help you think about and evaluate the information in your textbooks and other reading assignments. Many students use a text reading/study system such as P2R, SQ3R, or S-RUN-R to increase and monitor their comprehension. The strategies suggested in these systems get you more actively involved in your reading. You may find that you need to use only a simple system like P2R when reading your easier textbooks. However, a more complex system like SQ3R or S-RUN-R may be necessary to ensure good comprehension when you're reading your more difficult textbooks. Experiment with all the reading/study systems to find out which one works best for you. You may also choose to adapt one of these systems or design your own text reading/study system. If you find that you often get to the end of the page or the end of the chapter and don't remember or understand what you read, you need to get more actively involved in your reading assignments.

Activities

1. Go to the *Orientation to College Learning* Web site and download one copy of Activity 7–1 (Describe Your Textbook) from the Activities Packet. Complete the form as you preview one of your textbooks.

2. As you read your text assignments during the next week, experiment with the various reading/study systems that were described in this chapter. Begin each assignment with the easiest system (P2R) and proceed to use more complex systems (SQ3R or S-RUN-R) if you find

that you're not able to understand or remember the material. Which system did you find the most helpful for each text?

3. As you read your next text assignment, put a check mark in the margin every time you stop to think about what you've read and whether you understood it. After you complete the reading assignment, look at the placement of your check marks. Do they occur within paragraphs, mainly at the end of paragraphs, at the end of the page, or even less frequently? What types of comprehension problems did you experience? What strategies did you use to correct your comprehension problems? Did you notice any improvement in your comprehension of the material?

4. Use the three steps in the P2R system to read the text selection "Cultural Changes and Sustainability" available on the *Orientation to College Learning* Web site. Use one of the text-marking methods discussed or try a combination of them. Then choose one of the review methods that was suggested or use one of your own. Compare your marking, notes, and predicted questions with those of others in your group. Did you find the P2R system helpful in reading and understanding the text material?

5. Read the text selection "The Cytomembrane System," available on the *Orientation to College Learning* Web site, using the SQ3R reading/study method. Did you find the SQ3R system helpful in reading and understanding the text material? Why, or why not? Describe the process you used and your results in several paragraphs.

6. Read the text selection "The Old and Middle Kingdoms," available on the *Orientation to College Learning* Web site, using the S-RUN-R reading/study system. Don't forget to work on one headed section at a time. Compare your marking and notes with those of other students in your group. Did you find the S-RUN-R system helpful in reading and understanding the text material?

7. As you read your text assignments during the next week, experiment with the various reading/study systems that were described in this chapter. Begin each assignment with the easiest system (P2R) and proceed to use more complex systems (S-RUN-R and SQ3R) if you find that you're not able to understand and remember the material. You'll probably find that you didn't use the same system for all your texts. List the name of each of your texts and describe the system that you found to be most effective. Discuss your reasons with the members of your group.

8. If you're using InfoTrac College Edition, select a topic from one of your textbooks that you would like to know more about and do a search to locate an article that contains more information about the topic that you chose. Print the article and then read it using one of the reading/study systems. What did you learn about your topic? Did the material help clarify any of the information that was presented in your textbook? Include at least one example.

 9. Think of three examples of how you've applied what you learned in this chapter. Choose one strategy and describe how you applied it to your other course work using the Journal Entry Form that's located on the *Orientation to College Learning* Web site. Consider the following questions as you complete your entry. Why did you use this strategy? What did you do? How did it work? How did it affect your performance on the task? How did this approach compare to your previous approach? What changes would you make the next time you use this strategy?

 10. Now that you've completed Chapter 7, take a few minutes to repeat the "Where Are You Now?" activity, located on the *Orientation to College Learning* Web site. What changes did you make as a result of reading this chapter? How are you planning to apply what you've learned in this chapter?

Review Questions

Terms You Should Know:

Analysis	Critical reading	Read actively
Annotating	Evaluation	Review
Application	Facts	SQ3R
Bias	Opinions	S-RUN-R
Comprehension	P2R	Synthesis
Comprehension monitoring	Preview	

Completion: Fill in the blank to complete each of the following statements.

1. By connecting what you're reading to your _____ _____, you can improve your reading comprehension.

2. You can prevent boredom and increase your comprehension if you read your textbook chapter in _____-page chunks.

3. You need to turn the _____ into a question in the SQ3R reading/study system.

4. You should use the _____ reading/study system with your easy-to-read textbooks.

5. One of the disadvantages of using S-RUN-R is that it is very

    _____ _____ .

Multiple Choice: Circle the letter of the best answer for each of the following questions. Be sure to underline key words and eliminate wrong answers.

6. _____ refers to your evaluation of whether or not you understand what you read.
   A. Critical reading
   B. Previewing
   C. Comprehension monitoring
   D. Analysis

7. Previewing before reading a chapter can increase your comprehension by:
   A. 5 to 10 percent
   B. 10 to 20 percent
   C. 20 to 30 percent
   D. Previewing increases speed but not comprehension

Short Answer–Essay: On a separate sheet, answer each of the following questions.

8. List and define each of the five critical reading skills.

9. Why do some students have difficulty reading their textbooks? What should they do differently?

10. Compare and contrast the P2R, SQ3R, and S-RUN-R reading/study systems.

Chapter 8

MARKING YOUR TEXTBOOK

"Text marking helps me the most when reading. It keeps me alert and involved in my reading. I have to pick out the main ideas in the text, so I pay attention more. I've also noticed that when I highlight, the reading isn't boring and doesn't take as long. Also, when I'm reviewing, I can spend my time focusing more on the main points instead of rereading the whole chapter."

Suzette Pavlo
Student

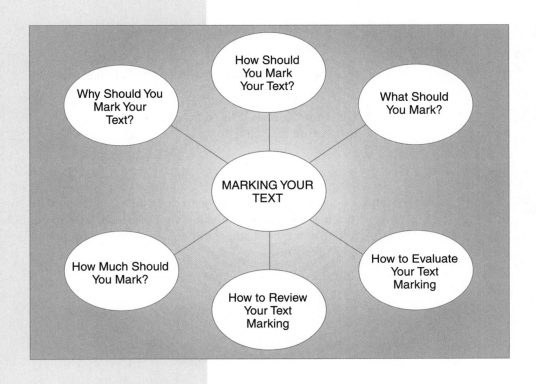

Where Are You Now?

Take a few minutes to answer *yes* or *no* to the following questions.

	YES	NO
1. Do you highlight or mark your textbook as you read?	_____	_____
2. Do you find that you often get to the end of a page and have no idea what you just read?	_____	_____
3. Do you begin to highlight or underline an important point before you finish the sentence?	_____	_____
4. Do you evaluate your text marking after an exam?	_____	_____
5. Does your marking make sense when you read it again before the exam?	_____	_____
6. Do you rehighlight or re-mark your text when you review for an exam?	_____	_____
7. Do you mark the headings and subheadings in your text?	_____	_____
8. Do you make notes in the margin when you read your text?	_____	_____
9. Do you tend to mark key words rather than phrases or entire sentences?	_____	_____
10. Do you ever reread the unmarked sections of your text before an exam?	_____	_____
TOTAL POINTS	_____	

Give yourself 1 point for each *yes* answer to questions 1, 4, 5, 6, 7, and 8 and 1 point for each *no* answer to questions 2, 3, 9, and 10. Now total up your points. A low score indicates that you need some help in text marking. A high score indicates that you are already using many good text-marking strategies.

WHY SHOULD YOU MARK YOUR TEXT?

You probably know some students whose textbooks look as new at the end of a course as they did at the beginning. Have you ever wondered why? One explanation is that those students believe text marking is a waste of time. They've heard that if you mark your text, you're just putting off learning the information. (Sometimes this reasoning provides a convenient excuse not to mark.) Other students don't mark their texts because they want to sell them at the end of the semester; they think marked textbooks are less valuable at the resale table. Textbook buyers don't really care if books are marked. But you should!

When done correctly, text marking promotes active reading, condenses the material for later review, increases your comprehension, and serves as a comprehension monitoring system.

PROMOTES ACTIVE READING

Marking your textbook is a useful activity because it promotes active reading. By now you probably have noticed that you're more actively involved in lecture classes because you're taking notes. By marking your textbooks as you read, you can achieve that same level of concentration and activity. Knowing that you should mark specific sections as you read helps keep you alert. It gives you a purpose for reading. Instead of daydreaming or thinking about something else you have to do, you're forced to concentrate on what you're reading. To mark your text effectively, you have to think about the content of the chapter. You constantly need to make decisions about what's important and what isn't. You may find that your reading takes on a whole new dimension when you mark your text.

CONDENSES THE MATERIAL

Text marking is also important because it condenses the text material for later review. Most students who don't mark their books don't go back and study the text before an exam. Without marking, they would have to reread everything. So, instead, they rely only on their lecture notes. Because most professors also test on text material, these students are at a decided disadvantage at exam time. By marking, you can reduce the amount of text material you need to review.

INCREASES COMPREHENSION

Text marking also improves your comprehension of the text material. Identifying and marking the main points and then looking for supporting details help you understand the text. If you highlight these same points after you've read the paragraph, you get a chance to read the information a second time. Have you noticed that your eyes follow your marker as you move it across the text? This second reading helps reinforce the key information. As you make notes or write questions in the margin, you get even more repetition on the important information.

SERVES AS A COMPREHENSION MONITORING SYSTEM

Text marking also provides you with feedback on whether you're paying attention as you read a particular section of your text. If everything is marked, you know you really weren't making decisions about the importance of the material. You may not have been able to determine what was important and what wasn't. If nothing is marked, you may not have understood the material well enough to pick out the important information or you may have been distracted. In these ways, text marking allows you to monitor your comprehension of the text material.

HOW SHOULD YOU MARK YOUR TEXT?

There are many methods for marking a textbook, but the two most common ones are underlining and highlighting. The first step in effective marking is to read and think about the text material. Text marking is a lot like taking lecture notes. You need to get actively involved in the material—read, think, decide, and then mark.

It's important to read an entire paragraph or headed section before you begin to mark your textbook. After you read a section, you need to decide what's important; then you can begin to mark. Many students really don't know how to mark a textbook, so as soon as they read something that looks as though it might be important, they start to mark. If you mark part of a sentence before you even finish reading it, you're actually interfering with your comprehension of the material. Until you get used to marking, try to read at least to the end of the sentence before you begin to mark. Work up to two sentences, then to the end of the paragraph, and finally to the entire headed section.

HIGHLIGHT

Highlighting the text as you read is probably the most efficient method of text marking. Because it takes so little extra time, more students are willing to do it. As you mark the text material, drag your highlighter across the printed words from left to right; in this way you'll be able to reread the sentence or phrase as you mark it. This second reading helps improve your comprehension and memory of the material. If you sweep backward across the line, you won't benefit from a second reading. If you decide to use highlighting to mark your textbooks, use a very soft shade like yellow or pastel pink. Although fluorescent markers do make the text material stand out, they also cause eye strain when you go back to reread your marking. Look at the example of highlighted text in Figure 8.1. Does the highlighting effectively show the important information?

FIGURE 8.1

• • • • • • • • • • • • • •

Example of Highlighted Text with Marginal Notes

WHY ARE THE OCEANS IMPORTANT?

Earth = "Ocean"

    As landlubbers, we tend to think of Earth in terms of land, but Earth is largely a water planet. A more accurate name for the planet would be Ocean, because salt-water oceans cover more than 71 percent of its surface.

"O" → survival of all life

1. dilute waste

2. regulate climate

    The oceans play key roles in the survival of virtually all life on Earth. Because of their size and currents, the oceans mix and dilute many human-produced wastes flowing or dumped into them to less harmful or even harmless levels, as long as they are not overloaded. Oceans also play a major role in regulating Earth's climate by distributing solar heat through ocean currents and by evaporation as part of the global hydrologic cycle. They also participate in other important nutrient cycles.

3. regulate temp

4. habitat ≈ 250,000 species

5. source nat. resources

    By serving as a gigantic reservoir for carbon dioxide, oceans help regulate the temperature of the troposphere. Oceans provide habitats for about 250,000 species of marine plants and animals, which are food for many organisms, including human beings. They also supply us with iron, sand, gravel, phosphates, magnesium, oil, natural gas, and many other valuable resources.

Text material adapted from G. T. Miller, *Living in the Environment: Principles, Connections, and Solutions,* 11th ed. (Pacific Grove, CA: Brooks/Cole, 2000), p. 189.

UNDERLINE

Some students use a highlighter, pen, or pencil to *underline* important text material. Underlining may not increase comprehension as much as highlighting does because you may not get a second reading when you underline your text. Many students focus more on drawing the line than on reading the text material as they underline. If you do decide to underline your text, don't use a ruler or straightedge to keep your lines straight—it will really slow you down. Although underlining does promote active reading and condense the material, it isn't as efficient or effective as highlighting.

MAKE MARGINAL NOTES

As you mark, you also may want to add *marginal notes,* summary statements in the margin of the text. You can also make notes to indicate that you agree or disagree with a point that the author made. You can put a question mark in the margin to indicate that you don't understand something or would like to ask about it in class, or use a star to indicate that the professor hinted that something would be on the test. Making brief notes in the margin will help increase your level of interaction with the text. However, don't overdo it. If you try to copy all the important information in the margin, you're defeating the purpose of marking. The marginal notes in Figure 8.1 summarize the main points made in the selection.

AVOID COMPLEX MARKING SYSTEMS

Learning to mark your textbook is not that difficult; however, some students make text marking more complicated than it needs to be. They use *complex marking systems* that lead to ineffective and inefficient marking. Have you ever seen a beautifully marked textbook? If this question made you think of one with three or four different colors of highlighting, you know exactly what I mean. During a workshop several years ago, I asked students to mark a text selection. One student immediately pulled out five different colored markers and began to read and mark the selection. It took this student four times as long as everyone else in the room to mark the selection. At the end of the session, I asked the student about her marking system. She explained that she used one color for main ideas, one color for key words, another for definitions, a fourth shade for examples, and a fifth for supporting details.

Although this type of system does force you to think about how to mark the text material, it actually can interfere with comprehension. If you spend too much time thinking about whether something is a main idea, a supporting detail, a definition, an example, or a key word, you may not be thinking much about the content of the selection. Thinking about what color you should use also distracts you from concentrating on the material itself. Using multi-colored highlighting systems can cause you to focus more on the system than the text material.

Other complex marking systems recommend using single lines, double lines, wavy lines, boxes, circles, curved brackets, square brackets, asterisks, numbers, and other marking symbols. These complex systems, like the multicolored ones, are very time-consuming and often lead to overmarking. Look at the example in Figure 8.2, which incorporates some of these methods. Deciding whether to use a single line or a double line, a box or a circle, or a number or an asterisk can interfere with your comprehension of the material. You spend too much time thinking about the system instead of the text content. Take another look at the marking in Figure 8.2. Did you notice that almost everything is marked? Using

FIGURE 8.2

Example of Overly Complex Marking

WHY ARE THE OCEANS IMPORTANT?

As landlubbers, we tend to think of Earth in terms of land, but Earth is largely a water planet. A more accurate name for the planet would be Ocean, because salt-water oceans cover more than 71 percent of its surface.

The oceans play key roles in the survival of virtually all life on Earth. Because of their size and currents, the oceans mix and dilute many human-produced wastes flowing or dumped into them to less harmful or even harmless levels, as long as they are not overloaded. Oceans also play a major role in regulating Earth's climate by distributing solar heat through ocean currents and by evaporation as part of the global hydrologic cycle. They also participate in other important nutrient cycles.

By serving as a gigantic reservoir for carbon dioxide, oceans help regulate the temperature of the troposphere. Oceans provide habitats for about 250,000 species of marine plants and animals, which are food for many organisms, including human beings. They also supply us with iron, sand, gravel, phosphates, magnesium, oil, natural gas, and many other valuable resources.

a simple system will help you focus on the important information, while reading actively and condensing the material for later review.

WHAT SHOULD YOU MARK?

Now that you know how to mark, the next step is figuring out what you should mark. As you read your text assignments, you probably caught yourself thinking, I wonder if I should mark this. Until you become more experienced at marking, it's better to mark a little too much rather than not enough. Remember the rule of thumb from note taking: When in doubt, write it out. The same thing applies to text marking. You also may want to follow a general rule for text marking: *If you think it might be on the test, mark it.* Of course, after the first test, you'll be able to evaluate your marking and make a more accurate decision about what to mark in the next chapter.

MARK HEADINGS

As you read your textbook, mark the headings and subheadings. If you're highlighting, highlight them as well. If you're underlining, you may want to draw a box around the headings. Typically, when students review their marked textbooks, they read only what they've marked. It's incredible, but many students never even look at the headings or subheadings as they review. Do you? The headings contain the most important information in the text. They present the topics to which all of the other marking refers. You wouldn't think of reviewing your lecture notes without looking at the headings, would you?

MARK MAIN IDEAS

The second most important information to mark is the main idea statements. Main ideas are the general statements that the author makes about the topic. The main idea statement, or topic sentence, is generally found in the first or second sentence of a paragraph. Unfortunately, many students overlook these statements because they don't contain a specific fact or buzzword. Look back at the text selection in Figure 8.1. Which sentence in each of the paragraphs states the main idea? If you said the first sentence, you were right for paragraphs 1 and 2. You may be having a hard time finding the main idea sentence in paragraph 3. That's because paragraph 3 doesn't contain a *stated main idea.* Sometimes authors don't directly state the main ideas; they only imply them. The *implied* (unstated) *main idea* in paragraph 3 is that the oceans provide other important resources to Earth. You'll find that it doesn't take much practice to learn to pick out the main idea statements in most of your textbooks. When they are unstated, you can figure them out from the information given in the paragraph. Ask yourself: What point is the author making here? Rereading your text marking should help you identify the stated main idea or figure out the implied main idea.

FOCUS ON SUPPORTING DETAILS

As you read and mark, you also should focus on definitions, examples, enumerations, facts and statistics, and signal words. Definitions are very important, and you'll need to understand what the technical terms in the chapter mean both to comprehend the text material and to answer test questions. You can highlight definitions as you read, or you may want to copy them onto index cards so that you can begin to learn them. Put the word on the front and the definition on the back, and then practice them out loud as you would with flash cards.

Examples are included in many textbooks because they help you understand abstract theories or concepts by bringing them down to a more concrete level. Examples are sometimes rather long and detailed or are set off in small print or in boxes, so students often view them as extraneous (outside or unrelated) information. However, examples can be critical to your understanding of the more abstract information in the text. You don't have to mark every word in the example; instead, mark just enough to see the connection between the example and the information to which it refers.

Lists or enumerations should always be marked. They may span several paragraphs or even several pages, but a main idea sentence will let you know what you should look for in a list. For example, the main idea sentence may state that there were three main adaptations that the vertebrates made. As you read, you should look for these adaptations so that you can mark all three.

Facts and statistics also are worth marking because they typically support the main ideas that the author is making and often end up on tests. Finally, it's important to mark signal words like *however, on the other hand,* and *but.* These *signal words* or transitions indicate that the author has shifted direction from positive to negative points. Leaving them out can result in misinterpretations during later review.

HOW MUCH SHOULD YOU MARK?

Now that you have a good idea of what to mark, it's important to discuss how much you should mark. It may sound as though you'll need to mark everything on the page, but don't panic. Even when you mark all the important information in a section, you'll still be able to condense the material. Learning to mark the right amount of text material is critical to effective marking. You should mark enough information so that you'll be able to review for an exam without ever reading any of the unmarked text again.

MARK MEANINGFUL PHRASES

When you identify information that you think is important, you should mark *meaningful phrases* rather than just key words. You can either mark a portion of the sentence, a phrase, or clause, or you can create your own meaningful phrase by linking key words together. Look at Sample 3 in Figure 8.3. Marking only the buzzwords (see Sample 1) really doesn't provide you with enough information from which to study. Mark enough of the sentence so that 1 month later it will still make sense. Fortunately, it's even easier to mark meaningful phrases in your textbook than it is to write them during a lecture because you have plenty of time to decide what you want to highlight.

AVOID UNDERMARKING

Sometimes students don't really understand how to mark a textbook, and they end up *marking too little* of the information. As you read, it may seem like marking only the important buzzwords in the text is effective marking. However, without the related details, the marking lacks meaning during later review (see Sample 1). Only the key words have been marked. Read only the highlighted information. Does this marking make sense? Has this student marked all of the important information in the selection?

Another type of undermarking results from *marking too selectively.* Some students do mark meaningful phrases when they mark. However, they miss important information by trying to pick out only one or two important points in each paragraph or headed section. These students may be trying to follow rules for how much to mark; they may have heard or read that you should mark only one main point in each paragraph or that you shouldn't mark more than 20 percent of the words on a page. In Sample 2 of Figure 8.3, the student marked only two pieces of information in the paragraph. Are these the only things you would have marked? Many students

FIGURE 8.3

• • • • • • • • • • • • • • •

Samples of Text Marking

Sample 1: Marking Too Little

The largest and most magnificent of all the pyramids was built under King Khufu. Constructed at Giza around 2540 B.C.E., this famous Great Pyramid covers thirteen acres, measures 756 feet at each side of its base, and stands 481 feet high. Its four sides are almost precisely oriented to the four points of the compass. The interior included a grand gallery to the burial chamber, which was built of granite with a lidless sarcophagus for the pharaoh's body. The Great Pyramid still stands as a visible symbol of the power of the Egyptian kings and the spiritual conviction that underlay Egyptian society. No pyramid built later ever matched its size or splendor.

Sample 2: Marking Too Selectively

The largest and most magnificent of all the pyramids was built under King Khufu. Constructed at Giza around 2540 B.C.E., this famous Great Pyramid covers thirteen acres, measures 756 feet at each side of its base, and stands 481 feet high. Its four sides are almost precisely oriented to the four points of the compass. The interior included a grand gallery to the burial chamber, which was built of granite with a lidless sarcophagus for the pharaoh's body. The Great Pyramid still stands as a visible symbol of the power of the Egyptian kings and the spiritual conviction that underlay Egyptian society. No pyramid built later ever matched its size or splendor.

Sample 3: Marking Meaningful Phrases

The largest and most magnificent of all the pyramids was built under King Khufu. Constructed at Giza around 2540 B.C.E., this famous Great Pyramid covers thirteen acres, measures 756 feet at each side of its base, and stands 481 feet high. Its four sides are almost precisely oriented to the four points of the compass. The interior included a grand gallery to the burial chamber, which was built of granite with a lidless sarcophagus for the pharaoh's body. The Great Pyramid still stands as a visible symbol of the power of the Egyptian kings and the spiritual conviction that underlay Egyptian society. No pyramid built later ever matched its size or splendor.

Source: William J. Duiker and Jackson J. Spielvogel, *World History*, 3d ed. (Belmont, CA: Wadsworth, 2001), pp. 19–20.

miss test questions, not because they don't study, but rather because their marking is too selective so they don't study *all* of the important information.

AVOID OVERMARKING

Overmarking can be just as bad as undermarking. If you mark everything on a page or mark whole sentences you aren't forcing yourself to think about the con-

MARK YOUR TEXT. Many students have difficulty writing in their textbooks. After years of being told not to write in books, it's difficult to actually do it. But it's an important strategy that saves time and improves your comprehension.

AVOID THE USED-BOOK TRAP. If at all possible, buy new texts for your classes. Many students who buy used texts rely on previous highlighting or notes that already exist in the text. It's very tempting, but it leads to passive reading. If you must buy used books, search for texts with little or no marking already in them.

DON'T OVERLOOK "EXTERNAL" TEXT MATERIAL. Some important information is found outside the regular body of the text. You need to read and mark any definitions for technical terms, even if they're in the lefthand margin. Don't omit information included in charts, graphs, and other diagrams. The information under photos, in footnotes, and in boxed features is also important to your understanding of the material.

MONITOR YOUR TEXT MARKING. You need to pause every so often (at the end of a paragraph, headed section, or page) and monitor your marking. If you look back and notice that you didn't mark anything or marked everything on the page, you probably need to go back and read it again. Your marking is a good indicator of whether or not you understood the material and your level of attention to it.

RE-MARK USED TEXTBOOKS. If you're forced to purchase a used textbook, you still should do your own marking. If the text is highlighted in yellow, you could use blue. If it's underlined, you could highlight. What someone else marked may not be what your professor will test on. Would you rely on a stranger's lecture notes?

MARK MATH AND SCIENCE TEXT-BOOKS. Box or highlight all formulas, as well as any problems that you want to review. Be sure you also mark the text material that explains or discusses that formula or problem. A lot of students ignore the prose material that's included in math and science texts. This material is as important as or perhaps even more important than the problems themselves.

MARK YOUR LITERATURE BOOKS. You can mark short stories, poetry, novels, and plays as you read. Instead of looking for main ideas and supporting details, look for lines that contain themes, major plot events, key information about the characters, examples of foreshadowing or irony, and so on. Marginal notes are especially effective for literary works.

PHOTOCOPY AND MARK OUTSIDE READINGS. Many professors assign reserved or library readings as part of the course material. Often one or two copies are available on reserve in the library for students to read. You may choose to read the articles and take notes on them. You could also copy them (if time on campus is tight) and highlight them as you read. Whatever you do, be sure to review the material before the exam.

tent of the material. Many times, overmarking is a signal that you aren't reading actively. If you mark everything, you aren't actively involved in making decisions about what's important or what isn't. Marking too much also reduces your chances of reviewing the text material before the exam. If you haven't condensed the text, you may be discouraged from reviewing it because there's just too much to reread.

HOW TO REVIEW YOUR TEXT MARKING

The most important reason for marking your textbook is to prepare it for later review. You may think that if you read the material carefully and spend lots of time studying it, you shouldn't have to highlight, underline, or even take notes. For most students, however, this is not the case. Even if you were to spend hours reciting and reviewing the information in one chapter of your textbook, you probably wouldn't remember very much of that information by the time you had to take the exam. Although you'll be able to remember "learned" material longer than material you read or hear only once, you still won't remember enough of it by test time. If you mark your text as you read it, it'll be much easier to review the material before your exam. You can review your text material by re-marking, taking notes, predicting quiz questions, and reciting.

RE-MARK YOUR TEXT

One of the most common methods of reviewing for exams is to reread highlighted or underlined material. Unfortunately, most students do this in a rather passive manner. They quickly scan the lines of marked text, assuming that the information somehow will be absorbed into their memory. Think about the last time you studied for a test. How did you review the text material?

To conduct an effective review, you need to remain actively involved in your reading. This means you should re-mark your textbook as you review. By holding a marker (or pen or pencil) in your hand, you're defining your reading activity. By planning to re-mark the text material, you're forcing yourself to read actively, to make decisions about the material that you marked before. As you reread the marked selections, you can determine whether or not the information is important enough to review again. Remember, the first time you read the chapter, everything was new to you. At that time, many things may have seemed important. After having completed the chapter, worked through text questions or a study guide, and listened to the professor's lecture, you should be able to reduce the text material even more.

There are a number of ways to re-mark your text. If you used yellow highlighting when you first read the chapter, you can use a different color for re-marking. (If some of the information is already learned, you need not re-mark it.) You might also underline, checkmark, star, or even bracket the information that you want to review again. If you decide to reread your marking a third time, re-mark the text again. Each time you reread the text material, you should re-mark it in order to remain actively involved and to further condense what you need to review again. Look at the text marking from a political science text (Figure 8.4). The material that's highlighted indicates the first marking, and the underlining indicates the re-marked material. Read only the underlined material. Does it effectively represent the key information in the selection?

TAKE NOTES ON YOUR MARKING

Taking notes as you review your marking is an excellent way—perhaps the best way—to remain actively involved in your reading. Not only does taking notes force you to decide whether the information is important, but also it requires you to condense the information and write it down. If you put the information in your own words, you also are using higher-level thinking skills to "translate"

FIGURE 8.4

• • • • • • • • •

Example of
Re-Marked Text
Material

The Class Bias of Congress

Technically, the requirements for becoming a senator or representative are minor. A representative must be twenty-five years old, a citizen for seven years, and an inhabitant of the state (but not necessarily the district) from which he or she is elected. A senator must be at least thirty years old, have been a citizen for nine years, and be an inhabitant of the state.

The pool of eligibles, however, is considerably narrower. In reality, Congress is far from a cross section. In fact, it is a remarkably homogeneous body, socially and economically. There are few blacks and few women. There are few members of the working class. Indeed, the wealth of senators and representatives is substantially higher than the national median income (about one-fourth of the members of the Senate are millionaires). Most have high-prestige occupations, such as law. Members of Congress are also older than the adult population as a whole.

Text material from T. Dye, H. Zeigler, and S. Lichter, *American Politics in the Media Age,* 4th ed. (Pacific Grove, CA: Brooks/Cole, 1992), pp. 195–196.

the text material. In addition, note taking allows you to organize the information so that it's more meaningful to you. You decide what to write down and how to arrange the information so that it makes sense to you. Finally, if you take notes, you can condense the critical information in a lengthy text chapter into a few sheets of notebook paper. In Chapter 9, you'll learn many new strategies and techniques for taking notes from text material. For now though, write the heading next to the margin, skip a space, and indent slightly to list each of the details.

PREDICT QUIZ QUESTIONS

After you finish reading and marking your text chapter, go back and review the important information by predicting and writing quiz questions in the margin. You can use these same questions to review for exams, of course, but they'll provide you with an excellent way to reinforce and learn the information before you even walk into class for the lecture.

There are three basics steps involved in predicting quiz questions. First, go back and reread the highlighted material for the first paragraph, identify an important point that you want to remember, and turn it into a question (see Step 1 in Figure 8.5). Next, write the question directly across from the information, in the margin of the textbook (see Step 2). Be sure you write questions that have stated answers in the text and not yes or no answers. Finally, underline the answer to the question in your text (see Step 3).

The more questions that you write, the more repetition you get on the material and the more you can test your learning. It's a good idea to write both broad and narrow questions. Write a broad question for each heading or subheading and then as many specific questions as you can in the space available. If your text doesn't have wide margins, you can still use this strategy. Write the questions on a long strip of paper (about 3 inches wide), which you line up with the top of the text page. Keep the question strip in the text on that page for later review (note the page number on each strip). You can also write each question on the front of an index card and the answer on the back (note the page number on the back, too).

Predicting quiz questions in the margin of your text provides you with at least three more interactions with the text material. You reread the highlighted material, think about its importance, turn it into a question, and then underline the answer. Of course, when you use the questions to check your learning, you're getting even more practice with the material. When I ask my students at the end of the semester to list the one strategy that they think has helped them the most, more than 25 percent list predicting quiz questions.

FIGURE 8.5

• • • • • • • • • • • • • • •

Example of Predicted Questions

STEP 2:
Write
question →

*What are the six
characteristics of goals?*

STEP 3:
Underline answer →

*Why should goals be
self chosen?*

*What happens if goals
are too challenging?*

*What factor can help
you determine how
challenging to make your
goals?*

*What are moderately
challenging goals?*

*What is another word
for realistic?*
*What is an example of
an unrealistic goal?*

CHARACTERISTICS OF GOALS

To be both useful and motivating, the goals you set must have some important characteristics. Your goals should be self-chosen, moderately challenging, realistic, measurable, specific, and positive. ← STEP 1: Identify information

1. **Goals should be self-chosen.** Goals that are set by your parents, teachers, or friends may not always work for you. You need to determine or choose your own goals; *you* need to decide what you want to accomplish. If you set your own goals, you will be more motivated to achieve them.

2. **Goals should be moderately challenging.** You probably were told to set high or even exceptionally high goals for yourself in college; you may have been told to "shoot for the stars" or "go for straight As." In fact, this may not be the best advice. If your goal is to achieve all As during your first semester in college, you may be disappointed. As soon as you "lose your A" in one class, you may feel that you failed to achieve your goal, and you may be tempted to give up.

   One way to set moderately challenging goals is to consider what you have done in the past. Of course, everyone is different, but high school grades are fairly good predictors of college success. Why were you successful in some classes yet unsuccessful in others? You may have been more motivated, so you may have worked harder. Of course, if you didn't work very hard in high school, you can do better in college if you choose to apply yourself; study skills can make a big difference. Even so, you should set goals that are moderately challenging—goals that will require you to achieve more than you did before but will not place undue pressure on you. Goals can always be revised if you discover you can achieve more than you originally set out to accomplish.

3. **Goals should be realistic.** Think about whether your goals are attainable. It would be unrealistic to expect to get a B or better in Calculus if your math background is very weak and your high school grades in math were never higher than a C. To set realistic goals, you must carefully evaluate your chances of achieving each goal. Using the five-step approach to setting goals (discussed later in this chapter) can help you make this decision.

HOW TO EVALUATE YOUR TEXT MARKING

Each time you evaluate your marking, you should consider whether you have marked the material in a meaningful way, whether you have condensed the text material, and whether the method you used was efficient and effective. You can test your marking before an exam and again after the exam. Each evaluation will give you more information about how well you're marking your textbook.

BE SURE YOUR MARKING MAKES SENSE

The first way to test your marking is to see whether it makes sense. Look back at a marked page in one of your textbooks. Read only the words that you marked. Does the information make sense? Now choose a page that you marked more than 2 weeks ago. Do you still understand the information that you marked? Reread the entire page. Does the marking retain the meaning of the selection? If it doesn't, check to see if you marked too little (only key words) or too selectively. Repeat this activity with material that you marked a month ago. If your marking doesn't make sense or include all of the important information in the text, you won't be able to properly prepare for your exam.

GET FEEDBACK ON YOUR MARKING

Another way to test your marking is to compare your marked section of text to a classmate's marking. Read your classmate's marked page. How does it compare to yours? Does it make more sense than yours? If it does, compare the marked information. You may find that your classmate included more information or was better able to create meaningful phrases than you were. Talk about why each of you chose to include or leave out specific information or words.

You can also evaluate your text marking by talking to your professor or to someone in your campus learning or tutoring center. Take your textbook with you and ask the person whether you're picking out the important information in the selection. If you aren't hitting the right material, ask your professor or learning center staff member to mark a portion of a page of text for you. Then you mark a section, while that person observes. Stop and ask questions about anything you aren't sure about. If you're just getting started marking a textbook, this additional feedback can let you know whether you're using effective strategies.

TEST YOUR MARKING AFTER AN EXAM

You also can test your marking after an exam using the *T Method*. That's often the time that students appreciate how much they condensed the material for review. Take your textbook with you when you go to take your exam. As soon as the exam is over, rush out into the hall, find a quiet corner, and sit down. Turn to any chapter that was heavily tested upon. Begin to reread that chapter. Read the unmarked and the marked areas of the page. Every time you come across something that was on the test, put a "T" in the margin of your book.

After you read through about a half of the chapter, stop and look at where the Ts appear. How many of them are in highlighted or marked areas? How many are in unmarked areas? If all the Ts are in the marked areas, you did a good job of marking. You were able to recognize as important the same pieces of information that the professor thought were important. By marking those points, you identified them for later review. If, on the other hand, a number of your Ts are in unmarked areas, you probably marked too little or too selectively as you read the chapter. Because those pieces of information were unmarked, you probably didn't review them before the test. Were you able to answer those questions correctly on the test?

SUMMARY

Marking your textbook increases your comprehension, your understanding, of the material because it promotes active reading. Because many students don't really know how to mark their textbooks, they tend to mark too little, too selectively, or mark almost everything. Strategic text marking involves thinking about what's important, deciding what to mark, and then using a simple method to identify that information. Reading to the end of the paragraph before you begin to highlight, underline, or take marginal notes will help you mark more efficiently and effectively. Avoid complex marking systems; you may find that you spend more time thinking about how to mark than about what you're reading and marking. Marking your text also allows you to condense the material for later review. Mark meaningful phrases and include main ideas as well as supporting details (much as you do when you take lecture notes). Learning how much to mark takes time and practice, so monitor your text marking after your first exam. If you missed a lot of questions because you never even reviewed the appropriate material, you may need to mark more information. Re-marking your text, taking notes, and predicting quiz questions are just a few ways to stay actively involved as you review your text marking.

1. Go to the *Orientation to College Learning* Web site and download one copy of Activity 8–1 from the Activities Packet. After marking the text excerpt, compare your marking with the marking in Figure 8.1.

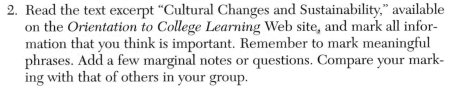 2. Read the text excerpt "Cultural Changes and Sustainability," available on the *Orientation to College Learning* Web site, and mark all information that you think is important. Remember to mark meaningful phrases. Add a few marginal notes or questions. Compare your marking with that of others in your group.

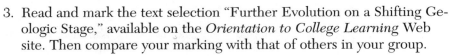 3. Read and mark the text selection "Further Evolution on a Shifting Geologic Stage," available on the *Orientation to College Learning* Web site. Then compare your marking with that of others in your group.

 4. Choose a selection from one of your textbooks that you read and marked at least a week ago. Re-mark the text material. How did you re-mark? How much more were you able to condense the information?

 5. Compare your text marking for the P2R section of Chapter 7 with the marking of the other members in your group. As a group, develop an "ideal" marking for the selection. How effective was your marking compared with the ideal? Did you include the key information? Did you use meaningful phrases? Did you condense the selection to its essence? What changes do you plan to make?

 6. Read and highlight the text material from Activity 3. Predict and write quiz questions in the margin and then underline the answer to each. Compare your marking, questions, and underlined answers with others in your group. How closely did your marking match that of the others in the group? How many of your questions were the same or similar to those of the others in the group? Did this activity increase your understanding and memory of the information?

 7. After your next exam, use the T Method to evaluate your marking. Write a paragraph explaining what you found. What do you plan to do differently the next time?

 8. If you're using InfoTrac College Edition, do a search on the topic *stress management* or choose a topic of your own. Locate two articles on the topic and print them. Read one of the articles and mark it using the strategies that you learned in this chapter. Read the other article

without marking it. Which article was easier to understand? What did you learn from each of the articles? Did you make a list of the key points? How do you plan to use this information to relieve some of the stress you are now experiencing?

9. Think of three examples of how you've applied what you learned in this chapter. Choose one strategy and describe how you applied it to your other course work using the Journal Entry Form that's located on the *Orientation to College Learning* Web site. Consider the following questions as you complete your entry. Why did you use this strategy? What did you do? How did it work? How did it affect your performance on the task? How did this approach compare with your previous approach? What changes would you make the next time you use this strategy?

10. Now that you've completed Chapter 8, take a few minutes to repeat the "Where Are You Now?" activity, located on the *Orientation to College Learning* Web site. What changes did you make as a result of reading this chapter? How are you planning to apply what you've learned in this chapter?

Review Questions

Terms You Should Know:

Complex marking systems	Marking too selectively	Stated main ideas
Highlighting	Meaningful phrases	T Method
Implied main ideas	Overmarking	Underlining
Marginal notes	Signal words	Undermarking
Marking too little		

Completion: Fill in the blank to complete each of the following statements.

1. You should read to the end of the _____ before you begin marking your text.

2. Complex marking systems can interfere with your _____.

3. One way to review your text marking is to _____ quiz questions in the margin of your text.

4. Marking only one sentence per paragraph is referred to as marking too _____.

5. When you are marking your text, you should read, _____, _____, and mark.

Multiple Choice: Circle the letter of the best answer for each of the following questions. Be sure to underline key words and eliminate wrong answers.

6. _____ main ideas are not directly stated in the text.
   A. Applied
   B. Implied
   C. Comprehensive
   D. Critical

7. Which of the following is not a disadvantage of underlining?
   A. It takes longer than highlighting.
   B. It interferes with your comprehension.
   C. You don't get a second reading.
   D. It can be overlooked when rewriting.

Short Answer–Essay: On a separate sheet, answer each of the following questions.

8. What are the three main reasons you should mark your text?

9. Why do some students have difficulty marking their textbooks? What should they do differently?

10. How should students evaluate their text marking?

Chapter 9

TAKING TEXT NOTES

"I now take text notes after I have completed reading the chapter. I don't wait until the night before the exam as I had done in the past. When I take text notes, I focus on the main points and ideas that are most important. I can relate my text notes to my lecture notes for comparison, which helps me learn the material better. I have found that taking text notes keeps me very actively involved in my reading."

Michelle Klimchock
Student

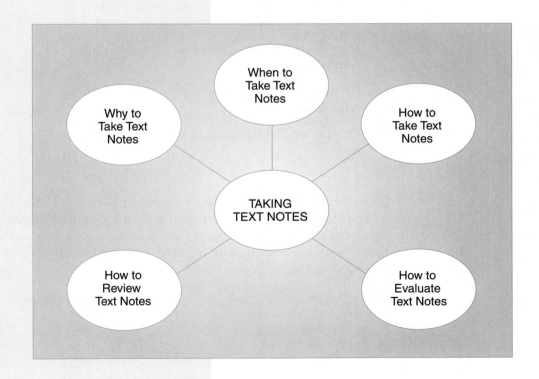

Where Are You Now?

Take a few minutes to answer *yes* or *no* to the following questions.

	YES	NO
1. Do you take notes on textbook material after you have highlighted the chapter or section?	____	____
2. Do you take text notes when you read the chapter for the first time?	____	____
3. Do you read the whole paragraph before you begin to take notes?	____	____
4. Do you evaluate your text notes after an exam?	____	____
5. Do you usually copy information from the text in the same wording that the author used in the book?	____	____
6. Do you recite your text notes when you review for an exam?	____	____
7. Do you create maps when you take notes on the textbook material?	____	____
8. Are your text notes a good summary of the text material?	____	____
9. Do you tend to write down only key words when you take notes?	____	____
10. Do you use formal outlining to take notes on your text?	____	____

TOTAL POINTS ____

Give yourself 1 point for each *yes* answer to questions 1, 3, 4, 6, 7, and 8 and 1 point for each *no* answer to questions 2, 5, 9, and 10. Now total up your points. A low score indicates that you need some help in taking notes on text material. A high score indicates that you are already using many good note-taking strategies.

WHY TO TAKE TEXT NOTES

Taking notes on text material is the most effective method for becoming an active reader. Note taking keeps you actively involved in the text material. It also helps you condense the information that you'll need to review before the exam. Finally, taking text notes allows you to develop a system of organization that is distinctly yours—a system that you design and that makes sense to you. This activity helps you clarify the meaning of the material and aids in your retention and retrieval of information.

PROMOTES ACTIVE READING

Taking text notes keeps you actively involved as you read because you know you'll have to write something down. It provides you with a purpose for reading that can help keep you alert and focused on the material. Note taking keeps you involved in what the author is saying because you have to make decisions about what's important—you need to identify both the main points and the supporting details. One of keys to taking good text notes is writing the information in your own words (as much as possible) in a format that's easy to study and remember. You have to think about the material, decide what's important, "translate" what the author is saying into words that make sense to you, and restructure the information in a new, easier-to-learn format. As you take text notes you increase your involvement with the text material and strengthen your memory of it.

INCREASES YOUR COMPREHENSION

Note taking also increases your comprehension of the material. To write the information in your own words, you have to analyze what the author has said and relate it to what you already know about the topic. This interaction with the text increases your level of comprehension of the material and your understanding of the concepts and ideas that are presented. Reading, thinking about the material, and then writing it in your own words also gives you more repetition on the material. This built-in review of the important information helps you understand it better. If you've already used the S-RUN-R reading/study system, which was described in Chapter 7, you know that the note-taking step helps to reinforce the important information in the material. Note taking requires you to use a number of active strategies that lead to increased comprehension.

SERVES AS A COMPREHENSION MONITORING SYSTEM

Note taking can also serve as an excellent *comprehension monitoring system.* Note taking provides you with feedback about how well you're concentrating on and understanding what you're reading. If you can't recall the important points to write down, you may not have been reading actively— you may have been daydreaming or thinking about something else. In addition, if you can't put the information into your own words, it could be a signal that you didn't really understand what you just read. You may need to reread the material or ask your professor, teaching assistant, or tutor to explain the information in that section. Keeping tabs on your reading can help you stay focused on the material as you read and can let you know when comprehension has broken down.

CONDENSES THE INFORMATION

Another reason for taking notes on textbook material is to condense the information for later review. You can condense the text material both by including only the key points in your notes and by writing the material in meaningful phrases. If you take text notes, you won't have to read the chapter again when you prepare for an exam. As you condense the material, you also have an opportunity to organize it in a way that makes sense to you. Your text notes, like your edited lecture notes, will provide you with a condensed version of the important information that you need to learn.

ORGANIZES THE INFORMATION

Unlike highlighting or underlining, taking text notes allows you to restructure and organize the information in a way that makes sense to you. When you highlight or underline your textbook, you're still operating inside the author's organizational structure. When you take notes, however, you can create an organizational structure of your own. Some note-taking strategies also force you to restructure the material in ways that show the relationships within the material. If you use some of the mapping and charting techniques that are described later in the chapter, you can organize the information into a visual display that clearly shows how the information is connected. This adds additional cues that can lead to improved memory of the material.

WHEN TO TAKE TEXT NOTES

There are benefits to taking notes at different points in your reading and study of the textbook. You can take notes when you first read the chapter, after the lecture, at the end of the week, or before the exam.

WHEN YOU FIRST READ THE CHAPTER

Some students take notes as they read the chapter instead of highlighting or underlining. Although note taking is a more active method, it is very time-consuming. If you try to take notes the first time you read the chapter, you may find that you write down more information than you'll need. After all, all the information will be new to you, and everything may seem important. After reading the entire chapter and taking notes on the lecture, you'll find that you can be more selective in what you write down. If you already have covered a section of the chapter in the lecture and have all the important information in your lecture notes, there's no need to write it all out again in your text notes. If you highlight the text when you first read it and then take notes afterward, you'll save time and have a better set of text notes. If you're using the S-RUN-R reading/study system, for example, you already may have discovered that taking notes after highlighting or underlining helps you condense the information even more.

AFTER THE LECTURE

You may prefer to take text notes right after the lecture. In this way, you can condense the information in the text while editing your lecture notes. If your professor's lectures follow the text fairly closely, you can fill in information that you may have missed during the lecture and at the same time note important points that were never touched on in class. It's not a good idea, though, to add all the additional text information to your lecture notes. If your professor tests mostly on lecture material, you want to spend most of your time studying your lecture notes. Instead, write your text notes in another notebook or on looseleaf notebook paper so that you can lay your text notes and your lecture notes out side by side when you're studying.

AT THE END OF THE WEEK

You may find that taking text notes at the end of the week serves as a good way of reviewing the information that you read (and marked) and that you took notes on during the lecture. At the end of the week, the material probably will be more familiar to you because you've had a chance to read, listen, discuss, edit your lecture notes, and think about the information. At that point, you should be able to take more selective and more organized notes on the text material. Follow along in your lecture notes as you take your text notes to avoid duplicating information.

WHEN YOU PREPARE FOR THE EXAM

Another good time to take your text notes is when you're preparing for your exam. Instead of just reading over the highlighted or underlined text material, take notes on it. By the time you're ready to prepare for the exam, you already may have learned a lot of the information that you originally highlighted or underlined. Not only will you save time by waiting to take notes, but you'll also benefit from the active review that requires you to determine what you still need to learn. Writing down this information will help you learn it, and allows you to condense what you need to study for the exam. Of course, you still need to practice the information in your notes by reciting it.

HOW TO TAKE TEXT NOTES

There are many different ways to take notes on text material. Some of the more useful methods are making written notes in the margin of the text, outlining, taking modified-block notes, or summarizing. You may also find that mapping and charting text material helps you learn and recall it more effectively than written notes. In this section, you'll learn when and how to use each of these note-taking techniques. Try each method as you do your own reading. Then decide which one works best for you.

WRITTEN NOTES

Taking written notes is probably the most common method students use for taking notes from text material. You already may be making notes in the margin of your text as you read. These marginal notes help you focus your reading and can serve as recall cues for your highlighting. Some students prefer to take notes outside of the text (on an index card or sheet of paper) in outline, modified-block, or summary form.

Outlining

One popular method of taking notes is outlining. If you want to use *formal outlining* to take your notes, you can use the author's organization to save time. Refer to the table of contents at the beginning of the book to find the main headings to use in your outline. These may be the chapter subdivisions or the main headings. Use Roman numerals (I, II, III, IV, and so on) for them in your outline.

Read and mark the first section in the chapter. Then write down the heading and use a capital letter (A, B, C, D) to indicate that it's a main point in your outline. Go back and jot down any other important information that you want to include. Number these points using Arabic numerals (1, 2, 3, and so on). If you wish, you can further break down your outline and indicate subpoints with lowercase letters (a, b, c). Dividing the material into main points and subpoints helps you condense and organize it for study.

Although formal outlining is useful, informal outlining is more efficient for taking notes (Figure 9.1). If you've been using the outline method for taking lecture notes, you already are familiar with the basic format for informally outlining text material. When you take notes on your text, you can rely on the author's organization or you can create your own. You can use the chapter subdivisions as your main points. You don't have to use every heading as a main point; some of them may be combined or omitted. Write the heading next to the left margin, go to the next line, and then indent to indicate supporting information. You don't need to use any numbers or letters in your *informal outline*. Don't forget, your outline will be much more helpful if you write meaningful phrases instead of copying entire sentences.

Block Notes

Some students prefer using the block method for taking text notes. If you already are using the block method to take lecture notes, you may find that it's just as effective for taking your text notes. The *block method* allows you to group all the important details for each heading rather compactly. Start by writing the heading next to the margin. Indent slightly on the next line and begin noting the details in meaningful phrases. Separate each detail by using a slash (/) or a dash (—). One advantage of block notes is your ability to focus totally on the text material. You don't have to spend any time thinking about where to write the information or how to label it. It's so easy—you write the heading and then jot down all of the important details.

FIGURE 9.1

● ● ● ● ● ● ● ● ●

Sample Notes in
Informal Outline
Form

Benthic Communities
  Rocky Intertidal Communities
    Intertidal zone
      land between highest and lowest marshes
      hundreds of species
    Problems living there
      wave shock — force of crashing waves
      temperature change
      ice grinding against shoreline
        higher altitudes
      intense sunlight
        in tropics
    Reasons for diversity
      large quantities of food available
        strong currents keep nutrients stirred
      large number of habitats available
        high, salty splash pools
        cool, dark crevices
        provide hiding places
          rest places
          attachment sites
          mating nooks
  Sand Beach and Cobble Communities
    Three types
      Sand beaches
        forbidding place for small organisms

The block method, however, may not be the best method for taking text notes. If you're a visual learner, you may have difficulty picturing the information in your notes because the information is crowded together, rather than spaced out in an easy-to-recall format.

Modified-Block Notes

The *modified-block method* may be even more effective. In this case you list all the important details directly under each other. Some students put a dash in front of each meaningful phrase, whereas others simply indent the list slightly. Look at the sample of modified-block notes in Figure 9.2. The information is well organized and includes sufficient detail to make it useful for later study. If there are too many details to list under just one heading, you need to create ad-

FIGURE 9.2

• • • • • • • • •

Sample Notes in
Modified-Block
Form

Levels of Depression

Depressive Episodes
— mildest form
— lasts several weeks or several months
— little pleasure — feel empty or worthless
— headaches, difficulty sleeping
— comes & goes without warning
— triggered by death or simple things
    (schedule change)
Dysthymic Disorder
— psychotic depression
— thought disorder
— more severe — can last a year or more
— occasional delusions
— psychomotor skills very slow
— no energy — want to stay in bed
— low risk of suicide but can be dangerous
— few friends, lonely, alone at home
Bipolar Disorder
— manic depression
— fluctuate back and forth
— similar to dysthymic but with manic
    episodes that alternate with depression
— manic episodes cause high energy
— thoughts flow quickly, get confused
— disappears (seems to) periodically

ditional headings or subheadings to organize the material in a way that makes it easier to study and learn.

Don't just copy the important information directly out of the textbook. If you force yourself to write meaningful phrases instead of whole sentences, you're more likely to put the information in your own words.

Summarizing

Some students prefer to summarize text information when taking notes. A *summary* is a condensed version of the information, generally written in sentence or paragraph form. If you decide to summarize your text information, you need to break down the chapter into shorter segments. You could write short summaries of each headed section or combine the information from several sections under a new heading that you create yourself. In any case, before you start writing your summary, read the entire section, think about what the author is saying, and decide what you think is important. Then write out the main points or key information in your own words. Of course, if you underline or highlight as you read the section, you may find that it's easier to focus on the key information to include in your summary.

Read the summary in Figure 9.3. Although Laura's summary is well written, it refers only to the key points made in the text; it doesn't contain the actual information. Many students make this same mistake when they begin writing summaries. Remember to include the actual points that the author is making. Don't just say that the text gives the reasons that you should mark your text—you need to list the reasons. "Vague" summaries are a common problem when students try to summarize an entire chapter in one or two paragraphs. However, some students make the same error even when dealing with shorter segments. (A better example is shown later in card A of Figure 9.4. It includes the main points and details contained in the text.)

End-of-chapter summaries found in many college textbooks only touch on the main concepts and ideas presented in the chapter. They don't include enough specific information to use them as a test review. However, as you learned in Chapter 7, reading the chapter summary is an important part of previewing your text.

FIGURE 9.3

• • • • • • • • •

Poor Example of a Summary

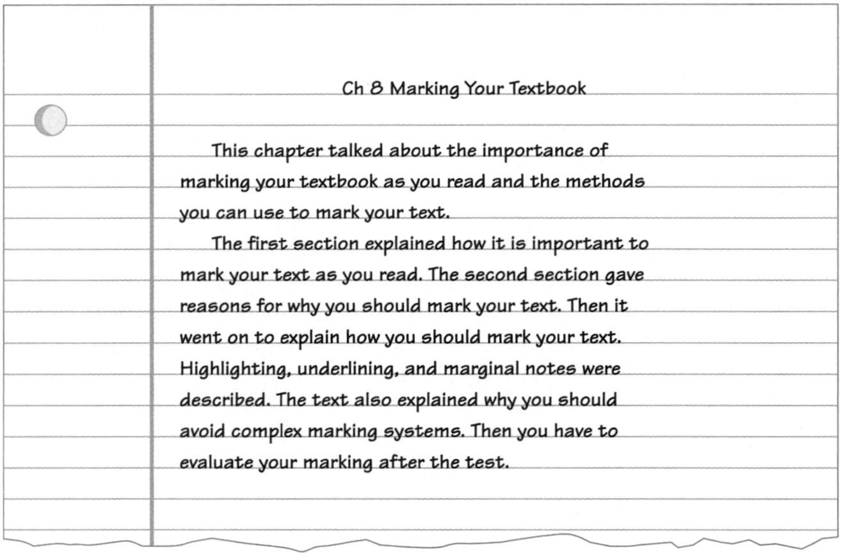

Ch 8 Marking Your Textbook

    This chapter talked about the importance of marking your textbook as you read and the methods you can use to mark your text.

    The first section explained how it is important to mark your text as you read. The second section gave reasons for why you should mark your text. Then it went on to explain how you should mark your text. Highlighting, underlining, and marginal notes were described. The text also explained why you should avoid complex marking systems. Then you have to evaluate your marking after the test.

Laura's Summary

Use Note Cards

Some students prefer to take notes on index cards rather than on notebook paper. As you'll see in later chapters, note cards or index cards can be used for many study techniques. They're especially effective for taking notes, though, because they make it easy to organize information and they're so easy to carry around. You can use note cards to organize all the important information on one particular heading or topic.

Center the heading at the top of the card and then jot down any important supporting information that you want to review. You may want to write a summary of the text material or take notes in the same way you would if you were writing notes on notebook paper. Look at the sample note cards in Figure 9.4. Card A summarizes the text information. Card B contains an infor-

FIGURE 9.4

• • • • • • • • •

Sample Note
Cards

> **Further Evolution**
>
> Major geologic events had an effect on land and sea life. During the Paleozoic Period the land masses Gondwana and Laurasia joined to form Pangea, a single world continent. All of the remaining surface of the Earth was covered by water — the Tethys Sea.
>
> As the continents collided, the overall diversity of species declined, and many habitats were lost. This resulted in a 96% reduction of marine species 240 million years ago. Climatic changes and changes in ocean currents affected all land & sea organisms.

Card A

> **Further Evolution**
>
> Major geologic events led to effects on evolution of life
> Paleozoic Pd - Gondwana & Laurasia → Pangea
>   (single world continent)
> rest of surface covered by Tethys Sea
> Collision of landmasses
>   1. habitats lost
>   2. diversity of life declined
>   3. reduced # species of marine animals by 96% (240 m yrs ago)
>   4. led to changes in climate & currents, which affected all lifeforms

Card B

mal outline on the same information. Which method do you think would work best for you?

MAPPING

Maps are visual displays of text information. They're a way of organizing the key information in the text into easy-to-read and easy-to-remember pictures or sketches. Although there are many different types of maps, only *line maps, hierarchical maps, and semantic webs,* will be described in this chapter. You may find that mapping is a great way to take notes. When you take exams, this strategy may help you recall the information that you learned because you can see a picture of it in your mind or remember how you set it up. Mapping is an even more active method than some of the ones we've discussed because you have to move outside the author's organizational framework and create your own.

Line or Wheel Maps

One of the easiest types of maps to create is the line or wheel map. A *line map* is a visual display of information drawn by adding lines or spokes that radiate out from a central hub. You already may be familiar with time lines from Chapter 3 (Time Management) and from history class. To create a line map for other types of text material, write the topic in the center of the paper and then add subordinate points on lines that radiate up, down, or out from it. Add supporting details by inserting lines that extend out from the previous lines. Many students like using line maps because they provide more space to write meaningful phrases.

You may need to create subheadings as you map the text information. The subheadings organize the information, separate the details into easier-to-remember chunks, and serve as additional cues to help you learn and retrieve the information. Christy created her own subheadings to better organize the text material in Figure 9.5. Take a few minutes and read a portion of the text excerpt that Christy used to create her map "Gender Stratification," available on the *Orientation to College Learning* Web site. As you will see, the author did not include the subheadings food source, social practices, and technology. Christy made some notes on the introductory material from the text at the top of her map. As you create your own line maps to take notes on text material, feel free to move outside of the author's organizational structure and create one that will make your map a well-organized study tool.

Hierarchical Maps

One of the most common forms of maps is the hierarchical map. *Hierarchical maps* provide a top-down display of information. You often see this form of map in science texts in the form of flowcharts or process charts. To create a hierarchical map, write the topic at the top of the page and put a box around it.

FIGURE 9.5

• • • • • • • • • • • • •

Christy's Line Map

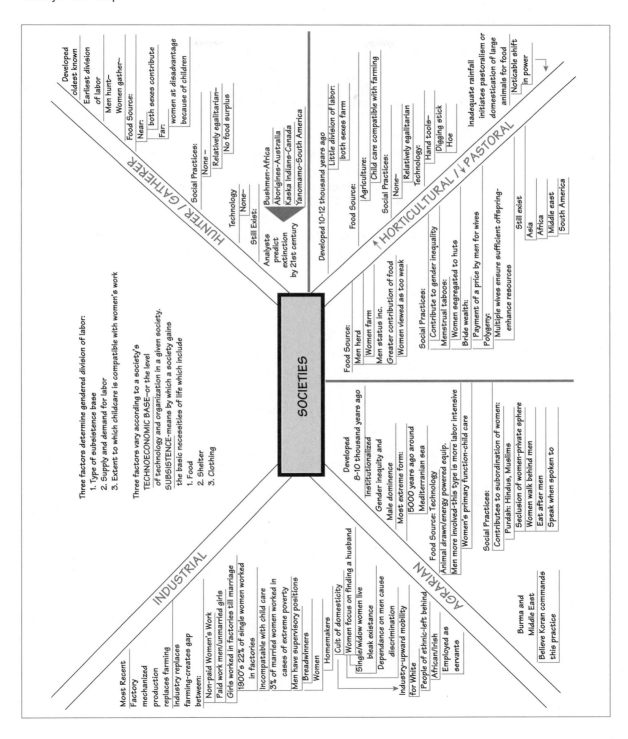

Then draw lines to indicate the subdivisions (the headings) and write and box each of them. You can then further divide each of these points into one or more subheadings and then add supporting points. Look at Figure 9.6, the hierarchical map that Wendy developed from the text material from a Special Education textbook. Look for the excerpt entitled "Chemically Dependent Youth" on the *Orientation to College Learning* Web site. You can see the natural progression from the main topic of the selection down to the supporting details.

Semantic Webs

One of the newest styles of mapping is the Semantic Web. Instead of using a top-down display, as in the hierarchical map, *Semantic Webs* radiate from a central focal point. There are four main components in a semantic web: the Core Question or Concept, the Web Strands, the Strand Supports, and the Strand Ties. The *Core Question* or *Concept* is the main focus of the text chapter or section. It may be the title of an article or chapter or the heading of the section that you decide to map. To start your web, write this word, phrase, or question in the center of a piece of paper and draw a circle or oval around it. The second component, the *Web*

FIGURE 9.6

• • • • • • • • • • • • • •

Wendy's Hierarchical Map

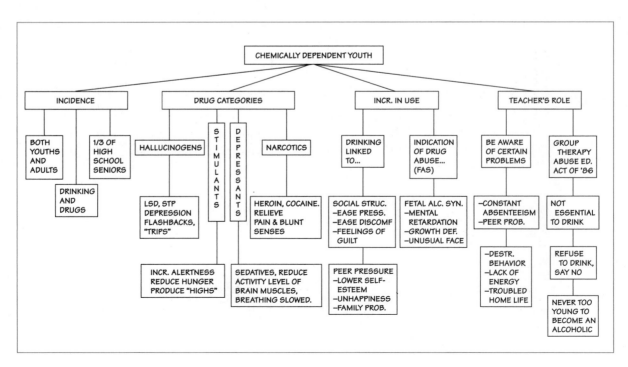

FIGURE 9.7

• • • • • • • • • • • • • • •

Kelly's Semantic Map

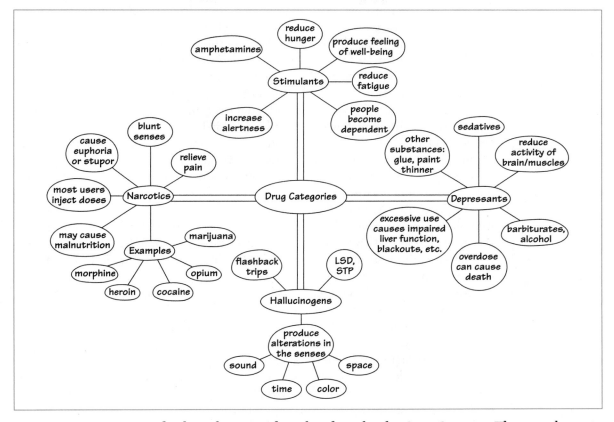

Strands, show the main ideas that describe the Core Concept. They are the main points that the author makes about the topic. In written notes, they would be the headings. They are joined to the Core Concept by lines that radiate from it. Circle each main point as well. The *Strand Supports* do just what their title implies; they support the Web Strands. They include the details that support the Web Strands. Finally, the *Strand Ties* are words or phrases that are written on the lines that connect some of the pieces of information. They define the relationships between the Core Concept, the Web Strands, and the Strand Supports.[1]

Look at Figure 9.7, the Semantic Web that Kelly produced for the "Chemically Dependent Youth" selection. Can you locate each of the components mentioned

---

[1]Adapted from G. Freeman and E. G. Reynolds, "Enriching Basal Reader Lessons with Semantic Webbing," *The Reading Teacher* 33 (1980): 677–684.

above? First, what is the Core Concept? If you look at the center of Kelly's web, you'll see that she used the phrase "Drug Categories." It also is easy to find the four Web Strands because Kelly used double lines to connect them to the center focal point. You may have noticed that Kelly used several levels of Strand Supports. She moved from "Narcotics" (a Web Strand) to "Examples" (a Strand Support) to "marijuana" (a detail supporting the Strand Support). Even though this last level of support was not in the "rules" for how to construct a Semantic Web, Kelly felt that the text information demanded further division. Don't leave out information you think is important just because it doesn't fit the formula for how to do the web. Instead, adapt the mapping technique to fit your text material. You can have second-level, third-level, and fourth-level strand supports if the text demands it. You may have noticed that Kelly didn't add Strand Ties to her map. She could have written "used to" on the line between "Narcotics" and "relieve pain," or "leads to" on the line that connects "Narcotics" to "blunt senses."

You probably will find that Strand Ties are useful for certain types of information but can be omitted at other times. After you complete your web, review the information that you noted. If you aren't sure how some of your information is related to the information connected to it, you may need to add Strand Ties to your map.

You may also find that color coding your maps can help you recall the information. Color coding will work on any type of map, but it's especially effective for semantic webs because you create "clusters" of information for each of the main ideas in the text material. You can either draw the ovals in color or use a highlighter or colored pencil to fill in each portion of the map. For example, you could color code all of the information related to narcotics orange, stimulants red, depressants blue, and hallucinogens green. Using a different color for each of the clusters in your map helps separate the details and provides you with an additional cue to trigger your memory of the material. It's important to use light colors if you're going to shade the information that you write—you still want to be able to read it clearly. For some material, you may find that the colors you choose are related to the material itself.

CHARTING

Another interesting method of note taking is charting. A *chart* is a graphic display of information that shows the similarities and differences of related information. You can't chart an entire chapter of a textbook, but you may be able to create a chart for several sections of a chapter. If you have a collection of topics or headings that are all related (types or forms of something), you may find that creating a chart helps you organize the information while noting the distinct similarities and differences of each topic.

To create a chart, first determine categories and headings. If you decided to chart the four drug categories from the excerpt on the Web site, you would write them along the left margin of your paper. The next step is not so easy. You need to read and think about the material in order to determine any areas of similarity among the topics.

Look at the example in Figure 9.8, which shows a portion of a *matrix*, a chart designed with rows and columns. Melissa listed the four periods of cognitive development down the left side of her chart and then looked carefully at the information in her text before determining the names of the categories. Since the text included information about the age, definition, development of skills and abilities, and key concepts or flaws for each period of cognitive development, she used those as the headings for the categories. If you were taking notes using written or mapping formats, these categories would be equivalent to subheadings that you would have created.

FIGURE 9.8

· · · · · · · · · · · · · · · ·

Melissa's Chart

Overview of Piaget's Stage Theory

Period	Age	Definition	Development	Key Concept or Flaw
Sensorimotor	birth to age 2	Ability to coordinate sensory inputs with motor actions	Symbolic thought Behavior dominated by innate reflexes	Key concept: Object permanence Recognizing that object continues to exist even when no longer visible
Preoperational	age 2 to age 7	Improve use of mental images Preoperational because of all the weaknesses	Development of symbolic thinking Not yet grasped concept of conservation: quantities remain constant regardless of shape or appearance	Key flaws: Centration: Focus on one part of problem Irreversibility: Inability to undo an action Egocentrism: Inability to share other's viewpoints Animism: Believe all things are living

TAKE NOTES IN YOUR OWN WORDS. Don't just copy the information in the text. By taking notes in your own words, you can further condense the material and make it more meaningful. You can also use your text notes to check your understanding of the material. If you can't put the material in your own words, you may not really understand it.

DON'T WRITE EVERYTHING YOU HIGHLIGHT. Your text notes should organize the material and include the most important information from the text. Remember, you want to condense the information. You don't need to write everything you mark. You should review your highlighting before the exam, too.

TAKE NOTES ON DIFFICULT MATERIAL ON INDEX CARDS. Writing your notes on index cards serves two purposes. First, you organize one headed section (or one specific topic) on each card and, second, you can carry them with you for quick reviews during work breaks, while commuting, and even before class.

ADD QUESTIONS TO NOTE CARDS. Take notes on the front of an index card for each headed section of your text material. Then write recall questions on the important material on the back. Study the material using the notes and then flip the cards over to self-test before class, a quiz, or an exam.

CREATE WORD CARDS. As you read (or even before you read) the chapter, make out a set of word cards for all of the new technical terminology. Write the word on the front of the card and the definition on the back (one per card). This will help improve your understanding of the terms and the text material. You can begin working on learning the definitions immediately.

TAKE NOTES ON LITERARY ASSIGNMENTS. Use a separate index card for each play, short story, or novel. Devise a list of categories of information that you want to record for each work. You may want to include the title, author, setting, theme, main characters, symbols, and a summary of the main plot line. Jot down any other important points that stand out and include your own reaction to what you read.

TAKE NOTES ON LIBRARY MATERIAL. Use note cards to take notes on outside reading material. Include the title of the article and the author at the top of your card and then take notes using one of the note-taking methods described in the chapter. Focus on the main ideas that are presented.

DON'T ELIMINATE MAPPING JUST BECAUSE IT'S NEW TO YOU. Mapping is a very effective technique for visual and kinesthetic learners. With a little practice, you may find that mapping is a very effective technique for learning course information. Try it a few times—you may find that you love it.

EXPAND CONCEPT MAPS. Many textbooks have concept maps at the beginning of every chapter. They serve as an overview of what the chapter is about. Copy the map onto your own paper so that you can add details to it as you read. This will help increase your comprehension and get you more actively involved in your reading.

HOW TO REVIEW TEXT NOTES

There are three main ways to review text notes, but simply "reading over them" is not one of them. Try reciting your notes, replicating your notes, and creating a recall column.

RECITE YOUR NOTES

One way to transfer the information in your notes into your long-term memory is to recite it. First, practice the information by reviewing the main and supporting points. Try to recall and recite the headings that you used to set up the information in your notes. Then recite the details under each heading. Look back at your notes to see whether you're correct. Then cover your notes and practice again. If you made note cards, carry them with you. Review them whenever you have a few minutes to spare. Then look away and try to recite (or mumble) the information. Try taping your notes to a mirror, or tack them to a bulletin board. Review them in the morning and then try to recite them as you walk to class.

REPLICATE YOUR NOTES

Another way to review text notes is to replicate them. Take a blank sheet of paper and try to reconstruct your notes. If you mapped the information in the text, you probably will find that it's fairly easy to recall the visual image that you created; try to remember the map and also how you set it up. If you made a detailed map, practice drawing it one section at a time. You also can practice writing out your modified-block notes, outlines, or charts. When you review charts or matrixes, don't try to learn all the information at once. Work on one column at a time. Practice matrixes by starting with a blank sheet of paper. Write in the headings and the categories. Then try to fill in one column across or one row down. Keep working on the matrix until you can write it from memory.

CREATE A RECALL COLUMN

If you took written notes, you can also write recall words or questions in the margin as a way of reviewing your notes. Be sure you create both general and specific questions in the recall column so that you can test yourself on all of the important information. You can develop the recall column when you first take notes or when you review for your exam. Just developing the questions requires you to go back and review the notes you took. Then you get another review of the material each time you test your memory using the recall cues. If you've already written your recall questions, review by covering your notes and writing or reciting the answers to the questions. Gavin, Beth, Chris, and Sara developed a set of notes and recall questions on text material from an anthropology textbook. A portion of those notes is shown in Figure 9.9. Did you notice that both general and specific questions are included?

HOW TO EVALUATE TEXT NOTES

There are a number of ways that you can evaluate your text notes. You can compare your notes to those of a classmate, ask your professor or a learning center professional to review them, or use the T Method to test the quality of your notes.

COMPARE YOUR NOTES WITH THOSE OF A CLASSMATE

You may find that comparing your text notes with those of a classmate can be very helpful. For one thing, you may notice some information that you omitted or even find out that you included a lot of unnecessary information. More important, you may get some new ideas about how to organize the text information. Looking at how other students arranged and organized the same text information can help you evaluate your own notes. You may have already made some changes in the way you take text notes after completing some of the group activities in this chapter.

CHECK WITH YOUR PROFESSOR OR LEARNING CENTER PROFESSIONAL

If you aren't sure how well your notes condense the important information in the chapter, you may want to get some feedback from your professor or someone in your college learning center. Ask your teaching assistant or your professor (or learning center professional) to review a few pages of your text notes and let you know how well you're doing at identifying, condensing, and organizing the information in the text. If you're working with a tutor, ask him or her to take a look at your notes. Getting feedback on what you're doing right and any mistakes you're making can help you become a better notetaker.

USE THE T METHOD

After an exam, you can evaluate your text notes using the *T Method* in much the same way you did your text marking. Go through your notes for one chapter and

FIGURE 9.9

• • • • • • • • • • • • • •

Text Notes with Recall Questions

	Types of Political Organizations
	Band Societies
What are the characteristics of band societies?	Characteristics
What is the occupation of bands?	• Least complex
	• small, nomadic groups of food collectors
How large are the groups?	• can range from 20 to several hundred
	• members share all belongings
How much role specialization is there?	• very little role specializations
What is egalitarian?	• egalitarian—few differences in status and wealth
	Political Integration
How much political integration occurs?	• have least—bands are independent
What is the political integration based on?	• based on kinship and marriage
What ties members of bands together?	• bound together by language and culture
What type of leadership occurs in bands?	Leadership roles
	• informal—no designated authority
Who serves as leader? Why?	• older men are leaders—respected for their wisdom and experience
Who makes decisions?	• decisions made by adult men
What are the powers of a head man?	• head man advises—has no power
What is an example of a band society?	Example
	! Kung of the Kalahari
What are the characteristics of tribal societies?	**Tribal Societies**
	Characteristics
What is their occupation?	• food producers
What are pop. like?	• populations—large, dense, sedentary

put a "T" in the margin every time you find the answer to a test question. Then go back through your textbook to check for any other answers to test questions. If all answers to the questions from the book were in your text notes, you did an excellent job of taking notes. If a number of the answers were not in your notes, you may want to go over your notes with your professor. The feedback you get can then help you improve the notes that you take on the next group of chapters so you'll be better prepared for your next exam.

SUMMARY

Taking text notes is an active and effective method of condensing your text. When done properly, taking text notes improves your comprehension, increases your memory, organizes the information, and condenses the material for later review. Although many students take notes as they read the chapter for the first time, that's not the most efficient way to take notes on your text. Since everything seems important during a first reading, students tend to write down much more information than they would after hearing the lecture, during a weekly review of material, or while reviewing to prepare for an exam. Taking written notes using the outline or modified-block methods, writing a summary, or making marginal notes are effective ways to take text notes. Concept maps and charts are especially effective for some students and some types of material. Creating hierarchical maps, semantic webs, line maps, and charts allows you to organize material in ways that can more easily be recalled for later use. Just taking written notes or creating maps and charts doesn't automatically mean that you've learned the information, though. Review your notes on a regular basis by reciting them, writing them from memory, or creating a recall column. Then test your notes for completeness, accuracy, and clarity after the exam.

Activities

1. During the next week of classes, experiment with taking notes at different times. Try taking notes on one part of a text chapter as you first read the chapter. Then try taking notes on a different part of the chapter after the lecture. Finally, wait until the end of the week and take notes on another section of the chapter. Note the time it took you to complete each task. What did you find? Which set of notes do you think is most useful? Why?

2. Refer to the text excerpt "Understanding Job Satisfaction," available on the *Orientation to College Learning* Web site. Take written notes on the first two pages on notebook paper. Then compare your notes with those of one or two of your classmates. What do you think of the notes you took? Do they contain the important information? Are they well organized? Are they easy to study from?

3. Go to the *Orientation to College Learning* Web site and download one copy of Activity 9–1 from the Activities Packet. Take notes on note cards using both the summary and the informal outline or the modified-block method. You may find that highlighting before you take notes will save you time and help you organize your notes. Then compare your notes to those of others in your group.

4. Using the text material on Desert Biomes available on the *Orientation to College Learning* Web site, work as a group to take text notes. First, highlight the text material and discuss what you think are the important points that should be included in the map. Also, create a set of subheadings to better organize the material. Once you know what you want to include in your map, ask each group member to create a line map, a semantic web, or a hierarchical map. Compare your map to the others to evaluate the organizational structure and the content you included. Which method do you think will work best for you?

5. Select a set of text notes that you took recently. Then divide the notes into three sections. Review the first section by reciting the information using the headings to prompt your memory. Review the second section by replicating your notes—rewriting them from memory. Finally, review the last section of notes by creating recall questions in the margin. Which review strategy was the most effective? Why? Write several paragraphs describing what you found.

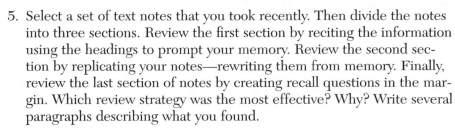
6. Read the excerpt "Chemically Dependent Youth" on the Web site and print a copy of the matrix on Drug Categories. Add another heading and complete the matrix by filling in each of the squares with the relevant information. Compare your chart with at least two of your classmates.

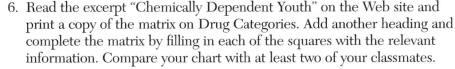
7. After your next exam, evaluate the quality of your text notes. Did your notes contain the information you needed to answer the questions on the exam? What changes do you plan to make so your notes will be more useful when you are preparing for your next exam?

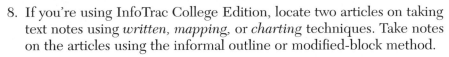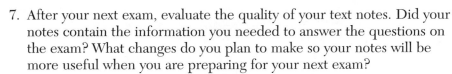
8. If you're using InfoTrac College Edition, locate two articles on taking text notes using *written, mapping,* or *charting* techniques. Take notes on the articles using the informal outline or modified-block method.

Then list three strategies that you plan to use. Be prepared to describe the process you used to locate the information and how you plan to use the strategies that you selected.

9. Think of three examples of how you've applied what you learned in this chapter. Choose one strategy and describe how you applied it to your other course work using the Journal Entry Form that is located on the *Orientation to College Learning* Web site. Consider the following questions as you complete your entry. Why did you use this strategy? What did you do? How did it work? How did it affect your performance on the task? How did this approach compare with your previous approach? What changes would you make the next time you use this strategy?

10. Now that you've completed Chapter 9, take a few minutes to repeat the "Where Are You Now?" activity, located on the *Orientation to College Learning* Web site. What changes did you make as a result of reading this chapter? How are you planning to apply what you've learned in this chapter?

Review Questions

Terms You Should Know:

Block method	Informal outlining	Strand Supports
Chart	Line map	Strand Ties
Comprehension monitoring system	Maps	Summary
Core Concept	Matrix	T Method
Formal outlining	Modified-block method	Web Strands
Hierarchical map	Semantic Web	Wheel map

Completion: Fill in the blank to complete each of the following statements.

1. You may not want to take text notes as you read the chapter for the first time because everything seems _____.

2. You can edit your _____ notes as you take your text notes.

3. Some students like to take text notes on _____ _____ because they can carry them around to review when they have a few extra minutes.

4. _____ _____ show the supporting details in a Semantic Web.

5. _____ cannot be used to take notes on entire chapters.

Multiple Choice: Circle the letter of the best answer for each of the following questions. Be sure to underline key words and eliminate wrong answers.

6. When you're writing a summary, be sure you use
   A. meaningful phrases.
   B. main ideas.
   C. paragraph form.
   D. recall questions in the margin.

7. Which of the following is a top-down method of taking text notes?
   A. Summaries
   B. Hierarchical maps
   C. Semantic Webs
   D. Charts

Short Answer–Essay: On a separate sheet, answer each of the following questions.

8. Why is note taking more effective than highlighting or underlining?

9. Why do some students have difficulty taking text notes? What should they do differently?

10. How should students review their text notes?

Chapter 10

PREPARING FOR EXAMS

"Recently I had a Psychology test. Before I took the test I used all the tips on preparing for exams and everything I learned about predicting exam questions. I made study sheets and question cards. Then I put myself on a five-day preparation schedule. I wrote and recited a lot. Going into the test, I felt very confident about my ability to do well on the test. As I was taking the test, I could remember something about each question. I received a C-average on my first couple of tests, but on this one I got a B. This proves to me if I can get myself to prepare properly now that I know how to, I can get the grades that I want."

Nelson Hernandez
Student

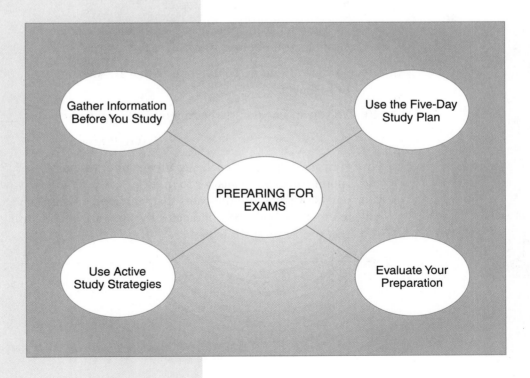

Where Are You Now?

Take a few minutes to answer *yes* or *no* to the following questions.

		YES	NO
1.	When preparing for exams, is your primary study method to read over the material?	_____	_____
2.	Do you tend to miss class the day before the exam?	_____	_____
3.	After an exam are you unsure of how well you did?	_____	_____
4.	Do you make up self-tests as a way of studying for exams?	_____	_____
5.	Do you study both by yourself and with a group before a very difficult exam?	_____	_____
6.	Do you tend to study only the day or night before the exam?	_____	_____
7.	Do you review your lecture notes and text material together according to the topic?	_____	_____
8.	Do you often know the answers to multiple-choice questions even before you look at the alternatives?	_____	_____
9.	Do you review by reciting out loud or by making up study sheets?	_____	_____
10.	Do you space your study time over several days?	_____	_____

TOTAL POINTS _____

Give yourself 1 point for each *yes* answer to questions 4, 5, 7, 8, 9, and 10 and 1 point for each *no* answer to questions 1, 2, 3, and 6. Now total up your points. A low score indicates that you need to learn how to study for college exams. A high score indicates that you are already using many good test preparation strategies.

GATHER INFORMATION BEFORE YOU STUDY

Before you begin to study for an exam, gather information about both the test and yourself. Learning about the type of test that will be given will help you know how best to prepare for it. In addition, knowing how you learn best can help you choose the most effective strategies to use. Together, this information can lead to better grades.

LEARN ABOUT THE EXAM

The first thing to do in preparing for an exam is find out what the exam will be like. If your professor hasn't already discussed the exam, ask about it. You need to know what types of questions you'll be expected to answer. Ask whether the exam is objective or essay or both. If the exam is an objective one, find out if all questions will be multiple choice or if some will be true/false, matching, or completion. The more you know, the better you can prepare.

You also need to know how many questions will be on the exam. If you have 100 questions on four chapters of Life Science, you can expect about 25 questions on each chapter. On the other hand, if you have only 20 questions on the same four chapters, you'll have only 5 questions per chapter. The more questions you have from each chapter, the greater the probability that they'll cover not only main ideas but also less important points from the chapters and your notes. If there are only a few questions from each chapter, they are more likely to cover the main ideas or concepts. However, you can't depend on this. Some professors who ask only three or four questions per chapter still test on "picky little things." And, don't forget: Even one essay question can cover a great deal of material.

LEVELS OF QUESTIONS

Many college students don't realize that professors test their understanding of the material at many different levels. Although most of the questions on your high school tests depended only on your ability to memorize, six different levels of questions are often found on college exams. Read the description of each in the list that follows.

1. *Knowledge-level questions* require only rote memory; they're the easiest type of question to answer. They include remembering terms, facts, dates, lists, and so on. To answer this type of question, you need

only to recognize or recall the information as it was written in the text or spoken in the lecture.[1]

2. *Comprehension-level questions* require you to do more than just recognize what was presented in the text or lecture. They require you to understand the material well enough to be able to identify concepts and issues even when they're phrased differently from the way you read them or heard them presented. To answer a comprehension-level question, you need to check its meaning carefully against what you learned.

3. *Application-level questions* require you to apply the information that you learned to a new situation. Application questions are common in math and science courses, but they may appear on any exam.

4. *Analysis-level questions* require you to break down a complex concept into its components or parts. Many essay questions involve analysis.

5. *Synthesis-level questions* require you to bring information together into a single unit or whole. Many essay questions involve synthesis.

6. *Evaluation-level questions* require you to make judgments about the value or worth of an idea. In most cases, both analysis and synthesis are required to answer an evaluation-level question. They are the most difficult type of question to answer and require the highest-level thinking skills.

LEARN ABOUT YOURSELF

As you decide which strategies to use when you prepare for an exam, you should also consider how you learn best. Refer to the section on learning styles in Chapter 1. Using your preferred learning style as you prepare for exams may help you stay more focused on the material and may make your study sessions more productive. Don't forget, though, that using a combination of learning styles is often most effective when you're dealing with a new type of course, a professor who doesn't teach to your style, or a type of test that you've had difficulty with in the past.

Think about how you currently prepare for exams. Do you generally prepare for all exams the same way, or do you prepare for different exams in different ways? You may, for example, spend more time, put in more effort, or use better strategies for exams that are in your major or for those that you feel are more important or critical to your college success. Think about the different

---

[1]Based on Bloom's Taxonomy in B. S. Bloom, ed., *Taxonomy of Educational Objectives: The Classification of Educational Goals. Handbook 1. Cognitive Domain* (New York: McKay, 1956).

ways that you and your classmates or friends prepare for exams. What strategies do you use now?

USE THE FIVE-DAY STUDY PLAN

Once you find out what the exam will be like, you should organize your study time. The *Five-Day Study Plan* provides you with a mechanism to space your learning over a period of days, divide the material so that you can work on it in small chunks, use active learning strategies to study the material, and monitor your learning.

Many students who have used this plan have reported dramatic improvements in their grades from one test to the next. The Five-Day Study Plan isn't a magic solution to all of your problems; rather, it's a well-structured plan that puts into practice what we know about how people learn and remember.

SPACE YOUR STUDY

How much time do you think you should spend studying for a four-chapter exam? How much time did you study for your last exam? Many students study about 1 to 3 hours the night before the exam. Compared with the time they put in on high school exams, this seems like a lot. Remember, though, that college exams may cover 10 to 20 times as much information as high school tests. Most college students need to spend 8 to 10 hours studying to get an A or B on an exam. Of course, this is only a general guideline. Some students constantly review material (daily and weekly) so that they don't need to put in quite as much time just before the exam. Other students may need to study even more. If you're taking a very challenging class (like Anatomy and Physiology or Organic Chemistry), you may need to double or even triple the suggested study time. As you'll see later in the chapter, it's not just the amount of time that makes the difference in your mastery of the material, but it's also what you do with that time.

If you're trying to figure out when you can find time to study 8 to 20 hours for one exam, don't panic. You don't need or really want to put in all of your study time on one day. It's much more effective to study over several days than to cram one day before an exam. Research studies have demonstrated that we learn better by spacing out our study over time. Instead of trying to study for 10 hours the night before an exam, try studying for 2 hours each day for 5 days before the exam (Figure 10.1). If you need to put in more time, add more time to each day's study session or add more days to your study plan.

To set up your study plan, count backward from your exam date to decide when you should begin to study. To get in 5 days of study before a Friday exam, you

FIGURE 10.1

• • • • • • • • •

Five-Day Study
Plan Overview

Tuesday			
	Prepare	CH 1	2 hrs
Wednesday			
	Prepare	CH 2	2 hrs
	Review	CH 1	30 min
Thursday			
	Prepare	CH 3	1-1/2 hrs
	Review	CH 2	30 min
	Review	CH 1	15 min
Friday			
	Prepare	CH 4	1 hr
	Review	CH 3	30 min
	Review	CH 2	15 min
	Review	CH 1	10 min
Sunday			
	Review	CH 4	30 min
	Review	CH 3	20 min
	Review	CH 2	10 min
	Review	CH 1	10 min
	Self-test		1 hr

would need to start studying on Sunday. When would you begin to study for a Monday exam? If you said Wednesday, you're right. If you said Tuesday, you could still be right. This is a flexible plan. If you work or even if you party on Saturdays, you can still use this plan. Just count back one more day to make up for the day that you decide to omit. However, never omit the day right before the exam; it's imperative to do a final review the day before the exam. Remember, we forget rapidly.

DIVIDE THE MATERIAL

The next step is to divide the material that will be on the exam. Make a list of the chapters, lecture topics, and outside readings that will be covered on the test. Then group or chunk them so that you study the lectures and readings covering the same topic at the same time. If your professor gave three lectures that related to the material in Chapter 1, you should study those lecture notes at the same time that you study Chapter 1 of the text. If your exam will cover four chapters, you can divide the material into four chunks, studying one chapter per day and then conducting a final review on the last day. How would you divide the material if your test covered only two chapters? You could study the first half of Chapter 1 on day 1, the second half of Chapter 1 on day 2, and so on. If you only had three chapters on the exam, you could use a four-day plan instead, or you could divide the oldest (or most difficult) chapter in half. How would you set up a plan for six chapters or eight chapters? Focusing on only one unit of material each day allows you to work on it more actively and concentrate all of your effort on it. Working on smaller units of material helps us learn and remember it better.

STUDY THE OLDEST MATERIAL FIRST

When you set up your five-day plan, be sure to start with the oldest chapter first. When you look carefully at the overview of the Five-Day Study Plan, you'll notice that the oldest chapters are given the most preparation time and the most review time. You need to spend more time on the old material because it's not as fresh in your mind. Even though you may have read it, marked it, and even taken notes on it, much of that material may seem new to you when you begin to review. If you covered Chapter 1 four weeks ago, you won't remember very much of it. In Figure 10.1, Chapters 3 and 4 are more familiar and therefore may require less preparation time and review. However, if Chapter 3 or 4 happens to be an especially difficult chapter, you may need to modify the plan and add some additional time for preparation and review.

PLAN ACTIVE STUDY TASKS

Look again at the framework for a Five-Day Study Plan in Figure 10.1. This plan includes both time to prepare a chapter and time to review that chapter several times before the exam. (Remember that "CH 1" means the text chapter, the lecture notes, and any other related materials.) The Five-Day Study Plan is a task-oriented plan. To be well prepared for a college exam, you need to use a variety of active study tasks to learn the material. If you don't plan active study tasks for the hours that you set aside for study, you may accomplish very little. Listing your study tasks helps you know what you need to accomplish each day. In many ways, it's like creating a "To Do" list for your study plan. You need to decide what you need to learn, what you already know, and what you need to work on again the next day. You also must determine which study strategies will be the most effective for learning the material. The type of course you have, the type of exam you'll have, and the type of questions must all be considered as you set up your plan.

Many college students know only one way to study for a test. They read over the material until they know it (at least they think they know it). Reading the material over and over is not only ineffective but also boring. If you've been rereading your text and lecture notes for hours before an exam and still not getting the grades you want, you need to change your strategy. Unlike reading over the material, writing and reciting strategies are excellent ways of putting information into long-term memory. In Figure 10.2 you can see some suggested preparation and review tasks for Wednesday and Thursday, the second and third days of this Five-Day Study Plan. Unfortunately, most students can't learn all the important information in their notes and in the chapter by going over it just one time.

Use Active Preparation Strategies

Preparation strategies help you identify what you need to learn, condense it, organize it, and write it. You can use the mnemonic ICOW to help you remember the role of preparation strategies. Preparation strategies are primarily writing strategies. Using at least three different preparation strategies allows you to work on the material in different ways. You can make word or question cards to

FIGURE 10.2

• • • • • • • • •

Actual Tasks for
Five-Day Study
Plan

Wednesday		
Prepare CH 2	1.	Re-mark highlighting
	2.	Make study sheets
	3.	Make word cards
	4.	Make question cards
Review CH 1	1.	Recite rehighlighted material
		*unknowns (recite main points)
	2.	Mark and recite study sheets
	3.	Recite word cards
	4.	Recite question cards
Thursday		
Prepare CH 3	1.	Re-mark highlighting
	2.	Make study sheets
	3.	Make word cards
	4.	Make question cards
Review CH 2	1.	Recite rehighlighted material
		*unknowns (recite main points)
	2.	Mark and recite study sheets
	3.	Recite word cards
	4.	Recite question cards
Review CH 1	1.	Make a list of information still not known from text or study sheets—recite
	2.	Recite cards still not known
	3.	Make self-test questions

learn key terms, facts, and details. You may also take notes on your text marking or even condense your lecture notes further as you reread them. Although these are all good preparation strategies, they tend to focus on material in an isolated way. You should also include at least one integrated study strategy in your plan. Making study sheets or planning possible essay questions allows you to study and learn the material in a more integrated manner. As you gather and organize the information on one topic or one question, you form many additional associations with the material. This helps you create additional cues to long-term memory, which makes it easier to retrieve the information during the exam. Preparation strategies are effective learning strategies because they force you to identify, condense, organize, and write the material.

Although the preparation strategies tend to emphasize the visual and kinesthetic learning styles, auditory learners still need to identify and condense the key information for later review. To use your preferred learning style, you may find it useful to read out loud as you re-mark your text or to recite key points as you create word cards or prepare concept maps and study sheets.

Use Active Review Strategies

During the review stage, you need to practice the material that you prepared earlier in your study plan. *Review strategies* are mainly recitation strategies that help you rehearse, understand, extend, and self-test your learning. They force you to recite the information out loud. You could get the same level of practice by writing the material again, but that's a bit more time-consuming. By reviewing all of the previous chapters each day, you can continue working on the material (often forming additional cues), gain a better understanding of it, keep it fresh in long-term memory, and monitor your learning. Each day, as you review the material, you continue to condense what you still don't know.

The review strategies tend to emphasize the auditory learning style because they rely so heavily on recitation (reciting out loud from memory). However, visual and kinesthetic learners can review by writing down the material, picturing the material, and looking at the material before and after reciting it out loud. As you'll see, many of the review strategies incorporate hands-on activities such as re-creating maps and charts, taking self-tests, working problems, and so on.

Since you'll be reviewing some of the material three or four times, it's also a good idea to vary your review strategies. Although you should use the same three or four strategies to prepare each chapter and to review each chapter the first time, you need to select different strategies to review the chapter the second, third, and fourth time. By working on the material different ways, you can create more new connections to it, use the learning style that may be the most effective, and make studying fun and interesting.

By reviewing the old material each day, you have more opportunities to learn it and keep it fresh in your long-term memory. Many students find that they really don't learn the course material until they've worked on it several times. Each time you review, you can also test your mastery of the material. If on day 2 you can't recite the main points in the study sheets that you prepared on day 1, you don't know the information. However, it's better to find that out on day 2 of your plan (instead of during the exam) because you'll have three more days to work on the material.

The tasks that are listed in Figure 10.2 are just a few examples of the types of tasks that you could use to study for an exam. The menu of active preparation and review strategies includes many other excellent strategies you can use in your study plan (Figure 10.3). You also may develop some excellent strategies of

FIGURE 10.3

• • • • • • • • •

Menu of Active
Study Tasks

PREPARATION STRATEGIES	REVIEW STRATEGIES
develop study sheets	recite study sheets
develop concept maps	replicate concept maps
make word cards	recite word cards
make question cards	recite question cards
make formula cards	practice writing formulas
make problem cards	work problems
make self-tests	take self-tests
do study guides	practice study guide info out loud
re-mark text material	take notes on re-marked text
do problems	make a list of 20 (30 or 40)
outline	recite list of 20 (30 or 40)
take notes	do "missed" problems
summarize	recite main points from outline
chart related material	recite notes from recall cues
list steps in the process	recite out loud
predict essay questions	re-create chart from memory
plan essay answers	recite steps from memory
write essay answers	answer essay questions
answer questions at end of chapter	practice reciting main points
prepare material for study group	write essay answers from memory
	recite answers
	explain material to group members

your own. Varying the activities you use when you study can keep you from feeling bored. You also may discover that many of these active strategies are fun and make learning interesting and exciting.

MONITOR YOUR LEARNING

One of the reasons that the Five-Day Study Plan is so effective is the built-in self-testing. As you review the old material each day, you should be testing your mastery of it. If you can't say it out loud or write it from memory, you don't really know it. Each time you recite your flash cards or practice the main points in your essay answer, you're checking to see what you do know and what you don't know. Although you may be disappointed that you don't get all the question cards correct the first time you review them, you will get some right. That tells you that you're learning the material and lets you know the strategy you're using is working. Have you ever tried to check your learning after just reading over the material? You may find that you don't really know very much of it.

Many students create their self-tests as a review strategy on day 2 or day 3 of the plan. Then they can take the test several times before the real exam. Self-testing gives you a feeling of accomplishment—makes you feel like all the hard work is paying off. That motivates you to keep going. You also will find that as you test your learning, you won't know some of the material. Identifying what you still don't know allows you to focus your efforts the next day on that material. Self-testing also allows you to practice retrieving information from your long-term memory. Since that's exactly what you'll have to do on the exam, the retrieval practice better prepares you for the test. Finally, taking a self-test on the last day of your study plan can help reduce any anxiety that you may be feeling about the exam. After all, if you take your test and do well, you'll know that you know the material.

USE ACTIVE STUDY STRATEGIES

In this section, you'll learn about a variety of active study strategies. Some of the strategies lend themselves to the preparation stage and others lend themselves to the review stage. You won't use all of these strategies to study for one exam; there are just too many of them. What you should do, however, is try each of them as you prepare for different exams during the semester. You probably will find that some strategies work better for you than others. You also may find that certain strategies work well for one class or exam but others are better for another.

FIGURE 10.4

• • • • • • • • • • • • • • • •

Effective Study Tools and Strategies for the Five-Day Study Plan

STUDY TOOL	PREPARATION STRATEGY	REVIEW STRATEGY*
Highlighting	Re-mark text and * unknowns	Recite main points out loud
Text notes	Dig through text and write main points and supporting details; develop recall column	Recite information, identifying connections among ideas from headings and/or recall columns
Summaries	Dig through text and lecture notes to identify the big picture and write out	Recite out loud or explain information to someone else
Concept maps	Design and draw	Sketch from memory or recite key points
Charts	Create charts	Re-create charts from memory on scrap paper
Geographic maps	Prepare copy of map without answers for self-test	Recite and/or write out answers; check original
Study sheets	Dig through text and lecture notes to select, condense, and organize material under main topics	Practice reciting out loud or in writing
End-of-chapter questions	Write out answers	Practice reciting answers
Word cards, question cards, formula cards, problem cards	Select information and write out cards	Recite out loud or in writing; shuffle cards and retest; test in reverse; retest missed items
Study groups	Prepare materials as agreed to by group	Explain your material to group and take notes on others' explanations; discuss
Self-tests	Select information and construct test	Take test in writing and/or recite out loud—retest
Predict essay questions	Predict specific essay questions; plan and prepare answers	Practice reciting main points and writing out answers
List of 20, 30, or 40+	Determine content and write out list	Recite out loud and write out troubling items

*Goal for review strategies is to recite and write out material from memory.
Adapted from chart developed by Patricia Luberto. Used with permission.

Your learning style, your professor's teaching style, and the type of exam you're going to have all influence how you need to study. Figure 10.4 includes many of the active study strategies that are discussed in the remainder of this chapter. Notice how each of the "Study Tools" can be used in both the preparation and the review stages. As you read about how to use these strategies, think about which ones you would use to prepare for exams in each of your courses this semester.

REREAD AND RE-MARK YOUR TEXT AND NOTES

Many students start preparing for a test by rereading their highlighting. You'll stay actively involved in your reading if you re-mark the text as you read it. You can further condense the material that you'll need to review again by determining what you do know and what you don't know. It certainly is possible that after several weeks of class, some of the information in the early chapters will be "old hat." You may not have to spend any more time on it at all. Don't spend time rereading the material that you didn't mark, though. Some students have trouble skipping this unmarked material, but you must learn to trust the marking that you did.

Mark the important information in your lecture notes as you reread them, too. You can condense them just as you did your text material. You may want to go through the chapter and your notes and reread the newly marked information the next day, too. This time, use another one of the methods to again condense what you need to learn. You can continue to reread and re-mark your text material and lecture notes every day. However, this is just the first step in learning the material. Remember, you need to write and recite to get the information into long-term memory—to learn it at the *recall level of learning*. At this level, you'll be able to recall the information without any additional cues.

If your professor tends to ask picky questions on small details, you may benefit from one quick rereading of your highlighting. This can be especially helpful if your exam is a multiple-choice test. To answer multiple-choice questions correctly, you often can rely on *recognition-level learning*. That means you don't need to recall the actual answer; you need only to *recognize* it from among the answers listed on the exam. If you've recently read that material, the answer may stand out or seem familiar to you. On the other hand, some professors rephrase the information on multiple-choice questions, too. Of course, if your exam is completion, short answer, or essay in design, that quick rereading won't be very helpful because you'll have to retrieve the information from long-term memory.

PREPARE WORD CARDS

Think back to the last objective test that you took. How many of the questions on the test required you to know the meaning of a word that was part of the specialized vocabulary for that unit of material? You may have been surprised to find a technical term somewhere in the question or in at least one of the possible answers. Many students don't spend much time on technical terminology because they know that they won't have to actually write out the definitions for an exam. What they don't realize, though, is that they're expected to know the meanings of those terms, and this understanding is necessary for answering many of the questions on the exam.

How do you learn all those terms? One way is to make *word cards.* By going through the chapter and writing out word cards, you're actively involved with the material. Just the process of writing them will help you learn them. Put the word on the front of a 3 × 5 card and then write a brief definition on the back. Put only one word on a card. You want to use them like flash cards, so they shouldn't be cluttered with information. If you're trying to save money, cut your cards in half.

Use Word Cards for Any Subject

You can make word cards for just about any subject. If you're in a psychology class, you may have 40 or 50 technical terms for just one chapter. In addition, you may want to make cards for famous psychologists and what they did, theories, or even research studies that were emphasized by your professor. In History, put people, dates, events, treaties, or anything else you need to learn on the cards. Make formula cards for math and science classes. Put the formula on one side and the name of the formula or when it's used on the other side. Of course, word cards are a great way to learn foreign-language vocabulary terms. Some students even put diagrams or sketches of things that they'll have to identify on the front of the card and the explanations on the back. Look at the examples of word cards from History, Biology, and Psychology in Figure 10.5. Word cards are easy to make, and they're quite effective in getting information into long-term memory.

Practice Your Word Cards

After you make your word cards, you need to learn them. Although you'll learn some of them just from writing them out, you won't learn all of them that way. Study them by practicing 10 or 15 at a time. Carry them around with you and recite or mumble them whenever you have a few minutes to spare. After you know that group, start on the next pack of 15.

Hold the stack of cards in your hand and look at the first term. Try to recite the definition out loud. Turn the card over to check your answer. If you were right, set that card aside. If you couldn't think of the answer or were not completely correct, read the definition out loud. Then put it on the bottom of the pile. Continue practicing the cards until you have none left in your hand. After you know all the terms, shuffle the cards to check your learning. Sometimes you remember the definition of one word because you got a clue to it from the previous term. Although it's good to learn information in chunks, sometimes you

FIGURE 10.5

• • • • • • • • •

Examples of
Word Cards

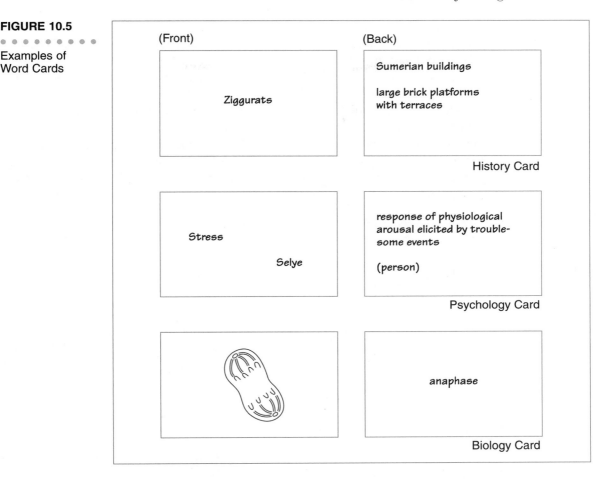

need to separate closely related information to make sure that you can distinguish among similar terms. If you also include the word card information in your maps, charts, study sheets, or outlines, you'll find that you can tie the information to a major concept. This will help reduce the effects of learning the information in isolation.

MAKE QUESTION CARDS

Making *question cards* is another active strategy for preparing for exams. Instead of just concentrating on terms, names, dates, and events, you can dig through your text and notes and write questions on all types of information. By making question cards, you actually are predicting what type of information you may need to know for the exam. You also may approach the material in a slightly different manner and focus more on understanding rather than on simple memorization.

You can make question cards on any type of information. Write the question on the front of the card and then write the answer on the back. Make at least 25 per chapter. If you already have prepared a stack of word cards for the chapter, concentrate on different information for your question cards. Focus on lists or on how things relate or how they differ. Look at the sample question cards for Business, History, and Biology in Figure 10.6. These questions emphasize steps in a process, lists of things, and causes and effects. You can also create problem cards for math and science classes. See Appendix D, on the *Orientation to College Learning* Web site, which contains information on how to study for Math exams.

FIGURE 10.6

• • • • • • • • • •

Sample Question
Cards

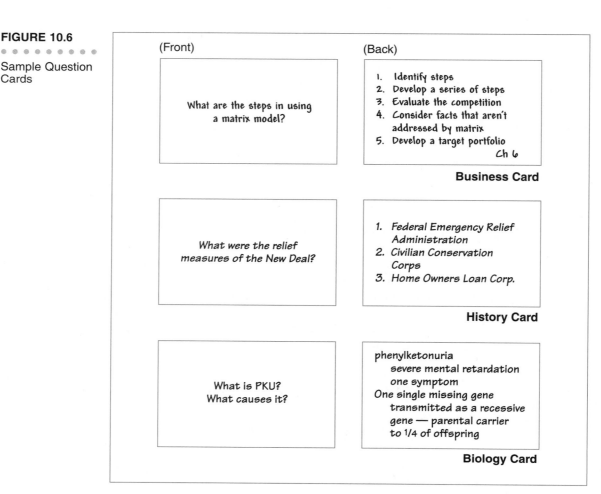

(Front)

What are the steps in using a matrix model?

(Back)

1. Identify steps
2. Develop a series of steps
3. Evaluate the competition
4. Consider facts that aren't addressed by matrix
5. Develop a target portfolio
    Ch 6

Business Card

What were the relief measures of the New Deal?

1. Federal Emergency Relief Administration
2. Civilian Conservation Corps
3. Home Owners Loan Corp.

History Card

What is PKU?
What causes it?

phenylketonuria
    severe mental retardation
    one symptom
One single missing gene
    transmitted as a recessive
    gene — parental carrier
    to 1/4 of offspring

Biology Card

Practice Your Question Cards

Use your question cards as you would flash cards. Practice answering the questions aloud until you know them all. You may want to write a page number or topic in the corner on the back so that you can refer to your text or notes if you get confused or think you need more review. You can use your question cards if you work in groups or with a study partner. If both you and your partner make question cards on the chapters, you'll be able to test each other on the material. You may be surprised because each of you will write different questions on the same material. Although you may have questions on the same information, you may approach it from a different angle. This can be helpful in preparing for the exam because you can test your learning in several ways. Your question cards are in fact another form of a self-test. Each time you recite the answer, you're prompting your memory for the information. If you've already predicted questions in the margin of your text and your lecture notes, use those to review for your exam, too.

CREATE STUDY SHEETS

Developing study sheets is one of the best ways to prepare for an exam. A *study sheet* is a 1-page compilation of all the important information on a particular topic. The sample study sheet on Mesopotamia in Figure 10.7 is the first of four study sheets prepared for one chapter of a Western Civilization exam.

It's easy to make study sheets. Put the topic at the top of the sheet and go through your text and lecture notes looking for all of the important information about that topic. Then combine the information in an organized manner. Creating a study sheet requires you to identify, condense, organize, and integrate the important information from both the text and your lecture notes into a single study sheet. When you create study sheets, you want to include both the material you already know and the material you need to learn. The already learned information will help you learn and remember the new information because it will serve as a hook to help you store and later as a cue to help you retrieve the new information. Study sheets allow you to work on information using high-level rehearsal strategies combined with organizational and elaboration strategies.

If you're using an outline or modified-block format, it's important to include headings and subheadings in your study sheet. The headings help you break up the information into manageable units and serve as cues to help you learn and remember the main points and details in your study sheet. How many study sheets you prepare depends a lot on how you organize or divide the information you need to learn. If you're preparing for a history exam, for example, you can make a study sheet on each main topic that was covered in lecture or each main sub-division of the chapter. You might have four study sheets for one chapter, or you could have six or seven.

FIGURE 10.7

• • • • • • • • •

Sample Study
Sheet

Mesopotamia

I.   Sumer (3500—2350 BC)

agricultural settlements T & E valley formed towns

first system of writing

(signs on clay tablets – cuneiform)

led to trade → cities

center of life – temple

religion – seasons – fertility   Great Mother

ex. Lady of Warka

govern – priests

Epic of Gilgamesh (most famous ruler) fiction

pessimistic (life struggle against disaster –

no afterlife)

1. quest — human is a questioner (ultimacy)

2. death — pos & neg moments

3. story — human is a mythmaker

II.   Akkad

Semitic King Sargon ruled (2350 to 2150)

art – bronze head of Nineveh

Stele of Naram – Sim

buildings – ziggurats

Many students get confused when they make study sheets. They simply jot down bits and pieces of information that seem important as they review the text and lecture material. These study sheets, as they call them, often contain long lists of unrelated details. Because the information is not organized under headings, it rarely contains sufficient detail about any one topic. These isolated facts, definitions, and theories are hard to learn and remember because they're not connected or related to anything else. It's important to work on information in both an isolated way (using word or question cards) and in an integrated way (using study sheets and by preparing essay questions and answers, which will be discussed in Chapter 12). Learning information in an integrated or connected way helps you prepare well for both objective and essay exams.

The second advantage of preparing study sheets is that you have concise "summaries" of the information, which can be used for review. Study sheets provide a quick way to review as you progress through your Five-Day Study

FIGURE 10.8

• • • • • • • • • • • • • •

Angela's Study Sheet

TYPES OF TERRESTRIAL BIOMES	DEFINITION	CLIMATE	TYPES OF PLANTS	TYPES OF ANIMALS
T_{UND}R_A TUNDRA	A biome found in polar regions and characterized by permafrost and a brief summer.	− average monthly temp − 10°C − winter is a way of life − summers are short and cool	− sphagnum mosses −lichens −herbs, grasses, flowers	− arctic hares − lemmings − arctic foxes − snowy owls − arctic wolves − polar bears
T_AI_G_A TAIGA	A biome character-ized by harsh winters, warmer summers, and a diverse array of plants.	− similar to tundra but summers are warmer − temperatures fluctuate wildly	−evergreens: spruce, fir, pine, and larch −deciduous trees: beech, aspen, willow and ash	− rodents, rabbits, moose, elk, deer − weasel, mink, lynx, wolves, bears − birds: eagles, falcons, buzzards, ducks
TEMPERATE FOREST	A biome found in the middle lati-tudes with rich soil and ample rainfall.	− mild winters − year-round rainfall	−shrubs, herbs −douglas fir −oak, hickory	− deer, boar, foxes, wild-cats, martens, lynx, elk, moose, caribou − birds

Plan, and they're useful when you prepare for comprehensive finals. After you prepare your study sheets, use them to review the important information. Practice reciting the information. If you have a lot of information on a study sheet, focus on the main headings first. Learn them and then use them to help you recall the details. File them away after the exam until you're ready to study for your finals.

Use Different Formats

You can use different formats in designing your study sheets. You may use an in-formal outline format like the Mesopotamia sample in Figure 10.7, a chart (or ma-trix) format, or even a map format. Look at a portion of the study sheet that Angela prepared to study biome types for her biology exam (Figure 10.8). Juanita combined information from her text and her lecture notes when she prepared a Semantic Web for an accounting class in Figure 10.9. She used the text to help or-ganize her map and then used information from her notes to fill in the details.If you already have made word cards or lists for the technical terms in the chapter,

FIGURE 10.9

• • • • • • • • • • • • • • • •

Juanita's Study Sheet

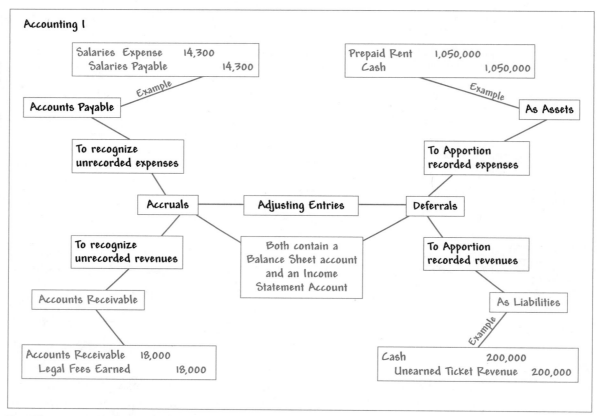

Note: Blue represents information taken from lecture notes.

you don't need to put long lists of definitions in your study sheets. Which method do you like better? If you already have been using one or more of these techniques for taking notes, you'll find that it doesn't take long to prepare your study sheets.

MAKE SELF-TESTS

Making *self-tests* is another active way to prepare for an exam. To make a self-test, you have to decide what information you need to know for the exam and then formulate questions about it. Most students tend to write either short answer or completion questions. Although both these types of questions help you focus on important information and test your recall of that information, they're not the types of questions that typically are on exams.

If you predict and prepare for questions only at the knowledge level, you may be unable to answer higher-level questions. That may explain why you may have felt well prepared for an exam but couldn't answer some of the questions. If you have to answer comprehension- or application-level questions on an exam, you should try to write questions at that level for your self-test. Writing higher-level questions does require more time and effort than writing knowledge-level questions, but it will better prepare you for the types of questions that you'll actually have to answer.

Use the Same Type of Questions

You can benefit even more from your self-tests if they're composed of the same types of questions that will be on the exam. For example, if you're going to have a Psychology exam that is 50 multiple-choice questions, you may be able to improve your score by writing multiple-choice test items rather than completion items. One advantage of actually making up multiple-choice items is that you have to generate 3 or 4 wrong answers in addition to the right answer. This can help improve your score on the exam because you're learning to distinguish between the correct answer and several possible but incorrect answers. In a sense you're predicting the incorrect answers or *distractors* that your professor may also use. If you choose the same ones that are on the actual test, you'll be able to eliminate them immediately.

In the same way, writing your own true/false items can help you tune in to key words that can be used or changed to make a statement false. Making up matching tests helps you make fine distinctions among terms, concepts, people, and so on. If you'll have to answer essay questions, you need to prepare by predicting and practicing possible essay test questions. A detailed discussion of how to prepare for essay tests will follow in Chapter 12.

Use Your Self-Test to Monitor Your Learning

Use your self-test to monitor your learning. One benefit of making self-tests is that you can use them over and over again to test your knowledge of the information. Write the answers on another sheet of paper or on the back of your self-test. Once you mark the answers on the test, you've changed the test into a review sheet. As you prepare the chapter, make a self-test and then take the test the next day to monitor what you've learned. Some students like to make up test questions as they prepare each chapter and then answer all of them the night before the test. This can provide an effective final review. Be sure, however, to leave some time to learn those items that you don't get right. Then test yourself again just to be sure.

USE RECITATION STRATEGIES

If you've been practicing your word or question cards, you've probably discovered that reciting is one of the best ways to get information into long-term memory. If you like using recitation strategies, there are a number of them that you can try. First, practice the important information by reciting it from your notes, text, or study sheets. Cover the information with your hand or look away, and then try to recite it, or use the questions in your recall column to test your memory. Seeing, saying, and hearing the information help you put it into long-term memory.

Teaching the information to someone else is another effective recitation strategy. If you're lucky enough to have a friend or relative who is willing to be your "guinea pig," you can take on the role of instructor and explain everything you know about the subject. One advantage of a human partner is that he or she can easily signal understanding or confusion. If your partner doesn't understand the information, you can try to explain it in another way. This may force you to rephrase the information in your own words, which helps you learn it, too.

You can teach the material to anything—a dog, a plant, or even a stuffed animal. Explaining the material out loud helps you clarify the information for yourself. Sit with your book and notes open and pretend that you're trying to explain the information to someone who doesn't understand it. Pretend that someone asked you a question about a particular topic, and answer it.

If you're being tutored or are part of a study group, remember one thing: The person who does the talking is the one who does the learning. Just listening to someone else explain something is a passive activity. When I was taking statistics in college, I walked to and from the parking lot with another classmate. I asked questions about something we had just covered, and he explained it to me. He then asked if I understood, and I always said, "yes," but often I was still not sure I did understand. Finally, one day I stopped my friend in the middle of explaining something and said, "Wait a minute. Let *me* explain it to you. If I make a mistake, stop me." After that I did the explaining. I found that I truly understood the information because I had to put it into my own words.

STUDY IN A GROUP

Many students who are taking difficult classes form study groups. They feel that by working together, each of them can help and be helped by others in the group. Study groups work the best if all members are committed to working hard. One advantage is that each member can share information. Not everyone has identical notes or can do all of the problems. By working together, group members help each other fill in gaps in their learning. By taking turns explaining information or by throwing out questions to other members of the group,

MORE ACTIVE STUDY STRATEGIES

PREPARE REVIEW CARDS. In some classes, students are permitted to take one index card to the exam with anything on it they wish. Even if you aren't permitted to do so, creating a review card may be an excellent final review strategy. To do it you need to identify those key pieces of information that are the most critical or that you still don't know. Writing and organizing the information on the card are active ways to review for your exam.

TURN DIAGRAMS INTO A SELF-TEST. Photocopy or trace any important diagrams that may be on the exam and label them with numbers instead of the names. Then use them to test your learning by reciting or writing the actual names of the bones, structures, or muscles, for example. Then you can use your labeled version as your answer key.

MAKE A LIST OF 20, 30, OR 40 OR MORE. Another final review strategy is to list the 20 to 40 or more most important things that you think will be on the test. It's important to list the actual information and not just the topic. Then review your list just before the exam as a final review and a way to focus your concentration. After the exam, check to see how many items on your list were on the exam. This strategy also helps you monitor your ability to predict what will be on the exam.

USE STUDY GUIDES TO TEST YOUR LEARNING. Many textbooks come with a study guide that includes word lists, questions, and practice tests. Don't actually fill in your study guide as you read the chapter. Instead, write the words on cards so you can shuffle them to learn them without cues. Then answer the questions and take the tests on notebook paper. That way you can use the study guide again to test your learning before the exam.

USE OLD EXAMS AS A RESOURCE. Use copies of old exams, which are often available in the library or your college learning center, to get more information about what the test will be like. You can get an idea about the kinds of questions the instructor uses, the topics that were emphasized, and the level of detail of questions. If the tests closely parallel your current material, take them for extra practice.

PREPARE TAPED SELF-TESTS. Read your test questions into a tape recorder, pause after each question while letting the tape run, and then read the answer. As you commute to school or work, you can take your tests. Try to answer the question out loud during the paused portion of the tape, listen to the answer, and check your learning.

GET YOUR FAMILY AND FRIENDS INVOLVED. Your family and friends can be a great resource to you as you prepare for tests. Ask a friend or family member to help you with your word or question cards. Teach the material to your friends, parents, or older children. Ask someone to quiz you by asking you the end-of-chapter questions or self-tests that you prepared.

each person gets a good review of the material. Sharing predictions about what will be on the test also can help all of the group members prepare.

The best way to work in a study group is to work as a group throughout the semester. If, however, you decide to work as a group just for exams, schedule your first meeting at least a week before the exam. Spend some time deciding what each member of the group should do in order to prepare for the next meeting. You may decide to divide the material so that each group member is responsible for one chapter and the related materials. During the next meeting, each student should present a short overview of the material and then drill the group on his or her portion of the material. If everyone works together, all members of the group should be well prepared for the exam. Remember, though— group sessions don't replace preparing alone. In many cases, they provide a clearer understanding of what you still need to learn on your own.

EVALUATE YOUR PREPARATION

Now that you've experimented with many of the test-preparation strategies, you need to evaluate their effectiveness. How comfortable you feel when you use certain strategies may indicate whether they fit your preferred learning style. How effective they are in helping you learn and master the material may indicate how well they fit your instructor's teaching style, and the course material itself. Finally, your performance on the exam may indicate how well your study strategies match your instructor's testing style.

EVALUATE AS YOU PREPARE

You can evaluate your study strategies even as you prepare for the exam. Monitor your learning each day of your Five-Day Study Plan. By reviewing the previously prepared and reviewed material the next day, you have an opportunity to test your learning. By reciting, writing, or taking self-tests, you can find out what you do know and what you don't know—what you need to continue to review. In addition, you can find out how successful your strategies actually are. If you study your lecture notes by simply reading over them for 2 hours, you may find that the next day you can't recall the key information when you try to recite from your recall column. If, on the other hand, you study your lecture notes by further condensing them and reciting key points, you may find that the next day you can easily recite the key information by using your recall column. It's easy to see which strategy works when you monitor your learning each day.

EVALUATE AFTER YOU COMPLETE YOUR PLAN

You can also evaluate your preparation strategies after you complete your study plan. Conducting a final review, taking a self-test, and even assessing how well prepared you feel are methods of evaluating your study plan. If you find yourself moving through the exam at a steady pace, knowing most of the answers, and thinking to yourself, "I knew this would be on the test," you did a good job of preparing. If, on the other hand, you find yourself moving slowly through the exam, skipping a lot of questions, and asking, "Where did these questions come from?" you probably didn't prepare properly for the exam. When things aren't going well during exams, many students tell themselves that they should have studied more (to them that means longer). Sometimes, though, it's not the time spent, but rather the way that time was spent and the strategies used that are the keys to success.

EVALUATE AFTER THE EXAM

After each exam, you should evaluate your entire study plan. Consider how much time you spent studying, the material you stressed or omitted, and the strategies that you used. Once your exam is graded and returned, you can make even better decisions about what worked and what didn't. Be sure to look at both the questions that you got right and those that you got wrong. Evaluating your study plan and your study strategies can help you do better on your next exam. By continuing to use the strategies that do work and replacing the ones that are less successful, you can improve your performance on future exams. You can't prepare for every exam the same way, though. Different courses, different professors, and even different types of material require you to tailor your study plan and study strategies to each specific exam.

SUMMARY

Preparing for exams requires you to be a strategic learner. If you prepare the same way that you did for high school tests, use the same strategies for all of your courses, or prepare the same way as your friends or classmates do, you may not get the grades you want or deserve. Before you prepare for an exam, you need to learn as much about the exam as you can. That way, you can design your study plan correctly. You need to plan what to study, when to study, and how to study. You may decide to study with a group for a math exam but study alone for your history exam. That's fine; you need to consider your learning style as well as the type of exam you'll have to determine how you can learn best. In any case, you should set up a Five-Day Study Plan to organize your study efforts and space out your learning over several days. Divide the material into smaller units so that you can concentrate your efforts and incorporate daily reviews. Use active study strategies as you prepare and review each of the chapters or units of material. Re-marking the text, taking notes, preparing word and question cards, making study sheets, developing self-tests, and reciting are just a few of the active strategies that will help you learn the material for your exam. You shouldn't study for every exam the same way. Choose the strategies and techniques that you think will work the best for you. Try different strategies for different subjects. Forget about just "reading over" the material, though; that won't help you remember it for the exam. By using a variety of active learning strategies, you can achieve your goal. You must be actively involved with the material to get it into long-term memory—to really learn it. Finally, evaluate your study plan as you prepare, during the exam, and before your next exam, and make some changes if your performance doesn't match your goals.

Activities

1. Set up a Five-Day Study Plan for an exam that you have coming up in the next few weeks. Decide when you're going to study; then divide up the material into four chunks. Use the overview in Figure 10.1 as a model. Select some active study tasks to add to your study plan from the menu in Figure 10.3, but feel free to create other strategies of your own.

2. Make a list of what successful students do when preparing for exams. Then compare your responses with other members of your group. Select the 20 best exam preparation strategies and create a list. How many of your strategies appeared on the group list?

3. Prepare a set of word cards for all the technical terms from one chapter in any of your texts. Practice reviewing the cards using the reciting and writing methods described previously. Then try to write or recite the definitions. How many did you get right? How many times did you need to practice the terms? Which strategy worked best for you? Describe what you found.

4. Select two headed sections from one of your texts or from one of the excerpts available on the *Orientation to College Learning* Web site. Review one section by reading over it a few times. Then review the second section by reciting the information or "teaching" it to someone

or something else. Which method was more effective in helping you learn the information? Why?

5. Work together to prepare a set of study sheets on the Five-Day Study Plan. Be sure that you combine the information from your text and your lecture notes. Share your study sheets with other members of the class. Did you include the same topics? What changes would you make the next time?

6. Develop a self-test on a cassette tape to play as you commute to and from school or work. Be sure to let the tape run for a few seconds after you record your question. Then record the correct answer. As you listen to the tape, recite the answer to each question out loud and then check it against the correct answer that you recorded. How did making the tape help you learn the information? How often were you able to play the tape and take your own self-test? How effective was this strategy in preparing you for the exam? Would you use this strategy again? Why, or why not?

7. Go to the *Orientation to College Learning* Web site and download one copy of Activity 10–5 from the Activities Packet. Evaluate the study plan that you used to prepare for one of your exams.

8. If you're using InfoTrac College Edition, use PowerTrac to locate a list of articles on test preparation. Test a number of key-word combinations until you narrow the hits to those that contain useful information on active test-preparation strategies. Make a list of the five best test-preparation strategies that you found. Why did you choose these strategies? What changes do you plan to make in how you study for your next exam?

9. Think of three examples of how you've applied what you learned in this chapter. Choose one strategy and describe how you applied it to your other course work using the Journal Entry Form that is located on the *Orientation to College Learning* Web site. Consider the following questions as you complete your entry. Why did you use this strategy? What did you do? How did it work? How did it affect your performance on the task? How did this approach compare to your previous approach? What changes would you make the next time you use this strategy?

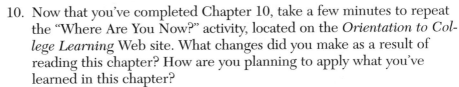

10. Now that you've completed Chapter 10, take a few minutes to repeat the "Where Are You Now?" activity, located on the *Orientation to College Learning* Web site. What changes did you make as a result of reading this chapter? How are you planning to apply what you've learned in this chapter?

Review Questions

Terms You Should Know:

Analysis-level questions
Application-level questions
Comprehension-level questions
Distractors
Evaluation-level questions
Five-Day Study Plan
Knowledge-level questions
Preparation strategies

Question cards
Recall-level learning
Recognition-level learning
Review strategies
Self-test
Study sheet
Synthesis-level questions
Word cards

Completion: Fill in the blank to complete each of the following statements.

1. You should study the _____ chapter on day 1 of the Five-Day Study Plan.

2. You should study for _____ to _____ hours for a college exam.

3. Studying your text and lecture material together is known as _____ study.

4. If you only have two chapters to study for an exam, you should prepare _____ on day 1.

5. The review strategies give you more opportunities for _____ your learning.

Multiple Choice: Circle the letter of the best answer for each of the following questions. Be sure to underline key words and eliminate wrong answers.

6. _____-level questions require you to understand the information so you can select the answer even when it is phrased differently on the exam.
   A. Knowledge
   B. Comprehension
   C. Application
   D. Analysis

7. Which of the following is the least effective time to evaluate your exam preparation?
    A. As you prepare for the exam
    B. After you finish studying
    C. During the exam
    D. After the exam

Short Answer–Essay: On a separate sheet, answer each of the following questions.

8. How are preparation strategies and review strategies different?

9. Why do some students have difficulty preparing for exams? What should they do differently?

10. Why is the Five-Day Study Plan so effective?

Chapter 11

TAKING OBJECTIVE TESTS

"Before reading this material, my test-taking skills were not very good. This text has helped me to learn different strategies that have helped me to improve my test grades. Before, I used to do the questions in order and would get frustrated when I didn't know one of the answers. Now I do the ones that I know and come back to the others. Crossing off wrong answers and underlining key words both help me come up with the right answers."

Amanda Fisher
Student

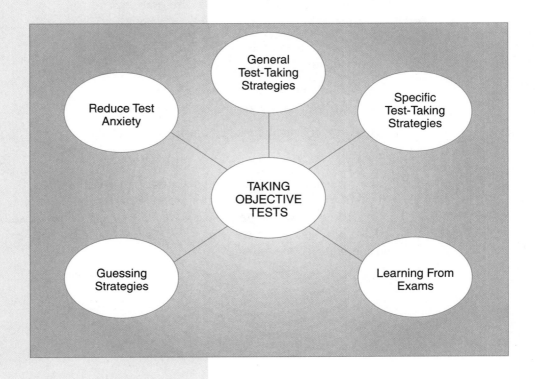

Where Are You Now?

Take a few minutes to answer *yes* or *no* to the following questions.

	YES	NO
1. Do you always read the directions before you begin to answer the questions on an objective exam?	___	___
2. Do you eliminate wrong answers on multiple-choice exams?	___	___
3. Does test anxiety interfere with your performance on exams?	___	___
4. Do you ever leave blanks on exams?	___	___
5. Do you use strategies to help you figure out the correct answer when you're unsure of it?	___	___
6. Do you ever find that you're unable to finish an exam before time runs out?	___	___
7. Do you go back over the entire exam before you turn it in?	___	___
8. After your exam is returned, do you go over it to evaluate your preparation and clarify your errors?	___	___
9. When you get your exam back, are you often surprised by the grade that you received?	___	___
10. Do you usually make careless errors on your exams?	___	___

TOTAL POINTS ___

Give yourself 1 point for each *yes* answer to questions 1, 2, 5, 7, and 8 and 1 point for each *no* answer to questions 3, 4, 6, 9, and 10. Now total up your points. A low score indicates that you need to develop some new skills for taking objective tests. A high score indicates that you are already using many good strategies.

REDUCE TEST ANXIETY

To perform well on objective tests, you have to be well prepared. However, several other factors also may contribute to your success or failure. One of these factors often is referred to as your "test-taking ability." Some students are more skilled at taking tests than others. They have learned strategies and techniques that improve their performance on exams. Another factor that can affect test performance is your level of comfort when you take an exam. Some students view exams as everyday events, whereas other students consider them to be monumental obstacles that must be overcome. These different attitudes toward exams may be, in part, a result of students' varying levels of test anxiety.

All students experience a certain level of test anxiety at one time or another, but some students experience high levels of anxiety, fear, and frustration before, during, and after taking exams. Understanding the real causes of test anxiety and developing coping techniques can help you reduce the amount of test anxiety you experience.

WHAT IS TEST ANXIETY?

Some students come into an exam feeling well prepared, well rested, and highly motivated. Other students, however, feel uncertain about their level of preparation and anxious about their performance on the test. We could say that they are experiencing test anxiety. *Test anxiety* involves both physical responses, such as rapid heart beat and shallow breathing, and emotional responses, such as worry and negative thoughts. What are some common symptoms of test anxiety? The following list was suggested by college students:

nausea	fainting	throwing up
light-headedness	going blank	shaking
sweaty palms	worrying about failing	headaches
butterflies	trouble concentrating	feeling tense
heart pounding	diarrhea	crying

Of course, not everyone exhibits all of these symptoms of test anxiety, but some students do experience one or more of them. Can you think of any others that could be added to the list?

Although many students experience test anxiety, we don't know for sure whether test anxiety really causes some students to perform less well on exams. The connection between test anxiety and poor test performance still is being investigated by many researchers. However, test anxiety does appear to be related to poor test performance in students who exhibit very high levels of anxiety. For most of us, though, test anxiety alone does not cause test failure.

Instead, lack of preparation (which can increase text anxiety) is the real cause of test failure.

WHAT CAUSES TEST ANXIETY?

What causes some students to experience test anxiety while others appear calm and collected on exams? Although there's no real answer to this question, several possible explanations may help us understand the problem. For some students, past experiences during exams lead to anxious feelings about subsequent exams. Failure accompanied by embarrassment and frustration in one testing situation can lead to anxiety in the next. Failure, by the way, doesn't mean the same thing for every student. When most people talk about failing an exam, they mean getting a grade that is below passing. For some students, however, getting a C or even a B is like failing; they fail to get the grade they wanted or needed. Excellent students often exhibit high levels of test anxiety because of the pressure they (or others) put on themselves to be the best.

The amount or level of anxiety that students experience also may depend on the value that they place on the exam. If doing well in the course is very important to you personally or professionally, you may view the exam as a critical or "must win" situation. On the other hand, if the class is seen as having little value or being unimportant to your future, you may experience little anxiety. This may explain why you may experience test anxiety in one class but not in others. Often, the greater the risk, the greater the stress.

Sometimes the type of test being given can lead to test anxiety. Some students become anxious during exams that require them to demonstrate their knowledge in ways in which they don't feel comfortable. For example, some students panic when they find that they have to take essay tests. Others become anxious over oral exams. And, some, like me, hate true/false tests. Different types of tests cause feelings of anxiety for different people. The added pressure of having to complete an exam within a limited time period also creates feelings of anxiety for many students.

IS TEST ANXIETY NORMAL?

With all of these factors contributing to test anxiety, it's hard to believe that any student doesn't feel some level of anxiety. Actually, just about everyone does. It's perfectly normal to be anxious about an exam. If you weren't a little anxious about your performance, you probably wouldn't study at all. A small amount of test anxiety is good. We can describe this state of anxiety as *facilitating test anxiety—*anxiety that facilitates or helps motivate us to prepare before and work hard

FIGURE 11.1

• • • • • • • • •

Test Anxiety
Cycle

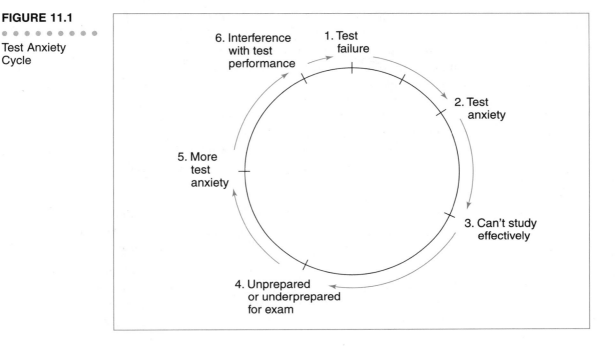

during the exam. On the other hand, a high level of test anxiety can interfere with your performance on an exam. We call this type of anxiety *debilitating test anxiety.* Like a debilitating illness, it prevents us from functioning in a normal way. High levels of test anxiety may interfere with your ability to concentrate on the exam, take the exam, or even prepare for it. If you're out in the hall throwing up, you're losing time you could have spent completing the exam.

Some students find that they really can't prepare for exams because they're so anxious about them. When they begin to study, they start to think about the exam, and they experience some of the physical and emotional symptoms that we've discussed. They have difficulty concentrating on the material during the study session in much the same way that they do during the exam. This leads to poor preparation, which then leads to another poor test grade, and so the cycle begins (Figure 11.1).

COPING WITH TEST ANXIETY

There are a number of ways that you can learn to cope with test anxiety. First of all, remember that some test anxiety is good, so your goal should be to reduce higher levels of anxiety to a level that becomes facilitating. Look again at the *test-anxiety cycle* in Figure 11.1. There really is only one point at which a test-anxious student could interrupt the cycle and therefore change the outcome. Where is it? If you said, "can't study effectively," you were correct. This is the only point at which you can effectively change the outcome of your next exam. By developing a structured study plan (such as the Five-Day Study Plan), you can be well prepared for the next exam. This will reduce your anxiety to a manageable level and allow you to focus on the exam questions rather than on the negative thoughts, worries, or physical symptoms that often interfere with your ability to concentrate on the exam itself. With good preparation and good concentration, you should do well. Once you know that you can do well on that exam, you won't be so anxious the next time—you'll be able to break the test-anxiety cycle.

1. **Prepare Well.** By using active study strategies like writing and reciting, you can master the material for your exam, and by monitoring your learning through self-tests, you can feel confident about your preparation.

2. **Use Relaxation Strategies.** Use breathing or muscle-relaxing techniques to calm yourself. Just taking a few deep breaths can help you calm down. If that doesn't work, try taking a breath and then blowing it out very slowly a few times until you find that you're able to control your breathing.

3. **Avoid Negative Thoughts.** Negative thoughts about failing the test, whether you studied the right material, or that you don't belong in school interfere with your ability to concentrate on the test itself. Negative thoughts compete with and distract you from concentrating on the exam.

4. **Recite a Positive Mental Script.** After you study for the test, prepare a positive statement or script. As soon as you begin to think any negative thoughts during the exam, yell "STOP" or "STOP IT" in your mind and then immediately start to repeat your positive script.

5. **Use Visualization.** Try to imagine the professor walking in with the exam, giving directions, and passing out the tests. Picture yourself starting the exam. As you go through this role playing, monitor your level of anxiety. If you begin to feel anxious, use one of the stress-reduction activities to calm yourself.

6. **Don't Arrive Too Early.** Enter the classroom about 5 minutes before the exam is to start. You'll have time to settle in and do a quick review but not enough time to allow yourself or others to make you nervous.

7. **Identify Your Triggers.** Identifying what triggers your feelings of anxiety can help you cope with them. If essay questions are your troublesome area, do the objective part of the test first. If your instructor makes you nervous by announcing the time every 5 minutes, tell him or her about your problem.

8. **Answer the Questions You Know First.** Test anxiety doesn't last forever; for most students the symptoms subside after about 15 or 20 minutes. If you use strategies to help reduce your anxiety and at the same time answer the ones you know, your anxiety need not affect your grade.

9. **Don't Let Test Anxiety Become An Excuse.** Some students blame test anxiety instead of themselves when things aren't going well. They blame their test failure on their anxiety rather than on their lack of preparation, poor class attendance, or poor preparation in high school. After all, that's easier than having to work hard and face the results of their efforts. Be sure you don't fall into that trap.

PEANUTS reprinted by permission of Newspaper Enterprise Association, Inc.

GENERAL TEST-TAKING STRATEGIES

Now that you've developed many good strategies for test preparation, you need to learn how to approach and take objective tests. Learning how to approach tests in a calm, logical way can help you increase your score. However, good test grades depend, first of all, on good test preparation, so let's quickly review some of the ways that you can prepare for your exam.

PREPARE WELL

In the previous chapter, you have learned a wide variety of general and specific strategies for how to study for a test. Rather than review all the strategies, let's focus on just a few. First, to acquire information or learn it, you must use active learning strategies. You need to spend the majority of your study time writing and reciting the information. Although reading the information out loud and copying your notes do help you rehearse the information, you'll gain a better understanding of the material if you use elaborative strategies such as mapping, note taking (in your own words), and explaining the information to someone else. Second, organizing the information so that it's more meaningful to you makes it easier to learn and remember. Third, spacing your study over a period of days, working on small units of material at one time, and planning additional opportunities for repetition all help you learn more effectively and reduce forgetting. Fourth, monitoring your progress by taking self-tests allows you to evaluate what you know and what you still need to learn. Finally, it's important to be in good physical condition when you take an exam. You should be well rested and properly nourished.

FOLLOW DIRECTIONS

Reading the directions before beginning an exam can make the difference between getting a good grade and failing the exam. The directions give you information on how many questions to answer, what form the answers must take, and special directions for some parts of the test. The directions for all parts of an exam aren't necessarily the same. Some sections of a multiple-choice exam, for example, may ask you to choose the best answer. Other sections may ask you to select all the correct answers or the only incorrect answer. Marking only the best answer when all correct choices are required may cost you 2 or 3 points per question. Occasionally, students lose points on true/false exams because they don't read the directions. If you mark the statement false without correcting the false statement (as required in the directions), you may not get credit for the answer. Errors like these can result in failure.

BUDGET YOUR TIME

If you budget your time during a test, you should be able to complete the entire test before time runs out. This is a problem for some students. They lose track of time or spend too much time on one part of the exam and end up leaving some questions undone. Being unable to finish even five 2-point questions on a test can mean the difference of one letter grade. Pacing yourself during the test also helps you maximize your score by letting you devote the most time to those parts of the exam that have the highest point values.

Consider Point Values

Previewing the exam gives you an idea of what you need to accomplish during the test period. Count the total number of questions that you have to answer. Then look at each section of the exam and check the point value for each question. Some students ignore the differences in point values among questions and treat all questions as if they were of equal weight. Occasionally, this has disastrous effects. If you use the following rule, you always will be able to determine how much time to spend on each question or section of the test:

> **Rule:** Percentage of the total points = Percentage of total time

Pace Yourself During the Exam

Even if your exam is all multiple-choice questions, you still need to budget your time. You want to complete the entire test and still have time to go back over it. Divide the time you have by the total number of questions and then shave off some for your review. You may have 40 questions to answer in a 50-minute period. If you allow 10 minutes for review, you can spend 1 minute on each question. *Pace* yourself during the exam—divide up the test and set time goals for each third, fourth, or fifth of the exam. For example, if you had 40 questions to answer in 40 minutes, you might divide the test at the end of each 10-question chunk. If your exam started at 2:00, you might jot 2:10 in the margin next to question 10, 2:20 in the margin next to 20, and 2:30 in the margin next to question 30. Each time you moved to the next chunk of questions, you would notice the time in the margin, check your watch, and monitor your progress. If you were working slowly, you would realize it early enough to speed up. If you realized that you were racing through the questions, you could slow down and spend more time on each question.

What to Do If Time Runs Out

You still may not be finished with the exam when time runs out. If you have one or two questions left to do, ask the professor for a few more minutes. Even though some professors are sticklers about time, they may allow you to finish the exam while they gather up their materials. If you know that you often have difficulty completing exams in the required time, discuss this with your professor ahead of time. Some professors allow students to arrive early and begin the exam before the rest of the class. If you have a reading problem or if English is your second language, you often can make special arrangements through your campus learning center or academic dean. Most professors are willing to make accommodations to help you succeed on exams, but you need to tell them what your needs are.

ANSWER THE EASIEST QUESTIONS FIRST

Another strategy for improving your grade on an objective test is to answer the easiest questions first. By immediately answering all questions that you know, you can maximize your score on the test. If you do run out of time, you'll be sure to receive points for the questions that you did know. In addition, you can reduce your test anxiety by answering the easiest questions first. By the time you go back to work on the more difficult questions, you'll feel more relaxed. This is because you build up your confidence as you complete the easy questions; you know that you know at least some or even many of the answers. One student reported that she used this strategy on an algebra exam. By the time she went back to the "difficult" questions, they didn't seem nearly as hard. Because she was more relaxed, she was able to think through the problems more logically and solve them correctly.

Some students panic if they read the first question on the test and realize they don't know the answer. Instead of allowing yourself to start thinking negative thoughts, just tell yourself "This is a hard question—I'll come back to it later." This type of positive thinking allows you to stay calm and focus on the rest of the test.

Work Strategically to Answer All Questions

As you move through the exam, skip the questions you aren't sure of and go on to the easier questions. If you know that you don't know an answer, don't spend a lot of time on the question. Mark the questions you skip by putting a dash or question mark in the margin or by circling the number. After you complete the rest of the test, go back to them. (If you're using an answer sheet, be sure you skip the same spaces there, too.) When you return to the questions you skipped, try to figure out the answers strategically. Think through each question. Eliminate any answer that you know is wrong and then try to figure out the correct answer.

Look for Clues in Other Questions

Many students find clues to other questions as they move through the test. You may even find the answer to an early question in one of the possible answers to a question three pages away. Even if you don't find the answer itself, you may find a clue or cue to help you answer the question. You may read a word in another question or in another possible answer that triggers your memory and helps you retrieve the information that you need. Even if you pick up a clue to only one or two questions as you move through the test, that can often make a difference in your grade.

SPECIFIC TEST-TAKING STRATEGIES

If you prepare well, reduce test anxiety, read and follow directions, pace yourself, and answer the easiest question first, you should do well on exams. However, some students still have trouble on objective exams because they lack specific test-taking skills for different types of objective tests. There are four levels of strategies that students should use when approaching test questions.

1. Prepare well enough to know the answer without even looking for it—think of it and then go find it.

2. Use problem-solving strategies to figure out the answer.

3. Use test-wise clues to improve your ability to select the right answer.

4. If all else fails, use strategic guessing to pick up a few additional points on the exam.

STRATEGIES FOR MULTIPLE-CHOICE TESTS

The most common type of objective test is the multiple-choice test. Many new college students have difficulty with these exams because they expect all of the questions to be at the knowledge level. They prepare by memorizing the material and often don't take the time to really learn and understand it. If you're able to recall the correct answers from memory without cues, multiple-choice exams will be easy for you. Most multiple-choice exams contain a *stem,* which is composed of a question or an incomplete sentence, and several *alternatives* or possible answers.

Many strategies are effective for taking multiple-choice exams; however, these strategies come in two different forms. The first group includes *problem-solving strategies* that can help you figure out the correct answer from the various distractors or decoys. The other group involves *test-wise strategies* that should be used only after you've tried all the other strategies first. Some students think of test-wise strategies as rules; they aren't. They should be used *only* in a guessing situation. After you read the directions and budget your time, use the following strategies for multiple-choice items.

Problem-Solving Strategies

Problem-solving strategies can help you logically and methodically identify the correct answer even if you don't know it when you first read the question.

1. **Read the question and all answers before you select the "correct" answer.** Some students lose points on multiple-choice exams because they don't read all possible answers before selecting the one that they think is correct. In most multiple-choice tests, you generally are asked to select the *best* answer. In that case, several of the choices may be correct or good answers, but only one answer is the "best" answer.

2. **Underline key words.** By underlining key words in the question, you can better focus your attention on what's being asked. In addition, you may find that underlining key words helps you identify a cue that triggers your long-term memory. Finally, taking the time to underline key words in both the question and the possible answers forces you to slow down and read the question and answers carefully.

3. **Work to eliminate incorrect alternatives rather than looking for the "right" answer.** After reading the question and all alternatives, begin looking for those that you know are wrong. When you're sure that one possible answer is a *distractor* (incorrect answer designed to appear correct), cross it off. Continue eliminating choices until only one answer remains. If you can eliminate all alternatives except one, you know you've found the correct answer.

4. **Connect the stem of the question to each alternative answer; then treat each statement as a true/false item.** If you're good at taking true/false tests, use the same strategies that work for you on the true/false items for the multiple-choice items. Identify key words, underline words or phrases that make the statement false, and watch for absolute, qualifying, and negative words. By examining each alternative as a separate statement, you may be able to improve your test score.

5. **Read the question, cover the alternatives, and think of the answer.** Some students find multiple-choice tests difficult because they allow the answers to confuse them. To avoid this problem, cover the answers with your hand, read the question, and think of the answer. Then read each alternative and ask yourself, "Does this mean the same thing as the answer that I know is correct?"

6. **Use caution when "all of the above" and "none of the above" are included as choices.** If you can eliminate even *one* alternative, you can eliminate "all of the above" as the correct answer. Similarly, if you're sure that at least one choice is correct, you can eliminate "none of the above." If you have three alternatives and you know that two of them are correct but aren't sure of the third, "all of the above" must be correct (assuming you can choose only one answer). If "all of the above" and "none of the above" are used only occasionally on the test, they are probably the correct choices. Watch for patterns like this on each exam.

Test-Wise Strategies

Use test-wise strategies to help you determine the correct choice when you can't figure it out. Many courses that are designed to prepare students to take the SATs or other standardized tests seem to specialize in these "test-smart" strategies. Some of them are very helpful; others aren't so useful. The key to using these strategies is to use them sparingly. Never follow a test-wise strategy that would require you to select one alternative when you're fairly sure that another alternative is the correct answer. Use these strategies *only* when you can't determine the correct answer by using the more conventional strategies.

Some of the more effective and useful test-wise strategies are listed below.

1. An answer that contains more specific, detailed information probably is correct. Vague or general alternatives are often used as distractors.

2. An answer that contains the most words, especially if it also contains the most specific information, probably is correct.

3. An answer that's in the middle probably is correct, especially if it has the most words.

4. An answer that's about in the middle numerically probably is correct.

5. An answer that contains an unfamiliar term probably is wrong.

6. An answer that contains a "typo," especially if there are very few typos in the test, probably is wrong.

7. An answer that's grammatically correct probably is right if the other choices are not grammatically correct.

8. An answer that contains a form of the word or a word similar to one in the stem of the question is probably correct.

9. If a question contains two opposite alternatives, one of them is probably correct.

10. If a question contains two alternatives that are almost identical (perhaps only one word is different), then one of them is probably correct.

STRATEGIES FOR TRUE/FALSE TESTS

Many students like true/false tests because they provide excellent odds for guessing correctly. However, some students have difficulty dealing with this type of test because the statements can be tricky. To make a statement incorrect, professors may change key words, omit key words, add absolute or qualifying words, add negative words, add extraneous information, and so on. Because there are so many ways to make a statement "false," students must consider all of them as they examine each statement.

Use the following basic guidelines when taking true/false tests:

1. **Always read the directions before beginning a true/false test.** Some instructors are very particular about how they expect students to mark true/false items. If you don't complete the exam according to the directions, you may not get credit for your answers.

2. **For a statement to be true, it must be all true.** If any part of the statement is false, the entire statement is false.

3. **True/false items are not all tricky.** Some students start to look for "tricks" or read too much into the question when a true/false item seems "too easy." If you're properly prepared for a test, some true/false items should appear to be easy.

4. **Identify the key words or phrases.** Many professors make a statement false by substituting another word or phrase for the correct one. By identifying and verifying the accuracy of key words, you can more easily decide whether a statement is true or false.

5. **Statements that contain absolute words are usually false.** Words like *always, all, none, never, only, every,* and *no* are examples of *absolute words.* Each of these words implies that there are no exceptions. Although the inclusion of these words in a true/false item doesn't guarantee that it's false, it usually indicates a false statement.

6. **Statements that contain qualifying words are usually true statements.** Words like *usually, often, may, can, sometimes, frequently, rarely, most, some, many, few,* and *generally* are examples of *qualifying words.* These words qualify or "temper" the statement to allow for exceptions and are generally associated with true statements. If you *know* that a statement is false, mark it *false,* even though it contains a qualifying word.

7. **Statements that contain negative words often are tricky and require careful attention.** Double negatives, which generally include the word *not* plus another word that contains a negative prefix often confuse students. If a statement contains a double negative, cross off the word *not* and the negative prefix (*in, il, ir,* or *un*) and then reread the statement in order to determine whether it's true or false.

8. **Always underline the word or words that make a statement false.** If you can't identify and mark the actual key words, absolute words, negative words, and so on that cause the statement to be incorrect, assume that it's correct and mark it true. There is one exception, however. If you know that a statement is false by omission (because a key word or phrase has been left out), mark the statement *false* even though you can't actually underline the words that make it false.

9. **Correct all false items on the exam if you have time to do so.** By correcting the statement, you show the professor and remind yourself what you were thinking during the exam. (By the time you get the exam back, you may not remember why you thought the item was false.)

10. **Professors usually include more true items than false items on an exam.** Many professors use tests to reinforce the main ideas that were presented in the course. If you absolutely can't figure out whether a statement is true or false, mark it true. Watch for patterns on each test.

STRATEGIES FOR MATCHING TESTS

With proper preparation and test-taking strategies, you should be able to get top scores on matching tests. Matching tests require you to recognize the correct answer from a list of alternatives. The answers to all questions are given. Before beginning a matching test, be sure that you read the directions. Usually, you're instructed to use each letter only once, but some matching tests allow for or require the repeated use of some letters.

Work from One Side

Matching tests often include a list of names or terms in one column and then a list of accomplishments or definitions in the other column. When you take a matching test, always work from one side only. Crossing off items in both columns leads to confusion and often results in careless errors or wasted time. You'll save time if you work from the column that has the most words (usually the definition column). If you work from the term column, you would have to scan more words in the definition column to find a correct match. If, instead, you work from the definition column, you would have to scan fewer words on each pass.

Answer the Questions You're Sure of First

When taking a matching test, it's crucial that you answer the questions or make the matches that you're absolutely sure of first. By skipping through the list and answering only the ones you're sure about, you improve your chances for a high or perfect score. If you make an error early in a matching test, you probably will make several more. Moreover, by eliminating all choices that you're sure of, you can narrow the alternatives for the remaining choices.

Eliminate and Cross Off Alternatives

As you go through the list of definitions, cross off the letter (not the word) of the ones that you use. Just put one diagonal line through the letter so that you can recheck your matches later. If you can eliminate five of the ten alternatives on your first pass through the list, you've improved your chances of getting the others right.

After you match all of the items you're sure of, start with the first unmatched definition that you have and try to match it with each remaining term. If you're sure of a match, make it; if not, skip over that definition and go on to the next one. Continue down the list until you can make one more match. Then go back through the list again. Having eliminated one more alternative, you may find that only one other term could possibly be correct for one of the definitions. Through the process of elimination, you should be able to make all the matches.

Recheck Your Work

After you've matched all items on the list, go back and check to be sure that you haven't accidentally used the same letter or number twice. Going through the letters or numbers and crossing off each one again can help you avoid careless errors. If necessary, rewrite the letters or numbers next to the original list and cross them off again.

GUESSING STRATEGIES

Even if you're well prepared for a test and use good test-taking strategies, you still may find that you can't answer some questions. When none of your test-taking strategies work, then you have to guess. Let's say there are four questions that you can't figure out on a 50-item multiple-choice test. Because each of those questions is worth 2 points, your unanswered questions add up to 8 points or almost one letter grade. Not answering them will result in at least an 8-point loss in your grade. Guessing doesn't guarantee that you'll get all of the questions right, but it certainly improves your odds of getting some of them right.

What is a guess anyway? Some students describe a guess as just putting down any letter they can think of to fill the slot. They choose randomly from among the alternatives. However, *strategic guessing* involves more active processes. Some students think they're guessing when they aren't sure of an answer but "kind of think" they know which one is right. These guesses may not really be guesses at all; they may be incomplete retrievals. When you read one alternative and it sort of sounds familiar or looks right, you may be making a faint connection to your long-term memory. You may be picking up on a cue different from the one that you previously used to retrieve the information, or you may be responding to the material on a different level. Nevertheless, your selection of that particular alternative may be more than a random guess. There are a number of strategies that you can use to pick up a few more points on a test even when you don't know the correct answer.

LOOK FOR PATTERNS

Pretend that you answered all of the easy questions on an exam and then went back and used problem-solving strategies to figure out the answers for a few more. Rather than just guessing randomly, look for patterns in the answers. Many professors never use the same letter more than two or three times in a row before shifting to a different response. So if you know that B is the correct response for the three previous questions and you eliminated C and D, A would be a more strategic guess than B. Go back and look at some of your old exams to see what types of patterns your professors use. Although you won't get all of the questions right, you should be able to add a few points to your test score.

CHECK FOR BALANCED ANSWER KEYS

Some professors always have *balanced answer keys;* they use exactly the same number of As, Bs, Cs, and Ds. If you find that there are three or four questions that you can't answer, count how many of each letter you've already used. You may find that you have fewer As than any other letter. By marking your remaining answers "A," you probably will pick up several additional points. Although this sounds like a great strategy, it works only if you're well enough prepared to get most of the answers right, thus revealing the patterns.

GUESSING DOESN'T REPLACE PROPER PREPARATION

Remember, guessing strategies are designed to help you pick up a few additional points when you absolutely can't figure out the correct answer any other way. They are *not* designed to replace proper preparation or substitute for more active problem-solving strategies that can lead you to the correct answer by providing you with clues or aiding your recall of the answer. Use them *only* after all other attempts to figure out the correct answer have failed.

LEARNING FROM EXAMS

Many students think that once an exam is over, the only thing that matters is the grade. However, exams are learning opportunities. Professors often use them to help reinforce the critical concepts that they're trying to present. Reviewing an exam after it's returned can help you learn more about the course content and

DON'T LEAVE THE EXAM EARLY.
Some students rush through the exam because they're afraid of running out of time. Others begin to panic as soon as the first student turns in his or her paper. You need to use all the exam time to get the best grade you can. You may be able to pick up a few more points by using problem-solving, test-wise, and guessing strategies.

GO BACK OVER DIFFICULT QUESTIONS. Use any additional time to rethink difficult questions on the exam. Underline key words in the question and in the alternatives. Eliminate wrong answers. Look for clues in other questions. Rephrase the question or the alternatives.

REDO MATH PROBLEMS TO CHECK YOUR WORK. Some students lose points on exams because of careless errors. If you have time, cover the problem with your hand and rework it. Then compare your answers. If they differ, check your work line by line until you locate your mistake.

DO A MEMORY SEARCH. When you can't figure out the answer to a question, try doing a memory search. Ask yourself whether the information was presented during the lecture or if it came from the text. Try to figure out from which topic the question came. Sometimes you can trigger a cue to long-term memory by identifying where or when you studied it.

USE CAUTION WHEN CHANGING ANSWERS. During a final review of the test, many students change answers because they start to have second thoughts about their original choices. This strategy often leads to changing correct answers to incorrect ones. Instead, use this rule: Don't change an answer unless you find that you misread the question or actually find the correct answer or a clue to it somewhere else on the exam.

REVIEW THE ENTIRE EXAM. When you complete the exam, take a few minutes to go back over it and check your answers. Some students make careless errors when they begin the exam because they're anxious; others do the same toward the end of the exam when they think they're running out of time. By reviewing your test, you may be able to correct some careless mistakes that would have cost you valuable points.

CHECK YOUR ANSWER SHEET AGAINST YOUR EXAM. Before you turn in your test paper, take a minute or two to check to be sure that you marked the correct answers on your answer sheet. It's easy to make mistakes when you're nervous or in a hurry. You want to get the points for all your correct answers. In the process, you may also catch some careless errors that you made.

ESTIMATE YOUR GRADE. Before leaving the exam, take a few minutes to estimate your grade. Learning to accurately predict your test score can help you eliminate feelings of panic that often occur after taking the exam. Some students become so nervous about the outcome of an exam that it interferes with their ability to concentrate on their other work.

clarify any errors that you made. You also can learn a great deal about your professor's testing methods and about your own test-taking skills.

EVALUATE YOUR PREPARATION

Your graded exam can be used to help you evaluate your preparation. By finding out where each question came from (the lecture or the textbook), you can determine whether you're focusing on the same topics and concepts as your professor. You also can check how well you mark and take notes by scanning the text or your text notes and looking for questions that were on the test. If you find that few of the test questions are contained in material that you highlighted or noted, you can adjust your marking for the next test. Determining how many of the questions came from the text and how many came from the lecture can help you decide how much time to spend on each type of material the next time you prepare. If, for example, your professor took 80 percent of the test questions from the lecture material, then you should have spent 80 percent of your study time on lecture notes and only 20 percent on text material.

You also can evaluate how well you were able to anticipate or predict test questions. Check your list of 20, 30, or 40 to see how many of the items were actually on the exam. Compare your exam to the self-tests that you designed. How many of the test questions did you predict? Think back to how you felt as you took the exam. Did you feel surprised by many of the items, or did you often find yourself thinking, "I knew this would be on the test"?

Finally, evaluate your test-taking skills. Did you read the directions, budget your time well, and answer the easy questions first? Did you work through the difficult items in a logical, systematic way, eliminating wrong answers? Were you able to identify key words in the questions that helped you figure out the correct answers? Did you review the exam and rework the difficult items? Knowing how effectively you were able to use the various test-taking strategies can help you improve your performance on the next exam.

LEARN FROM YOUR MISTAKES

Because you can learn a lot from exams, it's important to spend some time going over them. If you don't get to keep your exam, set up an appointment to review it with your professor. Unfortunately, too few students make use of their opportunity to review exams. Even if the professor goes over the answers in class, you need to see your own paper to analyze your errors. If you don't understand why something was marked wrong, ask the professor to explain it.

You'll benefit by learning more about the subject and by getting a better idea of what the professor expected.

GET HELP BEFORE THE NEXT EXAM

If your grade on the exam isn't up to par, go for help immediately. Your first stop should be your professor. Set up an appointment to discuss your exam. Go over the exam question by question until you have a clear understanding of what you need to do to improve your grade for the next exam. Tell your professor exactly what you did to prepare and ask for suggestions about what you may need to do differently. During the meeting you'll gain helpful tips on what to study and how to study, and your professor will find out that you're interested and trying to do better. He or she may offer to work with you before the next exam.

Your next stop should be your college learning center. Many learning centers offer individual assistance or workshops on test preparation, test anxiety, and test-taking strategies. You may need to request tutorial assistance. If you don't have a learning center on your campus, ask where you might go to get this type of help. Some departments or organizations offer tutoring services to students. Waiting to see if you do better on your next test can be very risky. If you don't do any better, you'll have two low grades to pull up. By finding out what you did wrong and by asking for help in correcting those mistakes, you can improve your performance on the next exam.

SUMMARY

Your preparation for exams is only one factor that influences your final grade. Some students appear to be good test takers and others don't. Why? One explanation involves how effectively they can handle the stress of taking exams. Test anxiety can affect your ability to prepare for and take exams. Some students get queasy, feel faint, worry, or even "go blank" during exams. Because of test anxiety, they can't completely focus on the exam questions and their grades suffer. Coping techniques such as doing relaxation exercises, visualizing, using positive self-scripts, and identifying anxiety triggers can help reduce your test anxiety. However, the most effective way to reduce test anxiety is being well prepared.

Following directions carefully is crucial during any testing situation. Too often, though, students skip this important step in order to save time or because of high levels of test anxiety. Budgeting your time during exams is also important so that you can complete all questions and still have time for a final review of the test. You can maximize your test score and pick up clues to more difficult questions by answering the easiest questions first. Using both problem-solving and test-wise strategies will help you gain points on matching, true/false, completion, and multiple-choice exams. Doing memory searches, eliminating wrong answers, and underlining key words are just a few ways to "figure out" the correct answer when you're not sure of it. However, when you still can't come up with the right choice, you should guess. You can often improve your exam score by using strategic guessing. If you've taken the time to prepare properly for your exam, take the time to "take" it, too. Use the full amount of time that's been allotted for the exam. Students who persevere— continue to work on difficult questions, think through confusing items, look for clues in other questions, and use other problem-solving and test-wise strategies—do better on exams. By estimating your grade and evaluating your preparation and performance, you can learn how to improve your grade on the next exam.

Activities

1. Go to the *Orientation to College Learning* Web site and follow the link to the Test Anxiety Scale. Answer each of the questions on line or by printing a copy of the questionnaire. Then follow the scoring instructions to determine your test anxiety level. What did you find?

2. Describe your test-taking experiences in high school. How did you do on tests? What strategies did you use when taking objective tests? How successful were the strategies? What changes do you plan to make in order to be as successful or more successful on college exams?

3. Go to the *Orientation to College Learning* Web site and click on the Activities Packets for Chapter 11. Take the practice tests to practice the test-taking strategies for true/false, multiple-choice, and matching tests found in Activities 11–3 to 11–6.

4. Compare the results of the practice tests with those of the other members of your group. What strategies did you use to figure out the correct

answers when you took true/false, multiple-choice, and matching tests? How did your strategy use compare with that of the others in your group?

5. Using the Internet, identify at least two sites that contain test-taking strategies or tips. Record the sites and either print out or copy 10 strategies for taking objective tests to share with your group.

6. Discuss the list of test-taking strategies you located on the Internet with the other members of your group. Select the best strategies from each list and create a group list of the 10 best test-taking strategies to present to the class. Develop a list of the best Internet sites to share with other members of the class.

7. Review one of the exams that recently was returned to you. Write a paragraph or two discussing what you were able to learn from the exam. Include information about how the test was designed, your preparation, and your test-taking skills.

8. If you're using InfoTrac College Edition, use Power/Trac to locate a recent article or research study on how test anxiety affects test performance. Describe the study and any suggestions that were included on how to cope with anxiety before and during college tests. List three strategies that you can use to reduce your own test anxiety. After using them before or during your next exam, describe any changes you noted in your performance or your ability to concentrate. Be prepared to present the information in class.

9. Think of three examples of how you've applied what you learned in this chapter. Choose one strategy and describe how you applied it to your other course work using the Journal Entry Form that is located on the *Orientation to College Learning* Web site. Consider the following questions as you complete your entry. Why did you use this strategy? What did you do? How did it work? How did it affect your performance on the task? How did this approach compare to your previous approach? What changes would you make the next time you use this strategy?

10. Now that you've completed Chapter 11, take a few minutes to repeat the "Where Are You Now?" activity, located on the *Orientation to College Learning* Web site. What changes did you make as a result of reading this chapter? How are you planning to apply what you've learned in this chapter?

Review Questions

Terms You Should Know:

Absolute words	Facilitating test anxiety	Stem
Alternatives	Memory search	Strategic guessing
Balanced answer keys	Pacing	Test anxiety
Debilitating test anxiety	Problem-solving strategies	Test anxiety cycle
Distractors	Qualifying words	Test-wise strategies

Completion: Fill in the blank to complete each of the following statements.

1. The real cause of test anxiety is _____ _____.

2. The best way to reduce test anxiety is to _____ _____.

3. The most important factor in determining how much time to spend on a question is the _____ _____.

4. On a matching test, you should always work from the side with the _____ words.

5. Unless you _____ the question or find the correct answer (or a clue to it) somewhere else on the test, you shouldn't change your answer.

Multiple Choice: Circle the letter of the best answer for each of the following questions. Be sure to underline key words and eliminate wrong answers.

6. _____ test anxiety is helpful because it makes you study for a test.
   A. Motivating
   B. Affective
   C. Facilitating
   D. Debilitating

7. _____ words generally make a statement false.
   A. Negative
   B. Absolute
   C. Qualifying
   D. Italicized

Short Answer–Essay: On a separate sheet, answer each of the following questions.

8. Why should students answer the easiest questions first?

9. How should students cope with test anxiety in order to improve their performance on exams?

10. What strategies should students use to maximize their scores on objective tests?

Chapter 12

PREPARING FOR ESSAY TESTS

"I never really prepared for essay exams before reading this chapter. Now I predict several questions for each chapter, list, and then outline the information. Then I create mnemonics to help me recall the information. I write the essay out to practice the main points. I used this strategy in Sociology because the exam was all essays. These strategies helped keep me well organized and prepared, and I felt confident answering the questions on the exam."

Rita Alvara
Student

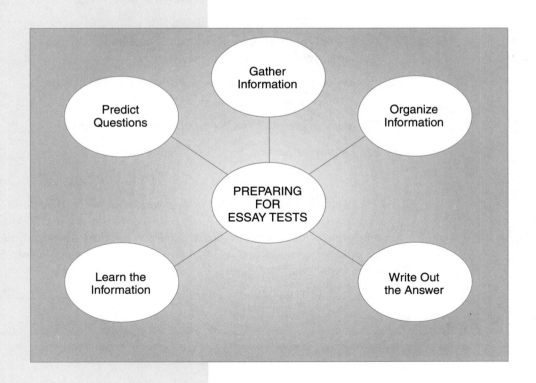

Where Are You Now?

Take a few minutes to answer *yes* or *no* to the following questions.

	YES	NO
1. Do you study differently for essay tests and objective tests?	____	____
2. Do you generally plan out your answers in your head rather than on paper?	____	____
3. Do you always write out essays before the test if the professor gives you the questions?	____	____
4. Do you predict possible essay questions before an exam?	____	____
5. Are you usually able to predict accurately which essay questions the professor will include?	____	____
6. Do you use memory techniques to help you remember the main points that you want to make in your answer?	____	____
7. Do you tend to rely on old exams and hope that the same questions will be used again?	____	____
8. Do you prepare sample essay answers and ask your professor to evaluate them before the exam?	____	____
9. Are you generally well prepared for essay exams?	____	____
10. Do you know how to study for an essay exam?	____	____
TOTAL POINTS	____	

Give yourself 1 point for each *yes* answer to all of the questions except 2 and 7 and 1 point for each *no* answer to questions 2 and 7. Now total up your points. A low score indicates that you need to develop some new skills for preparing for essay tests. A high score indicates that you already are using many good strategies.

PREDICT QUESTIONS

Essay tests are more difficult than objective tests for many students because they require recall learning. You need to *know* what you're writing about. You also need to be able to put what you know on paper in a rather short period of time. To prepare for an essay test, you should use many of the strategies presented in Chapter 10 for setting up a study plan and learning the material. Preparing for an essay test, though, involves more than just knowing the material. To write a good essay answer, you need to be able to organize your thoughts and ideas rapidly and then present them in a well-developed and well-written form. All these skills require training and practice. In this chapter you'll learn some additional strategies for preparing for essay exams. Predicting, planning, and actually writing out answers before the exam can help you improve your performance on essay exams.

An essay test requires you to write paragraph-style answers to the questions. Sometimes you'll be asked to write about topics that were presented either in the lecture or in the text. Other times, you'll be required to pull together bits and pieces of information from one or more lectures, several sections of your text, or even information from both lecture and the text to answer the question. Essay tests may require you to focus on rather specific information or to synthesize a large body of information.

If you aren't given the actual questions that will be on the exam, then the best way to study for an essay test is to predict test questions yourself. By anticipating questions that could be on the exam, you increase your chances of studying the same information on which you'll be tested. Of course, it's also to your advantage to prepare the answers in essay form so that you study the information in the same format that you'll be required to use on the test.

PREDICT EXTRA QUESTIONS

Deciding how many questions to predict isn't easy. Many factors need to be considered. A test that covers two chapters may require more or fewer questions than one that covers six chapters; the difference involves the depth or breadth of the questions. A good rule of thumb is to predict at least four times the number of questions that will be on the exam. If you'll have to answer two essay questions on the exam, then you should predict at least eight questions. Another approach is to predict three or four questions from each chapter. The more questions you predict, the greater your chances of accurately predicting the questions that the professor will put on the exam. Also, even if you don't predict the exact questions, you may find that you have predicted a question similar to the one on the test. In the process of preparing to answer your question, you may learn the information that you need to answer the question that the professor asks. The more questions that you predict and prepare, the better you'll do on the test.

PREDICT THE RIGHT KINDS OF QUESTIONS

It's equally important to predict the right kinds of questions. You should predict *broad questions* if the exam will cover large amounts of material. If the essay test will include ten questions on only two chapters of text, however, the questions may be more specific and require more detail about a more specific topic. If you go through your text and your notes, you should be able to come up with some ideas about topics that could become essay questions. Study guides (purchased guides or study guides provided by the professor) and end-of-chapter questions in the text also are valuable sources of essay questions. Your lecture notes are perhaps the best resource. Did the professor stress some particular topic? Were any comparisons drawn between one topic and a later one? Did the instructor ever hint that an understanding of one specific topic was critical to the mastery of the course? Asking the professor for sample questions and reviewing old exams can help you determine the types of questions that you should be predicting.

Narrow questions that focus on why or how something happened often are too limited in scope. Most essay questions ask you to discuss causes and effects, compare and contrast, explain the steps in a process, and so on. You'll be able to predict and answer essay questions more effectively if you understand the terms that commonly are used in essay questions. A chart of frequently used terms is presented in Figure 12.1. Although you don't need to memorize the terms and their definitions, you should become familiar with them.

PREDICT CHALLENGING QUESTIONS

Predicting good essay questions requires some practice; they must be not only thoughtful but also penetrating and challenging. Many students predict only knowledge-level questions—questions that require only the repetition of the information as it was stated in the text or the lecture. Although some professors do include some of these short-answer essays, most ask questions that require analysis, synthesis, and application. Look at these three questions:

1. What are two types of note-taking systems used for lecture classes?

2. Describe two types of note-taking systems that are used for lecture classes.

3. Compare and contrast the outline method and the block method of taking notes in lecture classes.

FIGURE 12.1

• • • • • • • • •

Frequently Used
Terms in Essay
Questions

Term	Definition
compare	Tell how two or more subjects are alike; provide similarities. Some professors also expect you to discuss differences—ask.
contrast	Tell how two or more subjects are different.
define	Give the meaning or definition.
describe	Provide details or characteristics about a subject.
discuss or explain	Give a detailed answer that may include definitions, main and supporting points, reasons, and examples.
evaluate	Discuss both positive and negative aspects of the topic and then make a judgment.
illustrate	Explain by giving examples.
justify	Prove by giving evidence that backs up or supports a point.
list or enumerate	Number and list the information rather than writing in paragraph form.
summarize	Provide a brief review of the main points.
trace	Describe the events or steps in order of occurrence.

The first question isn't really an essay question at all. It requires only a short answer and little other information about the topic. The second and third questions, on the other hand, require more in-depth mastery of the material. Several paragraphs or several pages may be needed to answer them properly.

To predict good questions, you have to know where to look for them. Although the questions themselves aren't often found in your textbook or lecture notes, clues to them are. Most essay questions center around main ideas or themes. The major headings in the text provide clues to these main ideas. You often can rephrase the headings to come up with predicted questions. Unlike the recall questions that you may write in the margin, a predicted essay question should be a more general "summing up" of all the material under that topic. Look for clues such as lists of reasons (positive and negative), similarities or differences, and sequences.

Students often get into the habit of predicting one essay question for each main topic or main heading in the text or lecture. One problem with this practice is that it may be too limiting for some essay tests. Learning the material in isolation, heading by heading, may not prepare you to answer a more general question that requires you to integrate the information. To prepare for tests

FIGURE 12.2
● ● ● ● ● ● ● ● ● ●
Predicted Essay
Questions on
Federalism

1. Explain the impact of the Thirteenth, Fourteenth, and Fifteenth Amendments with respect to limiting state power for individual freedom.

2. What are the advantages and disadvantages of Federalism?

3. How does Federalism increase political participation?

4. Name the three amendments passed by the Reconstruction Congress and describe what each amendment did to delegate Congress's power of security.

5. Explain the differences between delegated and reserved powers.

6. Explain both Hamilton's and Jefferson's views on Federalism and the Constitution; tell which one you agree with and why.

7. What was the greatest crisis of the American Federal system? Why did it happen? What were the results?

8. Name the court case in 1819 that involved the state of Maryland and the National Bank and tell what it established.

9. What is Federalism? How does it affect the American people?

10. Discuss the 1954 Supreme court case *Brown* v. *Board of Education.* What effect did this case have on civil rights in the United States?

where you may have only one or two long essays to answer, you need to learn to connect two or more of the main topics. By learning to write broad, general questions that incorporate information in several sections of the chapter, you prepare yourself for specific questions and broad ones.

Look at some of the questions in Figure 12.2 that one group of students predicted after reading a text excerpt on federalism. Which of these questions are broad, general questions? Which are narrow and need to be changed?

GATHER INFORMATION

Predicting essay questions is not the end of your preparation for an essay exam; it's just the beginning. The next step is to *gather information.* You need to find the main and supporting points required to answer the questions. You probably know some information to include in your answer, but you need to refer to your text and notes for more. This process of gathering information is valuable because it forces you to dig through the text and your lecture notes looking for relevant information. This active study technique may help you learn some of the other text information at the same time. Putting the information from the text and the lecture together also is a good technique for preparing for an essay test.

FIGURE 12.3

• • • • • • • • • • • • • • •

DaShawn's Example of Gathered Information

How did we obtain Alaska?	
Seward (L)	exercise commercial domination (T)
72 mill (L)	less than 2 cents an acre (T)
greatest steal (L)	feared Brit would buy it (T)
gold, fishery, timber (L)	convince British colonies to (T)
Folly or Icebox (L)	request annexation as well (T)
Bribe money (L)	
Union in 1960 (L)	
Russia (L)	

DaShawn's Gathered Information

TREAT EACH QUESTION SEPARATELY

An easy way to gather information is to treat each question separately. Write each question across the top of a large piece of paper. Then open your text and your notes to that section of the material. Start to look for information that you would use if you had to answer that question. Pretend that it's an open-book exam and you have the opportunity to look for the material that you're going to use. As you locate important points and details that would be useful in answering the question, write them down on your sheet of paper. Don't copy the information; rather, write it in meaningful phrases. If you use a two-column format, you'll be forced to write only meaningful phrases.

Figure 12.3 shows the information DaShawn gathered for the essay question that she predicted would be on her History exam. As you can see, the list of information is still far from the organized essay answer that she will need to write.

ORGANIZE INFORMATION

After gathering information for a number of questions, you may find that you have a huge amount of information to remember. By organizing the information and creating an outline for each question, you'll find it's easier to learn and remember

FIGURE 12.4
• • • • • • • • • •
Karen's
Organized
Information

Explain the research done by the experimenters at Santa Barbara
University. What conclusion was found?

∟ **significant differences in time ^{2C1} ∟ **three groups ^{2}
∟ **learned drive theory ^{3A} ∟ **saw no one ^{2A}
∟ **videotaped joggers ^{1} ∟ **saw woman reading ^{2B}
∟ **timed in two sections ^{1A} ∟ **saw woman watching ^{2C}
∟ **joggers—unaware experiment ^{1B} ∟ **Cotrell ^{3B}
∟ **fear of evaluation increases drive ^{3C} ∟ **conclusion ^{3}

Karen's Plan

the points you want to make for each question. Predicting essay questions and
planning the answers is a preparation strategy. You are identifying, organizing,
condensing, and writing the information.

LABEL EACH POINT

You can organize your gathered information by *labeling* each point. Look at each
piece of information that you wrote down and decide where it should go in your
essay. Find the point that you want to make first and label it 1. Any points that
support it should be marked 1A, 1B, and so on. Karen organized the information for one of her predicted Psychology questions (Figure 12.4).

OUTLINE YOUR ANSWER

Although Karen did organize her information (Figure 12.4), it still isn't in a form
that's easy to practice and remember. An informal outline is much more useful
for remembering the points that you want to make in your essay answer. The
easiest way to outline your answer is simply to list the *main points* (most important points) next to the margin and then list the *supporting details* indented
slightly underneath. Try to limit your main points to seven or fewer so you can
remember them. Three or four main points with good support for each should
be sufficient for most answers. Of course, if you need to know the five causes of
something, then you'll have five main points.

Look at the outline that Addie developed from the information that she
gathered to answer the question "What are the stages in the evolution and
growth of American cities?" (Figure 12.5). Addie used an *informal outline* style
to list the main points and secondary or supporting points.

FIGURE 12.5

Addie's Informal
Outline

> What are the stages in the evolution and growth of American cities?
> From beginning to about 1800s
> > Cities developed before commercial agriculture
> > Cities served as outposts of Western Europe
> > Development of coastal cities
>
> 1800 to 1860s
> > Manifest Destiny
> > Construction of canals and railroads
> > NYC became national metropolis
> > Northeastern cities as industrial centers
>
> 1860s to World War I
> > Industrialization continued after Civil War
> > Cities grew and developed
>
> World War I to World War II
> > The Great Depression
> > 9,000 banks closed losing $2.5 billion
> > Urban decay
> > Programs instituted by Pres. F.D.R. to help urban unemployed
>
> Post World War II
> > Returning veterans
> > Suburbs grew and flourished
> > SMSAs became MSAs
> > Urban population swelled

LEARN THE INFORMATION

Gathering and outlining the information that you would use to answer a question doesn't guarantee that you'll be able to replicate the answer on the test. The next step is to learn the information. By learning the key points you selected, you increase your chances of maximizing your score on the exam. It's not necessary to memorize your outline word for word. Reciting the main points and then practicing the details that you wish to add should enable you to remember the material for your exam.

IDENTIFY AND LEARN THE MAIN POINTS

Identify the main points in your outline and then learn them. The best way to learn the main points is to practice them over and over. Cover everything except the question with your hand or another sheet of paper. Ask yourself, "What are the main points that I want to make about this question?" Even better, try to write your outline without looking back. Practicing (reciting and writing) the information over a period of days will help you remember it during the exam. Once you know the main points, practice the details in your outline. Each of the main points can then serve as a cue to help you retrieve the details from long-term memory.

USE MNEMONIC DEVICES

If you have difficulty recalling certain points or remembering them in order, try using a *mnemonic device* (a memory cue) to improve your recall. Identify a key word in each of the main points that you made in your outline. Underline the words and then think of a way to remember them. Acrostics or catchphrases are useful for essay tests because they allow you to recall the information in order. Although these mnemonics don't replace learning the information, they do act as hooks or cues to help you recall what you learned. Lisa created the catchphrase, "Nancy sells every car for parts," to help her remember the six main points for her sociology answer (Figure 12.6). What mnemonics could you use to help you remember the main points in Addie's outline in Figure 12.5?

WRITE OUT THE ANSWER

Some students know how to answer a question; they know the information. However, when they actually are in the testing situation, they just can't seem to put that information on paper. If this has happened to you before, the problem may be about writing rather than about studying. To convincingly show the professor what you know, you may need to practice writing out the answers in paragraph form.

WHY YOU SHOULD WRITE OUT YOUR ANSWER

Writing out your answer before the exam will help you overcome some problems that cause students difficulty during exams. One of the most common problems is getting started. By practicing ahead of time, you can avoid this problem. When the

FIGURE 12.6

. . . .

Lisa's Gathered
Information and
Outline with
Mnemonic Cues

Explain the view Thomas Hobbes took on the problem of order and the social
contract.

1 social order is political natural law	3 equality among people
2 state of nature	4 people form a social contract
2A people are selfish and violent	4A agreement b/w societies
2C people become power hungry	4B people give up natural liberty
2B central concept is power	4C laws tell us how to act
3A state of nature is condition of war	5 if break laws we are denied
3B common fear of power	freedom
	6 power of state is order

TS Thomas Hobbes viewed order in society as a hunger for power
among people.

1. Social order is political natural law

2. State of nature
   A. people are selfish & violent
   B. central concept is power
   C. people become power hungry

3. Equality among people
   A. State of nature is condition of war
   B. Common fear of power

4. People form a social contract
   A. agreement b/w societies
   B. people give up natural liberty
   C. laws tell us how to act

5. If we break laws, we are deprived of freedom

6. Power of state is order

1. Natural
2. State
3. Equality
4. Contract
5. Freedom
6. Power

(Nancy sells every
car for parts.)

test begins, although you may not remember your first sentence word for word,
you'll know how to approach the question. Some students have difficulty deciding
how to phrase what they want to say and how to tie their points together. Doing
this before the exam will help you do a better job during the exam. Again, don't
try to memorize your answer word for word. If you forget one word or phrase, you
may find yourself unable to complete your answer. You want to practice writing
out the answer just to get the feel for how the whole thing fits together.

MORE TIPS FOR PREPARING ESSAY TESTS

PROPER PREPARATION IS THE KEY. Many students are anxious about essay tests, partially because they don't know how to prepare for them. Trying to write an essay answer requires recall learning. You can't just read over the material. Instead you need to predict questions, plan the answers, and learn the information.

REVIEW OLD EXAMS. Review old exams to get some ideas about the types of questions your professor tends to ask. Don't rely just on those questions, though, because few professors use the same questions over again. Use them, instead, as models to develop your own questions.

PREDICT YOUR OWN TEST QUESTIONS. Go through your text and lecture material and write five to ten essay questions that you think could be on the exam. The more questions you write, the greater the possibility several of your questions will be on the exam.

SET UP A STUDY GROUP. Some students find that working in a group is quite effective when preparing for essay exams. Compare your questions with those of the members of your study group or predict questions as a group. Other members of the group may find connections in the material that you hadn't considered.

WRITE AND COMPARE ESSAY ANSWERS. Ask each member of your study group to write out the answers to the questions that were predicted. Then exchange the answers during a group meeting and compare your answer to each question with the answers written by the others in your group.

DEVELOP AN INFORMAL OUTLINE. Organize your gathered information in an informal outline so that you can easily see the main points that you want to make when writing out your essay answer. List the main points of your answer and then several of the details in your outline. Keep your outline simple so that it's easy to recall.

RECITE THE MAIN POINTS OF YOUR ANSWER. Practice reciting the main points that you want to make for each of the answers that you developed. While you're driving to school or work, check your memory of the information. Just creating an outline doesn't mean you know the information.

PRACTICE USING YOUR OUTLINE

Practice writing your answer by referring to your outline. Your goal here is not to test your memory of the information but to practice stringing together your ideas. Turn each line from your outline (each meaningful phrase) into a sentence. Add additional sentences to provide more details, if you can. After you've successfully constructed an answer with the outline, try to write the answer again without it. On the evening before the exam, practice writing the answer one last time. By allowing yourself some time between your initial practice session and your final one, you test your ability both to recall the information and to present it in a well-written and well-organized manner. If you're able to construct a well-written answer without your outline the night before the exam, you'll feel reassured when you begin the actual exam.

WRITE OUT THE MOST DIFFICULT QUESTIONS

If you've predicted a large number of questions, you may not have time to write out all the answers ahead of time. If this happens, write out only the ones that you think you would have the greatest difficulty explaining. If a number of your questions seem fairly straightforward, you can probably eliminate this stage. Just be sure you review aloud the key points that you would make and think about how you might start the answers. Choose more complex questions for written practice. If you can present the information in the difficult questions in a well-written form, you probably can do equally well or better on the easier questions.

Figure 12.7 shows the practice essay that Lisa constructed from her outline in Figure 12.6. Notice how she moved from one main point to the next in constructing her answer.

PREPARE ANSWERS FOR ALL SAMPLE QUESTIONS

Some instructors pass out sample essay questions prior to an exam. These questions are a valuable source of information. You can use them to get an idea of the kinds of questions that will appear on the exam; however, they can be used to even greater advantage. Each sample question can be planned, practiced, and learned using the strategies described previously.

Even if the sample questions are not the ones on the actual test, chances are they're closely related. In the process of preparing to answer the sample question, you probably will learn the information to answer the actual test question. A good general rule is always to treat sample questions as if they were the actual exam questions. Don't assume, however, that you should focus your study only on those questions. Go ahead and predict some additional questions just in case.

After you've prepared several questions and written out the answers, go see your professor. Ask him or her to take a look at your predicted questions (or the sample test questions) and the answers that you wrote. Ask for feedback on how

FIGURE 12.7

● ● ● ● ● ● ● ● ●

Lisa's Practice
Essay

> Thomas Hobbes viewed order in society as a hunger for power among people. He looked at social order as a political natural law rather than a divine law. He said that people in a state of nature are naturally driven to satisfy their own needs and desires. He describes them as selfish and violent and will go to any measure to satisfy their needs. The central concept in the state of nature of human beings comes from power. To have power is the ability to get what we want, and we become power hungry and tear each other apart to accomplish this.
>
> There is an equality among people that gives everyone the ability to fulfill this need. The state of nature becomes a condition of war in which people fight with each other when they want the same thing. They then begin to have a fear of power, which is the only thing that makes society possible at this stage. When the power of fear does not exist anymore, people form a social contract in which they understand order as an agreement between societies. Under this social contract people give up their natural liberty and rely on a sovereignty under which they are protected. This sovereignty forms laws and the laws tell us how to act, and if we follow the laws, order will exist. If we break the laws, the state has the right to deny our freedom. To Hobbes, order is a power of state that keeps us in line.

you approached the question and how you presented your answer. Don't expect your professor to "grade" the paper for you; instead, look for tips or suggestions for how you might improve your essay for the exam. Getting feedback on your answers before the exam may result in much higher test grades and a better relationship with your instructors.

SUMMARY

Essay exams are often more difficult than objective exams because they require recall-level learning. You have to know the material well enough to write one paragraph, several paragraphs, or even several pages to answer the question. To be properly prepared for essay exams, you need to predict broad, challenging questions—questions that cover the main topics presented in the course. Developing questions that integrate or incorporate several headed sections of text or several topics presented during one or more lectures can help prepare you to answer the kinds of questions that often appear on essay exams.

After you predict a series of questions, you need to plan the answers. The first step is to gather information by digging through the text and your lecture notes. List any points that you would use to answer the question. Organize the information by labeling each point according to where you would use it in your answer. Then take a few minutes to write an outline of your answer. Seeing the information in this organized format will help you better learn and recall the points you want to make. Practice writing or reciting your outline to learn the main points you want to make and to test your ability to recall the details, too. Creating mnemonics can help you recall all the points in your outline. Finally, write answers to one or two of the most difficult questions just to get the feel for how the information in your outline fits together. Writing out several practice answers can help you learn how to move from one point to the next and, in so doing, reduce your anxiety about taking essay exams. By predicting possible essay questions and planning and practicing their answers, you'll be well prepared for your next essay exam.

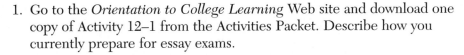

Activities

  1. Go to the *Orientation to College Learning* Web site and download one copy of Activity 12–1 from the Activities Packet. Describe how you currently prepare for essay exams.

 2. Predict three essay questions for an exam that you have coming up in the next few weeks. Write each question on a separate sheet of paper and then plan all three answers by gathering information, outlining, and planning mnemonics for the main points.

 3. Practice learning the information in your outline. Recite the main and supporting points out loud. Try to replicate your outline by writing it from memory. Which method helped you learn the information more effectively? Describe your results in one or two paragraphs.

 4. Write out the answers to at least two of the questions you predicted and planned for your exam. Set up an appointment with your professor to discuss the questions you predicted and the answers you

planned and wrote out. Write a paragraph describing your discussion and what you learned from the experience.

5. At least 1 week prior to your exam, prepare answers for the broad essay questions that you chose from either old exams, study guides, or sample questions provided by your course instructor. Discuss your answers with either your professor or a staff member in your college Learning Center. Using the feedback you received, revise your answers. What feedback did you get? What did you learn about the quality of your original answers? What changes did you make when you revised your answers?

6. Work as a group to develop a list of predicted essay questions for the material in Chapter 11 of this text. Use the chart of frequently used terms in essay questions (Figure 12.1) to help you develop a variety of broad general questions. Then choose one question and gather information for the answer individually. Work together to develop a group essay plan, including an outline. Then write the answer from the outline that you developed.

7. Exchange copies of the essay answer that you wrote for Activity 6 with the other members of your group. After reading each of the other answers describe how your answer compares. What were the strengths and/or weaknesses of your answer? What changes would you make?

8. If you're using InfoTrac College Edition, use the subject guide to identify a list of categories on a topic that has been emphasized in one of your classes. Using the category headings, predict five essay questions about the topic. Then locate one article that contains information about one of the essays that you predicted. Using the information from the article, develop a plan for an answer to your question.

9. Think of three examples of how you've applied what you learned in this chapter. Choose one strategy and describe how you applied it to your other course work using the Journal Entry Form that is located on the *Orientation to College Learning* Web site. Consider the following questions as you complete your entry. Why did you use this strategy? What did you do? How did it work? How did it affect your performance on the task? How did this approach compare with your previous approach? What changes would you make the next time you use this strategy?

10. Now that you've completed Chapter 12, take a few minutes to repeat the "Where Are You Now?" activity, located on the *Orientation to College Learning* Web site. What changes did you make as a result of reading this chapter? How are you planning to apply what you've learned in this chapter?

Review Questions

Terms You Should Know:

Broad questions	Evaluate	Mnemonic devices
Compare	Gather information	Narrow questions
Contrast	Illustrate	Summarize
Define	Informal outline	Supporting details
Describe	Justify	Trace
Enumerate	Main points	

Completion: Fill in the blank to complete each of the following statements.

1. One way to prepare for an essay exam is to predict _____ questions for every one that will be on the exam.

2. If you only have one essay question on an exam, you should predict _____ or _____ questions from every chapter.

3. Using a two-column format forces you to write the gathered information in _____ _____.

4. _____ are especially useful for recalling the main points in your outline.

5. After you create an outline for your answer, you must _____ the information.

Multiple Choice: Circle the letter of the best answer for each of the following questions. Be sure to underline key words and eliminate wrong answers.

6. If the word _____ is used in the question, you must explain by giving examples.
   A. describe
   B. illustrate
   C. justify
   D. trace

7. Which of the following is not a good source for predicted essay questions?
   A. Main headings in the textbook
   B. Main topics from your lecture notes
   C. Recall questions in your text and notes
   D. Old exams

Short Answer–Essay: On a separate sheet, answer each of the following questions.

8. How should you prepare for an exam that contains both objective and essay questions?

9. Why do some students have difficulty preparing for essay exams? What should they do differently?

10. What are the benefits of gathering information for predicted essay questions?

Chapter 13

TAKING ESSAY TESTS

"I feel that I am better prepared for essay exams now. I never really knew how to study for them or how to write out the answers. Often I would just write down anything that came to mind. Now that I have learned to plan in the margin before I write, essay tests don't seem as hard as they did before. I plan to use this strategy on all my future exams."

Kim Bednarski
Student

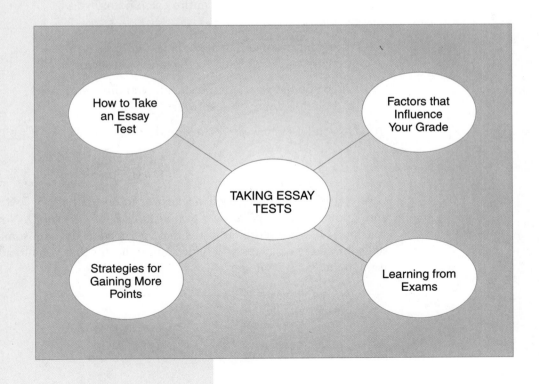

Where Are You Now?

Take a few minutes to answer *yes* or *no* to the following questions.

	YES	NO
1. Do you always read the directions before you begin to answer the questions on an essay exam?	_____	_____
2. Do you generally plan your answer in your head rather than on paper before you begin to write?	_____	_____
3. Do you usually score lower on essay exams than on objective exams?	_____	_____
4. Do you ever leave blanks on essay exams?	_____	_____
5. Do you organize your answer before you begin to write?	_____	_____
6. Do you generally find that you're unable to finish the exam before time runs out?	_____	_____
7. Do you go back over the entire exam before you turn it in?	_____	_____
8. After your exam is returned, do you go over it to evaluate your preparation and clarify your errors?	_____	_____
9. When you get your exam back, are you often surprised by the grade that you received?	_____	_____
10. Do you know how professors grade essay exams?	_____	_____

TOTAL POINTS _____

Give yourself 1 point for each *yes* answer to questions 1, 5, 7, 8, and 10 and 1 point for each *no* answer to questions 2, 3, 4, 6, and 9. Now total up your points. A low score indicates that you need to develop some new skills for taking essay tests. A high score indicates that you already are using many good strategies.

HOW TO TAKE AN ESSAY TEST

There are a number of strategies for taking essay exams that can help you retrieve, relate, and organize the information that you learned. Reading the directions, planning before you write, and organizing your answer can help you be successful on essay exams.

READ THE DIRECTIONS CAREFULLY

The first step in taking an essay exam is to read and follow the directions. Some students have actually failed essay exams, not because they didn't know the information, but because they didn't read and follow directions. Unfortunately, they just plunged into the exam without making sure they knew how to proceed. If you find that you tend to forget to read directions on tests, set up a special method to ensure that you read them. Some students use strategies like circling or underlining key words in the directions. Others sign their names, write their initials, or put a check mark at the end of the directions. Some students even jot down the directions in their own words before beginning the exam. All of these are good strategies because they ensure that you read the directions.

Find Out How Many Questions You Have to Answer

When you read the directions, be sure that you look to see how many questions you're expected to answer. On many essay exams, you're given a choice of questions to answer. Consider the following set of directions: *1. Answer two of the following questions.* (Six questions are given in total.) *2. Answer two questions from set A and two questions from set B.* (Three questions are included in set A, and three questions are included in set B.) In each of these cases you're being limited to a certain number of questions and, in the latter case, to a certain number of questions from two different sets.

   If you tried to answer all six questions in the time that you were given to answer two, you couldn't spend enough time on any one answer. As a result, you may earn a lower grade than your preparation warranted.

Don't Answer Additional Questions

Sometimes students who have extra time at the end of an exam go back and try to answer additional questions (more than the directions indicated). This is often a mistake. If the directions indicated that you were to answer two of the six questions, your professor isn't going to read all your answers and pick the best two on which to base your grade. In most cases, the professor will grade the first two answers and merely cross off or ignore the rest. This can really hurt your grade if your best answers were the fourth and fifth.

Follow Formatting Instructions

The test directions also may include information about how the essay is to be formatted. For example, you may be expected to answer each question on one side of a blue book page. The directions also may tell you to write on every other line, to include an example, or to include a brief outline. In some cases, students are given length limitations for their answers. Not following formatting instructions can cost you points on essay exams.

How Much Should You Write?

Although essay answers are often only one paragraph long, they can range from a few sentences to 10 pages long. The best guide for how much to write is how much space the professor provides on the examination paper. If there are three questions on one side of a page, a one-paragraph answer probably is expected. However, if you're not limited to just one side of the page, don't limit yourself to only the space that the professor has provided. Instead of trying to squeeze in or leave out additional information, continue your answer on the other side of the page. If there's only one question per page on your exam, then the professor probably expects you to fill the page in order to provide a satisfactory answer.

Many students are uncertain about how much to write when they're given only a sheet of questions and a blue book. If your professor has not stated a specific page limit for each question, you should consider the point value of the questions in order to determine how much to write. Obviously, a question worth 30 points will require a longer answer than one worth only 10 points. Occasionally, an essay test has only one question. This question is essentially worth 100 points. If you still feel unsure of how much to write, ask your professor what he or she expects.

PEANUTS is reprinted by permission of Newspaper Enterprise Association, Inc.

PLAN BEFORE YOU WRITE

If you take a few minutes to plan your answers before you write them, you'll find that you write better essay answers in a shorter period of time. When you first look at the essay test, read *all* essay questions before you decide which ones you want to answer. Circle the number of a question if you think you may want to answer it. Then jot down your ideas in a list in the margin.

Jot Down Ideas in the Margin

As you read each question, make notes in the margin, *marginal notes,* as the ideas for an answer pop into your mind. If you predicted one or more of the questions, jot down your mnemonic device, the key words, or the main points from the outline that you planned. You'll be able to make a better decision about which question or questions you should answer after you look at your notes. Look at the student example in Figure 13.1. Kesha listed the ideas that she thought of when she read the question. As you can see, she wrote down only key words and phrases.

Making notes as you read the questions can be very helpful. Sometimes it's hard to remember what you wanted to say about a particular question when you're ready to answer it. Reading the other questions and thinking about whether you should answer them can cause interference. Have you ever gone back to begin answering a question only to realize that you couldn't remember what you were going to say? If you think back to the analogy of your long-term memory as a filing cabinet, you may be able to understand better why this happens. When you read the first question, something in the question triggers an association that opens a particular file drawer for you and makes the information on that subject accessible to you. As you read other questions, however, that drawer is closed and others are opened. Sometimes, it's difficult to get the first drawer open again. The notes you jot in the margin also serve as additional cues to long-term memory. Each of the words you write down acts as an additional cue that can help you retrieve even more details for your answer. In addition to aiding your memory, making notes in the margin helps relieve test anxiety. Once you know that you can answer the question, you can relax and feel more comfortable about the exam.

FIGURE 13.1

Kesha's Marginal Notes

Question: What general and specific strategies should a student follow when taking a matching test?

Notes in margin:

- work from one side to other
- usually longest first
- don't work from side to side
- cross off answer if you use it
- do the ones you know 1st
- don't guess right away
- read directions
- read through all choices

Be Sure Your Notes Reflect All Parts of the Answer

After you've chosen to answer a question and have jotted your ideas in the margin, you should reread the question to make sure that your notes reflect all parts of the question. If you find that you've planned for only a part of the question, make additional notes in the margin. Some essays require you to answer two or three questions within one question. In that case, number each part of the question (1, 2, 3, and so on) and then write the numbers in pencil in the space under the question to make sure you don't forget to answer any parts. After you complete each part, erase that number.

Consider the following essay question from a chemistry test: *What differences, if any, exist between morphine and heroin in terms of chemical makeup, pharmacological effects, legal availability, and abuse?* Because there really are four parts to this question, you could put a "1" above *chemical makeup*, a "2" above *pharmacological effects,* and so on. If you find that you tend to forget to answer some parts of your essay questions, these strategies may help you improve your score on the next exam.

Be Sure You're Answering the Question That Was Asked

Also, at this point, you may want to go back to the question to make sure that your notes provide information that answers the specific question that was asked and not a different question. Some students lose points on essay answers because they haven't really answered the question that the professor asked; instead, they've written an answer to a different question. In the example above, you would need to be sure you were showing the differences between the drugs rather than just listing the chemical makeup of each. By rephrasing the question in your own words and then writing it below the professor's question, you can read both questions in order to verify your interpretation. Ask yourself, "What am I being asked to explain here?" After you plan your answer, go back and read the question again. As a final check, compare the information in your concluding sentence to the information required by the question. Even an excellent answer is wrong if it doesn't answer the question that was asked.

Organize Your Ideas Before Writing

After jotting down your ideas in the margin, you can organize your essay in just a few seconds. Simply number your ideas in the margin as Kesha did in Figure 13.2. Look at the ideas that you jotted down and ask yourself, "What's the first thing that I want to talk about?" After that, you can decide what to put second, third, and so on. You also may decide that some of your ideas actually support some of the others. You can indicate that some of your ideas are supporting points by marking them with an "A" or a "B" after the number.

Some students don't feel that they can take the time to plan their answers in the margin because they feel pressured for time during exams. However, you should be able to plan and organize an answer in just 1 or 2 minutes. For a

FIGURE 13.2

• • • • • • • • •

Kesha's Num-
bered Marginal
Notes

Question: What general and specific strategies should a student follow when taking a matching test?

Notes in margin:

③ — work from one side to other
④ — usually longest first
⑤ — don't work from side to side
— cross off answer if you use it

⑥ — do the ones you know 1st
⑦ — don't guess right away
① — read directions
② — read through all choices

longer essay, you can organize your ideas even more by writing a brief outline in the margin. Besides making it easier to write your answer, your outline lets you see where you need to add supporting details. Taking just a few minutes to plan and organize your answer before you begin to write can help you save time and earn extra points on the exam. One professor I know told his class that he would not even grade their papers if they didn't plan in the margin first. He found that the answers of the students who planned before they wrote were much better than those of the students who didn't plan.

WRITE YOUR ANSWER

Getting started is often the hardest part of writing an essay answer. So, start with the easiest question first. Write your essay answer as you would write an essay for one of your English classes. State your first main idea and then back it up with supporting details and examples. Then go on to your next main point.

Use a Basic One-Paragraph Design

The general format for a one-paragraph essay is shown in the left-hand column of Figure 13.3. Begin your essay with a *topic sentence* (TS) that states the central idea of your paragraph. After the topic sentence, state your first main point (M1). After stating your first main point, back it up with one or more supporting sentences. Each of these sentences may include details, facts, or examples that further explain your main point. Next, state your second main point, followed by a sentence or two of support. Your third main point should be made next, followed by relevant support. Additional main points and secondary supporting information also can be included here. Finally, end your paragraph with a concluding sentence. A well-developed paragraph should be from 8 to 11 sentences long. Of course, a paragraph can be shorter or longer, but by writing at least 8 sentences, you can ensure that you are including both main points and details.

FIGURE 13.3

Sample Essay
Design

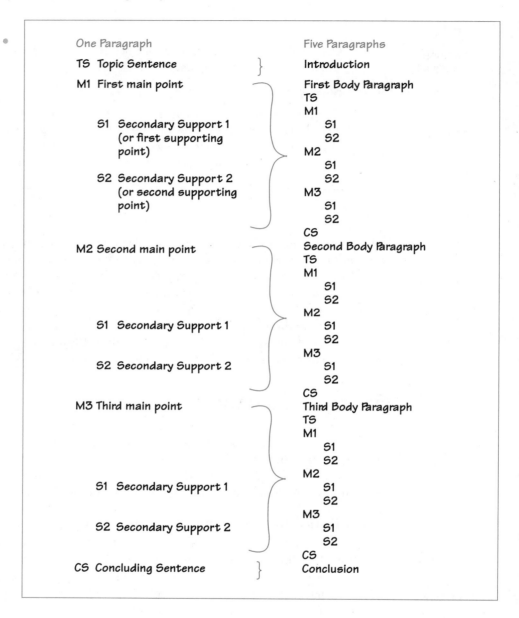

One Paragraph	Five Paragraphs
TS Topic Sentence }	Introduction
M1 First main point	First Body Paragraph
	TS
	M1
S1 Secondary Support 1 (or first supporting point)	S1
	S2
	M2
	S1
S2 Secondary Support 2 (or second supporting point)	S2
	M3
	S1
	S2
	CS
M2 Second main point	Second Body Paragraph
	TS
	M1
	S1
	S2
	M2
S1 Secondary Support 1	S1
	S2
	M3
S2 Secondary Support 2	S1
	S2
	CS
M3 Third main point	Third Body Paragraph
	TS
	M1
	S1
	S2
	M2
S1 Secondary Support 1	S1
	S2
	M3
S2 Secondary Support 2	S1
	S2
	CS
CS Concluding Sentence }	Conclusion

Modify the Design for Longer Essays

Not all essays can be answered in only one paragraph. You may be expected to write several paragraphs or several pages in order to answer a question properly. In that case, instead of having a topic sentence followed by several main points, each paragraph in your essay would focus on one of these main points. A one-paragraph answer can easily be expanded to a four- or five-paragraph answer simply by developing each point more fully. The topic sentence would be expanded to an introductory paragraph, each main-point sentence would be expanded to form a supporting paragraph, and the concluding sentence would become a concluding paragraph (see the right-hand column of Figure 13.3). A long essay, five or more pages, would be developed in much the same way. Remember, the shorter an essay answer is, the more general it tends to be. You can develop your ideas into a longer answer by adding more and more specific details and examples.

Turn the Question into a Statement

One strategy that may help you get started is to actually take the question, turn it into a statement, and add your answer to it. The resulting statement will become either your topic sentence (for a one-paragraph answer) or your *thesis statement* (for a short or long essay answer). Consider the following question: *How did Greek architecture and sculpture reflect the Greeks' concern for order, reason, and the ideal? What rules did they follow?* This question can be rephrased to form the following topic sentence: *The Greeks valued architecture and sculpture and tried to make them reflect their concern for order, reason, and the ideal.*

By generating a topic sentence or thesis statement that includes main points, you show your professor that you know the answer to the question. Turning the question into a topic sentence also helps you organize your own presentation of the material. In other words, you know where you're going with your answer.

Write Your First Main Point

The next step in writing your answer is to make your first *main point*. Take the idea that you labeled number 1 (or put first in your informal outline) and convert it into a sentence. Make it a general statement that can then be supported by details and examples. Look back at the sample plan in Figure 13.2. Kesha decided that "read directions" was the first main point she wanted to make. She converted her notes to the following sentence: "The first and most important thing a student should do is always read the directions."

Support Your Main Points

After you write your first main point, you need to add one or more sentences that contain *supporting points,* the specific information to back up your main point. Next, add an example if you can. You may use an example that was presented in the text or lecture, or you could include an example of your own. By using examples, you demonstrate to your professor that you understand the abstract material. Don't stop after you make one good point. Continue with other main points and follow each of them with details and examples just as you did for the first one. Your job on an essay exam is to prove each of your points by including the information you learned in lecture or from your textbook.

Although Kesha didn't list any supporting points in her original plan, she did back up her first main point with several supporting sentences; her next two sentences explain *why* it's so important to read the directions: "Some students see that they have matching on a test and automatically start matching without reading the directions. Directions may help a student out because not all answers are always used, and also because some answers may be used twice."

Add Transition Words

Add transition words to indicate each of your main points and to help your reader move from one idea to the next. Words like *first, second, third, next,* and *finally* are *transition words* often used to introduce the main points in your essay. They let your reader know that you're making a main point. *Moreover, in addition, also,* and *furthermore* tell your reader that you're adding support to the points that you already made. Occasionally, you may want to change direction or say something that contradicts the previous statement. In this case, you should begin your statement with a word or phrase like *however, but, on the other hand, nevertheless,* or *on the contrary.* Words like *consequently, therefore,* and *thus* indicate that you've reached a conclusion based on previous information.

You also can show connections by restating some of the key words in your question or topic sentence as you make additional points in your essay. If you're writing a long essay, it often is effective to restate parts of the question in each of your main points. You might say, for example: *The first main reason to answer the easiest question first is to maximize your points.* After explaining how that can be accomplished, you might restate the question for your second point as follows: *The second main reason for answering the easiest question first is to relieve test anxiety.* Each time you make a main point you can restate the question. Repeating key words and phrases helps organize your essay and reinforces the points that you want to make.

Add a Conclusion

Finally, you should end your paragraph or essay with a *conclusion,* a concluding sentence or paragraph that reminds your professor of the main points that you made. Professors form opinions of essays as they read, but they don't assign an actual grade until after they've read the entire answer. If you've made some of your best points early in your answer, it helps remind your professor of them just before he or she assigns a grade. Also, the concluding sentence or paragraph helps bring the answer to a logical ending, making the entire essay appear well thought out. Look at the sample essay in Figure 13.4. Which sentence is the topic sentence? Which sentences present the main points? Which sentences provide the secondary support? Which sentence presents the conclusion? Are transitions used? Which ones?

FIGURE 13.4

● ● ● ● ● ● ● ● ● ● ● ● ● ●

Sample Esssay

	Question: ①How did Greek <u>architecture</u> and ②<u>sculpture</u> reflect the Greeks' ᵃ·<u>concern</u> for order, ᵇ·reason, and the ᶜ·ideal? What <u>rules</u> did they follow? (30 points)
1 rules of	
proportion	Answer:
3 Parthenon	
2 human-ideal	The Greeks valued architecture and sculpture and tried to
4 perfect image	make them reflect their concern for order, reason, and the
5 virtual image	ideal. First, the Greeks followed very careful rules of proportion
	in creating their sculptures of gods and heroes. Every human
	figure was seven and one-half heads tall. The distances from
	the head to the chest, the chest to the groin, and the ankle to
	the foot all followed exact proportional measurements that
	had previously been determined. Also, the Greeks followed care-
	ful "rules" in the way they portrayed man and the gods in their
	sculpture. All works were idealized. They showed only the best
	human features. Second, the Greeks used the rules of propor-
	tion and measurement in creating their works of architecture.
	The Parthenon provides an excellent example of this order. The
	columns were spaced in proportion to the others in order to
	create a "perfect" image for the viewer. The number of columns
	across the side was equal to twice the number across the
	front plus one. This provided a sense of balance to the Greeks.
	Also, all of the columns leaned inward in order to maintain the
	illusion that they were exactly parallel and vertical. They were
	also thicker in the middle so that from the bottom of the hill,
	they appeared to be perfectly straight. Other similar "correc-
	tions" were made to the floor and the decorations in the frieze
	in order to maintain that "virtual image" that was so impor-
	tant to the Greeks. Both sculpture and architecture reflected
	the Greeks' concern for order, reason, and the ideal.

MORE TIPS FOR TAKING ESSAY TESTS

YOU CAN SUCCEED ON ESSAY EXAMS. Some students are intimidated by essay exams—perhaps because they haven't had to write an essay recently. It's true that you have to know the answer, but if you've predicted questions and prepared answers, you should be well prepared. By practicing writing your own essay answers, you've already taken your own self-test.

ASK ABOUT CONFUSING DIREC-TIONS. One of the most common mistakes that students make when taking essay tests is not following directions. Make sure you find out how many questions you need to answer, format requirements, and any limitations on length. If you're confused about any of the directions, ask your instructor to clarify them.

BUDGET YOUR TIME. It's critical to budget your time on essay exams. Wear a watch and pace yourself throughout the exam so that you don't spend too much time on one or two questions. You also need to consider the point value of each question.

ANSWER THE EASIEST QUESTIONS FIRST. As you preview the exam, look for questions that you predicted. Since you've already planned how to answer those questions, you should find them easy to do. Completing one or two easy questions will help build up your confidence. You'll also maximize your score before time runs out.

BE STRATEGIC WHEN ANSWERING DIFFICULT QUESTIONS. Put the question in your own words and do a memory search. Think about how some of the information that you learned when you prepared your predicted questions could be used to answer the exam questions. Just start writing—sometimes you can cue your memory of the material as you write.

INCLUDE ALL RELEVANT INFOR-MATION. Some students leave out important information because they think it's obvious. Pretend that you're writing the answer for a friend or family member who knows very little about the topic. Go into enough detail to explain each point you make.

PROOFREAD YOUR ANSWER. Be sure you take a few minutes to reread your answer before you turn in your exam. Some students are so nervous at the beginning of an exam that they make careless errors and leave out words, make spelling or grammar errors, or even forget some of the information that they learned.

LEARN FROM YOUR MISTAKES. After the exam is over, monitor your preparation. Go back and find out where the questions came from. Evaluate how well your predicted questions compared with the questions that were on the exam. Rewrite one or two of your answers and ask your professor to look them over and give you more feedback on their quality.

FACTORS THAT INFLUENCE YOUR GRADE

Many factors can influence your grade. Although the content of your answer carries the most weight, other factors—such as the organization of your answer, the format that you use, your writing ability, and how neatly you write your answer—can affect your grade. Some professors are as interested in how well you present the information as they are in the information itself. Knowing what your professor will be looking for in your answer can help you write better essay exams.

CONTENT

The *content*—the information that you include in your answer—is of course the most important factor in determining your grade. When you're planning and writing your answer, include as much *relevant information,* main points and supporting details related to the question, as you can. Many students make the mistake of including only some of the information that they know. They incorrectly assume that their professor will think that some information is just obvious and should not be included in the answer. Assuming that your professor will know what you mean even with little explanation also may result in a lower test score. It's important to explain key terms and back up the statements that you make. One way to avoid being too general is to pretend that your professor doesn't know the answer to the question. If you tell yourself that you're writing the essay for someone who doesn't know anything about the topic, you'll be sure to include all the pertinent information. Remember, your job on an essay test is to show the professor how much you know about the question.

As tempting as it may be, avoid including irrelevant information. Some students try to impress the professor by including everything that they know about a topic even if it isn't relevant to the question. Some professors will simply overlook the irrelevant information or make a note that it's unnecessary or off the topic. Other professors, however, may penalize students because, to them, it seems the students really don't know the answer to the question that was asked.

ORGANIZATION

The *organization* (order) of your essay answer also is an important factor in the grade you receive.

FIGURE 13.5

• • • • • • • • • • • • • • •

Two Sample Essay Answers

Question: Compare and contrast short- and long-term memory.

Sample 1:

Short-term memory and long-term memory are much alike. They both allow you to remember information that you have read or heard. In short-term memory, we can only hold things for 15 to 30 seconds. Long-term memory is memory that has an unlimited capacity. You can get information into long-term memory by spacing study, using associations, using mnemonics, etc. Short-term memory is not permanent, and unless information is rehearsed, repeated, and meaningful it is lost. ROY G. BIV is an example of a mnemonic device for the color spectrum. Mnemonics like ROY G. BIV are devices that aid retrieval. We have limited capacity in our short-term memory. Its capacity is the magical number 7. A good example is a telephone number. Once we get information into our long-term memory it is permanent. To get it into long-term memory we must learn the information. We can expand our short-term memory by chunking. This is when we categorize information into one thing instead of leaving it separate. They are also both kinds of memory.

Grade _____

Sample 2:

Short- and long-term memory have some similarities and a number of differences. Short- and long-term memory are two types of memory. To get information into either short-term memory or long-term memory, you must encode it; you must make it meaningful. Short-term memory and long-term memory are also similar in that each is plagued by interference and forgetting. But short-term memory and long-term memory are different, too. Although it is easy to get information into short-term memory, you must rehearse and organize it in order to get it into long-term storage. The capacity of short-term memory is very limited. It can hold only seven plus or minus two bits of information at one time. If you try to hold onto more than five to nine things at a time, displacement of some of the earlier information will occur. However, we can increase the capacity of short-term memory by chunking the information. For example, it was easier to remember the list of letters after we put them into meaningful groups. Long-term memory, on the other hand, has an unlimited capacity. Long-term memory can hold billions of bits of information at one time. While information remains in long-term memory permanently, it can only be retained in short-term memory for about 15 to 30 seconds. Without rehearsal, the information is quickly forgotten. For example, if you look up a phone number and then get a busy signal after you dial it, you may have to look the number up again when you decide to try again. Although short- and long-term memory are similar in some ways, they are very different in both their capacity and durability.

Grade _____

Take a few minutes to read the two sample essay answers in Figure 13.5. After reading sample 1, assign it a grade of A, B, C, D, or F. Then read sample 2 and assign a grade for it also.

How well an answer is organized does affect how it will be graded. After I ask the students in my class or a workshop to evaluate the sample essay answers, I tally the grades. The first sample almost always is assigned mostly Cs, Ds, and Fs, whereas the second sample receives As and Bs as the most common grades. A number of students indicate that after reading the second essay answer, they decided to change their grade on the first one. In almost every instance, this change resulted in lowering the grade. The students felt that the second answer was so much better than the first that it made the first one look bad. When asked why the second answer was better, the most common response was that it had more information.

When you first read the two essays, sample 2 probably seemed to contain much more information. However, if you look very closely, the two answers contain about the same information. The second essay appears to contain more information because it's so well organized. Some students think the first essay should receive a lower grade even though it contains most of the relevant information because it was poorly organized. Do you think that some of your professors approach grading this way?

When professors grade essay exams, they expect to read a well-organized answer. If they're looking for particular points to be made, they expect those points to be noted easily as the answer is read. Few professors will take the time to read an essay over and over again to *find* the information that they're looking for. Some professors penalize students intentionally for poorly organized answers. They feel justified in giving a poorly organized answer a lower grade because they think the student who wrote it didn't know the information as well as the student who wrote the more clearly organized answer. In other cases, though, students are unintentionally penalized because the essay answer is so jumbled that it becomes difficult to follow the argument, and the professor misses some of the information.

FORMAT

The *format* of your answer may also affect your grade. The directions on an essay test are sometimes rather vague. Professors assume that students know how to write essays, and they don't go into detail about what form of answer they expect. Students, however, sometimes don't really know what is expected. In some classes, writing the correct information in list format would earn a student an A. In other cases, though, this student might be penalized for not answering the question in the appropriate form. Penalties for not using paragraph form vary greatly from one professor to another. If the directions are not clear, ask!

MECHANICS

Mechanics—sentence structure, grammar, punctuation, and spelling—are other factors that influence your grade. They probably are given more weight in English courses, but professors from every discipline—engineering, biology, business, and so on—are influenced by these factors. Poor sentence construction and grammar can make it difficult to understand the information that you're trying to relate. Even problems in punctuation and spelling affect how well your written answer matches what you want to say.

Your professors also may be influenced by these kinds of errors in less obvious ways. How well you're able to write your answer—how free of errors in mechanics it is—says something about you as a student. Essay answers that include numerous errors in sentence construction, grammar, spelling, and punctuation can give your professor the impression that you're not a very well-educated student. Unfortunately, this impression can "spill over" to the evaluation of the content of your answer as well. This shouldn't happen, but it does. Some professors may find themselves thinking, "If this person can't even write a complete sentence, how can he or she understand philosophy (or psychology, sociology, history, and so on)?"

NEATNESS

Neatness also may influence your grade. Most professors expect students to write clearly and neatly, observe margins, and present the material in a "professional" manner. Very few of them are willing to spend hours attempting to decipher unreadable handwriting. If your professor can't read your essay, you'll lose points simply because he or she won't be able to understand the points you're trying to make. You also may lose points just because you make a "bad impression" by writing in an awkward and messy manner. Nicely written papers have been getting better grades than messy ones for years. Teachers seem to believe that good students care about their work and take the time to write in a careful and skillful manner, whereas poor students don't.

STRATEGIES FOR GAINING MORE POINTS

In this section you'll learn some strategies that may help you gain additional points on an essay exam. Even if you're well prepared, you may find that during the test you have difficulty getting what you know down on paper. Occasionally, students draw a complete blank on an essay question, think of an important point after they've completed their answer, run out of time, or even run out of space. The following tips may be helpful if you find yourself in one of these situations.

USE THE EXAM AS A RESOURCE

Many college exams are a combination of objective and essay questions. Students sometimes overlook the objective questions, which are a valuable source of information. By referring to the multiple-choice, true/false, and matching questions, you may find a great deal of specific information that you can use in your essay. Don't be afraid to look back at them for names, dates, terms, or even key ideas. Professors often include in the objective part of the exam information that relates to the essay questions. In fact, some of these details may even be found in the incorrect choices for the multiple-choice items. Even if the actual information isn't available, reading some of the questions and possible alternatives may help you recall some of the information that you need. Words or phrases in the questions may act as cues for your long-term memory.

ALWAYS WRITE SOMETHING

There are times when even well-prepared students are surprised by an essay question and draw a complete blank. Before you give up and resign yourself to accepting a failing grade, try to think through the question. Look for key words in the question that might give you some clues to the answer. Think about the main topics of the lectures and the chapters that were covered. Try to recall the maps you made, the study sheets you prepared, and the questions you predicted. Sometimes you actually can recall the answer after you do a memory search. However, if you still have no idea what the answer to a question is, you should write something. Many professors give students a few points for just trying. In addition, you may find that you know more than you thought. Even though you may not think you know the information the professor is looking for, you may be right on target. Sometimes in the process of writing "anything" to fill the space, you trigger something in your memory that suddenly makes the actual answer pop into your head.

LEAVE EXTRA SPACE

When you're answering a question on the test paper itself, it's important to leave reasonable margins on all sides of the answer. First of all, this makes your answer look better. Also, it allows you to add information after you've completed your answer. If you must add further information at the end of your essay, place an asterisk (*) or number next to it and also in the paragraph at the spot where the information belongs. You may earn more points if the additional material is read within the context of the answer rather than at the end. You also benefit from leaving wide margins because your professor has space to provide you with feedback about your answer. If no space is available, professors tend to include comments only at the end or not at all.

If you're using a blue book for your answers, leave at least three lines between each answer. Again, you'll have room to write in another point if you think of something after completing the question.

Sometimes you may find that you need even more space than is provided on the exam. You may write larger than other students or have more information to present. Before writing on the back of the page or on additional blue book pages, check with your instructor to see whether there are any space limitations. If your instructor hasn't limited you to one side of a page or to the space provided on the exam sheet, continue your answer on the back. Be sure to indicate that you're continuing your answer. Use an arrow, write the word "over," or write "continued on back." If you write parts of several answers on the back, number them so that they'll be easily recognized.

WHAT IF YOU RUN OUT OF TIME?

No matter how carefully you budget your time, you occasionally may run out of time during an essay exam. The first thing you should do is ask your professor whether you can have additional time to complete the test. Some professors will allow you to continue working until the next class begins. Others may even allow you to come to their offices to complete your test. If, however, your professor says that you must finish in the time allotted, you can still pick up most of the points on an essay answer. Let's say you've started writing your last essay answer out in paragraph form. When you have only about 5 minutes left, simply list the remaining points that you wanted to make. Add a little note to the professor that says something like, "I'm sorry that I didn't have time to finish my essay. These are the additional points that I wanted to make." Some professors will give you full credit for your answer, assuming it's a good one, even though you didn't write all of it out. This is a better strategy than just writing until time runs out and answering only half of the question.

LEARNING FROM EXAMS

You can learn a great deal from your essay answers after the test is returned to you. You may think that once the test is over, you should simply move on and concentrate on the next unit of work. You probably think that if you just try harder the next time, you'll be able to do a better job. Unfortunately, some students just don't know how to write an "A" answer for some of their classes. They may do very well on the exams in one class, but for some reason that they can't explain, they just aren't able to get the grades they want in another class. Looking carefully and analytically at your returned tests can provide you with information on how to improve your answers on future exams.

WHAT CAN YOU LEARN?

One of the most important things you'll learn from your returned exam is how closely your answer matched what the professor wanted. If you got a good grade on the exam, you probably are doing a good job of presenting the information that the professor wanted. If, on the other hand, your grade was lower than you expected, you need to find out where you went wrong. It's important to understand why you got the grade you did. You may want to evaluate your answer on the basis of the factors that influence grades (described earlier in this chapter) and then discuss it with your professor. Of course, the key to improving your score on future exams is to find out what you need to do differently.

HOW TO EVALUATE YOUR ANSWER

There are several good ways to evaluate the quality of your essay answer. One method is to compare your answer with those of your peers. Sometimes just reading another student's essay can teach you a lot about what the professor expects. Find a student in your class who got an A on the exam. Explain to this student that you were disappointed in your grade and you just want to get a better idea of what you should do differently. Ask the student to explain how he or she answered the question and ask whether you may read his or her essay.

Once you get a better idea of what the professor expected, set up an appointment to discuss your test with your professor. Don't go into the meeting with the expectation of getting extra points. Instead, focus on finding out how you should have answered the question in order to gain the maximum number of points. In this way, you and the professor are on the same side; you're working toward the same goal. Often, when you "fight" for additional points, you and the professor may find yourselves acting as opponents or adversaries. If that type of atmosphere is generated, you may gain a point or two on the exam, but you'll probably lose the opportunity to learn how to write a better answer.

Another place you should go for help is your college learning center. The learning center staff can help you evaluate and improve your essay answers. Also, the learning center may offer tutorial services in the course content area and writing assistance that will help you learn to correct sentence construction, grammar, and mechanics errors.

REWRITE YOUR ANSWERS FOR COMPARISON

An excellent strategy for learning to write better essay answers is to rewrite your answers to the test questions after you get the exam back. Use your text and your notes to put together the best answer that you can. Take time to organize the information and check your sentence structure, mechanics, and spelling. Then go back to your professor and ask him or her to read your new answer. Ask what your grade would have been if you had written *that answer* for the exam. You need to find out whether you understand what your professor expects for an "A" answer. If you still don't succeed in meeting your professor's expectations, you now have another opportunity to discuss why your answer wasn't a good one. You may want to rewrite the answer one more time and then meet with your professor to discuss it.

Students who use this strategy find that it provides several rewards. First, they learn what their professors expect for an "A" answer and how to prepare for and write one. They also demonstrate to their professors that they are motivated enough to do extra work in order to excel in the course. This leaves the professor with a very positive impression about them as students. Some are even rewarded with bonus points for demonstrating that they can write an excellent answer. In addition, most of these students report that they score much higher grades on the remainder of their essay exams.

SUMMARY

If you're well prepared, essay tests can be even easier than objective tests. Some students lose points on essay tests, not because they don't know the material, but because they don't know how to take essay tests. First, read the directions to determine how many questions to answer, their point values, and any special limitations or formatting requirements. Most professors give students a choice of questions to answer, so consider them all before you decide which ones to answer. As you read each question, though, jot down any ideas that pop into your head. Use a basic essay design to construct your answer. Turn the question into a thesis statement or topic sentence (for one-paragraph answers) and then write your first main point. Be sure to back it up with reasons, details, facts, and examples. Continue in the same manner until you've included all the relevant information that you know. Take a few minutes to sum up your main points and then proofread your answer. Although many students believe that the content of their answer is the only factor the professor uses to determine a grade, it's only one of many factors that actually influence that decision.

Even the best-prepared students need to use some strategies to gain extra points on exams. You can use the objective part of your exam (if you have one) as a resource. If you don't know the answer to an essay question, you should still write something. Leaving a blank on an essay test can cost you one or more letter grades because essay questions generally carry high point values on exams.

When your exam is returned to you, you can learn how well your preparation and your style of writing essay answers match your professor's expectations. Discuss your answer with your professor or compare your answer with those of several classmates. If you didn't get the grade you expected or feel you deserved, you need to find out what you did wrong so that you can improve your score on future exams.

Activities

1. Describe the steps that you generally use when taking essay exams. What new strategies do you plan to use on future exams? Why?

2. Go to the *Orientation to College Learning* Web site and download one copy of Activity 13–1 from the Activities Packet. Jot down your ideas in the margin as you read the questions. Then work with a group to organize them by creating an informal outline.

3. Practice turning your ideas into sentences by converting your first numbered response to each question in Activity 2 into a sentence. Then compare each of your main point sentences to those of others in your group. How similar were your responses?

4. Take a few minutes and answer the following essay question: *Compare and contrast a catchword and a catchphrase.* Then read each of the essay answers available on the *Orientation to College Learning* Web site, and evaluate them using the criteria that were discussed in this chapter.

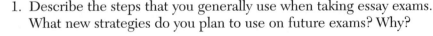

Evaluate each answer and assign a grade from 1 to 10 points (no grade is used more than once). Jot down a few notes to justify your decision. Which are the three best essays, in order? Which are the three worst essays, in order? Be prepared to defend your choices with your group.

5. Analyze and critique the grade that you got on one of your essay answers from a recent exam. Consider some of the following questions as you examine your answer: What factors influenced your grade? What mistakes did you make? What did you learn from your peers and your professor?

6. Rewrite your essay answer. Use your text and notes to locate the correct information for your answer. Improve or correct organization, sentence structure, grammar, spelling, and punctuation errors. Attach a photocopy of the original answer to your new answer and add a note describing the kinds of changes that you made.

7. Develop a two-column chart to list all your strengths and weaknesses when taking essay exams. Select three of the strengths on your list and describe how each can help you be successful when taking essay exams. Then select three of the weaknesses that you listed and develop a plan to improve or overcome them. List the steps in your plan.

8. If you're using InfoTrac College Edition, locate several articles that contain information on how to take an essay exam. List three new strategies that you plan to use for your next essay exam. How would you use each strategy when taking your next essay exam?

9. Think of three examples of how you've applied what you learned in this chapter. Choose one strategy and describe how you applied it to your other course work using the Journal Entry Form that is located on the *Orientation to College Learning* Web site. Consider the following questions as you complete your entry. Why did you use this strategy? What did you do? How did it work? How did it affect your performance on the task? How does this approach compare with your previous approach? What changes would you make the next time you use this strategy?

10. Now that you've completed Chapter 13, take a few minutes to repeat the "Where Are You Now?" activity, located on the *Orientation to College Learning* Web site. What changes did you make as a result of reading this chapter? How are you planning to apply what you've learned in this chapter?

Review Questions

Terms You Should Know:

Conclusion	Mechanics	Thesis statement
Content	Neatness	Topic sentence
Format	Organization	Transition words
Main point	Relevant information	
Marginal notes	Supporting points	

Completion: Fill in the blank to complete each of the following statements.

1. You should answer the _____ questions first on an essay exam.

2. Doing an informal outline in the margin can help you _____ your essay answer before you begin to write.

3. Jotting ideas in the margin can actually help you _____ which questions to answer.

4. It's important to include all _____ information on an essay exam.

5. A good essay answer includes both _____ and _____ points.

Multiple Choice: Circle the letter of the best answer for each of the following questions. Be sure to underline key words and eliminate wrong answers.

6. A good _____ tells the professor you know the answer to the question.
   A. outline
   B. paragraph
   C. thesis statement
   D. transition

7. Which of the following is the second most important factor in determining your grade?
   A. Sentence structure
   B. Organization
   C. Spelling
   D. Neatness

Short Answer–Essay: On a separate sheet, answer each of the following questions.

8. Why should students plan in the margin before answering essay questions?

9. Why do some students have difficulty taking essay exams? What should they do differently?

10. Why should students rewrite their answers after the exam is returned?

Chapter 14

PREPARING FOR FINAL EXAMS

"Preparing for finals would have been so much harder had I not planned and spaced out my studying. I also set up a specific time to start studying and I stuck to it. I'm not even worried about finals because of this. When my friends are running around cramming for finals, I just have to check my calendar to see exactly what I have scheduled to do. It's so easy."

Brian Shomo
Student

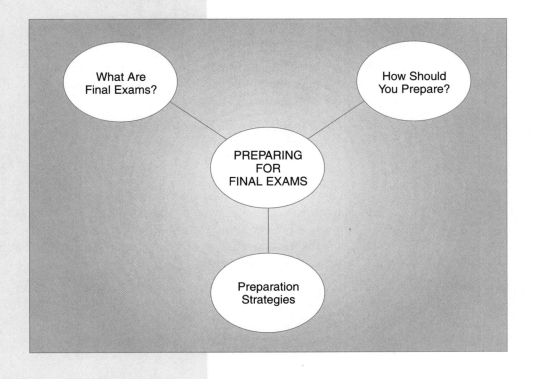

Where Are You Now?

Take a few minutes to answer *yes* or *no* to the following questions.

	YES	NO
1. Do you work ahead before finals to free up study time?	____	____
2. Do you tend to give up at the end of the semester and spend little or no time preparing for finals?	____	____
3. Do you usually score lower on final exams than on the other exams given during the semester?	____	____
4. Do you set up a plan to prepare for your finals?	____	____
5. Do you put most of your effort into the course in which you have the lowest grade?	____	____
6. Do you generally spend a lot of time partying at the end of the semester when you know you should be studying?	____	____
7. Do you review all your old exams before your final?	____	____
8. Do you use a four- or five-day study plan to prepare for each of your finals?	____	____
9. Do you put so much effort into one exam that you don't have the time or energy to prepare for one or more of the others?	____	____
10. Do you realistically consider your chances of success before preparing for final exams?	____	____
TOTAL POINTS	____	

Give yourself 1 point for each *yes* answer to questions 1, 4, 7, 8, and 10 and 1 point for each *no* answer to questions 2, 3, 5, 6, and 9. Now total up your points. A low score indicates that you need to develop some new skills for preparing for final exams. A high score indicates that you already are using many good strategies.

WHAT ARE FINAL EXAMS?

Final exams are end-of-semester tests that help professors evaluate your progress. They are used by some professors to monitor your mastery of the concepts and ideas presented in the course. Other professors use them to make decisions about grades, to determine whether students should move on to the next class, or even to monitor their own teaching. Although final exams may be one of many routine exams given during the semester, they often are longer, both in number of questions and in time allotted for the test, and more difficult. Comprehensive final exams may survey all material covered in the course. Final exams range in value from about 20 percent of your grade all the way up to 100 percent. In some courses they count as much as two regular exams; in others, they are the *only* exam and determine your entire grade.

Many courses include only a midterm and a final, with each one determining half of the course grade. However, sometimes the final carries more weight in determining your grade because it's the second exam. If you score higher on the final, you'll probably receive a higher grade in the course, and vice versa. Although finals are more challenging than most of the regular exams that you have during the semester, you can still use many of the same strategies that you used for your other exams to prepare for them. However, if you have four or five final exams in a one-week period, you need to begin your preparation even earlier—perhaps several weeks before your first exam.

HOW SHOULD YOU PREPARE?

Many students change their patterns of sleeping, eating, studying, socializing, working, and so on before final exams. For example, they may limit their time with friends, cut out television, and spend more time in the library in order to fit more study time into each day. They believe that their performance on finals is critical to their ultimate success in one or more of their courses. By starting your preparation early and managing your time efficiently, making academics your first priority, and putting your effort into the right courses, you can improve your grades on your final exams as well as your overall GPA.

MANAGE YOUR TIME EFFICIENTLY

You can make the end of the semester much less stressful by using time-management techniques to reduce the overload that many students experience.

Two or three weeks before your first final, sit down and make out a new calendar for the end of the semester. Write down all assignments, papers, projects, and exams that you still need to complete. Then make a list of all your outstanding assignments and realistically estimate the amount of time that you think you'll need to complete them.

Pick several assignments to complete early. Even if they aren't due for 2 weeks, finish them as soon as possible to reduce the amount of work that you'll have to complete right before exams begin. You need to be able to begin concentrating on your finals at least 5 days before the first one is scheduled. That means you need to complete most of your regular work about a week before it's due. Doing some of your reading early, completing a term paper, or working ahead in several classes can help create the extra time that you'll need.

MAKE ACADEMICS YOUR TOP PRIORITY

Many students get tired at the end of the semester. College is hard work, and it takes its toll on many students. One of the biggest mistakes that some students make, though, is to decide to rest up before finals week. They slack off and even get behind in their work just when they need to be pushing harder to get ahead. Although they may feel better for a day or two after this hiatus from work, most of them realize too late that it was a mistake. Suddenly they have only a few days to complete all of the assignments that have piled up and to prepare for their finals. They feel overwhelmed and stressed out. Even though they push hard at the end, they just don't have enough hours in the day to do all the work that needs to be done, so something suffers. Often they give up on one or more assignments or on one of their courses, and their grades drop.

Rather than easing off at the end of the semester, you need to push hard. If you work as hard as you can for 1 week about 2 weeks before your first final, you'll be able to complete many of the assignments on your list and still have a few days to rest up before you begin to study for your final exams. During this week, plan daily tasks. Some students still like to use "To Do" lists; others get really serious and use hourly calendars to schedule their assignments. In either event, schedule regular study hours and set daily study goals.

The 2 weeks before finals tend to be a rather slow period for end-of-semester projects, so it's a good time to get ahead in your work. Look at your assignment calendar and locate a "light" week near the end of the semester. It may be 3 weeks before finals for you. Whichever week is the lightest week for you, that's when you should get a head start on your outstanding assignments. Don't forget to break down tasks, switch subjects, and plan rewards to maintain your motivation.

SET PRIORITIES FOR EXAMS

You can increase your chances for academic success by *setting priorities*. Reevaluate your goals for each of your classes. Look closely at where you stand in each course. You may be able to figure out exactly what your grade is by averaging all your scores on exams, homework, and papers. If you can't determine your grade on your own, set up an appointment with your professor to go over your grade. You need to know what your grade is before you can determine how much time and effort you need to put into each of your final exams.

Do a Practice Exercise

Pretend that you have the following test grades in your classes so far this semester. The final exam in each class has the same weight as the other exams. For which final exam or exams should you work the hardest, put in the most time? Make a decision before you go on with your reading.

Exams deserving the most preparation time: _____ , _____ .

Class A	82	84	83
Class B	81	76	79
Class C	74	84	85
Class D	14	40	56

Most students think they should put the greatest amount of time and effort into the final for class D. For the second most important final exam, some students select class A and others choose between B and C. The majority of students, however, select A and D as the finals that they would put ahead of the others. Why? They realize that they are failing class D. To pass the class, they need to get a good grade on the final.

Unfortunately, some college students actually let all their other exams go (spend very little, if any, time on them) in order to "ace" the final in their worst class and "save" their grade. In most cases, however, students who have failed all previous exams in a course are unlikely to score high enough on the final exam to improve their grade. In this exercise, what grade would you have to get in order to pass class D? Because each exam carries the same weight, it's easy to figure this out. Add up the points that you already have (14 + 40 + 56). After the first three exams, you have accumulated 110 points in class D. To score a passing grade (with 60 as passing), you would need a total of 240 points (4 times 60). So what would you need to get on the final to achieve your goal of 240 points? If you said 130 points, you were right. As you can see, not only is it impossible to score 130 points, it also is highly unlikely that any student with scores of 14, 40, and 56 would even score 100 on the final exam.

Consider All Your Options

By evaluating your grade in this class before you begin to study, you can determine that there really is no hope of passing the class. It would be better to try to drop (withdraw from) the class and concentrate on your other courses. Check with your professor before you drop a class, though. Some professors do take improvement into consideration and may actually "drop" the first exam when calculating your grade. If only the second, third, and final exams were counted, there could be hope of passing class D. Before dropping a class, ask your professor whether there is any chance that you can pass the class. If the answer is no, then drop the course or just forget about it. Don't study for the exam; don't even go to take it. Instead, put your time and energy into your other classes. It's a mistake to believe that you should *never* give up on a course.

Setting Priorities Can Improve Your GPA

By setting your priorities appropriately, you actually may improve your GPA. You should put the greatest effort into the courses in which you have a borderline grade, in courses where the final actually can make a difference. Many students think that they should put their greatest effort into class A because it's the class with the highest grade (an 83 average). Although class A is the course in which you have the highest grade, the grade is a pretty solid B. What grade would you have to get on the final in order to get an A (90 average) in this class? Look at the following calculation:

$$\begin{array}{rl} 360 & \text{what you need for an A (if all four exams are given equal weight)} \\ \underline{-249} & \text{the total points you now have in Class A} \\ 111 & \text{total points that you need} \end{array}$$

As you can see, here again it's impossible to gain enough points on the final to significantly affect the grade; an A cannot be achieved, even with a perfect score. The two classes where you should put your effort are the middle two classes (B and C). In each of these courses, you have a borderline grade (78.6 in class B and 81 in class C). Because your grade is close to the cutoff for a B, the results of your final exam will determine your grade. If you want to get a B in class B, you need to score only an 84 (320 minus 236) on the final. With previous grades of 81, 76, and 79, an 84 seems to be a realistic goal requiring only a little extra effort. To keep the low B that you already have in class C, you need to get only a 77 (320 minus 243). Putting in the extra effort in class C certainly could pay off.

You can determine the grade you need in each of your courses by adding up all of the points you have so far and subtracting that total from the total points that you need. If you want an A in a course that has only three exams, you need 270 points, assuming a 90 is an A ($3 \times 90 = 270$). In a course with five exams, you need 460 points, assuming a 92 is an A ($5 \times 92 = 460$). The total points that you need can be calculated by multiplying the total number of exams by the lowest numerical value for the grade that you want to earn. If your grade is composed of homework, quizzes, papers, and other assignments, in addition to exam grades, ask your professor how to calculate your grade and how to determine what you need on the final.

ATTEND ALL CLASSES

You can improve your performance on final exams by attending class. Missing class is never a good idea, but missing class just before finals is extremely unwise. Some students miss class because they feel they need that time to catch up or study for other courses. This may be a wise choice once in a while, but it's not a good choice before final exams. Many professors squeeze extra information into their lectures during the last week or two of classes in order to present all material that will be on the final. Others review or discuss what will be on the final, as well as what won't be on the final. Knowing what to study and also knowing what you don't have to spend time on can help you use your study time more effectively. In addition, you may benefit from questions that other students ask during class and the answers that the professor gives.

REDUCE ANXIETY

Don't let the thought of final exams make you panic. Many students experience anxiety during final exams. Why do you think this happens? For one thing, final exams, especially comprehensive finals, are a new experience for many students. In addition, finals are more important than most exams because they can determine your grade in the course. Because they carry more value, they involve more risk. Because they involve more risk, they cause more feelings of anxiety. Finally, students experience more anxiety during finals because they are tired and "run down" at the end of the semester.

Some anxiety is a normal part of finals week. Although you can't expect to eliminate all feelings of anxiety, you can do things to keep test anxiety from interfering with your performance on exams. If final exams are a new experience for you, talk to your professor, advisor, or someone in your college learning center about what to expect. Ask some of your friends to describe their experiences with final exams and how they compared with regular exams. The more you know about the exams, the more prepared you'll be for them. If one of your finals will determine your grade in the course, be sure to make that exam your top priority. The strategies for test preparation that you learned will help you be well prepared for the exam, and being well prepared is the best way to reduce your feelings of anxiety. Although anxiety may be an obstacle during final exams, you have many resources to help you overcome it.

330 • Chapter Fourteen   Preparing for Final Exams

PREPARATION STRATEGIES

Although cramming for finals is a common phenomenon, it's not the best way to prepare for finals. If you cram for finals, you may find that after one or two days it becomes very hard to keep up that kind of pace. You may get tired of the long days and nights of study and give up on later exams. Cramming makes inefficient use of your time, causes feelings of frustration, and results in lots of memory interference. It's a form of massed practice, and massed practice isn't an efficient method of learning information. You have less opportunity to organize, practice, and test your retrieval of the information.

Cramming is especially ineffective when you have more than one exam on the same day. Few students have a finals schedule that includes only one exam per day; usually, students have at least two exams on the same day. In most cases, then, cramming is not a useful strategy for preparing for exams. What alternatives are there? By spacing your study over several days, you can study for each of your exams using the *Five-Day Study Plan* and, at the same time, maintain your motivation throughout exam week.

MAKE A FINAL EXAM STUDY SCHEDULE

One of the first things you need to do is set up a schedule of your exams. Check your syllabi or final exam schedule several weeks in advance and write each exam time on a calendar. Occasionally, students find that they have more than one exam scheduled for the same time. If this happens, check with your professors about alternative exam times. More often, students find that they have more than one exam on the same day. It's relatively common to have two exams on one day, but some students find that they have three exams (or more) on one day. Having too many exams on the same day can negatively affect your performance during finals. By the time you begin the third exam, you may be exhausted, frazzled, or emotionally drained. To put it another way, you won't be at your best. Some schools have policies that help eliminate these conflicts; the faculty and administration recognize that students can't properly demonstrate what they've learned if the testing situation works against them. Check with your professor, academic dean, or someone in the registrar's office if you have exam conflicts.

Make out a *reminder sheet* (on 8½-by-11-inch paper) for each exam that you have to take. Write the name of the course, day and date, time, place, and any materials that you need to take with you. Post these on your door or bulletin board. Some students get so stressed out during finals week that they forget when or where their exams are scheduled. Having all the information for each of your exams clearly organized and posted may help reduce some of your anxiety. If your final exams are scheduled for times and places that are different from your regular class hours, these reminder sheets will be especially helpful.

SET UP A STUDY SCHEDULE

By setting up a *study schedule,* you can properly prepare for each of your exams without feeling rushed or anxious. Use the Five-Day Study Plan to space out your study. By dividing up your day, you can prepare for several exams at the same time.

Don't Start to Prepare Too Early

When you start to study can affect your performance on final exams. Some students decide to get a jump on finals by preparing several weeks in advance. This strategy has both positive and negative effects. On the positive side, you can review a lot more material a lot more times if you start early. On the negative side, though, you can forget a lot of the material before the exam if you begin to prepare *too* early. If you do begin your preparation more than a week before the exam, you need to review the material that you prepared first when you're closer to the exam. One way to make good use of early preparation time is by preparing study sheets, maps, self-tests, word cards, and so on. Begin your actual review of these materials 4 to 5 days before the exam.

Space Your Study to Aid Retention

Spacing your study as you prepare for finals is crucial to getting information into your long-term memory in a logical and organized manner. Because of the large amount of information that you may need to master for a comprehensive final, you need to learn information in small chunks and review it often. If you try to cram 15 chapters of biology into one long (8- to 10-hour) study session, you may find that you only partially know the material. By studying one chunk of the material each day and then reviewing it again over the next few days, you can monitor your learning and reinforce the information that you still don't know.

Split Your Day When Preparing for Several Exams

Rather than studying for one exam at a time, you need to learn how to prepare for several exams at the same time. This isn't an impossible task as some students think, but rather one that requires a little planning and a lot of perseverance. Count back 5 or 6 days from each of your final exams to determine your starting date. You may find that you're on day 3 of your study plan for Biology when you start day 1 of your study plan for English Literature.

By splitting your day, you can effectively prepare for several exams at the same time. If you have your other work done, you should be able to devote all your time to preparing for exams. This doesn't mean that you'll study nonstop from the time you wake up until the time you go to sleep. Rather, *splitting your day* means that you should be able to schedule three or four 2-hour blocks of time each day to prepare for your exams. Let's pretend that you have the finals schedule shown in Figure 14.1. If you use a Five-Day Study Plan, you shouldn't

FIGURE 14.1

• • • • • • • • • • • • • • •

Final Exam Study Schedule

Algebra	Monday	December 14	9:00 to 11:00
English	Wednesday	December 16	9:00 to 11:00
Biology	Thursday	December 17	12:30 to 2:30
Study Skills	Friday	December 18	12:30 to 2:30

Final Exam Study Plan

Wed Dec. 9	Thurs Dec. 10	Fri Dec. 11	Sat Dec. 12	Sun Dec. 13	Mon Dec. 14	Tues Dec. 15	Wed Dec. 16	Thurs Dec. 17	Fri Dec. 18
Day 1 Algebra	Day 2 Algebra	Day 3 Algebra	Day 4 Algebra	Day 5 Algebra					
		Day 1 English	Day 2 English	Day 3 English	Day 4 English	Day 5 English			
				Day 1 Biology	Day 2 Biology	Day 3 Biology	Day 4 Biology	Day 5 Biology	
					Day 1 SS	Day 2 SS	Day 3 SS	Day 4 SS	Day 5 SS
					Take Alg Final	No Exam	Take Engl Final	Take Bio Final	Take SS Final

have to prepare for more than three exams at one time. Your hardest and busiest days on this schedule are Sunday, Monday, and Tuesday. By carefully planning your time, you can prepare for each exam and still have sufficient time for sleep, meals, and some relaxation.

Students often ask me to help them figure out when to study for finals. If I were helping you plan a study schedule, I would recommend that you divide your day according to the three courses on which you're working. Assigning one course to the morning, one to the afternoon, and one to the evening allows you to study for each test in a regular time slot. By studying the same material at the same time of day, you can separate course material for one exam from that of your other courses and thereby prevent some of the interference that often occurs during finals week. It's also a good idea to work on your hardest subject early in the day, when you're the most alert. By the time you spend 4 to 6 hours on your other two classes, you won't be able to concentrate as well on the material from the third class.

Sample Study Schedule

Look at the sample study schedule in Figure 14.2. If this were your exam schedule, I would suggest that you set up your study time this way. Because you have finals early in the final exam period, begin to prepare for your final exams during the last week of regular classes. You may still be busy completing reading assignments or even papers or projects that are due at the end of the semester. If you need to prepare for more than one exam during this week, try to complete your regular assignments early. By Sunday of exam week, schedule time to prepare for three final exams. Even in this schedule you have some flexibility. There's even room in this schedule (listed as optional study time) to put more time in on your high-priority classes. Because Biology is a very difficult class, I would schedule that study time first. You could then review it again later in the day, putting in another hour or two. Notice, incidentally, how each study block is followed by at least a 1-hour break. You need time to rest and allow the information to *consolidate* (get organized in long-term memory) or "sink in" before you start to study again.

You also may notice that day 5 of Biology is scheduled for the morning of the exam. Because the exam is scheduled for an afternoon time slot, you could (and should) do your final review that morning. If you do have afternoon or evening exams, doing that final review just before the exam is a good way to keep the information fresh in your memory. However, it's not the best time to do your self-test. If you don't *know* a lot of the material that morning there isn't enough time left to learn it. Instead, do your self-test the day before the exam. Then you still have time to work on any information you missed.

FIGURE 14.2

Sample Study Schedule

Time	Wednesday (9)	Thursday (10)	Friday (11)	Saturday (12)	Sunday (13)	Monday (14)	Tuesday (15)	Wednesday (16)	Thursday (17)	Friday (18)	Saturday (19)
9:00	class		class			Algebra		English	Day 5	Day 5	
10:00	class		class	sleep		FINAL		FINAL	Bio	Study Skills	
11:00	class		class			break		break	break	break	
12:00	lunch	lunch	lunch			lunch		lunch	lunch	lunch	
1:00	class		class		Day 1	Day 2	Day 3	Day 4	Biology FINAL	Study Skills FINAL	
2:00		class			Bio	Bio	Bio	Bio			
3:00			Day 1	Day 2	break	break	break	break	break		
4:00			Engl	Engl	Day 3	Day 4	Day 5				
5:00		Dinner	Dinner	Dinner	Engl	Engl	Engl				
6:00					Dinner	Dinner	Dinner	Dinner	Dinner		
7:00	Day 1	Day 2	Day 3	Day 4	Day 5	Day 1	Day 2	Day 3	Day 4		
8:00	Alg	Alg	Alg	Alg	Alg	Study Skills	Study Skills	Study Skills	Study Skills		
9:00					break	break	break	break	break		
10:00					OPTIONAL	OPTIONAL	OPTIONAL	OPTIONAL	OPTIONAL		
11:00					Study Time	Study Time	Study Time	Study Time	Study Time		

PREPARE FOR COMPREHENSIVE FINALS

Check to see whether your final is comprehensive (includes previously tested material) or covers only new material. Some professors include both old and new material on final exams. Knowing how much of the exam is based on old material is critical to effective preparation. If you have a comprehensive final, find out *how much* of the exam is comprehensive. Many instructors give final exams that are partially comprehensive. If, for example, you had an exam that covered 12 chapters (and accompanying lecture notes and so on), you would prepare differently depending on whether the exam was 100 percent comprehensive, 75 percent comprehensive, 50 percent comprehensive, or 25 percent comprehensive.

Preparing for 25 Percent Comprehensive Finals

Let's say that you're going to have an exam that is only *25 percent comprehensive.* That means that 75 percent of the test questions cover *new* (not yet tested) *material,* while 25 percent of the test questions cover *old* (already tested) *material.* If the exam is composed of 100 multiple-choice items that cover 12 chapters, how many of the questions will be on old material? Of course, 25 of them will be. That means that 75 questions will be on the new material, which, for this example, will be Chapters 10, 11, and 12.

If you were going to set up a Five-Day Study Plan for this final, which chapters would you study on each of the first 4 days, assuming that you save the last day for a final review and self-test? Many students make the mistake of dividing the material into four equal chunks (as they did for regular exams). In the case of a comprehensive final, however, this would be very poor planning. Because 75 percent of the questions will come from the new material, 75 percent of your time should be spent on those chapters.

It may seem strange to spend only 25 percent of your study time on the first nine chapters of the text (and accompanying lecture notes, and so on); however, that is the appropriate time to devote to the old material. Look at the three study plans in Figure 14.3. In the first plan, the student divided up the study time equally. In

FIGURE 14.3

Sample Study Plans

Plan 1		Plan 2		Plan 3	
Day 1	Ch 1–3	Day 1	Ch 10–12	Day 1	Ch 1–9
Day 2	CH 4–6	Day 2	CH 7–9	Day 2	CH 10
Day 3	CH 7–9	Day 3	CH 4–6	Day 3	CH 11
Day 4	CH 10–12	Day 4	CH 1–3	Day 4	CH 12

the second study plan, the student divided the study time equally but reversed the order of the review. She thought that by beginning with the new material, she would get to spend 5 days reviewing it. Even so, the total time spent on the old material is still disproportionate to the number of related questions on the test. In the third study plan, the proportion of time spent on each section of the material is more appropriately divided to reflect the weight (number of test questions and point value) of each section. The correct way to divide the time would be to spend day 1 preparing Chapters 1–9, day 2 on Chapter 10, day 3 on Chapter 11, and day 4 on Chapter 12. Because each of the four chunks of material (1–9, 10, 11, and 12) is weighted the same on the exam, they should be given equal preparation time.

The number of questions taken from each chapter often signals how detailed or specific each question will be. Typically, the fewer the questions from each chapter, the more general they tend to be. If you have only 25 questions covering nine chapters of text, you have less than three questions per chapter on the exam. On the other hand, if you have 75 test questions based on the last three chapters, you have approximately 25 questions for each chapter. Although the student who spends 3 days preparing and reviewing the first nine chapters may know that material very well, he or she will not know the last three chapters well enough (with only 1 day of preparation) to get a high score on the exam. A quick review of the old material followed by intense study of the new material is necessary for exams that are only slightly comprehensive.

How can you review nine (or more) chapters of material in only a 2- or 3-hour study session? Obviously, you don't have time to reread all your highlighting or even all your lecture notes (and rereading is not a good way to review anyway). If you prepared properly for each of the exams that covered those chapters, you should have study sheets, word and question cards, and self-tests from which to study. The best way to prepare for those chapters, then, is to review the material that you already prepared when studying for the earlier exams. In addition, if you have copies of your old tests or are permitted to review them in your professor's office, do so. Many instructors use questions from the original exams again on the final.

Preparing for Other Comprehensive Finals

Now that you know how to divide your time correctly between old and new material for 25 percent comprehensive finals, let's look at other combinations. Let's say that you're going to have a *50 percent comprehensive* final. One-half of the test questions will be based on Chapters 1–14 and the other half will come from the last four chapters in the text (15–18). How would you divide your study time, assuming you have the same 4 days to prepare and 1 day for a final review of the material? To figure out the proper ratio of time to chapters, think about how many chapters will be covered in each quarter of the exam. Because half of the test questions will come from the first 14 chapters, you can effectively divide those chapters in two. You would prepare Chapters 1–7 on day 1 and Chapters 8–14 on day 2. You would then prepare Chapters 15 and 16 on day 3 and Chapters 17 and 18 on day 4. Deciding which chunk of chapters to review first depends on your past performance. If you got high grades on the exams on Chapters 1 to 14, you may want to work on the new chapters first, to get more repetition on that material. If you didn't do well on the old tests, you should start with those chapters because they are less fresh in your mind and will require even more review. Remember to review each chunk of material on each of the succeeding days to aid retention.

An exam that's 75 *percent comprehensive* requires more time on old material than on new material. Let's use the following example. If you had 100 questions that covered 19 chapters of text, how much time would you spend on the old material if only Chapters 16–19 were still untested? In this case, you would spend the first 3 days of your study plan reviewing the first 15 chapters (because 75 percent of the questions will come from those chapters) and only the last day on the new material (because only 25 percent of the questions will be drawn from those chapters). Even though you have not yet been tested on the last three chapters, you shouldn't spend a disproportionate amount of your time on them because so few questions will be taken from each one. However, if you did really well on the exams for the "old" chapters, you should review Chapters 16 to 19 first. That way you'll have more time to learn the "new," not-yet-tested material during each daily review. By spacing your study and allocating the appropriate amount of time to each of the chapters, you can maximize your test score on any type of comprehensive final exam.

USE ACTIVE STUDY STRATEGIES

Use active strategies when you review your text and lecture materials. Write and recite in order to move information into long-term memory. Test your understanding of the material by using flash cards, self-tests, and recitation. If you already took good notes on your textbook and prepared study sheets combining the information from your text and your notes, you won't need to go back and review the text again. If you prepared questions in the margin or word and question cards for each of your chapters, take them out again to review for your final. Rather than rereading the notes that you took and the study sheets or maps that you prepared, create new ones. This time use your notes and study sheets as your starting points. In the process of making new study sheets, you'll effectively review the material. If you made self-tests for each chapter, use them again to find out what you already know and what you still need to learn.

STAY MOTIVATED

As you prepare for each of your finals, use strategies to stay motivated. If you get tired or discouraged, give yourself a pep talk. Surround yourself with other motivated people. Join a study group or check in with friends who also have made a commitment to work hard during finals week. One of the worst things you can do is hang around with other students who don't have very many exams or who don't plan to study. They will constantly distract you and may, without meaning to, tempt you to neglect your studies and "party" with them. Even though it's hard to say no to your friends, you have to. Remember that your academic goals must come first. If you have a heavy exam schedule, save the partying for when you're finished. Many students don't realize that partying every night after they study can be very harmful. You won't do as well on your exams without enough sleep. Don't drink during finals preparation; hangovers can throw off your study schedule, interfere with your concentration and retrieval during exams, and even affect whether you get to the exam on time.

WORK HARD DURING EACH EXAM

Work hard during each of your exams. Stay in the testing room for the entire time period. Review your answers and use problem-solving strategies to try to figure out the correct answer for any question that you aren't sure about. Concentrate on only one exam at a time. Don't think about the exam that you had yesterday or the one that's coming up tomorrow. If you feel anxious, use one of the relaxation strategies that you learned. Focus all your energy and all your effort on the exam. After the exam, take a break before beginning your next study session. Don't allow your performance on one exam to interfere with your ability or commitment to prepare for another one. If you leave an exam angry or upset about your performance, accept the fact that you may not achieve your goal in that class, but don't give up on all of your other classes. You may be able to do even better than you expected on one of your other exams.

MONITOR YOUR PROGRESS

After the exam is over, evaluate your performance. Write down a few notes about how you thought you did on the exam. Note any areas where you think you had difficulty and then review your notes or study sheets to check your answers. At the beginning of the next semester, visit your professor and ask to look at your exam. If you had problems with some areas, ask your professor to go over

MORE TIPS FOR PREPARING FOR FINAL EXAMS

PUT ACADEMICS FIRST THIS WEEK. Put family activities, cleaning, and social events on hold until after your last exam. You'll have several weeks between semesters to catch up on things once your exams are over. By focusing your attention on your final exams, you can increase your chances for academic success.

USE GOOD TIME-MANAGEMENT STRATEGIES. At the end of the semester, it's even more important to make the best use of your time. You need to set up a schedule to complete all your outstanding assignments. Write down what you plan to do each hour of the day.

SET PRIORITIES FOR STUDY. You don't need to study for every final exam the same way. If the final is unlikely to change your grade in the course, spend less time preparing for that exam. Put more effort, instead, into those courses where the final will determine the grade. You still need to study for all your exams, but use your time to your best advantage.

ASK FOR TIME OFF IF YOU NEED IT. You may need to take a vacation day from work or even from household tasks in order to prepare for one or two of your

most important final exams. Think about how hard you worked the entire semester to get to this point. With a little extra time to prepare, you can make all that hard work pay off.

USE THE FIVE-DAY STUDY PLAN. Most students have two to five exams spaced within a 3- or 4-day time period. Some students have two exams on the same day. Although it's tempting to study for one exam at a time by cramming, you already know that's not the most effective way to learn. Split your day to use the Five-Day Study Plan for each of your exams.

STAY HEALTHY TO DO YOUR BEST. Some students skip meals and pull one all-nighter after another to cram for finals. This strategy often results in poor test preparation and performance. You need to eat properly, get enough sleep, and get some exercise during final exam week so that you can do your best on each exam.

PLAN REWARDS. Make a list of things you want to do when finals are over. Ask your family and friends what they'd like to do, too. Setting goals for special activities or even some rest and relaxation can help keep you motivated through your exams.

them with you. Even though the course is over and your grade is already assigned, you still may benefit from this review. You can decide whether the plan that you set up or the strategies that you used were effective. If they were, use those strategies again in a similar class. If they weren't effective, revise them for future exams.

SUMMARY

The key to preparing for final exams is good time management. Most students are still attending classes, preparing daily assignments, and completing term papers and projects as final exam period approaches. Because final exams are often critical in determining your final course grade, you need enough time to prepare for each one as carefully as or more carefully than you did for your regular exams. To do this, you may need to make some changes in your daily routine. About 2 weeks before your first final, you need to make academics your first priority. Push hard and get ahead in your work. Your goal is to complete most of your outstanding assignments 5 days before your first exam. At the same time, you need to evaluate your status in each course. By calculating your current grade, you can determine whether the final exam will make a difference in your overall course grade. Setting your priorities before you begin to study can help you decide how much time to put into studying for each of your final exams.

Use the Five-Day Study Plan to prepare for each exam. Set up a final exam study schedule. With most of your regular assignments already completed, you should have plenty of time to schedule three to four (2-hour) study blocks each day. Spacing your study and splitting your day will help you stay on task, reduce anxiety, and prevent interference as you prepare for several exams at the same time. Cramming for one exam after another just doesn't work.

Comprehensive final exams are more difficult than other tests because they cover so much material. However, if you divide your study time properly and use the material that you prepared from each of your old exams, you can do as well or even better on the finals. Developing strategies to stay motivated is also especially important during final exam week. As you take each of your finals, put forth your best effort. Concentrate on each exam, monitor your progress to evaluate the strategies you used, and then make any necessary adjustments for the next exam. If you learn from your successes and your mistakes, the experience you gain will help you cope with the intensity and the stress of final exams—each semester, you'll do it even better!

Activities

1. Write a paragraph that describes how you prepared in previous semesters or how you think you will prepare for final exams this semester. Then list five things that you generally do differently (or that you think you will do differently) to prepare for final exams as compared with other exams.

2. Work as a group to list 10 strategies that students should use when preparing for final exams. How many of the strategies do you already use? Which ones do you plan to use for your final exams this semester?

3. Make a list of all the assignments, projects, and exams you need to complete before the end of the semester. Then list your home and work responsibilities for the 10 days before your first final exam. What tasks can you postpone until your finals are over? Mark them and decide when you will complete each of them. What tasks can you omit entirely? Develop a plan to manage your time more effectively for the 2-week period surrounding final exams.

4. Go to the *Orientation to College Learning* Web site and download one copy of Activity 14–3 from the Activities Packet. List the grades you have in each of your classes and total your points earned. Then set priorities for your final exams. Write a paragraph describing how you determined the rank order for your finals.

5. Look at Tanya's and Joel's study schedules available on the *Orientation to College Learning* Web site. Although both students attempted to develop a good study plan for their final exams, they made some common mistakes. What are the strengths and weaknesses of each plan? What changes would you make if they asked you to set up a study schedule for them?

6. Go to the *Orientation to College Learning* Web site and download one copy of the Final Exam Planning Calendar. Write in all of your fixed commitments, classes, and exams. Then set up Five-Day Study Plans for each of your exams.

7. List some of the obstacles that you'll have to overcome during finals week, the strategies or resources that you plan to use to overcome them, and the rewards that you anticipate.

8. If you're using InfoTrac College Edition, locate additional information on time management or stress management. After reading several of the articles that you found, make a list of 10 strategies or tips that college students could use to help them prepare for final exams. Include the titles of the articles that you found most helpful. Be prepared to share your lists with your group.

9. Think of three examples of how you've applied what you learned in this chapter. Choose one strategy and describe how you applied it to your other course work using the Journal Entry Form that is located on the *Orientation to College Learning* Web site. Consider the

following questions as you complete your entry. Why did you use this strategy? What did you do? How did it work? How did it affect your performance on the task? How does this approach compare with your previous approach? What changes would you make the next time you use this strategy?

10. Now that you've completed Chapter 14, take a few minutes to repeat the "Where Are You Now?" activity, located on the *Orientation to College Learning* Web site. What changes did you make as a result of reading this chapter? How are you planning to apply what you've learned in this chapter?

Review Questions

Terms You Should Know:

Comprehensive final exam
Consolidation
Exam reminder sheet
50 percent comprehensive
Final exam planning calendar
Final exam study schedule
Final exams
Five-Day Study Plan

New material
Old material
Setting priorities
75 percent comprehensive
Spacing your study
Splitting your day
25 percent comprehensive

Completion: Fill in the blank to complete each of the following statements.

1. You can prepare for several final exams at the same time by _____ your day.

2. You should generally review the _____ material early in your study plan so that you can get more repetition on it.

3. When setting up your study schedule, plan _____ hour(s) for each exam each day.

4. Courses with _____ grades should be your highest priority.

5. A 25 percent comprehensive final includes _____ questions out of 100 on the old material.

Multiple Choice: Circle the letter of the best answer for each of the following questions. Be sure to underline key words and eliminate wrong answers.

6. If you're failing a course, you should:
   A. rank that course as your top priority.
   B. drop the course.
   C. check with the professor to ask if there is any chance you could pass.
   D. stop attending, don't study, and don't take the final.

7. On the sample study schedule (Figure 14.2), optional review time can be used for:
   A. additional practice for all of your exams.
   B. additional practice for your top-priority exam.
   C. preparation time for a fifth course.
   D. all of the above.

Short Answer–Essay: On a separate sheet, answer each of the following questions.

8. Why do students experience so much anxiety at the end of the semester?

9. Why do some students have difficulty taking final exams? What should they do differently?

10. How should students prepare for 25 percent, 50 percent, 75 percent, and 100 percent comprehensive finals?

INDEX